The Coming of Night

Alex Janaway

Published by Browncoat Books 2014
Copyright © 2014 Alex Janaway
Map illustration by Laura Watton
All rights reserved.
ISBN: 0992813727
ISBN-13: 978-0-9928137-2-7

For Siobhan.
Who, let's face it, is the reason I do everything.

Go to www.alexjanaway.com to find out more
about the author and his upcoming releases

ACKNOWLEDGMENTS

Thanks to Helen, Laura and Liz. And Punkass, just because.

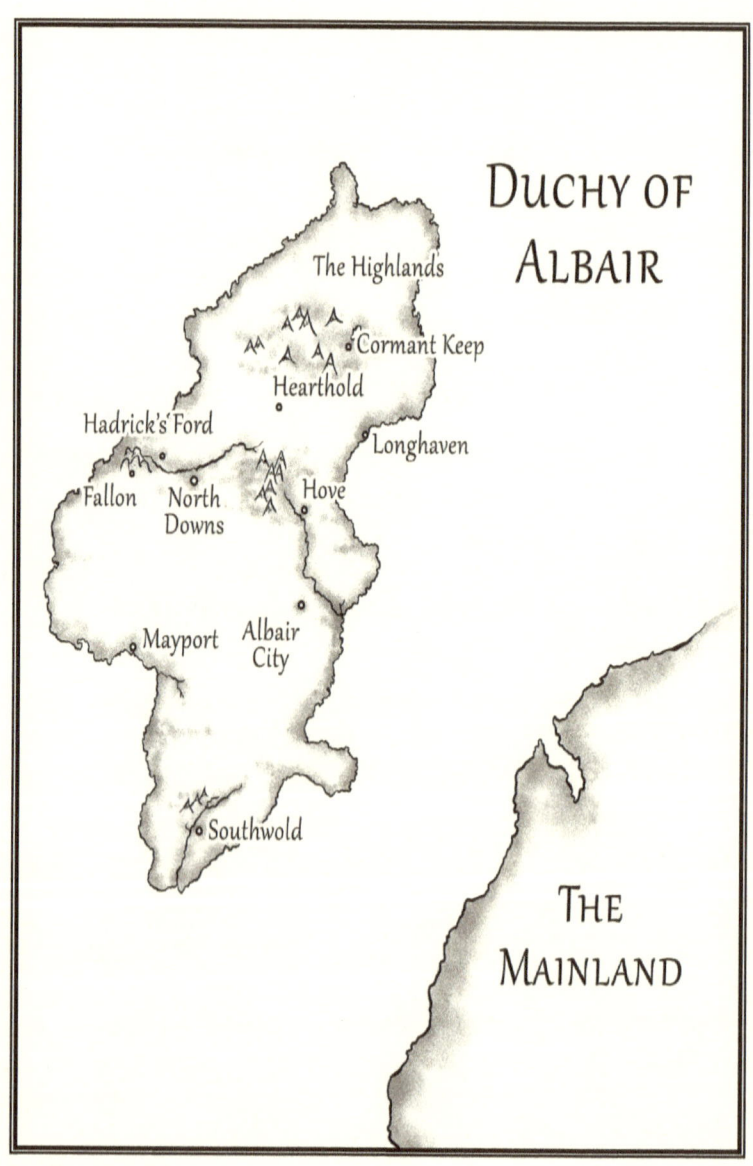

DUCHY OF ALBAIR

The Highlands

Cormant Keep

Hearthold

Hadrick's Ford

Longhaven

Fallon　North
Downs　Hove

Mayport　Albair
City

Southwold

THE
MAINLAND

THIRTY YEARS BEFORE

Archmage Tennebran negotiated his way through a series of collapsed columns. Shattered and in many cases bloodstained, they lay strewn across the main hallway of the Temple of Dawn. They certainly made an effective barricade, once or twice he had to hitch his robes up to allow his legs to pass over a lump of stone. Stone that had once been so lovingly crafted and fashioned into flutes, symbols and of histories become legend. He was surprised that the whole ceiling had not come down, such was the devastation visited upon the infrastructure. He was tempted to erect a shielding spell over his head just in case, but then thought better of it. During these times it was not wise to perform acts of magic without the direst need

Normally the temple had been well supplied with braziers and brackets, but now there was little illumination to guide his steps, only the starlight entering from the shattered doorway to his rear and the glow of the torches that were ahead of him. Looking to his left and right, gazing into the dim recesses of the temple wings, he could make out further rows of columns, as well constructed as the ones that lay around him. That, at least, answered why the building had remained standing. The flames ahead cast a chaotic scene of shadows that danced and mutated before his eyes. They added to his discomfort; he couldn't shake the impression that he had entered into the hell of one of the many religions that flourished in the city. He tried to ignore the bodies that were scattered about. These once living forms were twisted and broken, each as different and as gruesome as the next. Many torsos lacked limbs and many limbs lacked bodies. In the outer darkness, he was allowed a small relief as the dead humps beyond his night vision kept their injuries to themselves, shadowed and black as they were. Tennebran could not guess at the number of deceased.

Ahead now, the torches that acted as a beacon began to define the figures that held them. Six in total; six men gathered in a loose ring around something he as yet could not see. Before this group stood another figure, his back to the wizard. Tennebran completed his journey and joined him. He regarded his companion: a stocky, moustachioed, man of middle years, wearing a battered, round helmet, the standard garb of the City Watch, his arms folded across his broad chest. He was staring intently at the scene before him. Tennebran waited patiently to be acknowledged.

'We got called out about an hour ago,' said the

watchman, his gaze still fixed towards the circle of flames. 'We knew enough to not take any chances these days, so my whole shift was deployed. That's including the reserves. Got everyone wearing full kit and carrying all their issue weapons. You'd think we were going to war. I've been a watchman all my life, made a career out of it. Killed a few souls in my time too, though most of them deserved it. This,' he paused a moment, 'if this is what war is like, then I'm damn glad I never joined the army.'

Tennebran continued to regard the man, he realised that the watchman was rambling, letting his jumbled thoughts spill out. He was clearly suffering from shock.

'Captain?' said Tennebran softly. 'Where is the rest of your shift? How many did you lose?'

The watchman lifted his head and turned to stare at the wizard. His eyes narrowed and something like recognition passed across his face. He turned his head back to the scene before him.

'This is my shift. All that's left of it. The other forty are dead.'

Tennebran was shocked. He shouldn't have been. But forty? What had happened here?

The watchman continued to talk. 'When we arrived they had pretty much finished butchering the congregation. Good in a way, as it meant they didn't leave any alive this time. Meant the contagion didn't spread into the wounded. Also meant they could turn their full attention on us,' said the watchman. 'This was the last one we killed. The biggest and the meanest. Broke one of my men in half, just picked him up and snapped him in the middle, whilst the rest of us were skewering it in a dozen places. Didn't think it would die. That's why we're standing here, just to make sure it's gone. Then we're going to burn it.'

Tennebran regarded the man for a few moments longer then forced himself to look at the creature that was lying within the circle of light. He did so reluctantly. He had seen too many of these already and each one frightened him to his very core. As he studied the dead form he inwardly shuddered. To think, this had once been a man, probably the High Priest himself. The creature before him still retained the basic shape of a human. Two arms, blood red, heavily muscled; the hands bore talons, not fingers. Two legs thickly furred with cloven hooves where feet had once been. And the head, oversized, distorted, ears tapering to points. A snout replaced the nose. There was a huge gaping maw of a mouth, filled with bloodstained, razor sharp teeth, bits of flesh still hanging from some of the incisors. The eyes were open, black as night. There was no pupil, nothing to show it had once possessed a window into the human soul within. These eyes were windows into a world without souls, without any goodness or compassion. Evil. Evil in its purest form. That was what Tennebran saw, but more than that, it was what he felt, what he knew to be the case. Whatever had taken the priest; it had never known human emotion and never would.

'Burn it,' he said.

The captain of the Watch nodded to his men. They poured oil over the body and threw torches upon it. The fire caught quickly. Tennebran turned and walked away from the circle of watchmen. He had no desire to inhale the scent of putrid, burning flesh. He had been subjected to it too many times in the past few months already. The fire began to flare up and as he walked back along the corridor of pillars, the light chasing the shadows from him. Behind, the group of watchmen stood silently and still, the brightness of the fire obscuring the details of their shapes, turning them once more into black, formless figures.

Tennebran entered his private chambers within the Ducal palace. In times gone past there would have been a number of wards set upon the entrance, now he made do with a lock and key. The wards needed renewing often; another luxury he could no longer risk. As it was he felt reasonably secure, ensconced in the northern tower overlooking the river that bisected the city north to south. The palace was well guarded and the walls were high and broad. The city gates themselves were shut and seldom opened to their fullest extent, any traffic to and from the outside world being conducted through the smaller, more defensible postern gates.

Deep in thought, he crossed to a table by the window and helped himself from the carafe of wine upon it. As he poured the red liquid into a grand looking goblet, he dimly noted that a fire had been set in the hearth and was burning merrily. More flames, the one true devourer of existence, he thought to himself. Placing the carafe back on the table he stepped up to the window and gazed into the night. He drank from the goblet and allowed himself to savour the vintage. Fiery, rich in berries with a lingering aftertaste. A vintage Sirah from the south of the continent, if he was any judge.

'I took the liberty of lighting your fire,' said a cultured, low-toned voice from behind him. 'And bringing up the bottle. I guessed that you might need it after hearing of your departure for the temple.'

Turning, Tennebran allowed his eyes a few moments to refocus on the fireplace. Before it there were two high backed chairs, facing one another and to either side of the grate. He had clearly been too wrapped up in his own thoughts to have noticed that the left hand chair was occupied.

Nodding to the seated man, he raised his cup to acknowledge the gift. 'Indeed, my lord Duke, the liberty is yours by right. As is my thanks for this gift of wine.'

The Duke stood, refilled his own goblet and joined Tennebran by the window. In the night, a number of fires could be seen burning throughout the city. Some were the lights of pickets that had been placed at certain points. Others were the result of more chaotic and no doubt more violent measures.

'Was it bad?' asked the Duke.

'Yes, my lord Henry. Bad enough,' replied Tennebran who turned to regard the Duke.

'I should have been out there tonight.'

Tennebran shook his head. 'No, my lord, you should not. The situation is chaotic. Your protection cannot be guaranteed. There are not enough men and those we have are fighting for their lives. If you were lost, that would be a greater tragedy than the one we have already.'

Lord Henry remained staring out of the window and so the wizard was left with a profile view. A black shock of hair combed back tightly against the head did little to frame his face upon which grew a small, well clipped goatee that was displaying white hairs in increasing numbers. A dignified, noble looking nose, slightly too large for the face and ramrod straight in profile added an exclamation to his grim expression. The feature which Tennebran did appreciate was a pair of warm, brown eyes that lent the younger man the aspect of a scholar. The Duke of Albair was thirty years of age and had ruled his island nation for only two years. His ascent to power had come with the death of his father and older brother, lost in a storm as they crossed the channel between Albair and the continent. A man of learning, he had led a quiet, contented existence as Warden of the Eastern Marches. He had expected his brother, a jovial and charismatic man, to take over from his father on their return. In fact, the reason for the trip had been a ceremony given by the local lords to witness and acknowledge the passing of the Dukedom.

It was a fickle fate that the passing of the Dukedom did indeed occur, if not into the hands of the right brother. It was not too long after that that the first signs of the troubles began to manifest themselves. Whispers and rumours of a plague – or a curse. Tales of people becoming wild, becoming monsters, becoming the murderers of the very people they had once known and loved.

'My soldiers brought me word that some escaped and are now roaming the city causing panic and mayhem,' he said grimly, and nodded towards the city. 'The fires before me seem to bear testament to that.'

'The high priest was warned - was ordered not to attempt anything like that,' said Tennebran. 'They all were. And instead, half of the temple leaders decided that a display of faith would heal the hurts of the world. How much more hurt have they caused by their folly?'

'I doubt that the half who did not participate in their rituals will ever unbar their doors again after tonight's hell,' surmised Duke Henry.

'I doubt they'll have much of a congregation left when word gets out as to the cause of this,' replied Tennebran.

'After tonight I am faced with little choice. I must ensure the protection of the public; instil some belief that I can protect them against these creatures. Else all will fall into chaos,' said Duke Henry.

'I fear that what you say is right, my lord. We have discussed what must be done and whilst it fills my heart with such a hollowness, I must confess,' the wizard shrugged his shoulders. 'I do not know what else to advise.'

'And what of your colleagues?' asked the Duke. 'Do they not have anything else to suggest?'

Tennebran shook his head.

'No, my lord. In all the lands, each looks to the defence of their homes by different means. Magic is not to be trusted. All we have discovered is that magic imbued upon a thing is not affected. Only objects can be wielded with safety.'

'And have you prepared the stones?' interrupted the Duke.

'Yes, Lord Henry. I have used and imparted as much magic as I dare. As have my colleagues across the seas. But we can do no more. Now only the most powerful of my kind attempt to converse by way of our magic. Each time we do, we place a great burden upon ourselves. We can feel the weight of the darkness upon us, trying to beat through our defences. It is only the years of mental discipline and devotion to my craft that has kept it from entering and possessing my body. I fear we shall not commune by way of our convocation again.'

'Then there is little else that I can ask of you, Uncle, except of course your counsel,' said Duke Henry.

'And that you have, sire. If only for a short time.'

'What do you mean?' asked the Duke.

Tennebran smiled wistfully.

'I know that the proclamation you will make tomorrow is a hard one. Yet one you would not enforce upon me. But I am as much a threat to you as any you will hunt down. I am powerful and therefore so is the potential of the destruction I might cause,' he said.

'So must I destroy you as well?' asked Duke Henry.

'I must confess that a practical man would suggest this as the best course of action. However, fifty years of age and a lifetime's devotion to my arts, leaves me somewhat loath to sacrifice myself just yet. But I cannot stay. I would not put you in danger; you are the last of the family line. I will leave tomorrow morning.'

'And go where?'

'I do not know, just away from here. Far away. I must confine my magic as best I can. But I still have my intellect. Perhaps I can think of a way to stop this madness, to discover its source. I have some time left in me.'

'And if you do gain this knowledge, will you return home?'

Tennebran nodded.

'Yes, nephew. If I can, I will return. Now, leave me to enjoy a final night of comfort and fine wine. I have one last piece of counsel for you. In the dark days ahead, in all the hard decisions that you must make, do not forget your humanity. Do not let your heart harden else you will lose your soul anyway.'

Staring intently into Tennebran's eyes Duke Henry nodded.

'I will.'

'And don't close yourself off from the world either,' continued Tennebran. 'We might have a degree of security on our island but only in maintaining our alliances with the continent can we hope to mount a collective defence. Only in numbers can we be strong enough to resist. Understand?'

'I do, Uncle.'

Tennebran detected a note of irritation in Duke Henry's voice. He smiled and shook his head. 'I'm sorry, Henry. Here I am lecturing you as if you were still a boy. And you are most certainly not that. I apologise. It is not for me to dictate.'

The Duke returned the smile.

'It is good for a Duke to be spoken down to occasionally. It keeps his feet on the ground.'

'Then I am doubly sorry that I take my leave of you now. I'd like to spend some time alone, enjoying this place and its comforts. Just for a short while, before I go.'

Reaching out Tennebran grasped the hand of the Duke.

'Good luck, Uncle,' said Duke Henry. Releasing his grip and smiling sadly he strode out of the room.

Watching him go, the wizard took another sip of his wine, savouring the taste once more. He turned and gazed out onto the city, the lights of the fires continued to burn bright. He could see his own dim reflection in the window. There was a time when men found him intimidating. Looking at his face, all he saw now was a gaunt face and a tired old man.

'Aye, lad, to you as well,' he whispered.

CHAPTER ONE

'So which one?'

'The left.'

'Why?'

'It looks smarter.'

'Well what's that have to do with anything?'

'Because,' Enna rocked back on her haunches and gazed at the sky, 'it'll work out the best route.'

Erik threw his hands in the air in exasperation. 'It's a frog, Enna! It's only got to go two feet across the puddle.' He lowered his hands and leaned closer to his friend. 'Besides,' he lowered his voice conspiratorially, 'mine's got bigger back legs.' He sat back crossing his arms and looking pleased with himself. 'You're buggered.'

Enna continued to rock backwards and forwards and stare upwards. The sky was starting to grow dark. The shadows were beginning to lengthen. The bell would sound soon, she thought.

'Okay, fine,' she answered enjoying his mistaken

confidence.

Erik rubbed his hands and blew his cheeks out in excitement.

'You are such a boy, Erik,' said Enna, shaking her head.

'I am only ten,' responded Erik, matter of factly. 'A kid, just like you.' He prodded Enna. She doubled up and giggled; her long red hair covering a freckled face and obscuring her green eyes. 'I'm thirteen, actually,' she responded.

Behind them a deep resonant gong emanated from the south-eastern watchtower. Before the peel had finished, its call was echoed by each of the three watchtowers stationed around the stockade.

Enna looked up, smiled sweetly at Erik and shrugged her shoulders.

'Oh well,' she said.

Erik looked nonplussed. 'But hang on. What about the race?' He pointed his two index fingers at the frogs that remained imprisoned under a glass jar.

Enna stood up and ruffled Erik's tousled mop of dark brown hair. His innocent face gazed at her in disappointment.

'Let them go, Erik. You can race me back to the gates if you like.'

Erik beamed at her, pushed himself up off the ground and reached down to collect the jar. The two released frogs didn't move and appeared unaware of their new-found freedom.

'Go on, then,' said Erik, 'you get a head start!' He

pushed Enna who let out a mock scream and began to run back towards the stockade. Erik watched her go and counted out three seconds under his breath. 'Here I come!' he shouted, and tore after Enna. The girl was well on her way and possessed a decent turn of speed. She had already begun to dodge and weave around the other villagers as they made their way towards the gates.

By the puddle, the two frogs remained motionless, except for the pulses of their breathing. The one Enna had picked twitched and then leapt into the water.

Enna lost the race to the gates. She hadn't really tried that hard to win. After giving Erik a congratulatory hug, the boy had grinned at her and ran off to his home. She watched him go but lingered where she was, enjoying the last of the midsummer warm. She stood on the simple bridge that spanned the ten-foot ditch that surrounded the palisade. The ditch was steeply sided and embedded in its bottom were rows of fire-hardened wooden spikes. The palisade itself was made of thick wooden trunks that had been cut from the surrounding forests. They had been transported whole to the village before being lowered into the earthen mound ringing the inside of the ditch. The wall and ditch had proven effective against attempted incursions by the beasts. In the past, some had tried to scale the wall only to be forced back by spears and had fallen, impaling themselves on the spikes below. Those that had survived had learned by their mistakes and seldom troubled the settlement, preferring to haunt the woods and valleys surrounding North Downs.

Enna liked to watch the closing of the gates. She had heard some of the adults complaining that it felt they were shutting themselves into their own tombs. For her it always provided a sense of safety and comfort, watching those thick oak portals shut every night, watching the huge bar being placed into its brackets on either side. She had always thought of the gates as being incredibly huge, some four yards in height, and framed within the walls of the stockade. They were made of the same thick oak that measured near enough five yards tall. Added to this was the walkway, the width of two men standing shoulder to shoulder, which spanned the entire perimeter. To Enna it seemed like the entrance to some grand castle or a city, like the ones the adults would talk about that lay far to the south. She had never been of course. As she had grown through the years, the impressive nature of the stockade had diminished. But her father had assured her that the gates and walls of their home were big, by anyone's standards.

'And more than big enough to keep you safe, my sweet,' he would say. 'Why, even an army would have to force its way in by siege if it wanted entry.'

'So they won't get in either?' she would ask him.

'No lass,' he said quietly, 'they can't get in either. And if they did,' he would reach over and pat his rack of smithy tools, 'they'd have me and my hammers to contend with!' At this point in the often-repeated ritual, Enna would giggle and clap her hands.

When the last of the villagers had gone through and the gates had been sealed shut, Enna did her nightly rounds of the perimeter. She knew that the same procedure would have been followed for the western gate. It was the same every night. People weren't likely to forget. Even so Enna liked to check. She would walk around the stockade walls to the opposite gate, see that it was shut and then continued round back to where she had started. When she had first started doing it, when she was six, mother had chided her for being silly and foolish. Her father, however, had laughed, telling his wife that Enna was simply displaying a sense of commitment to the community and was showing some much needed caution and responsibility. At that he would fold his large, well-muscled arms and smile at his wife. That was the signal the conversation was at an end and that Enna had his tacit permission. Since then, barring illness, Enna had conducted her patrol with diligence, regardless of the seasons and the weather. Her patrols had become a permanent fixture of the nightly routine of the stockade and a few minutes later she reached the western gate. The nightwatch, wrapped up in their thick woollen cloaks, were in the process of lighting the torches that were placed at regular intervals around the walls. They always started with the two gate lights first. One of the cloaked figures looked down from the walkway at Enna.

'All's well, Enna,' said a male voice. 'You can run off home now.'

'Thanks, Borric,' she replied, 'but I'll just walk back to the east gate first.'

Borric chuckled. 'Course you will. And tell Jenna that I'll be having one of her oatcakes come midnight. I saw her trying to hide them from me when she came past.'

'Okay.' She waved and continued on her way. She returned to the far gate and delivered the message. Jenna laughed and thanked her. In the village of North Downs, all adults from the age of sixteen to sixty shared the load of watch keeping. That meant some one hundred souls to man the stockade walls, six adults a night, every night of the year. Four had positions in each of the corner watchtowers and two patrolling and doing chores. Enna was quite looking forward to when she would be old enough to take on her duties. She would feel like a proper guard, prowling the battlements of her own citadel. Just like they must do in Albair City.

As she daydreamed past the homes of her friends and neighbours, she passed the open door of Mistress Tabawick. Inside, the local healer was holding a class for the youngsters of the village. Mistress Esther Tabawick was in her early thirties and had a talent for understanding the restorative properties of countless plants and herbs found around the region. More than that, however, she was also responsible for teaching the youngsters in their formative years. She would show them how to count, do simple mathematics, teach them plant-lore and more importantly she would recount the histories of Albair and the lands close to it. For most people these days, the only history worth knowing began some twenty years before Enna was born. That was when the bad times had begun and the plague had struck. Many of the older folk liked to reminisce about the times before then, when life was safer and more optimistic. The younger adults such as her mother didn't really like to listen to them prattle on; Enna loved it.

'No point in wishing your life a way for a world long gone,' she would say.

Enna on the other hand was fascinated by the past. And to be honest, when she listened to the older adults, their lives didn't seem particularly different than now. They died of the same illnesses and had the extra worry of war, beasts and nature. Well, they didn't have war to worry about anymore. Nature was still nature. And the beasts, well, they had changed.

It was on this subject that Mistress Tabawick was lecturing the half-dozen youngsters. It was the tale of how the world came to be as it was. The story of the plague. The children listened, their attention held rapt. The tale was one that each would have had told to them as toddlers, in simpler words, by their parents. Of the coming of the Possessed, or demons, as some called them. It was difficult to tell what they were; they came in many different forms. The story was well known to all of them. And if they had nightmares, well, the adults felt that was no bad thing. Everyone, from the oldest spinster to the youngest babe had, likely as not, heard the cries coming from the woods at one point or another in their lives. Without stopping her flow, the woman glanced up at Enna with piercing blue eyes, nodded her recognition and then looked away again. Enna nodded back and hurried on. She knew the story well enough.

Some thirty years ago, anyone who was able to perform magic had become struck by a curse. They had all turned into monsters. Some of them were disease bearers, carrying a virulent sickness that wasted and ruined a person within days. In a short space of time, civilisation had crumbled. Many had died in the first years.

Those that had changed would kill indiscriminately, and those they did not kill would often quickly turn into others like them. Those settlements that had time to react had built walls, and those that had walls built them higher. Villages like North Downs had been luckier than most. Having no magic users itself, and none nearby for many miles around, had given the people time to protect themselves. Other places had not been so lucky. It was said that whole communities had been wiped out in the space of a night. That fully half the population of Albair had succumbed to or died from the plague.

For a time all communications had ceased and travel between settlements had stopped. People had looked inward to their own survival, unsure whether the world was ending and when their time would come. Then slowly links were re-established. Bodies of heavily armoured soldiers rode the land bringing word of the new order of things. It appeared that the monsters preferred the dark to travel abroad. In the hours of daylight, a man could risk travel across open country. Therefore each settlement must look to its own affairs and its people must reach safety before the day's end. To be abroad at night invited death. The creatures could smell a man out and would hunt remorselessly. The night was their domain now. Darkness was death. And as for those that carried the plague, those with the taint of magic: they were not suffered to live.

Ahead of her now, Enna spied the village smithy, her home. A building of two parts, one of which housed her family, a simple single storey, three room structure, similar in appearance to most others in North Downs. It had two shuttered windows, one to either side of the doorway and another one around the side. The other half of the smithy was an open sided barn, extending out from the left side of the house. Its roof had shallow slopes and the forge that her father used made up the other end of the barn opposite the house. While the rest of the building was made of wood, the fireplace was made of fired clay bricks. His tools were hanging in a rack to one side of the forge and close by, in the centre of the barn, sat the anvil. Her father kept a tidy workspace. A number of iron ingots were stacked neatly to one side, whilst hanging off the rafters was a collection of horseshoes, plough-bits, shovelheads, picks and saws.

A large, well-worn and pitted metal sharpening wheel sat idle in the yard behind the barn. On a small workbench set up against the wall of the house, her father kept a collection of spearheads and arrowheads. Replacements for a situation none hoped would arise. North Downs had not lost a life to the monsters in over six years. It was a respite from the horror that none were naive enough to believe would continue. Her father was in the back yard chopping wood. His huge calloused hands gripped a single bladed wood-axe, some two and a half feet in length. To Enna the axe was a heavy and unwieldy tool but her father made the use of it seem easy.

As she walked up to him, he swung his axe in a steady over-head motion and brought it down on to the chock of wood, resting on the wide tree-stump he used as a chopping block. The chock spilt in two and fell onto its sides, rocking gently on the stump. He rested the axe against his side, wiped his brow with the back of his hand, scratched his stubbled chin and smiled at his daughter.

Michalis was of the average height but a life-time of metalwork had made him broad and muscular. Apprenticed to his father, a journeyman who had settled in North Downs when the plague had struck, Michalis had known no other life. But his father had given him an appreciation of the wider world and its opportunities. Something he did not want his daughter to lack. Michalis and his wife Sarah, though married thirteen years, had only Enna. Some might have thought the blacksmith would have wished a son to whom he might pass on his knowledge. In fact, he did not mind at all. Enna knew she was the apple of his eye; and he had often told her how proud he was of her. He hoped that perhaps one day, in the future, she might travel. That she might see all of Albair, visit the capital and gaze in wonder at the trade ships that Michalis's father had told him of. She would dearly love to do that one day, but not yet. He'd have her for a few more years to come. And woe betide any potential suitor who wished to chain her to North Downs before then!

'Evening, Dad,' said Enna.

'Young lady, you've been playing with Erik again,

haven't you?' It was a statement rather than a question.

Enna dipped her head and tilted it to one side. She knew her father thought it endearing. 'Maybe,' she replied lightly.

'No maybe about it. You clothes are filthy and there's mud on your hands. That means you've been with Erik. The pair of you are bloody nightmares. Get inside and get cleaned up. No doubt your mother will have a fit and I'm sure as not going to even try and stop her.' He inclined his head towards the door of the house. 'In you go. I'll see you in a few minutes once I'm done here.'

'Yes, Dad,' she said brightly and made for the door.

'Hang on!' he called after her sternly. Enna stopped and looked back. Michalis raised his eyebrows questioningly.

Enna grinned in understanding and tramped back to her father. He leant over and put an arm round his daughter's shoulders. She leant in close and gave him a kiss on his sweaty cheek. Michalis released his hold and Enna turned and ran into the house.

As predicted, Sarah went mad at Enna's arrival. 'How many times have I told you, madam?' she scolded. Sarah shared the same red hair and green eyes of her daughter, but whereas Enna's face spent much of her time smiling, Sarah's showed a life of stress and worry. She had lost her father to the beasts early and had never truly come to terms with the loss. She fretted about the safety of her family and worried whenever her daughter strayed far from the stockade walls.

'Sorry, Mother. I didn't think it would be so wet and the sun was out,' pleaded Enna, half-heartedly. She couldn't charm her mum like she could her dad.

'And I bet you didn't stop to think that every time you go out to play with Erik I end up shouting at you for getting dirty?' said Sarah. 'Well, you'll be doing the washing tomorrow morning.'

'Yes, Mother,' said Enna, meekly.

Sarah pointed at her daughter's room. 'Go on and get changed. And wash your hands. Supper is in five minutes.'

Enna turned and walked to her room. It was one advantage of being an only child. Most of her friends had to share a similar space with their brothers and sisters. As it was, she had lots of room to spread her stuff around and a big bed all to herself. She stripped off her woollen shift and dug another one out of her clothes chest at the end of the bed. She then washed her hands and face in the wooden bowl that lay on the table in one corner of the room. Happy that her hands were free from dirt she took a red ribbon from the table and tied her hair back. Mum always threatened to cut off Enna's hair rather than let her locks continuously end up lying in the midst of whatever meal was consumed that evening.

As she washed and changed, she did so without a light. As the room darkened she relied on her own night vision to accomplish her tasks. Night came quickly to these parts, and at this time of year it stayed longer too. She reached up to the window and closed the shutter boards, latching and testing them firmly. Enna opened her door and was met by a gentle glow of light coming from the cooking fire and two candles sat at the table dinner table. The light did not chase the darkness away but allowed for comfortable and unhindered movement across the room. And was more than enough to eat by. She walked over and joined her father who was already sat across the table from her. He was busy slicing off several pieces of bread from a thick brown loaf sitting in the centre of the table. He picked one up and placed it on the side of Enna's plate. Sarah was busying herself by the fire and presently removed a pot full of steaming stew. She ladled a generous portion onto Michalis's plate, a smaller helping for Enna and a similar sized one for herself.

She then placed the pot close to the fire before joining them. At this unbidden signal, both father and daughter tucked into their food. Sarah poured them both out a measure of ale before sitting at the end of the table. Enna's mother took pride in her cooking abilities and was always pleased to see her family devour the food she had prepared. After a few minutes of dedicated eating, Michalis pushed his plate away and gave his wife a warm smile.

'Ah, that filled a hole!' he declared.

Sarah snorted. 'Only 'til the morning, love.'

'Well, a man needs energy, doesn't he?' argued Michalis. 'Got to keep my wife in the manner to which she has become accustomed.'

'Oh well, that won't be too hard!' she shot back.

'Love...' he replied, an edge of consternation in his

voice.

'Just make sure you've got enough energy to take care of me tonight,' she warned.

Michalis smiled and Enna could detect a gleam in her father's eyes. She had followed the exchange whilst mopping up the last of her stew with the bread. Her parents often talked like this and she knew the two of them were up to something but she never quite understood what it meant.

Turning to study his daughter for a moment, Michalis began to pick at a fingernail.

'I heard today that the magistrate is coming over tomorrow. Looks like it's time for the Testing again.'

Sarah nodded. 'Yes, Mistress Tabawick told me that she'd received the message by carrier bird today.'

'Young lady, you're thirteen now. A grown up. This will be the last time for you, won't it?' Michalis was trying to sound light but Enna could detect an edge to his voice.

'Yes, Dad, I guess,' responded Enna.

Once every year the magistrate out of Fallow would come and test the children of the county. The Testing, as it had become known, was when youngsters were examined for signs of magical ability. If they were found to possess any, they were killed. It was a hard concept to deal with, but the people of Albair had come to accept it as a necessary evil, as a means of ensuring their own survival. That didn't stop the outpouring of terror and grief from the parents whose children were taken. Other members of the community would offer support and care but the taint would never leave the family. The fear was

25

that somehow the plague may be present in the parents as well. It was generally accepted that by the age of ten, any latent ability would have displayed itself. Children were tested until they reached thirteen, just to be certain.

'You'd think after thirty years we must have bred it out of our systems by now,' mused Sarah, quietly. She didn't look up from her plate where she still played with her food.

Michalis shook his head in response. His eyes shifted between Enna and her mother. 'It doesn't work like that, love. Sure, it often follows in blood-lines, but it can pop up in any generation, of any family.'

'And that's what makes it so frightening. That we might never be rid of it,' said Sarah, looking now directly at her husband.

He coughed and reached his hand over to his wife.

'Well, let's not worry about it. Our wee one's alright, aren't you, pet?' he smiled, looking at his daughter for support.

'Yes, Dad. I want to be a soldier anyway. You know that.'

Michalis laughed. 'See, wife? Our daughter is going to become a mighty warrior. She'll be keeping us safe!'

Sarah smiled weakly and squeezed Michalis's hand.

'Anyway,' he continued, 'me and your mother have got some things to talk about. Why don't you get yourself off to bed, my sweet?'

'Fine. But only because I'm tired,' replied Enna. She walked round the table and kissed both her parents goodnight. She was usually allowed to stay up longer but whenever her dad got that gleam in his eye it was always the same. She'd mentioned it to Jenna, who had laughed uproariously and told her to go speak to Mistress Tabawick about it. After closing her room door, she found herself in darkness except for a gentle glow coming from under the bottom edge of the door. She crossed quickly to where her bed was, threw off her shift and crawled under the blankets. She heard the voices of her parents murmuring and then the sound of them standing up from the table. After a few minutes, the glow from the next room lessened and then went out.

She really must speak to Mistress Tabawick about that, she thought to herself before shutting her eyes and drifting off to sleep.

On the walkway on the western edge of the village, Borric leaned against the palisade wall, gazing out into the night. Looking left and right he could make out the two watchtowers and the dark shapes of his fellow watch keepers. From the hills in the distance he heard a long, high-pitched howl. It rose in intensity and became almost a shriek. Borric felt himself stiffen and he clutched the shaft of his spear tightly. Looking left and right again, he could see that the others had also leaned forward, craning out over the tower railings. It was always difficult to judge distance in the dark. He prayed to all the Gods long forsaken, that the howling would come no closer.

CHAPTER TWO

It was mid-afternoon when the Magistrate was sighted, appearing from the forest trail to the west. Word spread quickly and a crowd gathered at the gateway to watch him arrive. As soon as Enna heard, she was up and running from the smithy before her mother could call her back. She knew if her mum had her way she'd already be sitting in the tub being scrubbed to within an inch of her life. Enna couldn't quite understand it herself. Why her mother insisted on going to the effort seemed mad. Looking nice if you were just about to change into a Possessed made no sense, nor did trying to impress the magistrate; as if looking pretty would stop him getting you put to the sword. Erik had joked that apparently it was important to look one's best if you are about to be publicly executed. As it was she had been outside with her dad when the news had come. Her father had not tried to stop her. At least he had a bit of faith in her. The Testing wouldn't take place immediately, more than enough time for her to be preened for the parade.

She raced through the village and got herself onto the walkway to the left of the gate. She joined Borric who had also found himself a spot.

'Afternoon, lass. Come to watch the big arrival?' he asked, smiling at her.

She grinned back at him. Borric laughed and ruffled her hair.

As the party grew closer Enna squinted to make out the numbers. There were seven riders in all: two in the lead, one following a few yards behind and then another group of four, two to a side. They would have come from the town of Fallow, a good fifteen miles away. The party would have left early to make sure they arrived in plenty of time before the light began to fade. It was said that Fallow had its own stone walls and a thousand people lived there. How they all got along with each other enclosed in such a small space always concerned Enna, let alone what it must be like to be in Albair City! Her dad had promised to take her to Fallow when she was a little older. She was ready now. She was a teenager!

She began to discern the riders' features. The man riding by himself was the Magistrate. He had been in office for the past five years as best as she could remember. As well as conducting the Testing, his job was to act as the chief representative for the Duke, making sure crimes were punished and arguments settled. He was a grim-faced man, slightly over-weight and had a receding hairline, which was covered by his pot-shaped helmet.

He wore a cream-coloured padded jerkin and had a short sword strapped to his side. Enna felt he looked quite silly and clearly wasn't a fighting man. Not so his companions. Those six were members of the Ducal Guard, not local constables. The Testing was considered of such importance that the Duke would trust the task to none but his own retinue. Just looking at them, Enna thought they must surely be the best soldiers in all the lands. Far better than the Hunters, who were simply gangs of brutes with no real training or discipline. The soldiers rode steadily and swayed with ease on their saddles. Each man wore a pot helmet re-enforced with a nose-piece and cheek guards. Their blue surcoats bore the symbol of the Hawk, the ducal seal, on their left breasts. Underneath they wore chain hauberks that reached to their knees. Each man carried a spear in one hand. Strapped to their horses were sheathed long swords and kite shaped wooden shields. Enna was impressed, as she always was. She dreamt often of one day being able to join the Ducal Guard and ride around the land protecting her kin. Not that there had ever been women on the guard, but she wouldn't let that stop her. As they drew near the gate the crowd parted to allow them access. They would head straight for the inn. It was there that they would conduct the Testing and then overnight before heading back the following morning.

'You know why the Magistrate is done up like a sword practice target, Enna?' asked Borric, beside her.

Enna shook her head.

Borric leaned down and spoke softly. 'Word has it

that two weeks ago he was Testing up in Hadrick's Ford. He had a nine-year-old boy before him. His last of the day. He was tired and wanted to get home. He touched the boy with the Stone and the thing glowed red-hot and burnt his hand.'

Enna stared up at him, a look of alarm on her face. Borric smiled, a mischievous glint in his eye.

'Well, that shouldn't have surprised him. He has been witness to many cursed children. What did surprise him was when the child looked at him and screamed. Screamed and began to change before his very eyes! Seems that the boy might have already been showing some ability, but his parents had not wanted to draw attention to it. Odd though, from what I've always heard, usually the change happens pretty quickly once magic has been employed. It's almost like the creature was biding its time before it took hold.' Borric sighed theatrically and stood. 'They lost three soldiers putting the creature down. Some of those,' he indicated the approaching soldiers, 'are no doubt replacements for the ones that fell. The Magistrate almost lost his life in the process. Guess he's not taking any chances this time.' He gave a short laugh and patted Enna on the shoulder.

When she became a Ducal Guard she wouldn't be taking any chances either, Enna mused. She turned back from Borric and watched them ride underneath her and out the other side. Warner, who owned the inn, and Mistress Tabawick met them just beyond the portal. After a few pleasantries were exchanged, the party carried on the short distance to the inn. Enna sighed, waved to

Borric who nodded back, and headed for home to face the expected telling off by her mum.

An hour later, a freshly washed and dressed Enna and her parents joined the expectant crowd before the inn. Everyone stood around a cleared, horseshoe-shaped area before the entrance. Four of the soldiers stood either side of the doorway. As was expected, all the families of young children were at the front so that they could be called forward. She glanced around and spied Erik on the opposite side of the gathering to her. He stuck his tongue out at her and she responded by thumbing her nose at him. At which point, Erik's mother intervened by giving him a cuff to the head. A few moments later, the Magistrate stepped out from the inn. He no longer wore the helmet and his remaining hair fell down about his ears in sweaty tangles. Behind him came Mistress Tabawick looking solemn and Warner looking agitated. He always got that way when important people turned up at his place, noted Enna. The Magistrate took position in front of the soldiers and gave a gentle cough to get the attention of the crowd. Not that he needed to, as all conversation had stopped at his appearance. He began to speak.

'Good people of North Downs, as I have many times before, I come to you to conduct the Testing. The Testing that has been mandated by Duke Henry himself. I bring before you the Testing Stone,' at which point he put his hand into a leather pouch attached to his belt. From it he withdrew an ebony-coloured stone, about the size of a fist, that was thick around the middle and tapered to sharp points at both ends. He held the shard up for the crowd to see. Even though all the people of North Downs had seen it before, there was a tangible air of excitement, for this object was imbued with magic. Magic was a dark power; the summoner of evil. The irony of using such a tool to defeat magic was not lost on many of the villagers. To use the Stone, it simply needed to touch the flesh of a person. In so doing it could sense and react to any latent magic present within them. The story went that contact with anyone cursed with magic would cause the stone to glow red. Not that she had ever seen it happen. As far as she knew no one in the village had ever been singled out with the Stone. It did make her feel slightly better that this was the case.

The Magistrate continued. 'As is customary, the good Mistress will call out those who are to be tested, one by one. They will be taken into the inn by my soldiers and I will conduct the test myself. Once it is done, your children will be returned to you. I'm sure you have heard of the incident at Hadrick's Ford. The danger is as great as ever. Do not doubt it. If, Duke forbid, the stone reveals a tainted soul, then you will not see them return from this doorway. My men know their duty. We would spare you the pain.'

At this point Enna's mother grabbed her hand and squeezed it tightly. Behind her, her father rested his hands gently on her shoulders. Enna tried to imagine what it must have been like for the Magistrate and his men. Facing a creature that had but moments before seemed like a normal little boy. She had to admit the man must have some bravery about him to continue to do the job he did. She could feel her mother's hand shake with worry. Enna was used to the tension in her mother at these times. As she had grown older, she had become aware of the shared glances, the unspoken words and odd behaviour of her parents. They are both being far too concerned, she thought. I'm thirteen now, past the danger age, and I've never shown one bit of magical ability. Besides, I'm going to be a soldier, hardly what someone possessed would be thinking, is it?

Meanwhile, the Magistrate had finished his speech to the crowd.

'We will begin at once,' he announced. At that, he turned and walked back into the inn with two of the soldiers following. The other two took up positions either side of the entrance. Mistress Tabawick stepped forward and looked slowly around the crowd.

'My friends, I will call out the children one by one. As always I know who needs to be tested.' Her gaze rested on Enna's friend. 'Erik, you first, come with me.'

She held out her hand and, after a few moments where Erik's parents fussed over him, he stepped forward and took it in his. As he walked towards the inn, Erik turned and winked at Enna. She blew him a kiss in return. A couple of minutes later Erik was led back out. His mother gave a cry of relief and ran to fetch him. Others applauded, though the parents of other children did so with only half-hearted enthusiasm. Enna's turn came ten minutes later after six more children had passed the Test.

Mistress Tabawick had called her name out and Enna's parents had given her a hug before gently propelling her towards the teacher. As she passed through the doorway, she studied the soldiers on guard with interest. She wasn't sure if she could wear all that armour. She might have to get a special set made for her when she joined up.

Enna was led into the main room of the inn and was asked to stand by the fireplace in the middle of a cleared area. Tables and chairs had been removed and stacked up against the walls. It was unusual to see the fire lit at this time of the day, though the circumstances dictated otherwise. Two of the guards carried lit brands that they held low and steady before them so as to lessen the chance of inadvertently setting light to something. Borric had told her that the reason for this was that many of the Possessed did not like fire. If a testee were to turn then it would be the first line of defence. They would also burn the inn for good measure. Enna was quite sure Warner wouldn't be so happy about that.

'Enna.' Mistress Tabawick bent down and grasped Enna's right hand gently. 'Just like always, the Magistrate will bend down and touch you with the Stone. It'll take a few moments, and no doubt that'll be it. Don't worry and don't be afraid. And remember, it's your last time ever.'

Enna cocked her head and fixed the woman with an intense face and thin lips. 'I'm not scared, Mistress.'

Mistress Tabawick laughed gently, stood up, and took a few paces back to clear the area around Enna.

The Magistrate then stepped forward and with a solemn expression gazed down on Enna. She noticed that he held himself stiffly and seemed to hold himself back from getting too close from her. As he produced the shard, the air of expectation grew around her. The soldiers tensed themselves and readied their spears, those carrying the brands edged closer. The Magistrate leaned forward and pressed the pitch-black rock against the exposed skin of her arm. It felt cold to the touch, just like it always did.

It shattered with a loud crack, fragments flying in all directions away from Enna. The Magistrate leapt back from her with a shriek. Mistress Tabawick cried out and covered her face with her arms to ward from the small projectiles. The soldiers shouted at each other and closed in on Enna who, rather than being terrified, felt shocked and confused. That was not what was supposed to happen. She had ever heard of a Testing Stone exploding before. As the armed men came towards her she began to back up against the fire. She could feel the heat of the flames against her and knew she could go no further.

'Quickly, stop her before she changes!' shouted one of the soldiers.

Outside, the crowd had heard the commotion and their voices rose in a nervous clamour.

'Wait!' commanded Mistress Tabawick.

The men halted at the tone of her voice and flicked nervous glances at each other.

Mistress Tabawick stepped forward and grabbed hold of the Magistrate who was rubbing blood from his eyes. His forehead had been punctured by a number of fragments and small rivulets of blood were working their way down his face.

'Magistrate, what does this mean?' she asked of the still shaking man.

'I do not know,' he replied, an edge of hysteria in his voice. 'This has never happened before. I do not know.'

'Well, if she were tainted would it not have glowed red? Has it not always done this in the past?' she asked quickly. Enna watched her closely and was grateful. Clearly her teacher was trying to regain order, trying to protect her from harm.

'Yes, yes,' replied the Magistrate. He was regaining his old composure and his brusque official voice was starting to reassert itself. 'A hundred times, a thousand. I don't know. But yes, every time a child tainted with magic has caused the stone to glow red.'

'But never shatter?' pressed Mistress Tabawick.

'No, never,' conceded the man.

'So we cannot presume that she has the mark of magic.'

'We cannot take the chance, what but magic could cause that stone to shatter so?'

'You are right, Magistrate,' said Mistress Tabawick. 'But perhaps it is the magic in the stone that caused it? Perhaps it was no longer functioning correctly?'

The Magistrate chewed his lip. He was clearly rattled, the incident at Hadrick's Ford fresh in his memory.

One of the soldiers stepped forward. 'M'lord, we must act before it is too late. If she changes later, when we are not prepared, lives may be lost.'

The Magistrate nodded irritably. 'Yes, I know,

corporal. But she has not changed yet. The Stones are old, perhaps they are failing?'

'And if not then we risk a slaughter,' argued the corporal.

'But if they are,' interjected Mistress Tabawick, 'and if you do not bring this to the attention of the Duke, more innocent children may die in the panic of the moment. And you, who discovered it first, would shoulder the guilt of knowing you could have stopped it.'

The Magistrate shot her a warning glance. 'Do not presume to tell me my responsibilities, mistress. I know what I must do.'

Mistress Tabawick stepped back in deference, but it was clear her words had had an effect.

The Magistrate continued to ponder.

'Sir?' asked the soldier.

The Magistrate nodded to himself and then looked around at those present.

'Corporal, there appears to be no immediate danger and this is an unexpected event. There is no precedent for it, no protocol to follow. But I will not cause a panic or mistakes will be made. In this kind of situation, those mistakes have often proved to be hazardous to health. '

Michalis burst into the room. He had forced his way past the two worried soldiers at the door and was followed by his wife.

'What have you done?' he demanded of the room.

Mistress Tabawick stepped forward, her hands raised in a placating gesture.

'It is all fine, Michalis, Sarah. Enna is fine. Something

has caused the stone to shatter. We are not sure what.'

'Then what are those men doing around my daughter?' he growled, menace in his voice.

'Nothing as yet,' said the Magistate who looked at the soldiers. 'Stand back,' he ordered.

The soldiers moved away from Enna and lowered their weapons slightly. Sarah ran forward and grabbed Enna in a tearful embrace.

'As I was saying,' continued the Magistrate, 'it would seem proper that this matter is investigated further. I will send a message back to Fallow and from there a summons will be issued for a Hunter Band to come. I have word one is three days ride to the south of here. They also have possession of a stone. I will turn over the responsibility to what happens afterwards to them. And there is the question of the other children to be Tested. In the meantime,' he turned to look at Enna. 'It would seem best that this child was kept under supervision in her home.'

'There is nothing wrong with her!' said Sarah, angrily.

'Perhaps not,' agreed the Magistrate. 'But do you expect your fellow villagers to believe so?'

Mistress Tabawick sighed and nodded. 'He is right Sarah. For all that Michalis and your family are a part of this community, the village cannot afford to take chances.'

Sarah began to cry once more and hugged Enna to her. At the doorway, Michalis tensed his shoulders in anger. But he nodded his agreement.

'I will speak to the village on your family's behalf,

Michalis,' said Mistress Tabawick. 'And I will leave a guard, to provide...protection for you,' added the Magistrate.

That evening Enna lay in her bed and thought about the day's events. Next door she could hear her mother weeping. She had been doing that since they had gotten home. Now that she had had time to think about it, she was certain that there was nothing to worry about. She had never made anything magical happen in her life. She had never been able to tell the future and she certainly couldn't speak to animals. So how could she be a wizard? It had been quite horrid when they had finally left the inn in the presence of four of the soldiers. Mistress Tabawick had gone before them and had spoken to the village about what had happened, how nothing had been proved, and that it was just taking precautions having Enna stay at home. The girl wasn't sure how much of an effect it had had. The rest of the village had watched in silence as they had walked by. Even Erik had looked scared. They had been friends forever and it really hurt to think he didn't like her anymore. Still, when the Hunters arrived, she was sure that things would be sorted out. Enna listened for the guard outside their door to be replaced. She heard the voices and the clink of metal. Satisfied that the soldiers were doing their duty correctly, she fell asleep.
That night in the village of North Downs, there were few houses that did not leave a light on.

CHAPTER THREE

The sun was already high in the sky when Enna emerged from her room. She guessed her parents had deliberately let her sleep what with all the trouble going on. Her mother was busying herself over the stove.

'Morning, Mum,' yawned Enna as she rubbed sleep from her eyes. Sarah looked up and forced a smile for her daughter. Enna noticed that her eyes were red. Probably from all that crying.

'Morning, pet. Come on, sit yourself down.' Sarah pulled out the bench from under the table and Enna plonked herself down. Her mother laid out a spoon, bowl and mug. 'So your father has gone over to the inn this morning. He's going to find out what is happening.'

Sarah poured some milk into the mug and then started to ladle porridge into Enna's bowl.

'Any honey?' asked Enna.

'Yes, hold on.'

41

Sarah grabbed a small pot from the shelf above the stove and placed it on the table. Enna took off the top and used her spoon to scoop out a large helping of honey. Sarah sat opposite her and watched her daughter in silence.

'Has the soldier outside had breakfast?' asked Enna as she drizzled the honey over her porridge.

Her mother raised an eyebrow. 'No, I shouldn't think so. He's been out there for a good few hours now.'

'Aren't you going to invite him in?'

'I most certainly am not!' declared Sarah.

'Go on, Mum, I could talk to him about joining.'

'I am not feeding your jailer, and I doubt if he'd really want to come inside as it is.'

'Mother, please!'

'No, he can get his breakfast when he gets replaced.'

Sarah said it with the tone that Enna knew well. If she carried on, it would probably mean going back to her room without finishing her breakfast. She fell silent and started to think of excuses to go outside and speak to the soldier.

At that point her father stepped through the door. He smiled weakly at his wife and daughter, shut the door behind him and then took up the third seat at the table. He placed his hands flat on the table, puffed his checks out and blew out a long breath. He looked up at his family.

'The Magistrate left this morning with three of his men in tow. Hardly a surprise, I didn't think he'd want to stay around here. They were galloping out in a hurry and my bet is they won't take that long to get back to Fallow. Then they'll send word to the Hunter band.'

'So how long before they get here?' asked Sarah.

'It depends if the Hunters are near a settlement. If so then a bird can get to them in a day. If not, riders will have to get to them. I'd say four days, at best.'

'So Enna has to stay locked away 'til then?' asked Sarah, her voice began to quaver.

'I spoke to Esther Tabawick, she thinks it's best. The village is feeling mightily unsettled. People are talking to me, Sarah, it's not that they wish us ill. They just fear for their own families.'

'And doesn't ours count?' asked Sarah, tears flowing freely.

Michalis reached over to grab her hand.

'Yes, it does. And that's why Esther and the village haven't thrown us out into the night. They have every right to. That's the way of the world now.'

'Well, it's not right!' shouted Sarah.

'It's okay, Mother. I'll be okay.' Enna reached over and squeezed her mother's hand.

Michalis smiled fondly at his daughter.

'See, my love? She's still our little girl. Sensible beyond her years and far braver than the pair of us!'

Sarah choked out a laugh through her sobbing and wiped her eyes.

'Well, this won't do. If our young lady has got to stay here she can help with chores for a change.'

'Oh, Mum!' protested Enna.

After scrubbing the floor until it gleamed, Enna had been allowed to help her father in the smithy. Initially, the soldier on guard had not wanted to allow her out of the house but Enna's father had argued hard that he would be able to keep a far better eye on her outside, and that he had access to fire and weapons if need be. Enna had found the exchange quite funny. Fancy her dad trying to reassure that soldier that if she caused any trouble he would reach over with his hammer, smack her on the head and throw her into the furnace! All her dad ever had to do was just use the threat of a spanking. That always kept her in line.

The soldier had eventually relented and was now sat on a barrel by the side door, munching an apple and watching with mild interest as her father went about his business. Right now, as part of the agreement, he was using his metalworker to sharpen the soldier's knife. As Michalis bent over the spinning stone wheel, Enna worked the rope that imparted rotation to the heavy object. She pulled down on the rope steadily and at an even pace, ensuring that the metalworker rotated at a constant speed. Her father was bent over the wheel, his face a mask of concentration as he moved the edge of the blade across the stone. He'd stop occasionally, examine the metal and then reapply it to the worker.

Enna remembered her father telling her that different blades required different types of cutting edge. A scythe needed to be sharp as it sliced through stalks and vines; a shovel needed a more robust, rounded edge to force its way into stony soil, anything finer would be a waste of time. A sword's edge needed to be sharp, but mustn't be overdone as the edge would become too brittle; it needed flexibility. A knife could afford to be sharper on the edges, so it could be employed for more mundane domestic usage, as long as its point was well defined. That way, when it came to fighting, it could be rammed home into the enemy. Enna had taken this advice to heart; it was important for a soldier to take care of their weapons.

'Okay, Enna, that's enough,' said Michalis, wiping his brow with his left forearm. He held the knife up to the light and gave it a final inspection. He grunted his contentment and returned it to the soldier. The man nodded his appreciation and returned it to its sheath.

Enna waited for her father to return to her side and for a few moments watched him arrange his tools.

'Dad?'

'Yes, Enna?'

'Tell me again about the Hunter Bands?'

Michalis stopped and regarded Enna. A faint smile played on his lips.

'I wondered when you might ask me about them, love.'

Michalis leant down and picked her up. Whilst she was now a good size for her age, he lifted her easily and gently placed her on top of his anvil. Enna giggled, placed her hands under her thighs and swung her legs backwards and forwards. Her dad would always do this before they had a talk about something exciting.

'Well, now,' he began, reaching over for a rag to wipe

his arms as he did so, 'I've only seen one once before, years back, before you were born. There are three such Bands that wander through the lands of Albair. They were formed a few years into the plague, after those settlements, like ours, that could defend themselves had settled into the new ways of life. They were formed by the orders of the Duke himself. Their task was simple, to seek out and destroy the creatures wherever they could.'

'But that's easy,' interrupted Enna. 'All you have to do is go outside at night and they'll come to you.'

'They won't if they feel outnumbered. They tend to hold up by themselves in their lairs, but the Possessed aren't stupid, they have animal cunning. They'll gather together for a hunt, just a couple, when they smell one of us. But remember, they only do this at night, when they have the advantage and then only an army would want to take them on. We haven't had the soldiers to make that size of force since before all this started. What the Hunter Bands do is track them to their daytime lairs, catch them when they are asleep and kill them through surprise and use of numbers. It's a dangerous job,' Michalis stretched and then hunkered down in front of his daughter.

'A man has to be driven to do this job, to face the Possessed again and again. That's why the Hunter Bands only recruit a certain type of soul. Each of the Hunters has suffered a loss, be it wives, children, family or close friends. Each of them has a rage within them, a desire for vengeance. That is what the Hunter Bands look for, someone who'll stop at nothing, risk everything, to see the Possessed destroyed. The Band gives that someone a place to use their rage, a means of controlling and focusing their strength. But they are not soldiers, they are free men. And women, so I hear. That's why they have a reputation of being a bit rough round the edges.'

'So how do they take orders, then?'

'Each Band has a captain and a lieutenant. They are chosen from amongst the Band by the Band, and in turn it is up to them to decide who has what it takes to join them. Soldiers are good fighters, Enna.' Michalis inclined his head to the man who was now listening on their conversation. 'But the Bands are the best at what they do. They exist to fight and destroy the Possessed. It is all they live for.'

'They're only the best because they have an edge,' said the soldier who had eased off the barrel and joined them. Michalis stood up and appraised the man.

'An edge?' he asked.

'Well, apart from the fact that they are psychotic, they are given special chemicals. Some kind of explosive stuff that they use on the creatures. Very expensive. I saw it used once, bloody great bang and lots of flames. But you have to get close to use it. So not only are you likely to blow yourself up, but if you miss, then the bloody Possessed will get you. Hah!' He reached over and patted Enna on the head. She shrunk back a little but was also surprised that the soldier seemed to have forgotten to be afraid of her.

'My advice, steer clear of them buggers and let them get on with it.'

'I'm going to be a soldier when I'm older,' said Enna,

keen to show her agreement.

The man looked at her with an amused expression. He grinned and ruffled her hair.

'Good lass. Sensible decision!' He turned and wandered back to his post by the barrel. Enna was quite pleased and smiled at her father. Michalis smiled back, but his eyes betrayed his sadness.

It was an especially dark night. The clouds had come in thick and black, threatening a big downpour at some point. Borric rolled his shoulders and tilted his head from side to side, stretching tired muscles and trying to keep himself awake. From his vantage point on the south-western watchtower he gazed out across the fields and the woods beyond. There was little he could make out, such was the lack of natural light. After only a couple of hundred paces he could not see much more than black smudges and shapes. The watchtower he was in was nothing more than a raised and covered platform some ten feet higher than the top of the palisade. It had a chest-high railing running around its sides and a torch was placed against the left-hand outward facing edge of the roof support. The woods themselves were lost in the inky depths. The torches were the only sources of illumination and Borric was grateful for them.

Jenna was doing her rounds along the wall now, having just passed him. She was checking to make sure each torch was burning well and did not need replacing. Borric sighed and nibbled on a nail. Jenna's night-time rounds had caused him to think of Enna. Since the

Testing he hadn't seen her, and had missed the usual drill of her inspecting the walls every night. Everyone had been on edge since then and had become as fearful of the danger within the walls as the ones without. Poor lass. Enna was thirteen, she should have been okay. He hoped that perhaps she might still be proved safe. The sooner the Hunter Band got here the better; things would be swiftly resolved. But it just went to show that nothing had really got any better, even after thirty years of the plague. When a smart girl like her was being treated like a murderer, you knew that no one was really any safer now than back at the start of it all.

He placed his hand on top of the palisade and leaned into his spear, which was supported vertically by his other hand. He felt a droplet of water on his hand. Borric tensed and looked up. Sure enough further fat drops hit his hand and face. Great, he had hoped that the rain would not hit until dawn. He reached behind his head and pulled his hood forward. He moved closer to the edge of the railing that faced the western wall and watched the nearest torch some twenty paces away to see what effect the rain would cause. The gentle fall began to build in strength. The torches in the watchtowers were sheltered by the roof but if the rain got any heavier the torches on the walls themselves would soon begin to sputter out. Borric was not overly worried; rain was a fact of life. They would have to rely on the watchtowers and their own eyes and ears until the rain had passed.

As he watched and counted the minutes, the rain became a downpour. One by one the lines of torches to either side of him began to die out. The rain was creating quite a noise as it struck his platform and lines of water were streaming through the many gaps in the roof. Borric drew his cloak about him and wondered how long it would be before it became too sodden and allowed the rain to soak through to his clothes proper. Turning to look below and behind him on the southern wall, he saw Jenna, similarly cloaked against the weather, busy collecting up the wet torches. She would take them back to her home and give them a chance to dry out. He gazed back out into the night. The rain had gotten worse, if that were possible. He could barely see beyond a few dozen paces in each direction.

Looking down and along the wall, most of the ditch was also covered in shadow. At the end he could make out the light coming from the northern tower. Jenna looked up at him and waved as she passed under his platform and commenced her walk towards the northern end of the wall. She collected the nearest torch, and placed it into a large sack that she carried slung over her left shoulder. As she moved off, Borric resumed his vigil. He rubbed his eyes and yawned. As his eyes attempted to refocus, he caught sight of a swift blur off to his left.

'Damn me,' he whispered.

He shook his head, opened his eyes wide and leaned forward. Staring out into the murk he could see nothing, just sheets of rain and layers of mud. A soft thud to his right caused him to spin round and look along the walkway. He couldn't see Jenna anymore. That wasn't right; she couldn't have gone that far along. Perhaps she had fallen off? A rising sense of panic gripped him. He moved to the rear right of his platform and leaned forward, trying to locate her on the ground. He scanned left to right, moving his gaze further along the line of the palisade. There! He spotted her sack. It lay in the mud, torches scattered around it. Straining harder he looked for his friend. Perhaps she was hurt, maybe she was stunned. He saw her! She lay face down in between an alley separating two houses. He could make out her legs and lower torso; she was resting on her side facing away from him. That's it; she must have slipped and knocked herself out on the fall. Suddenly Jenna jerked and she was dragged back into the alley way. Fear gripped Borric. Perhaps someone had found her and was trying to help. But it had been so fast. There had been no cry for assistance.

He leaned back into his tower and swiftly peered back out into the gloom. More blurs of movement against the darkness of the tree line in the middle distance. Borric knew what they were yet couldn't accept it. He stepped back and looked along the palisade. Perhaps the other lookouts had seen them too. They could alert everyone before it was too late. Then he saw them.

'Oh, God's help us,' he whispered.

Dark, monstrous shapes were already in the ditch. Others were crawling up the palisade wall, sharp claws digging deep into the wood to gain purchase. Again he stepped back, trying to make himself invisible. Indecision gripped him. Then a bell tolled. One of the other towers had seen the danger and had reacted. The ringing shook him out of his stupor. He gripped his own bell rope and began to swing it violently. Yanking the rope backwards and forwards, as if that act alone would be enough to stop the horror. The bell's ring added to the first and then it was joined by the others as the discordant cacophony was joined by the shouting of the confused and the screams of the terrified.

'Oh my gods,' said Borric, in quiet hysteria. 'They're coming, they're coming!'

Enna was jerked awake by her mother. It was still dark outside and she blinked at the light pouring in from the main room.

'Mother?'

Sarah shook her head frantically and then cast about for Enna's thick cloak. She scooped it up and beckoned to her.

'Come here, Enna. Quickly!' Her mum had the same panicked air that she had had after the Testing.

As she jumped off the bed and moved to her mother, Enna registered the bells and the shouts of people outside the house. Above her head, the ran added a rapid, violent drumbeat.

'What's going on? What's happening?'

'Not now. Just do as I say!' commanded her mother.

The cloak was bundled about her and she was hustled into the front room. Her father burst in from the door leading to the smithy. He was carrying a long handled woodcutting axe in one hand and his knapsack in the other. He threw the bag to Sarah.

'Quickly, fill it up with food.'

Enna started to feel hollow in her stomach..

'Dad? What's happening? Are we running away?'

Michalis moved to his daughter, knelt down before her and placed his free hand on her shoulder.

'You know those bells, Enna. Something bad has come. That it should happen this night. I don't think it's a coincidence. Either way, I don't want to find out.'

He stood and looked at Sarah. 'Done?'

Her mother closed the flap of the bag. 'Bread and cheese.'

'Good. Now, the soldier left to guard us ran back to the inn. He told us to stay in the house. This is our chance,' said Michalis.

'But they've sent for a Hunter Band. They'll want to see me, won't they?' asked Enna.

Michalis shook he is head. 'And they'll want to take you as well. They aren't like the Magistrate. They won't stay their hands. We get out now. Get away from here.'

Enna looked to her mother. Her face was unreadable as she locked her eyes on Michalis. She gave a small nod. He nodded back, a grim look on his face.

'Stay close to me. We're heading to the south wall. Whatever you see, whatever you hear, ignore it.' At that he opened the door, and stepped out into the night and the sheets of heavy rain. Her mother placed a reassuring hand on her shoulder and squeezed.

Her father stepped back in and beckoned to them.

'It's clear. We go to the right. Stay close to the walls.'

The family ran out into the night, Michalis in the lead,

then Enna followed closely by her mother. They moved swiftly along a lane which snaked away from the main street. It was already sticky underfoot and water puddled everywhere. Enna could not believe how quickly her home, that had seemed so safe and normal just the day before had turned into a nightmare. She watched every alley, every shadow, expecting a monster to leap out and devour her. She could see figures moving across her vision, but she didn't recognise them, the rain obscured everything. Her father stopped at the corner of the house they were moving past. He hunkered down and tilted his head round the side and looked down the alleyway. He was quickly up again and was moving round the corner. They followed him along what was nothing more than a tight passageway between two single story buildings. Up ahead she could see that the alley ended at the perimeter track of the village. They stopped once more at the alley mouth. Michalis looked out left and right and then turned to his family.

'Alright. Straight across from here is the old tool shed. We're going to get inside. We'll be able to take a moment to get your breath.'

Enna remembered that the tool shed was built up against the wall. She didn't think it was used anymore. As a hiding place it was okay but there wasn't anywhere to go. The next moment, they were up and running. Michalis barely slowed as he reached the door, pushed it open and ushered them inside. Enna and her mother stood in the darkness. They were breathing hard but both were trying to keep calm and as silent as possible.

'All here, Michalis?' a voice asked from behind Enna. She started and held her mother tightly.

'We're here. Not exactly the way we planned this, Mistress,' he responded.

'No, and I fear that it's no accident,' agreed Mistress Tabawick.

'Mistress Tabawick' whispered Enna. Her mind as well as her heart was racing now. What was going on? What had they'd been planning?

'Yes, child, it's me.' Enna felt a reassuring hand pat her shoulder. 'Michalis, our work was not discovered. I suggest we do not wait.'

Enna heard her father move to the palisade wall. As her eyes adjusted to the dark, she could see his shape, hunkered down, his back to her. She heard a soft scraping sound, followed by a soft grunt of effort. Suddenly her father was highlighted further by the soft glow of night light. He had taken away a piece of the wall. He shifted his position and revealed a small area where part of the palisade wall had been removed. His hands moved to one side of the hole and began tugging at the wood.

Enna sensed Mistress Tabawick lean down next to her. 'Your father and I did this today. We knew that the wall was weak here,' she whispered.

Her father wrested another chunk of wood away and the hole widened. It appeared big enough for them to squeeze through.

'I'll go first. Then you, Enna, then your mother,' said Michalis.

'I'll come after you,' added Mistress Tabawick.

Michalis nodded and bent down further, readying himself to move through the hole.

A loud thump stunned them into silence. A few moments later, an insistent scratching noise came from above. Something had landed on the roof of the shed and was waiting there. The relative safety of their hideout was lost and the small group could sense that the thing would burst through at any moment. Enna saw her father tense up and reach for his forester's axe. Her mother clutched onto her hand tightly, so tightly that Enna wanted to cry out but she had to be brave. Instead she let tears form in her eyes.

The scratching stopped. She strained to catch the lightest tremor or vibration, desperately hoping that the monster above would launch itself into the night and go hunting for someone else in the village. She felt terrible for thinking it but it didn't make the emotion any less real. There! Something. The faintest sound. It was sniffing. Sniffing so close that is sounded as if the thing had its head right above the roof. Sniffing that was swiftly replaced by a guttural grunting. It knew they were there. It was too late. They would die in here.

'Run!' shouted Mistress Tabawick. She stood and launched herself at the door. She slammed into it and was running out into the night of death. The thing above howled in glee. The shed shook as it launched itself off the roof. Enna saw little but a black blur pursuing her old teacher. Her father's hand grabbed her and spun her round.

'After me', he whispered urgently.

He picked up what seemed like a long pole, pushed it out and then followed it through the hole, hands first, then his arms, then his head. Spreading his arms to either side of the palisade wall he used his strength to lever out the rest of his body. When he was out, he perched on the edge of the palisade mound, the ditch wall sloping steeply down before him. He reached back through the hole, grabbed his axe and then his knapsack and dropped them into the ditch. Sarah urged Enna through the hole. She scrambled through, dimly aware of the mud covering her hands and the rain falling on her head. She felt a brief moment of freefall as she slid off the edge of the palisade ditch before landing in her father's outstretched arms. He placed her down and reached up to grab her mother. Sarah dropped into the ditch with a squelch that sent splats of mud onto Enna's cloak and dress. Michalis took hold of the pole that had been resting against the ditch wall. Enna could see that there were shorter bits of wood that had been placed along the pole running at right angles to it. She understood immediately. It was a simple ladder. Michalis placed it against the opposite wall and pushed its end firmly into the ground and then bracing it at a steep angle against the vertical slope.

'Sarah,' he beckoned.

She stepped forward, a determined set to her face, reached up and grabbed a rung near the top and hauled herself onto the ladder. With Michalis holding the ladder firm in one hand and placing a supporting hand on her rump on the other, Sarah swiftly took two climbing steps and then dragged herself over the edge. Michalis reached down and passed up their meagre belongings. He then reached for Enna.

'You next, hold on tight and pull yourself up. I'll be right behind.' He picked her up and raised her as high as he could so that she was already two thirds up the ladder. She grabbed on tight to the crossbeam and for a few moments her arms had to take the weight as her feet tried to find purchase. She felt her father grab her feet and guide them to a perch. Looking up she saw her mother reaching down with one hand. Enna took it and was hauled, none too roughly back up onto level ground, her mother grunting with the effort.

As she waited for her father to climb up, Enna looked about her. The dark and the rain gave an eerie sense of isolation. Like they were in a bubble, like the ones she used to play with when her mother did the washing. Sarah had often told her tales about what it would be liked to be trapped in one, usually the tale would involve a young princess. Those stories didn't really mean much to her anymore. She knew what was happening behind the walls but she could not sense it. She couldn't see any damage on this side or indeed either of the gates; they had come about at a point almost equal in distance to either. As it was they were located further round the curve of the palisade. For the first time she had a moment to really comprehend what this night meant. She was under no illusion that everyone she had ever known would be dead. She felt that she ought to be crying at this but somehow she just didn't have it in her. She was too frightened.

Michalis hauled himself over the lip, his left leg

swinging round to give him purchase and he was up, gathering his pack and axe and then grabbing Enna's hand. They were off across the open ground in a moment. They ran quickly, fear giving strength to their legs, and were soon entering the tree line. Enna had expected that they would stop, rest up and watch. She was proved wrong. They kept going into the undergrowth, their pace slower now, her father keeping them behind him as he forced a path through low-lying branches and skirted round bushes and smaller shrubs. She felt her mother trying to keep the branches from springing back but every few paces Enna would feel the slap of sodden leaves and twigs. Sometimes they connected harder and gave her a hard sting. For several minutes this continued before she found she was standing on flattened ground. At this point her night sight was well adjusted and she could see they were on a game trail. They stopped for a few moments whilst Michalis glanced up and down the trail. Enna listened intently, hearing only the rustle of the wind as it flowed through the trees. Thankfully the rain had passed.

'This way,' ordered Michalis, and they began to follow him along the northern route. The going was better now and they made good time. Enna was able to take more stock of their situation as they moved. Her father and Mistress Tabawick had planned an escape for this night all along. That's why they had packs prepared so quickly. She wondered if her mother, the quiet but reassuring presence behind her, had known. Either way, they would have all been dead by now. The monsters had been all over the place and she imagined that the gates would have been impossible to get through.

Although, now she thought about it, she had never heard of an attack on a settlement like this before. The tales she had listened to described the monsters as being indiscriminate in their attacks. They were just animals. They might hunt in loose packs but nothing more. But the ones that had attacked them must have thought about what they were doing. They must have understood that to get in they would have to do it together. Perhaps they were getting smarter? That was something really scary to think about. It meant they had been really lucky. But wasn't it odd, though? That they came just after the shattering of the shard? Was that a coincidence too? Enna didn't think of herself as superstitious, the world was clearly a messed up place nowadays, but surely it was nothing to do with her that they had come. Like they had sensed it? That it had acted as some kind of signal? She hoped not. Because if that was the case, then it was her fault that everyone had died. She felt herself starting to well up with tears and her legs go weak. Instead she took deep breaths and steeled herself. Her mother and father needed her to be strong if they were to get out of this. She wouldn't let them down.

A noise shocked Enna out of her reverie and she uttered a gasp before her mother placed a hand over her mouth. Something was crashing through the undergrowth to the left. Her father pushed them both down to the ground and then followed suit. She could feel the tension pouring off him.

From out of the darkness, a figure burst into the moonlight. It seemed to be holding a long branch in one hand. Enna quickly changed her assessment when the top of a spear point flashed. This wasn't a Possessed! The figure, a man judging by the heavy breathing, was blundering past them. Her father reacted quickly; looming up beside the man as he passed, he snagged an arm around the figure's waist. There was a loud shriek and the two fell heavily to the ground, the spear flying from the runner's hand. Whoever it was tried to wriggle out from beneath her father. Michalis clamped his hand firmly over the mouth of the man and whispered urgently in his ear. The man stopped moving and Michalis released his hand.

'Michalis?'

'It is and my family too.'

Enna recognised that voice! It was Borric.

'Borric, are you hurt?' asked Michalis.

Borric sat up as his father climbed off of him.

'No. I'm okay. Just bruised a little.' He searched round for his spear, found it and levered himself up. 'We shouldn't stay here.'

'What happened, Borric? How did it happen?' asked Michalis.

Borric shook his head and glanced over to Enna and Sarah.

'I don't know. It happened too fast. They came from everywhere. I rang the bell. Then one of those things saw me. It was coming along the wall, so I jumped, damned well cleared the ditch too! I was lucky, the ground was so damned soft, didn't break anything. Then I started running.' Borric snorted. 'Think I was going round in circles.'

'Did you see anyone else? Did anyone make it out?' asked Sarah.

'No. I don't know. I didn't look back. I could hear screaming,' Borric replied.

'Alright,' said Michalis. He reached down to collect his axe. Something stopped him. He listened a moment more then stood upright, taking his axe in both hands and planting his feet in a wide stance.

'What is it?' whispered Borric.

'You were followed.'

'No. No. Come on. We must go, now.'

'It's too late. Listen.'

The group stood still. Enna strained her ears, and tried to pick out whatever here father had noticed. It was difficult to do as her heart had started to pound. There! You could just pick it out. It was a hard, guttural breathing, coming from the same direction as Borric. There was no movement she could sense. This thing was tracking them and was taking its time.

'Sarah. When I say, I want you to take Enna and run.'

'Michalis…'

'Just do it,' he replied harshly. Enna had never heard her father speak with such a tone. It was hard and determined.

Borric, gripping his spear tightly, glanced at Michalis.

'What do we do?'

'We kill this thing and give my wife and daughter a chance to live.'

'We could run.'

Michalis shook his head.

The breathing had stopped. The forest was silent and waiting. A Possessed emerged from the gloom. Tall and rangy, the creature was hairless; its skin so pale it seemed almost translucent, there was a gentle shine of moonlight on its bare pate. It stood quite still, regarding them with black eyes, its chest rising gently, oddly misshapen ribs standing out with each breath. It shrugged its shoulders and flexed its arms. Enna saw that it hands were unnaturally long and its fingers tapered into wicked looking talons. The creature smiled, its mouth cracking open far too widely to reveal two lines of bright white serrated teeth.

'Sarah, go!' ordered Michalis.

Sarah took hold of Enna's hand and started to move. The creature tracked their movement and took a step towards them.

'Go!' cried Michalis. He charged at the Possessed. It swung round to meet him and whipped out an arm. It caught Michalis a glancing blow to his side which lifted him clean off the ground and sent him flying off to the side.

Ignoring the shock to his body, Michalis heard Enna scream and looked up to see the Possessed turn back and lope towards his family. Sarah pulled Enna's arm and they started to run up the trail.

Coming up to its side, Borric yelled and thrust his spear at the creature. The blade hit its hip sliding diagonally across, opening up flesh as it travelled. Borric's thrust had extended his balance and his left side was undefended. The Possessed leapt up and latched itself to him. Its legs wrapped around the lower part of his torso and Borric squealed as its hands buried themselves into his back. It leant forward and bit savagely into his neck and stared to tear at his flesh. Borric's knees buckled and his spear dropped to the ground, his arms held out in supplication. Michalis limped up behind the creature, raised his axe high and brought it down hard. It buried itself into its back and the Possessed reared up and howled. Michalis tried to wrench the axe free, but instead the creature released its hold of Borric and scuttled away taking the axe with it.

Michalis clutched his side, his breath was coming in short, painful gasps. He looked behind him to where his family had fled. He could not see them. That was good. Searching for a weapon, he leaned down and gathered up the spear. Borric was dead. His throat had been ripped clean out and his lifeless eyes gazed up into nothing. The Possessed was in front of him, it was bent over, trying to reach behind itself to pull the axe out.

Seeing his chance, Michalis barrelled towards it, the spear held tightly and aimed directly its chest. The Possessed reacted instantly; it stood up and held its arms out pointed forward. Michalis smashed into the creature, the spear rising upwards at an angle entered just below the ribcage. His momentum forced the shaft clean through the thin body and the blade exploded out the back. Michalis felt its talons enter his body coming in from both sides. He did not truly register the thin claws as they pieced his heart. As his body slammed into the Possessed, the force of the impact lifted it into the air and the pair of them careened backwards into a large oak, the spear head driving through into bark.

The Possessed squirmed and pulled its claws free. Unable to get purchase, the creature was pinned in place by the unyielding wood against its back and Michalis's body; his full weight was slumped against it and his hands held the spear in a death grip. The Possessed screamed its frustration and struggled fiercely even as it began to lose strength. After several minutes, the Possessed ceased its movement. Its hands fell to its side and its lifeless head tilted back against the tree.

CHAPTER FOUR

The spyglass sight swept along the line of the west wall. It afforded the user reasonable vision up to a hundred yards before beginning to blur. At this distance, it was easy to identify where the Possessed had scaled the walls and gained access to the settlement. There were long raking claw marks upon the surface of the wood, where areas of timber showed up white against the dark bark. In one particular place, the parapet was stained with blood.

Avery Miller turned his head away from the eye piece, spat out a stream of dark, tobacco-stained saliva onto the ground, his gaze never leaving the walls. He shifted his squatting position so that his weight was supported against the large tree trunk on his left. He could smell, as well as feel, the damp wood after the night's rain. The musty odour always gave him a feeling of comfort. Perhaps it was something to do with the washing away of dirt and the purity of the water. But then that sounded all too much like romanticised bullshit to him. His legs were starting to complain at the strain of maintaining his position; the muscles of his thighs were aching and would soon begin to shake. His trousers were just starting to dry out and he had no intention of getting them sodden again by putting his knees on the gathered detritus of the wood.

There were footfalls behind him and Jess Woodhall, Miller's second-in-command, joined him in a low squat, resting his hand before him on the ground to steady himself.

'No movement on the east side. The smoke is coming from a building not too far from the centre, best as I can figure it. East gate is open, no forced entry. Looks like someone tried to make a run for it. Got tracks leading off into the trees a little further to the north, following a game trail.'

Miller nodded as he continued to scan the walls. 'West gate still shut. So they climbed. See any evidence on that side?'

The other man shook his head. 'Nope, guessing they must have used this side, hoping to get over the wall quick, probably one or two of the black ones getting there first, taking out the sentries, reducing the chances of getting spotted too early.'

Miller raised an eyebrow but conceded the point.

'Fuckers are getting smarter.'

'Looks like. Was a time they would have just come at it all ways. Remember when we got four of those hairy guys in the pit trap? Just came right at us. Didn't even stop to wonder why we were stood in the open like that. Easiest job we ever had.'

Miller grunted. 'Now they'll stop, split up and circle round. Block off your chance to escape.' He lowered the spyglass, retracted it and tucked it inside his jacket. He lifted himself up slightly and angled himself round to the rear of the tree trunk and then stood unsteadily.

'Well, might as well see what's left. Usual clearance formation.'

'Bigger job than we're used to. Don't think we've handled a settlement like this before. Don't you reckon we should just fire the place up?'

Miller shrugged. 'Bigger places than this got cleansed back in the old days, Jess. Ain't no different.'

'Even so, Boss. It's worth going in extra careful - may be more than we can handle at once.'

'Reckon they're long gone but careful is all right. Won't hurt the boys, getting some practice.'

'Think we might start seeing more of this?' asked Woodhall.

Reaching into a pouch at his side, Miller pulled out another plug of tobacco and stuffed it into the side of his mouth.

'As I said. They're getting smarter. Come on, let's go.'

The two men turned back into the depths of the wood line. To either side, armed flankers left their concealed positions and moved in behind them.

'That stuff'll rot your mouth and kill you, you know,' said Woodhall.

'Add it to the list,' replied Miller.

Miller led his troop out of the tree line in front of the eastern gate. Thirty horses emerged almost abreast and halted. Miller looked down the line and signalled to Woodhall. The man nodded and peeled off from the line. Nine more riders followed him. The group made their way around the cleared perimeter and positioned themselves facing the western gate. Those in the main group peeled off into a line. Miller took the centre position and looked left and right down the line of his force.

The riders wore a mixed selection of clothing. Unlike regular troops, the Hunter Bands operated with a degree of independence and never felt themselves part of a properly military structure. Every one of them chose to be part of the group and could leave whenever they wanted. Subsequently they armoured themselves as they saw fit. Some liked to stay light and flexible, restricting themselves to toughened leather and occasional chain pieces. Some of them, inevitably the bigger ones, the 'heavies', went for the whole kit: metal helms, chain coats and gauntlets. These were the ones who would be expected to close with the Possessed and take them on hand to hand. At that point, if the others had done their job, the creature would have been weakened enough to slow them down. The armour was there to protect against wild or desperate swings. If the Possessed were still lively, it wouldn't really matter how well protected you were.

A number of the riders readied wicked looking lances

with barbed heads. Two pairs of Hunters were spreading out nets. Some notched arrows to bows whilst others readied swords, axes and hammers. Miller himself carried a bastard sword, sheathed and currently resting against his back, and a hunting knife strapped to his right thigh.

Reaching behind him he pulled round his crossbow. Taking the hook on the end of a strap fitted to his belt, he attached it to the bowstring. He then took his right foot out of his saddle stirrup, lowered the crossbow down and put his foot through the weapon's stirrup. He then straightened his leg while leaning back in his saddle. It was a lazy manoeuvre; he should have done it standing on the ground. But even in his forties he was still possessed of a powerful body. Some in the Band liked to joke about his age but this simple act let them know he was still up to the job. The bow itself was heavier than most and fired a larger bolt. It wasn't meant for precision or great distance, rather the projectile was designed to pack a punch at short range. Perfect for taking out two hundred plus pounds worth of Possessed. Some of the stronger men in the group also used this weapon as it was perfect whether fighting inside or outdoors

With a grunt, he pulled the string into position and it caught in the trigger and cocked. Pulling out and replacing his foot in the stirrup, he removed the hook then reached down into a pouch hung on the left side of his saddle. He withdrew a black-shafted bolt that looked like a miniature version of the lances. Placing it into the groove of the bow, he rested it gently on his lap.

Satisfied all was ready, he raised his right hand high and urged his mount into a gentle walk. He lowered his hand and took a grip on the crossbow while holding the reins in his left. He swayed in the saddle, making himself relax. The tension would be building up in all the men now. None of them were greenhorns and all of them had faced off against Possessed before, but there was always that slow, inevitable growth of nerves. The twinge in the stomach, the cold sensation in your gums. That expectation that at any moment some hellish creature could burst from hiding, headed straight for you. Miller had come to terms with it, by and large. But he didn't want to ever become inured to it. He'd lose his edge if he did, and whatever was left of his fragile humanity.

As they neared the entrance to North Downs, Miller could see through the open gates. The rain had stained the wood dark and the mud had spattered the bottom sections. But the bloodstains higher up were easy to see. About head height, he reckoned, a spray line stretched two foot along the right-hand gate. Probably a neck wound had caused that, maybe the head had been taken clean off. No sign of the bodies though. Within he could see some clutter; an overturned cart, a smashed barrel. Stopping a few yards away he paused to think through their next move. The place looked quiet. But that meant nothing. Plenty of places to hide. Easy to get pounced on. But he wanted to see inside. Like Jess had said, a place like this was unusual. He wanted to see for himself what had gone on.

'I'm not taking horses in there,' he said to his men.

'Capture teams and lancers can take care of the nags. If we find any of them, we'll flush 'em out and then the riders chase 'em down. Everyone else, dismount and we go in on foot. Usual groups.'

He gently swung off his horse, still holding onto his weapon, its business end held vertical. When he gained his footing, he took it in both hands and lowered it back to horizontal. As he stepped forward, his men formed up around him. Leaving the six riders outside, he lead the rest into the settlement. As he stepped through, he swung his crossbow right and left, covering his arcs. Four more of his men bearing bows quickly followed through, spreading out to his right and left. Miller quickly turned to check the parapets above them. Nothing. The main street ran right through to the western gate. Jess would be sending guys over the gate to target any Possessed heading their way and sending them back towards the main group.

'Light 'em up.'

Beside him the four archers removed their armour-piercing bodkin arrows and replaced them with fire arrows. Made of resin-soaked material, tied just below the arrowhead, they were designed to be used against wooden structures. They served a dual purpose as many of the Possessed had a fear of fire. The Hunter Bands had had success against those beasts that had thick fur, which made it easier for the flames to catch. One of the heavily armoured hunters stepped forward with a torch and lit each arrow. The resin meant the flame burnt slowly and would not easily blow out. That said, the archers did not have to apply the same pull to their bows as for a bodkin and had to take care to remember, else the speed of the flight would sometimes extinguish the arrow.

'Two groups.' Miller picked out half of his mean including two of the archers. 'You lot do a sweep of the perimeter. The rest of us are going straight down the middle'.

The six men of Miller's group took up their places in a much practiced fashion. As they moved down the muddy thoroughfare, Miller took up the middle position. To his flanks, spearmen took station. Their job would be to hold off any attack and give the archers directly behind them a chance to get a bead and loose. The rearguard was made up of two heavies who would step in to finish the job. This meant that Miller would be the first to engage any frontal assault. Just the way he liked it. He always wanted to be a part of the kill, it was the same for any of his men. But being the leader meant that sometimes he had to stand back. He just had to take the satisfaction where he could.

As they reached the entrance to the first building, Miller could see clearly the devastation that had been wrought on the dwellings. Most of the doors were opened; many had been smashed in, likewise some of the window shutters. Further down the street he could see the smoking building. He turned his attention to the first building. It was not large, probably just a one room. The door hung off one hinge and opened inwards. He stepped across the threshold, his crossbow held up to his eyeline and swept the room. To his right was a table, undisturbed it held a number of utensils; a wooden plate and mug, a knife and fork. In front of him was the fireplace. Cold and clean, a small cooking pot was suspended over the grate. To his left sat a single bed. The occupant lay in the midst of his own blood. Miller moved inside, his bow tracking left and right, following up close behind the spearmen entered and took station at the door. Outside, the others took up defensive positions, facing towards the street. Satisfied the room held no hidden terrors, Miller made his way across to the bed. A man, roughly the same age as Miller, lay on his back. His stomach had been ripped open and his entrails lay in a pile on the floor. His throat had a chunk bitten out of it.

There but for the grace of the gods go I, thought Miller. It was always those they found in their beds that bought the memories back to him. He had not been at home the night the creature had attacked. Instead he was making his way back from a grain delivery in the next town. It had been in the early days, when many still believed the plague to be nothing more than rumours or a simple sickness. He had found his wife and daughter in the same way. Both mauled in their beds. They had never had a chance to react. The Possessed were quick, they didn't worry about torture. He always wondered who had died first, because the second would have seen it happen. They would have had to watch the terror unfolding. That was what angered him the most. His older brother Thomas had dragged him screaming from his home. It had taken him a week to recover. His brother had dug the graves and cared for him in his grief. Two weeks later

Thomas was killed.

Miller turned from the body. 'This one ain't coming back,' he stated.

He walked outside and looked about. One of his heavies, carrying a torch, approached. He was a foot taller than Miller, with shaggy blonde hair and piercing blue-eyes.

'What you got, Hall?' asked Miller.

'Ain't nothing moving, boss.' Hall tilted his head towards the eastern end of the village. 'And Woody has got some boys on the gate.'

Miller glanced towards the gate and could make out two bowmen on the parapet, one on either side.

'We move down the line.'

They continued for the next twenty minutes, entering each dwelling, shack or outbuilding in turn. In many they found a number of bodies, in one or two, entire families had been caught. Some had been torn apart and left. Others had been fed upon. As yet they had found no survivors and no evidence of turners, those who had been wounded by the Possessed and then subsequently infected with whatever caused the possession.

It wasn't till they reached the centre that they found bodies lying on the street. The Hunters stood in a circle before the smouldering inn. The only two storey structure in the village, black smoke drifted out from the shattered doorway. Before it were three bodies. Two of them were villagers whilst a third was dressed in military gear.

Hall kneeled down and studied the man. 'Ducal guard.' That answered the question of what had happened to the Magistrate's men. Miller had been scornful of the pompous man, especially when he had refused to travel back with his group. As it turned out, if he had stayed, he'd have ended up like the rest. Sometimes it clearly paid to be a coward.

Miller nodded. These were the reason they were here. They had received the word of an aberration, that some local girl had caused the stone to go shatter. It seemed to him clear cut. Deal with her first then talk about it later. Why they needed his approval he didn't know.

Harvey, one of the archers, was staring into the dark recess of the inn. 'Boss! Looks like we got a last stand in here.'

Stepping forward he peered into the gloom. He could make out tables and chairs piled by the door and windows. He could also make out inert forms lying on the floor.

'A lot of bodies. If there's trouble, I reckon it'll be here,' he said to his men. Moving forward the group entered the building. This time the archers took post by the door whilst the rest moved in deeper. Lying amongst the wreckage were more soldiers. With them were one or two of the local men folk. It was clear that a number of people had taken refuge in the inn. That figures, thought Miller. This would be where the magistrate would have stayed.

'Looks like they piled all this up as a barricade and fired it,' said Harvey, a sallow-faced man with broad shoulders and an arm that could pull a bowstring back like it was just a sapling branch.

'Didn't do much good,' added Hall.

Miller spotted what appeared to be the owner of the inn against the bar. Least the big apron gave it away. Both his arms had been ripped from his sockets. His right was not far away and nearby that was his blade. Miller couldn't see the left arm anywhere. As he glanced idly around he registered that he could see only male bodies.

'Anyone see the women and children?' he asked.

To a chorus of 'no' he walked over to the doorway leading to the kitchens. Another door leading out had been blocked, but there were no signs of forced entry. No doubt it led to a courtyard or some such. He headed back to the bar and found what he had been looking for. A large cellar door lay shut in the floor. He thought for a moment.

'Right, clear the upstairs first. We leave this till last.' He detailed the spearmen and Hall to sweep upstairs.

As they ascended, Miller walked behind the bar and stood before the hatch. Looking under the bar he found a mug. He reached under, gathered it up and placed it on the counter. He looked up and saw Harvey grinning at him. Hefting his crossbow in his right hand he filled up the mug from the nearest barrel and took a long draught. Looking at Harvey, he placed the mug back on the counter.

'You get some when the sweep's done.'

'Yes, Boss. Whatever you say,' replied Harvey, still grinning.

Moments later, his men came tramping back downstairs.

Hall shook his head. 'Place is clean. Lots of beds vacated in a hurry.'

'Right then.' He indicated to the hatch before him. 'We go down. Hall, you get the other side and lift it up. You two,' he nodded at Hall's companions, 'get them spears either side of me. Anything down there is going to know we're up here.'

He took up position in front of the hatch, his crossbow now pointed towards it, his feet braced. To either side the spear heads extended a foot a so beyond him, their bearers taking up a similar braced stance in the area between the bar and kitchens. Leaning over the counter, the other heavy held the torch.

Hall got into a squatting position, reached down took hold of the iron ring and looked up at Miller, who nodded in return.

With a grunt he hauled the hatch up, quickly stepping back as it landed with a thump. Miller edged forward, his weapon brought to eye level. A familiar stench hit his nostrils, a mix of iron, bile and excrement. The stench of death. He could see steps leading steeply down but not the bottom.

'Light.'

The torch flared as it fell into the cellar and guttered as it hit the earth floor below. The light flickered for a moment before steadying. As waves of shadow and light vied at the edges of the torch's corona, Miller knew he could never go into that cellar. He wasn't afraid; he just didn't need to see anymore. His sanity wouldn't take it. The cellar floor was thick with congealed blood. Limbs and torsos lay scattered, their distribution and quantity suggesting a number of bodies. What stopped him, the thing he could never truly deal with, lay just on the edge of his vision. A small arm, a child's arm, lay palm down on the ground. He felt the familiar pains of loss build inside him. He tore his gaze away and looked into the questioning eyes of Harvey. A low growl quickly drew him back. The warning was too late.

A black shape burst from the hatch. It slammed hard into Miller causing him to tumble backward against the two spearmen. He felt claws dig into his jerkin and a blast of hot, fetid breath. Then just as quickly the weight was off him. Somehow he had kept hold of the cross bow and it was pushed up against his chest, the bolt inches from his chin. He sat up and swivelled round. The black Possessed, having leapt over the bar, was crouched low in the middle of the bar area facing off against Harvey and his companion. It was one of the smaller creatures, more nimble than the larger types; all teeth and whirling limbs. Hall had been knocked back against the fire place and was lying in a heap. The other heavy was now blocking the doorway. Miller could see the danger, the windows were clear. He could already see the creature tensing to leap.

'Take it!' he roared, loosing his bolt into the back of the creature. The two archers fired. At short range they couldn't miss. But the Possessed was already on the move. It flew towards Harvey and leapt onto his chest even as the bolt slammed into its back. In one swift motion, it bit into his neck and was leaping out of the window.

'Go. Kill the bastard!' Miller shouted.

The spearmen were already up and running. The heavy had disappeared back outside. He left the crossbow on the floor, pushed himself up and jogged out. He reached behind his shoulder and drew his blade.

Emerging into the daylight he halted quickly. His men surrounded the beast and had it pinned against the wall of the opposite building. One arrow shaft protruded from its chest and the second had broken off in its shoulder. What had truly stopped it was the bolt. It had buried itself in the spine. Miller grunted; a lucky shot. The Possessed was hissing and spitting. Its arms lashed out against the hunters who stayed just out of reach, sending in stabs when its defences opened.

Miller lowered his sword. 'Stop playing with the thing. Get it done.'

The spearmen took a moment to step slightly apart and then thrust into the beast. One head penetrated the left side; the other was blocked by an arm and ended skewering the beast in the belly. As it howled and writhed, the heavy stepped up and brought his axe in an overhead arc, burying itself in the Possessed's head. The creature twitched briefly then its body relaxed.

Miller spat and nodded. Sheathing his sword he returned to the inn. The remaining archer was helping up Hall.

'Scratches?'

Hall shook his head. Getting scratches was not a good thing. It usually ended badly for those that did.

Miller turned his attention to Harvey. The man lay

with his back beneath the window. He was already bled out.

'Alright, you two. Torch this place.'

'Harvey?' asked Hall.

'Leave him here. And drag that other one inside.'

He walked back to the exit and paused. He looked back towards the bar area and the hatchway leading to the cellar. He'd forgotten his crossbow. He walked over and collected the weapon. Behind him his men were creating a pile of wood to burn. He stared at the hatch wondering how the creature had gotten in there. Perhaps in the carnage it had smelt them out, lifted the hatch and dropped in. More likely it was a turner. Someone had gotten bit and the wound had taken. They would have changed and slaughtered the others before they had a chance to escape. Then it had feasted. That's why they had found it down there. It had no reason to leave. He sighed. What a way to go.

The archer had removed his oil bottle and was pouring the liquid over the wood. He left them to it as he returned outside.

He stretched and rolled his shoulders. He watched as their kill was dragged by its arms into the inn and left near the fire pile. Coming down from the excitement of the last few minutes he started to relax. A throbbing in his arm indicated where he had landed badly in his backward tumble. He contemplated whether to reload his bow. *Damn fool, 'course you bloody load it. Remember what just happened?* He slotted his foot into the stirrup and took hold of the string. A chorus of shouting stopped him. He released the tension and stood up. The shouting had come from behind the inn, some distance. It must have been the other search group. He tried to gauge what direction they were moving in.

Looking towards the men on the western gate, he called up. 'You see anything?'

He could see the pair, bows now ready, straining to catch sight of the commotion. One of them lowered his weapon and raised his hand.

'Nothing. Must be headed west!'

Further shouting behind him confirmed it.

Leaving his weapon unloaded, he withdrew his sword for the second time.

Ordering his men gathering at the inn doorway to stay and finish the job, he began to run back down the main street. He could still hear the calls of his men to his right as they continued a pursuit. Ahead his mounted forces had already begun to react. A net had been spread evenly across the entrance and made taught; behind it two lancers were ready to move forward. At that moment, another Possessed, this one long legged and green scaled, came bowling from a side alley and paused, swinging its head right to left, taking in both the gate then the advancing swordsman. Miller didn't falter. To show any kind of fear or weakness was all the encouragement these things needed.

'Come on!' he roared, and charged towards the beast. It reacted swiftly by launching itself at the palisade wall, its powerful rear legs pushing it high into the air. It easily reached the walkway, hauling itself up and then over the parapet.

The Hunters were already reacting. The lancers were turning their horses and the netting was being removed from the gateway. Miller ran to it and then through as space was made. He paused outside as there was no way he could catch the beast now. As it was, the second capture team was already moving to intercept. The creature had landed awkwardly in the mud when clearing the ditch, falling on its side. As it scrabbled to gain purchase, the horsemen passed either side and let the net drop cleanly on top of it. Each corner of the net was weighted, and as the Possessed howled and struggled to get free, it only succeeded in snaring itself even further as the weight of the net held it firm.

Its struggles were brief as the two lancers brought their weapons to bear. While the mud meant they could not build speed, the lancers knew their business. As the weapons closed with the target, the riders leaned in with their bodies and drove the lances hard into the creature. They continued past, the lance-shafts left quivering in the flesh of the Possessed, and quickly slowed their mounts. They retrieved short javelins from their saddles and walked their horses back towards the wounded prey.

The capture team, already turned and carrying similar weapons, joined their colleagues. As they closed with the beast, each man drew back his javelin, waited for a clean shot, and launched it the short distance into the body of the Possessed. They then withdrew and watched the beast closely. It had stopped moving after the second javelin had pierced its skin. But it was still devious and deadly. It was best to let it bleed out and wait for the heavies to step in and finish it off.

All this Miller witnessed before he sheathed his blade. He forced himself to breathe deeply as he regained his wind. Behind him were gathered the men of the second sweep party, in similar states of breathlessness. One of them joined Miller.

'Leapt out a barn attic. Straight over our heads and was off down the street before we got a bead in 'im'.

Miller nodded. 'Anyone hurt?'

'No, all fine.'

'We lost Harvey.'

'Shit.'

'Yeah. Okay. Get your breath back and finish your sweep.'

'Yes, boss.'

He cupped his hands and called over to the riders. 'We got a fire going. Drag that sack of shit in there and throw it in as well.'

One of the riders raised a hand in acknowledgement and Miller turned and walked slowly back towards the inn. He could see smoke billowing from the building and his men gathered outside. As he reached them, Hall handed him back his crossbow. The group stood and watched the blaze grow. It was possible that it might spread to adjoining buildings, but Miller figured they would be too wet for the fire to take. To be honest, he wasn't bothered either way. This place was dead anyway.

He hefted his crossbow, now reloaded.

'We finish our sweep and get out of here.'

As the group took up their previous formation, he was pleased to see that no one had shown any sign of irritation at his orders. They were all tired, but the loss of a comrade and the long experience of their work meant they knew what had to be done.

The rest of the search proved to be uneventful. When they reached the far gate, Miller ordered it open. He then sent his group back along the street with orders to wait for and assist the perimeter group.

Woodhall walked his horse up to the gate and dismounted. He looked up at the two archers on the parapet.

'Down you come. Don't shoot yourselves on the way.' He turned to Miller 'I heard we lost Harvey.'

'Yep. Bastard got past me.'

Woodhall sighed. 'Clearing a house is never simple.'

'Never is.' Miller turned his head and spat.

'Reckon the ones we caught were turners.'

'Uh huh.'

'How many you think got in here?'

Woodhall scratched his head. 'Lot of tracks in the mud. A lot. Not sure I've seen so many together before.'

'That's a problem.'

Woodhall grunted.

'Big one. We run across a pack like that we're fucked.'

'Then let's not. So I guess we can forget about checking that girl out.'

'Maybe. Found some human tracks. Heading off into the woods.

Miller shook his head.

'If they went in there, they wouldn't have lasted long. Something would have found 'em.'

'Guess so.'

Miller looked at his friend.

'Ain't got time to be looking for lost causes. I want to see if we can't track this pack. See if we can't wear 'em down some. I'm going for my horse. Walk your guys back round. We're done here.'

'Yes, sir.'

Woodhall mounted his horse and called his men. Miller made his way back through the centre of North Downs. As he passed the now blazing inn he could feel the heat against the side of his face. He didn't stop. He didn't think about the man he had lost. There was no point.

CHAPTER FIVE

Outside the rain hammered down; a constant, rapid staccato against the rocks. Enna huddled in close to her mother, the pair of them gazing out into the dark from the shelter of a small cave looking out into the forest. They had discovered it as they paralleled a high, sheer ridgeline running north and east. Finally having a chance to rest, she reflected on how they had come to this point.

A dark storm was pursuing them from the west and they had begun to despair of finding shelter. On the move constantly since her father's death, Enna was struggling. Sleep was reduced to nothing more than snatched minutes and she felt exhausted. Her mother drove them on remorselessly. They had to get out of the forest but had done themselves no favours in fleeing north; it only drove them deeper into it. It was a miracle that they had not been found by any Possessed.

Her mother had seen the cave. As they moved

through the trees, they kept to the edge of the ridge where the scree slope met the forest. The undergrowth was thick and the ground treacherous, but better to stay in or as near the daylight as possible.

'There!' her mother had pointed up and to the left. Enna had seen the small opening, mid-way up the rock-face. They had scrambled over to it and had, to their joy, found the makings of a route: nothing more than a goat-path, leading up to the entrance. Together they climbed, fear and necessity driving them up the precarious path. A few minutes later the wind picked up, thunder rolled and the storm arrived.

Now, as the wind howled and the rain lashed the trees, Enna wondered what would happen next. Once the storm clouds had hit, it had grown very dark, and there would be no more protection from the sun. But they were dry. Perhaps the storm will help get rid of our scent or something, she thought. Maybe we left them all behind, maybe they were all in the south? That would at least explain why they had not been discovered.

She looked behind her into the back of the cave. It was tight in there, only half her height. The roof was jagged and sharp, though the floor was relatively smooth, and there were signs of life. Fur, its colour lost in the dark, was scattered all over, on the ground and caught on the cave walls. She supposed it was from a goat. She dreaded to think if they belonged to a mountain lion. Or *what if the goats were eaten by the lion?* She was being foolish, there'd been no bones on the floor and if this was home to something vicious there would have been evidence.

Wouldn't there? A flash of lightning illuminated the space, throwing light into the rear of the cave, and giving her the briefest glimpse of a hole, large enough for her to crawl into. A tunnel! It sat a little to the right and bottom of the cave wall, running off into the dark, not a few feet away from her.

'Mother!' she whispered. 'This cave goes back aways. Where do you think it leads?'

Her mother turned around, looked for a moment and shook her head.

'I'd rather not think about it. Nowhere,' she pulled Enna back to her. 'If anything was sharing this with us, I'd think they would have announced themselves by now.'

Enna hummed. Her mum was probably right. She resumed her vigil, gazing out into the forest. Another flash of light, another bolt of lightning, scratched the sky. It lit up the trees, and the cave and the bare rock of the ridge. And, just for a moment, a shape emerging from the trees. Not a shape, a figure.

Enna's breath caught and she squeezed her mother's arm.

'Enna, what?'

'There's something down there. I saw it!" replied Enna.

Her mother acted without hesitation.

'Get back, quickly.'

Enna scuttled deeper into the cave and banged her head against the roof. She bit her lip and hunkered down. She watched as her mother pushed herself against the right-hand side of the cave mouth and peered out. She withdrew her head and worked her way back towards Enna.

'It's found the trail we used. It's... sniffing,' she whispered urgently.

'What should we do?' asked Enna.

'I don't know. Wait, be quiet. It might not-' she stopped. 'It's wet here. Look, put your hand down... there.' Enna felt her hand taken and pressed on the floor next to tunnel mouth. It was wet.

'That's running water. It's coming from somewhere. Quickly go through!' Enna's mother pushed her towards the hole.

'But what if it leads nowhere?' Enna asked.

'We don't have time. Go. I'm right behind you.'

Enna scrambled into the hole and started to crawl. Any night vision she had was swiftly gone and she had to extend her arms out to feel her way ahead, her head kept low. What if this just stops? she thought. Fear came unbidden. She imagined herself being trapped in the dark, the tunnel narrowing and her body caught, no way forward, no way back. And then the creature comes, she could hear the breathing, it was going to grab her legs, pull her back and tear her open or eat her from the feet up. Enna bit back a scream. She had to keep moving. The tunnel continued, the rainwater still trickling beneath her fingers, making wet slapping sounds under her hands. And the breathing she heard was her own.

As she crawled, she realised that she was starting to climb, that she was reaching forwards and up, seeking handholds and straining to lever herself up. Climbing was good, the world was above. She stopped and looked back.

'Mother, the tunnel is going up!'

'I know,' came the hissed reply. 'Keep going, it's behind me.'

Enna forced herself on, fear giving energy to her tired muscles. As she scrambled on, her eyes could make out a glow ahead of her, like her vision was blurred. Drawing near, her eyes made sense of it. She could see! But the passage was ending, it was just a blank wall. No, she realised, it wasn't. As she reached into the grey light, it played upon her hands. Looking up, her face was splashed by raindrops and water cascaded down the sides of a near vertical chimney. She wriggled about, reached up and gripping the sides, pulled herself into a standing position.

'Can you climb out?' asked her mother, her head poking out from the end of the tunnel.

'Yes, I'll try.' Enna turned around, looking for somewhere to put her feet. She found a protrusion of rock, stepped onto it and climbed up into the chimney. She looked about her, found another handhold and a place to put her foot. The going was easier than she had thought. Her shoulders almost touched the sides and though it was slick with water there was plenty of clefts, gaps and lumps to grab on to. Her confidence grew, the higher she climbed. She found she could lean against the rock behind, and pushing with her legs, pull up with her hands. Looking up, it was getting lighter. A gentle breeze played against her face, and she heard the rush of the wind.

A bloodcurdling snarl erupted from beneath her, flowing over her and onwards, reverberating off the walls. Her foot slipped and her heart flew into her mouth as her body shunted down the chimney. It came to a stop just as rapidly. 'Huh' she breathed. She felt a pressure on her foot, a tight grip.

'I've got you,' grunted her mother, strain in her voice.

The pressure on Enna's foot increased, forcing it upwards. Pressing herself against the rock she lifted the leg free and jammed it back in place. Pushing up, she commenced her climb once more.

Her head breached the mouth of the chimney and the wind whipped her hair into her face. Gods but it had never felt so good. The rain had ceased. The world around her was still dark but she was out! She freed her arms and placing them to either side of the hole, dragged herself up and out. She lay on grass. Her fingers ran through the wet, soft stalks. She looked about, the grass ended just a few inches away from her and then... nothing. She sat up onto her knees. Behind her and to either side was another cliff face. A mixture of bare rock and peppered with sprouts of grass and weeds, swaying in the wind. She was on a ledge, overlooking what, she could not say.

'Enna.'

She looked over. Her mother was climbing out of the hole. She crawled over, took her mother's arm and pulled. She spilled out into the ledge, her breath ragged.

'It was right behind me. I could hear it,' she said. 'Where are we?'

'I don't know, I didn't look yet,' replied Enna.

Her mother scuttled to the edge and looked over. Enna joined her, pulling the hair from her eyes, and looked down. Below them a river surged and beyond that, on the far side, the forest continued. They were on the far side of the ridge, part of a bluff forcing its way into the water.

'What do we do?' she asked.

Her mother looked back toward the hole. 'We can't stay here.'

Surely she didn't mean to jump? Who knows what's under the water, how shallow it is? Enna thought.

Another growl came from the hole. It was close.

'Come on. Stand up.' Her mother grabbed her arm and hauled her up. 'We've got to jump.'

Enna shook her head. 'But... '

'We have to.'

Enna stole another look at the hole. Talons emerged, groping their way into the night sky.

Enna felt her mother's hands on her shoulders. Then they shoved. Enna pitched forward, lost her balance and fell. She let out a shriek and slammed into the water. It was cold, her breath driven from her lungs by the shock. The current grabbed her as she flailed to the surface. As she breached, she sucked in a mouthful of air between bouts of coughing. Amidst the sound of the river she heard a loud splash, and her mother's head appeared not far from her. *Thank the Gods.* She kicked hard to stay afloat and spread her arms wide and down to give her lift. As water slapped into her face and the river carried her away, she looked up and back toward the bluff. As it receded from view, she spied the Possessed, crouched on the ledge. For a moment she feared it would dive in after them. But it remained motionless. It was too far away but she could swear its eyes were upon her.

A hand grabbed her arm.

'Enna, stay close to me.'

'Should we swim to the other side?'

'Not yet. Let the river carry us.'

Enna was not sure how long they stayed in the water, but as she worked to keep herself afloat, she felt safer. The forest swept by them, and above, the storm cleared from the sky. Stars and moonlight bathed the water, the glow comforting. She felt the pull of the river lessen as it widened. Spreading out as it moved beyond the ridgeline and its rocky banks replaced with trees and inlets.

'Enna?' her mother asked.

'Hmm?'

'I'm tired. Let's get out of the water.'

'Which side?'

'The right.'

Together they struck out for the bank. It took just a few strokes before their feet touched the riverbank and, supporting each along, they climbed out and onto the riverbank itself. They collapsed against the wide trunk of an oak tree.

'Will we be safe here?' Enna asked.

Her mother shook her head.

'I don't know. But we've gone a long way. We should be fine 'til morning.'

Her mother reached over her shoulder and unclasped her cloak, letting it fall to the ground.

'We need to get undressed or we'll catch our death.' She stood, pulled her tunic off and hung it on a branch. 'The sun will dry it some before we have to set off. Come on.'

Enna stood and stripped, handing over her clothes, britches and socks. Once done her mother sat her down and wrapped her arms round her.

'All done. Now stay close to me. We can keep each other warm.'

Enna snuggled in close.

'I can't believe you pushed me in, mum,' she said. 'Anything could've happened.'

Her mother stroked her cheek.

'I had no choice. It was the river or the monster.'

'It was a fast choice you had to make. I didn't know what to do.

'One day, my angel, you might understand. There is nothing stronger than a mother's love for her child. It will drive you to do things you never thought possible.'

CHAPTER SIX

Three days.

Three days had passed and they had seen no sign of the Possessed. No sign of anyone. It must be over. It was a miracle. The gods were finally being kind to them. Enna thanked them all.

Two miracles in fact. Because on this late afternoon they had found a road, a well-travelled trail, a length of rutted brown earth, running east to west. After following the river for so long, Enna had started to despair that they would ever find another soul. There had been no sign of any human life, no settlements, nothing. The land was wild. At least they'd been able to forage some. There were plenty of autumn berries to pick, plenty of apples. They'd even found a pear tree or two.

Walking east along the road, a final miracle confronted them. Up ahead was a trader caravan. It was camped on the side of the road in a large open area of cleared ground, set well away from any vegetation. Smoke from a cook fire drifted up into the darkening sky. Enna beamed at her mother.

'Thank the Gods,' her mother said. She gripped hold of Enna's hand and together they walked towards the caravan. As they drew nearer, Enna looked over the camp. A dozen wagons were corralled in a circle, the gaps between them made as tight as possible. Some were covered with hide, others no more than flatbeds, carrying crates and barrels. The horses had been unhitched and tethered within the safety of the circle. There were two men stood by an entrance to the circle; both carried spears and wore helmets of some sort. They watched Enna and her mother approach for a while, and then one turned and shouted into the camp. Another man emerged and walked out towards them. They met thirty yards from the camp.

'Afternoon,' said the man, dipping his head. He was of middle years, with a mop of curly brown hair and a short-cropped beard showing grey. He was big bellied, his belt cinched tight about his waist, causing the fat to spill over the top of it. Enna didn't think that could be comfortable.

'Good afternoon to you, sir,' said her mother.

He looked them up and down. Enna felt a little self-conscious. To say they looked bedraggled was being too kind to them.

'You two looks like you've been in the wars.' He scratched his beard. 'Where have you come from then?'

'From North Downs,' said her mother.

The man raised an eyebrow.

'North Downs, you say. That's a ways west of here. Long ways west.'

Her mother coughed. It was an unpleasant, hacking sound.

'We were attacked. Possessed got into the town, huh? You ran a fair distance, I'll give you that.'

'We did. And we have been lost. You are the first people we've seen for days.'

The man shrugged.

'Not a surprise. We're roughly halfway between Longhaven and Hearthold. You have to spend nights out on the road to do it. Not to everyone's taste.' He paused for a moment, looking them up and down once more.

'I imagine you'll be wanting to shelter with us tonight?'

'Yes, yes, sir. We would like that very much.'

'No skin off my nose. We caught a deer yesterday. Plenty of meat to go round. Never let it be said that I don't show charity in these trying times.'

'Thank you so much,' said Enna's mother, squeezing her hand tightly. 'Say thank you, Enna.'

'Thank you, sir,' she replied, with genuine gratitude.

The man grunted.

'North Downs? Possessed attack? Not sure I believe you. But the road ain't no place for women on their own. Not unless you pay for more than thirty guards to go with you. Costs me dear to have to keep so many on. But what can you do? You'll be safe with us tonight. No Possessed has ever bothered me with the number of spears I have at my back. Come on in.'

He turned and they followed him into the camp.

They did eat well that night. The caravan master was an honourable man and ensured they had blankets and a quiet space to themselves. It felt good to have something hot, and not made of fruit, in her stomach. It was now very late, sometime after midnight. Her mother lay asleep next to her, face drawn and haggard, mouth hanging open, utterly exhausted. She had been coughing more, a wet, rattling sound, and Enna was concerned that she had picked something up during their nights in the wild. Enna couldn't sleep. She wasn't sure what it was, but she had spent hours just lying on the ground, restless. A strange sensation, almost like pins and needles, buzzed in her head. *I might as well walk it off. Perhaps it'll clear my head.* She stood and walked to the nearest wagon, ducked under it and crawled to the far side. Looking out from the perimeter of the encircled wagons, there were at least four guards she could see. They were gathered by a large, well stoked fire. It blazed away like a bright beacon and she could feel the heat it generated, warming her face. She knew another fire was built on the far side with yet more men. The caravan master was right about his guards. He had plenty, more armed men than she had ever seen in one place. You'd need them to travel on the open road after dark. She was tempted to join them by the fire, but something stopped her. What was it? That damned buzzing in her head was still there. She lay under a wagon and stared out into the dark. The land was cleared of vegetation well back from the trail. This was a deliberately placed site, green with grass, the wood cut well back to afford a good clear view of the tree line, perhaps a quarter of a mile away. She stared at that tree line for some time. She didn't know why. She put it down to nerves. Her stomach had gone cold, like when she had butterflies.

There was a change. At first she couldn't put her finger on it. Something about the night. Then it struck her. She realised that other than the crackle of the watch fires and the soft talk of the sentries off to one side, there was no noise. All the usual sounds of small creatures moving amongst the undergrowth had stopped. There was no breeze to mask this, and no suggestion of rain in the sky. The sound had just stopped. She strained her eyes, probing the darkened ground around her. Was that a shadow, a shape she saw moving across the open ground? Am I imagining it? She felt panic rising inside of her. She forced it down, wriggled back out from under the cart and raced to her mother. She shook her awake. 'We have to go. We have to go now!' she whispered frantically.

It took some moments for her mother to come to. She started to question her daughter, but instead Enna placed a finger on her mother's lips and dragged her up. Her mother gave another cough, she clutched Enna's arm weakly.

'Enna, I...'

'Mother, trust me,' she said softly. Pausing only to grab a few apples from a nearby stores wagon, Enna led them through the camp, past sleeping drivers and the snoring wagon master. They wriggled between two wagons on the far side, heading for a small, rocky mound to the north.

As they ran out, a sentry called after them. His voice was joined by others as the camp awoke. First there were shouted questions, then cries of alarm. An inhuman howl echoed behind them, its call taken up by others, joining their own twisted voices to the noise. Enna scrambled up the mound, using the rocks to haul herself up. At the top of the mound she helped her mother who had fallen some way behind. She was breathing heavily. They took a moment, pressed against the hard, uncomfortable surface of the mound, hidden from the view of the caravan. Enna looked ahead of her. The ground ahead was undulating, punctuated by more of the mounds, many crowned by small stands of trees. The buzzing in her head was still strong, but the way ahead felt safe. She did not think anything was out there.

'Come on,' she said, helping her unresisting mother to stand. They ran down the slope. Those concerned shouts from the camp changed in nature, becoming panicked, and then turning to screams. Neither she nor her mother looked back.

CHAPTER SEVEN

The autumn rains had truly started early. The lands had been plagued by an unusual number of storms during the preceding months but they usually ended as swiftly as they had started. Now, though, the rain had a more persistent quality and, coupled with the cooler weather, it meant that the nights were becoming miserable and less easy to tolerate. The ground was losing its residual heat, built up from the day's warming, and the cloud cover meant there was little of that at the best of times. In the northern Highlands of the Duchy, it was often moot as to which season it was. Spring blended into summer and summer was often a brief interlude before autumn's swift move into the hard, grim winters. Those that lived in the northern settlements seldom had the opportunity to enjoy long, hot summer days. Their time was spent moving with the herds of cattle that roamed over the hills or maintaining the few vegetable crops that would take. It was a wild place and sparsely populated. This had worked to the advantage of the inhabitants. It meant there were fewer instances of Possession and the hill farmers felt more confident about being far from their beds. They were hardy, tough and used to the dangers that nature threw at them. The terrors of the recent years were but one more problem to deal with.

It was fortunate then, that a group of three highlanders, passing through their southernmost grazing lands, were alerted by their cattle dogs to a discovery. The dogs, muscular and wearing short-haired coats of light, wheaten-coloured fur, were typical of the Highland breeds. Loyal and intelligent, they were natural hunters and acted as excellent guards. They could smell Possessed a mile off.

'What we got, lads?' asked the eldest of the men. The dogs were capering around a small rock outcropping midway down the slope the men were traversing. The lands for many miles around were made up of bare rock, steep slopes and grasses. The outcropping itself was insignificant, and was far too small to be the lair of any beast.

'They seem more excited than worried, Merrett,' observed one of his companions.

Merrett chewed his lips. 'Aye, guess we should have a look then.'

He led the way down the slope towards the rocks. Each man carried a spear which they used as a walking aid whilst on each man's back was carried a bow and a covered quiver of arrows. As they neared, he whistled to the dogs, who obediently lay down, their tails wagging and tongues lolling.

Merrett halted and scratched his beard. The man, who had spoken before, indicated with his spear butt.

'Looks like a body.'

'Ah, that it does, Adrian. Go on then, Conor. Have a look.' The last and youngest of the trio glanced over with a look of mild alarm.

'Stop your fretting. If they're dead, they're dead. If they're not, I'd imagine they'd have turned by now.'

'What if it's a beast laid a trap?'

'Then we poke these spears into it and kill it where it lays,' said Adrian.

'And the boys will help shred it. Go on, now. Or I'll tell your mother.'

Conor shook his head in irritation and moved towards the prone form. He held his spear out in front of him and stopped when he reached prodding distance.

'Okay, you can come over.'

His companions joined him and Merrett squatted down next to the body.

'A woman.' He leant forwards and picked up her arm. It hung limply in his hands as he felt for a pulse. He shook his head. 'No. She's gone.'

'What about the girl?' asked Conor.

'Well,' Merrett leaned over, gripped the farthest shoulder of the woman and pulled her towards him to rest on her back. He then bent over the girl who had been shielded by the older woman's body. This time Merrett didn't test for a pulse.

'She's breathing.'

He rolled back onto his haunches, blew out a whistle and looked around him.

'Where do you reckon they come from, Merrett?' asked Adrian.

'Between us we'd recognise anybody living within three days march of here. And I'm sure I've never seen these two before. Besides, look at the state of 'em. They've been abroad for a while.'

'Traders. Got lost from a caravan, maybe?' said Conor.

Merrett shrugged. 'Maybe.' He stood using his spear as a lever. 'Standing out here ain't going to solve the question. You two fix up a litter and we'll look to get this one home.'

As his companions got to work, Merrett called for his dogs. They bounded over enthusiastically. They had some rounding up to do before heading back. He wanted to make sure they were well on their way before nightfall.

It was pitch black. There was no sense of space but there was a measure of time. It was the breathing, heavy and laboured. Always present, but never in the same place. First from behind, then in front, then just by the shoulder. Close and then drawing farther away. Up ahead a pin-prick of light. Drawing closer. And as it did so the breathing changed in pitch and tone. It became shrill, more desperate. Faster and shallower. It turned again, this time not breathing but screaming. As the light drew even nearer, so the screaming became longer with fewer pauses. Then the light was close, it filled the space in all directions and the screaming wouldn't stop.

And the light changed. It lost its intensity, it gained form. All around shapes began to appear. Alien. Then familiar. A quick blink of darkness then the world was revealed. Enna was screaming, it was her. And she lay in a bed. In a room she did not know surrounded by strangers who tried to comfort her, even as she struggled to be free of the blankets wrapped tightly about her.

And then, overcome with fatigue and sorrow, Enna stopped struggling and laid back. She was exhausted and she knew her mind was on fire. But she also knew what this meant. She was alive and her mother was dead.

She closed her eyes. Her breathing became less ragged. She felt a wet cloth against her forehead. She sucked in the cold sensation and revelled in it. It calmed her down. She felt cared for in a way that only her mother could do. In a time that seemed long ago. She dimly listened to the soothing voices and allowed herself to fall back into the darkness. But this time she felt no fear.

'So what do you think, hen?' asked Merrett.

The woman sat at the side of bed removed the cloth from Enna's head and squeezed the water out of into a small bowl by her feet. 'She'll be fine now. I dare say she'll be sleeping naturally for a day or so yet and then wake up as famished as a new born babe.'

'And then I think we'll be needing to ask her some questions.'

'Well, you can wait for that, husband. If that was her

mother you found out there, I can't imagine she'll want to talk about much. So, did you go and fetch the body?'

'Aye. I'd have thought the wolves would've been at it but they didn't. We've already buried her. Craig and Denny prepared a spot.'

'Well, that's good. So I guess you'll be wanting feeding now.'

Merrett smiled. 'I think I've earned my appetite.'

His wife stood and together they left the room.

Two days later Enna, sat up in the bed with two pillows behind her back, ploughing her way through a second helping of broth. This was her lunchtime meal and she'd already had two bowls of porridge earlier in the day. After that meal she'd slept some more and had been woken by the herder's wife, Mary, with the steaming mix of vegetables and meat only a short while ago. She had wolfed down the food and the slab of bread that had gone with it. She hadn't really had time to savour the taste and textures of the meal but Mary had quickly returned with the second bowl, with amusement in her eyes. As she handed it over she had instructed Enna to take her time and actually try and chew her food. Enna felt sufficiently sated to do just that and allowed herself the chance to enjoy the experience. It had indeed been a long time since she had had anything hot, or indeed anything which hadn't been pulled straight from a tree, or ripped from the earth.

'Good, eh?'

Enna looked up and nodded enthusiastically at the

man leaning against the doorframe.

'Been a while?'

Again she nodded but this time kept her attention fixed on the food.

'Mind if I sit?'

She shook her head.

The man came over and sat at the end of her bed.

'This was my son's bed. Hasn't been used since he grew up and found a house for himself, in another place north of here. Could have done something with the room I guess. But well, you get sentimental for such things. It's not that we have many visitors staying over these past few years. But there you go.'

Enna glanced up at him. She got the impression he had started to ramble a bit and was waiting for him to ask the obvious questions. He seemed older than her father, maybe ten years or so, his hair was grey and there was a bald patch in the middle of his head that spread all the way to the front. He wasn't well built but had a wiry, muscled frame from what she could see through his short sleeved woollen tunic. His eyes seemed keen and kindly enough.

'My name's Merrett, by the way. You've already met my wife Mary.'

Enna continued to eat. Then she remembered her manners.

'Enna.'

'Well then, Enna. Now that we've been introduced, I dare say you'll be wanting to know where you are?'

'North.'

'Yes. I imagine that's true, judging by your accent.'

'I watched the sun and I counted the days. Well I did after the first few anyway. We were too busy running to think about much. But then I started counting. I guess it was easier cos I got hungry and started thinking about when last I ate.'

'So how many days did you count, Enna?'

'Twelve. I think.'

Merrett sat back a little and rubbed his chin.

'So you've been travelling north all that time? You've come a long way, then.'

Enna tore off a chunk of bread and started mopping up the last of the liquid in her bowl.

'I don't think we were always going north. Mum kept changing directions. We were with a caravan for a night.'

'A caravan, you say?'

She nodded.

'Traders?'

'Yes. But they found us anyway.'

'Who did? Who found you?'

'The Possessed.'

'They were chasing you? What, all that time?'

Enna was now chewing on her bread so just shrugged.

'But Possessed don't do that. I've never heard of it.'

'We thought we might have lost them when we used the river. We floated down it for a whole day. On a big branch we had found, it had lots of smaller branches and we could lie on top of them and not be wet. It was warm that day.'

'You and your mother?'

'Uh huh.'

'Enna...your mother.'

'I know. She's dead, isn't she?'

'We brought her back. Got her buried in the cemetery. Nice and safe.'

He stopped and studied her for a moment. Enna looked back and met his gaze. He had the same look that her father got when he was wrestling with a problem.

'You feel up to going to see her?'

'Yes. Please.'

Merrett nodded and stood up.

'Then I'll see if Mary can't rustle you up something to wear. I'll be by to fetch you soon,' he turned, and walked out the room, shutting the door behind him. Enna placed the bowl and plate on the small table beside her. This seemed like a nice place and she felt her mother would have been happy. She had been crying the last night they'd been together. Her mother had lain on the ground by the rock, exhausted. She had pulled Enna to her and began to weep. As they lay there, Enna felt her mother's hand gently stroke her, it was a feeble and light touch but it was all she could do for her daughter. Enna had lain there, tired as she was, and concentrated on every stroke, wanting to feel the sensation of her mother's love for her. As time wore on, Enna's own tiredness began to take hold, she drifted in and out of consciousness. At some point she realised that her mother had stopped stroking her, the hand resting limply against her back. As Sarah grew cold, Enna had stopped fighting and let the darkness take her.

Enna stood in the bedroom wearing a simple grey dress, a white tunic and a thick shawl. On her feet were a pair of sturdy leather boots and woollen socks. All supplied by Mary, courtesy of a neighbour's daughter. Merrett, wearing a cloak swept over one shoulder, entered the room and inspected her. He nodded appreciatively.

'A true lass of the high country!'

He held out his hand and gestured for her to walk through. Together they left Merrett's cottage and walked into what looked like a small hamlet. Each house was built on a single level out of sturdy blocks of stone and topped off with tightly worked thatch. Many of the dwellings had small gardens and fenced off areas where vegetables were grown or livestock kept. Surrounding this hamlet was a stone wall about twelve feet in height. Here and there along its length, buildings had been constructed using it as their rear wall. A simple wooden gate in its centre lay open. To the left side of it stood a wooden watchtower. Enna noted that it was unmanned and that the gate itself was open. Even in daylight this shocked her. She looked up in alarm at Merrett. He caught her expression and smiled.

'Aye. I know what you're thinking. But things are quieter up here. We don't get much trouble. Besides, you haven't seen what's behind you.'

He took her shoulders and gently turned her around. Before her stood a large, imposing keep. She had never seen one before but her father had told her stories and had described what they were used for. She remembered him saying that larger towns had some form of building like this. A place of refuge and defence, where the local lord or magistrate would live. The grandest of these keeps was to be found at Albair city, the Ducal Palace. This particular keep was a rather dour building when compared to her imagined splendour of the Duke's residence. It had four storeys and a set of battlements above that. There were no windows below the fourth storey. Instead there a number of thin arrow slits dotted along its length. She could see that above the double doors was a portcullis with wicked looking spikes.

'Cormant Keep. This is where we took refuge in the dark days. Kept us nice and safe. The laird still lives there – you'll see him in a while. But that's not all.' He turned her around and walked her towards the open gates. As they got nearer Enna could make out what lay beyond. A humped, stone road bordered by short walls made of the same stuff. A bridge. And beneath it lay water. As they walked through the gates she took in the scene before her. As she looked left and right she could see the curve of the land and the water surrounding it.

'Is this an island?' she asked.

Merrett nodded.

'Yes. A patch of soil lying amidst the water of this lake. Good fishing too. And all around us we have the hills. And look, no trees hiding the horizon. It isn't easy for something to be creeping up on us without somebody spotting it.'

They began to walk over the stone bridge. Up on the slopes ahead, Enna could make out a flock of sheep being driven by a herder and his dog. She looked back on the lake and saw how the island was actually very near to the shoreline. Behind it, the lake spread out for what must be half a mile, bordered all around by slopes leading up to high hilltops. She could see a boat bobbing in the middle; a figure hunched forward tugging on their fishing rod. Enna found it hard to come to terms with all that she was seeing after the hardships she had been through. She never really thought she'd see such a life again. As they walked off the bridge she saw how the shoreline, whilst rocky and bearing the marks of higher water levels, also had patches of dry and green land stretching some way back before starting to rise. It was at the end of a short path leading off the well-worn trail leading up westwards into the hills where lay the graveyard.

'We've buried all our people here for the last twenty years or so. Before that it was reserved for those in the keep. Then of course we all started moving in. And now this is where you'll find your mother.'

The graveyard was bordered with a crude waist high stone wall: just big enough to keep out curious livestock. They entered through a wooden gate and Enna noted how the first few rows bore stones, raised rectangles well weathered from age. Looking at the inscriptions, she could see these were for the staff and retainers of previous lairds. She guessed that a laird was a type of baron or lord. A number of larger plots off to the right seemed like they belonged to those lairds.

As they moved further through the graveyard, the graves became simpler and, she guessed, more recent.

Small stones placed into the ground recorded husbands, wives and children but did not talk of rank or roles. Ahead the graves ended but the space within the enclosed area stretched on for some time. They arrived at a freshly dug plot. The soil still brown, the marks of a shovel where it had tamped it down were clear and defined.

'This is her,' said Merrett.

Enna gazed at the grave and wasn't sure how she was supposed to feel. She knew her mother was dead and gone. But she couldn't find the tears to shed. She had cried for her father. She hadn't had time to say goodbye. But she had watched her mother slowly give up and waste away. She was glad that her mother had passed on. Her suffering was over.

'We haven't got a place stone for her yet. Well, we don't even know her name,' said Merrett.

'Sarah.'

'A lovely name. Anything you want to say? Anything else you would want us to write?'

Enna shrugged. 'She was my mother. My dad's name was Michalis. They're both gone now.'

'Well. That'll do then.' Merrett looked about him. 'So do you want a moment to yourself?'

'No, that's okay. I don't need to.'

'You're a tough one. Alright then. Let's take you to see Donald. You up to telling your tale?'

'Yes. Not much to tell. But I will.'

'Good enough. Come on then, lass. I'll see to the stone after we're done.'

As they turned and walked back to the island, Enna

114

wondered why she felt so hollow. She knew there was something wrong with her. It had started back at home, a small knot in her stomach. She knew it was because of what had happened at the testing. But she'd still been with her parents and somehow she felt everything would be alright. Now they were gone, the thing had grown inside of her. As she entered the hamlet and walked towards the keep, she figured out the problem. She just didn't know what she was supposed to do now.

The inside of the keep was dark and smelt of smoke and must. The floors were laid with worn but uneven flagstones. There was little illumination other than what was allowed in by the doors, so the place had a perpetual gloom to it. She was also surprised by how cold it was. Certainly colder inside than out. She had also expected the doorway to lead into a great hall or something. Instead it was a reasonably wide passage with a doorway immediately on the inside to the left of the entrance. The door was open and within she could see a spiked wheel with dark, well-oiled chains leading up into the ceiling.

'That'll be the portcullis room,' remarked Merrett. 'You'll find the kitchens and armoury on this level.' As they passed along the corridor, it opened up to a larger chamber, further rooms opened up into it with steps set into the wall leading both down and up.

'Downstairs you'll find storage chambers and below that we even have some dungeons. But last time we used them was when young Conor got drunk, so we threw him in there for the night to sleep it off,' Merrett chuckled. 'Poor lad spent the whole night hearing scratching and swore blind there were Possessed down there. Ach, what's a few rats between friends?'

'I like rats,' commented Enna, as she looked around.

'Good for you. And they don't taste half as bad as people say. As long as you cook them right. Anyway, up the stairs we go.'

They ascended the steps and reached the first floor landing. A corridor and rooms led off it but they continued on up to the next floor. On this landing, a short passage led to an open doorway. Inside was a much larger room. This was more what Enna was expecting. A long table dominated the centre of what appeared to be more like a small hall. A number of benches ran along each side of the table but at the front a large, grand-looking chair stood by itself. Around the sides, the walls were decorated with a number of tapestries depicting various woodland scenes which seemed to mostly involve hunting. One stood out in particular, as its theme appeared to be a fight between two groups of men. She could spot that each side wore different coloured cloth. Men were waving swords and pikes, dogs like the ones she had seen walking about outside were biting at legs; in one part of the scene she could see a head flying off a body.

'Everyone always stops and looks at that one.' A new voice came from the far side of the hall. 'It's sad, really. Most of our lives are taken up with the other scenes of daily survival and life. But it's always those brief moments of violence that draw interest.'

Enna turned to watch the new arrival as he entered

through a doorway on the far side of the room. He wore a cream shirt and dark brown britches finished off with brown leather boots. He looked a lot like Merrett, his hair was grey too but longer and swept back from his head. Enna, whilst not used to seeing nobility, could see he carried himself with an air of authority and command. But his smile seemed nice enough.

'That particular one was made to commemorate one of the many number of conflicts with our neighbours of old,' he continued. 'Though you'll find that in recent times none of the surviving families have really had much inclination. All the old enmities were forgotten as we withdrew into our keeps to weather the storm. Although, I can imagine a time, long from now, when perhaps things have gone back to the way they were. And I can imagine that this reticence to fight one another will suddenly cure itself and we'll be back squabbling amongst ourselves.' He joined them at the tapestry.

Merrett sighed. 'You don't have a very optimistic outlook, do you, cousin?'

The man lifted his hands in mock surprise.

'Why, Merrett, you misunderstand me. I hold a very optimistic view, have I not just said how I predict a time when these monsters no longer stalk the land and plague our families?'

'Very well, M'lord. I stand corrected,' Merrett laughed. He gestured towards Enna. 'This is our foundling, her name is Enna.' The man inclined his head. 'And this is our Laird, Donald.'

Enna made an awkward attempt at a curtsey. She

wasn't sure if she got it right. She couldn't remember doing one before.

Donald laughed at her, and Enna felt her face flush.

'No, no, young Enna. I don't mean to embarrass you, rather I can't remember a time when I've been curtsied to.'

'It's true. We don't really go in for that in these parts,' added Merrett.

'Be that as it may, I thank you, Enna,' said Donald sincerely. 'So, as my cousin has already told you, I am the laird of this keep and the lands around it. We belong to the clan Maelwick, although we have become much reduced of late. And the lands we used to claim for ourselves are not as secure as they once were.' He gave her another swift smile but his eyes did not share its warmth. 'So what do you think of our island?'

'I like it. I wish we had a place like this in my village. We could have fought them off if we had.'

'Ah, well now. Here we come to it. Come, let us sit.' He led them to the head of the table. He indicated for Enna to set on the end of the bench nearest the right side of the chair. He took this for himself whilst Merrett settled himself down on the bench opposite. Already set on the table was a jug of water and three cups. Donald poured some out into each cup himself and set one before Enna. He then leaned forward, rested his arms on the table and clasped his hands.

'Merrett has already told me what he has learned from you. But, from what he has gained, it has but deepened the mystery of your arrival here. I would like, if you are able, for you to tell me as much of your story as you can bear. I understand it may be difficult for you but believe me, in these times the need to be forthcoming has never been greater.'

Enna nodded her head. She understood why they would want to hear why a young girl would be so far away from home. And in her case, for almost exactly the right reasons. She didn't really know these people and how would they react when they heard about her Testing. They might just throw her into the lake. So maybe she should leave that part out. Enna started her tale about the destruction of her village. Merrett hissed and Donald sat back when she told them of the massed attack of the Possessed. They, like her, had never heard of such an occurrence before.

She almost slipped up when she mentioned the presence of the Magistrate and his men for the Testing but quickly recovered by making a dismissive comment about her having had the test the year before. She then continued with how her family had fled their home and the loss of her father. She struggled to put the rest of her tale into order. This part had become jumbled as she and her mother had travelled north. Not really knowing where to go, rather just trying to stay ahead of the beasts. They hadn't time to consider it at first but, after two escapes, they had begun to realise that they were being deliberately tracked.

'Why did you not head for the settlement the caravan was going to?' asked Merrett. He looked at Donald. 'No doubt it was Hearthold.' Donald nodded in agreement and looked back towards Enna.

Enna shrugged. 'In the dark we just kept running, in the morning we were lost again. We didn't really have time to think about following the trail. I should have done though.'

'And then, soon after, you entered the Highlands?' asked Donald.

'Yes, I think so. At that point my mother was really weak. She had become ill shortly after having crossed the river, days before. The climbing was really hard on her and we could find less to eat.'

Donald leaned forward again.

'Lass, you said that the attack on your village came when?'

'It was the end of August,' Enna replied, although she was not sure on the date.

'Well, we are into autumn now. I would hazard that you have been running for three weeks.'

This shocked Enna. She hadn't really figured out how long they had been running for.

'And you've come a long way. By rather a zigzag route by the sound of it. There aren't many settlements between here and where you came from. You were lucky to have found us.' Donald steepled his fingers and rested his chin upon the tips. 'But what you say worries me greatly – why were these creatures following you? It makes no sense. Perhaps you are mistaken.'

This was too much for Enna. 'I lost my family and my friends to these things, and then they almost caught us three times!' Enna cried angrily.

Donald and Merrett reeled back in surprise at her outburst.

'I am sorry, Enna. I did not mean to question your honesty,' said Donald. 'But you must understand, there has never been an example of the behaviour you have described. The creatures have always been things of passion and animal instincts. What you describe suggests intelligence and drive that none of us have ever witnessed.'

'And why do they pursue you so doggedly, lass?' asked Merrett.

Enna cursed herself. She shouldn't have mentioned all the times they had been pursued. They were getting suspicious. Normally she was much better at making up tales. But the horrors of the last few weeks had robbed her of her imagination. All she knew was that they mustn't learn that the Testing had gone wrong.

She sighed.

'I really don't know. We were too busy running to ask why this was happening to us.'

Donald nodded and placed his hands on the table.

'Very well, Enna. I don't think there is much more we can discover today. Go home with Merrett. Tomorrow I want you to go and speak to someone else about these matters. He has rather more experience than I do in such things. I'll go and speak to him myself today. But no doubt he'll want the full story from you.'

At that Donald stood to signal the end of the discussion.

Merrett leaned in to Enna.

'Lass, I just need a moment with Donald. Can you find your way back to the keep entrance?'

Enna nodded.

'Good, then. I'll see you there in a minute or two. Off you go now.'

He gently pushed her away and Enna made for the stairs. She looked back to find the two men watching her go. At the door, she made to walk down the steps but stopped after the first couple. She waited a moment and then quietly tiptoed back towards the doorway. She strained to hear what was said but all she could discern was a low murmur. One word she did pick out was 'Testing'. That gave her a start. She almost risked peeking her head round but thought better of it. Instead she turned and quickly made her way back to the stairs and down to the main doors. As she waited she chewed her lip. She didn't really know what she could do. If she ran, there was no telling what would happen. At least here she felt safe. But then she had felt that way at home. She knew now how even her own neighbours, people she had known all her life, could turn against her if she posed a threat. These people looked pretty tough, and she could easily being imagined being thrown in the lake like the stories she heard about witches of old. That didn't sound like fun. She would just have to wait, maybe gather some supplies, and be ready to run if things turned against her.

A few moments later Merrett joined her. He smiled and placed an arm around her.

'Come on then, lass, I'll show you a bit more of our little world.'

Enna didn't detect any of the concern his face had shown earlier, but she decided to push the matter.

'Is everything alright? I really don't know what else I can tell you.'

Merrett shook his head.

'It's fine. No need to worry. We'll get it sorted out tomorrow.'

'Who are we going to see?'

'Our very own local madman!' laughed Merrett.

'Really?'

'Well. I suppose he is, amongst other things. As I said, not to worry. We'll be heading up to see him in the morning.'

'Where does he live?'

'Oh about a mile or so away, round the other side of the lake actually. It won't take us long to get there. The question is, do you want to walk round or row across?'

Enna shrugged. 'What's quicker?'

Merrett scratched his chin. 'Hmm. Depends what sort of hurry you're in. If you were sprinting you might get there first, but I don't see why anyone would want to bother.'

'So, we are rowing, then?'

'Good idea.'

That night, Enna lay in her bed thinking about what might happen in the morning. She was seriously considering her earlier plan to leave. Why would they want to take her to see a madman? It made no sense and she was pretty sure it could only end badly for her.

Merrett hadn't volunteered any more information to her and, excusing himself to tend to matters agricultural, left here in the care of Mary. She fussed over Enna for a while before allowing her free rein of the island. Enna had spent an hour or so wondering around the settlement. Her first impression had been of a small hamlet. It was actually a bit bigger than that. She spent some time counting how many homes were accommodated within the walls. She counted thirty or so houses of varying size and upkeep. She guessed there must be a hundred or so living here. There wasn't much space left what with the gardens as well. People were friendly and bid her good day though there were not many people around.

Earlier, Mary had said that during the daytime both men and women alike could be found out in the hills looking after flocks of cattle, sheep and goats, hunting game or fishing. It was a matter of what work suited people best. The coming of the Possessed had meant certain divisions of labour had to be changed. Enna had then casually asked when the next Testing was. She wanted to make sure she was nowhere close to it.

Mary shrugged at that. 'Well, whenever we need one.'

'You have a Testing stone? All to yourselves?'

'Not quite that. But you're not far off the truth.' At that Mary bustled off to continue with her chores.

As she wandered around, Enna had been able to find a small leather bag with a shoulder strap. It had been left inside a shed that looked like it hadn't been used in a while. She had placed it over her head and had been able to acquire a few items. A small fish knife, some string and a fish hook. She had even wandered into the keep and had been able to take a loaf of bread and some dried meats. She had walked out the main gate and then followed a path round to the back of the keep which led to a pier sat out into the lake. She went past it and had to scramble over some rocks and then buried the bag under some rocks up against the keep wall.

So all in all Enna was pleased with her preparations. By placing the bag by the pier, she intended to slip away by boat. Just let them try and sniff her out, she thought. She'd realised pretty quickly that the cattle dogs they used would be really good at hunting, just as they were good at sniffing out Possessed. So now, if she needed to, she could slip out and be off. She fell asleep planning her escape.

CHAPTER EIGHT

Enna and Merrett left Cormant at dawn. Accompanying them was Merrett's dog, Jagger. A bright, well-muscled thing that stayed close to his master's side and wagged his tail happily whenever Enna made to stroke him. Much of the settlement was still hidden in gloom and murk. There were some signs of life, with a few lights showing through wooden window slats. It was chilly and Enna was wrapped up in her thick woollen shawl. Merrett nodded to the man on watch in the tower, who climbed down and let them out the gate. They walked round to the pier and Merrett helped her into the front of one of three rowing boats tied to the side. Jagger hopped in after her whilst Merrett untied the tether and stepped easily into the middle. He gathered the mooring rope and placed it beside him, then drew out the two oars that were resting lengthways along the boat. He pushed off with one and as the boat drifted out he fitted the two oars into their rests and began to pull the boat out onto the lake.

Enna wrapped the shawl around her and absent-mindedly stroked Jagger's head, the dog having sat himself close to her, no doubt realising he might be made a fuss of. As the boat cut a path through the centre of the lake, she watched as mist rose from the water. Ripples and the lightest of splashes marked where fish came to the top to feed. Looking up, Enna could see streaks of light through the light cloud cover coming from the east. This early in the morning, the sun had yet to clear the line of hills bordering the lake. The gentle stroke of the oars and the creaking of the boat caused Enna to believe she might still be dreaming. She was certainly tired enough. A quick wet nosed sniff to her ear from Jagger dispelled this notion. She looked over at him and gave his chin a scratch.

'Oh, he likes you,' said Merrett.

Enna glanced behind and Merrett smiled back at her.

'Our cattle dogs are tough animals. Very loyal. Seems he's already adopted you.'

Enna reached over and gave Jagger a squeeze. It felt nice to have him around. The rest of the trip was conducted in silence. Enna was happy just to sit there and watch the quiet world go by. Slowly the far side, which had been largely screened by the mist, began to appear. Firstly, as a series of dark humps, and then the familiar rocky shore and various draws, gullies and slopes began to take shape.

'Lass, take the mooring rope, would you?'

Enna reached down beside her to take the rope. She noted that there wasn't any pier on this side of the water.

'Where do you want me to tie this off?'

'Oh, don't worry about that. When we beach, I need you to jump off and start pulling the boat up. We'll just leave it on the shore.'

'Alright.'

Enna readied herself and as the boat covered the last few feet to land, she could feel the vibrations of the boat scraping along the beach. It jerked to a stop and she stood up half jumping, half pushing herself over the bow. Her boots splashed in the last few inches of water underneath her and she ran a few steps onto dry land. Jagger jumped off after her and stood his ground, tail wagging enthusiastically. She pulled on the rope but didn't feel that she did much, the weight of both the boat and Merrett was too great. Merrett stood, picked up his knapsack and spear and stepped steadily from the boat. He walked round to the front and, one handed, yanked the boat onto the shingle. Enna staggered back as the tension on the rope was lost.

'Sorry, lass. Here.' He passed her his spear to hold and took the rope from her hands. He coiled it and placed it inside and then with two hands this time, gave the boat another pull and brought it up a foot further onto the shore.

'So. On we go.'

Merrett took the lead and made for a meandering path

leading up a steep gorse slope. As the climber, Jagger took the lead and trotted ahead of his master. Enna suspected Jagger knew the way quite well.

She was a little out of breath when they reached the top and she realised that the hill was in fact a false horizon. Ahead of her was a steadily climbing, wide patch of rock and gorse that spread to the left and right. Ahead, this flat plain of rock ended in a series of short cliffs. They made their way across the ground, taking care to avoid the various cracks and depressions that covered the landscape. As they got nearer, she spied that the cliffs were dotted with small openings and cave mouths. From one or two of the smaller ones she could see birds coming and going.

Their route took them towards a jumble of large boulders that created a natural canyon to negotiate through. The path in between was tight enough to allow only one person at a time. Jagger went first; Merrett indicated that Enna should go next. Being smaller, she found the gap easy to move through. At the end of this short path, the way opened up into a small enclosed area and beyond that a cave. A man sat cross-legged before the entrance. He was dressed in a similar manner to the men of Cormant and was puffing away on a pipe. To one side of the entrance a fire pit was lit and a crude kettle was suspended over it. A cloak was drawn about him but Enna could easily see he had a very slender frame. This wasn't surprising; he looked as old as the hills. Bald, apart from a ring of grey hair encircling his head at about the level of his ears. Jagger bounded up to him and he reached out to pat the dog. His face was weathered and had a great many wrinkles; the skin on his hand looked like it was paper thin. Merrett moved up to stand next to Enna.

'Morning, Tenn.'

The man named Tenn nodded back and raised his pipe.

'Morning, Merrett. This the girl?'

'Yes. Enna is her name.'

The old man fixed her with his stare. Enna gazed back into a set of dark blue eyes. They glittered with an intelligence and life that belied the age of their owner. She felt very intimidated.

'So, young lady. I've already had a version of the tale from Donald. He came round yesterday afternoon having spoken to you. It seems like you've had quite an adventure.'

'I wouldn't call it that,' she responded.

Tenn took a draw from his pipe. 'No, I guess you wouldn't.'

He stood up slowly, a look of pain moving across his features.

'Getting old?' asked Merrett.

Tenn waved a dismiss hand at him.

'You're one to talk, Merrett. I remember you when you still had some colour in your hair. And less of a stomach. Anyways, why don't you pop inside and get some mugs. The tea's been brewing for half an hour so I dare say it's ready. And as for you, Enna. Why don't you settle yourself by the fire? Let's hear your story, shall we?' He lowered himself back down into his cross-legged position but left a space through into the cave. Merrett walked past and went inside.

Enna did as she was told and found a flat spot near the pit, the heat keeping the chill away. Tenn continued to regard her. Moments later Merrett came out with three mugs that he set on the ground before the kettle. He used the hem of his cloak to take the kettle off its hook and poured out three steaming cups of liquid. He put the kettle back and placed a mug in front of Enna and handed another to Tenn. He then took the third, stood up and leaned against the rock behind him, Jagger laid out by his side.

'Off you go then,' urged Tenn.

So for the second time in as many days, she retold the events of the last few weeks. This time round, although she knew Merrett had heard her before, she tried not to dwell on the long pursuit that followed the attack on North Downs. Tenn listened quietly, puffing on his pipe and occasionally sipping from his mug. Once she finished, she reached for her tea and took a sip. It was lukewarm but had been sweetened with something. It tasted good and she finished it all before putting the mug back down.

'Well, she's got an appetite on her,' said Merrett.

'That she has,' agreed Tenn. 'So I can imagine you are wondering why the good folk of Cormant would want to involve a mad old man who lives in a cave?'

Enna bit her lip. 'Yes?'

'Quite right too. Well, let's say I might be old and live in a cave and some would have you believe I'm mad. But I'm not without my uses and I do know a thing or two about certain subjects.'

'For example,' Merrett added, 'you might be surprised to know that we don't have Testings. At least not the way you do.'

'I know, Mary said you had your own Stone.'

'Hmm, not really,' said Merrett smiling at Tenn.

'What he means to say, young lady, is that in return for some of the bare essentials of life, I perform that service for them,' said Tenn.

'What do you mean?' said Enna. 'It needs magic to do that and we don't have wizards anymore.'

'True enough,' agreed Tann. 'Well, almost true.' He then forced himself from his sitting position, the same pained expression passed over his face.

'Now, Enna. I've heard your story. And I've no reason to doubt what you say. But there are many things which concern me. Especially regarding this dogged persistence shown by the Possessed in trying to hunt you down. Now whether or not you say this is nothing more than coincidence is not the point. If something is happening, and these creatures are tracking you, who's to say they won't track you here? I can imagine the good people of Cormant would not be best pleased.'

'Aye to that,' responded Merrett.

'If you don't mind. I'd like to take a closer look at you. Tell me, Enna, you have been Tested, have you not?'

'Last year.'

'And nothing happened. All was well?'

Enna felt butterflies in her stomach but tried to hold his gaze.

'They touched my arm and nothing happened. Nothing ever has.'

'Hmm.' Tenn looked at Merrett.

'Enna and I will go for a chat in the cave. Help yourself to some more tea, Merrett, I shouldn't think we'll be long.'

'Don't mind if I do.'

Tenn turned and walked into the cave entrance. Enna felt her panic rising. She didn't know who this man was but she knew she was trapped. If she made a run for it Merrett would probably grab her and if not, Jagger would be on her in an instant. She forced herself to stay calm and stick with her story. They probably don't have a testing stone anyway. They probably expect this man to guess if children are going to turn or not, she thought to herself.

She followed him in and allowed her eyes to adjust to the gloom. The light coming in from the entrance helped but it took a couple of seconds before she could see that the cave mouth quickly opened out to an almost circular chamber. Placed on and around the sides of the walls were various bits and pieces of furniture, books, utensils and tools. Some of these she could only guess at their use.

On the far right side was a cot with a large number of blankets. In the centre of the room was a small rug made of thick pile. Tenn took up station on the far side of it.

'This is where I meditate. At my age it needs to be comfortable,' he said, with a wry smile. 'When Donald came to me yesterday he was worried. And he has every right to be if the story, which you gave me a slightly altered version of, is true.'

Enna felt her face flush. This was what a cornered rat must feel like.

'The folk of Cormant use me to Test their children. Within this cave,' he looked around him. 'I can do so without fear of...consequences. My name, my full name, is Tennebran. And I am a magician, a sorcerer, a mage. There are a number of names but for the sake of brevity, I am a magic user. Best if you still call me Tenn.'

She should have been shocked, fearful even, but she wasn't. Just looking at him suggested he was either a mad old hermit who truly believed what he was saying or perhaps, in truth, he was a wizard.

'People like you are why we have Testing,' said Enna. She really wasn't sure how to react to this man. If what he said was true then he could turn at any moment. He was the reason that this whole nightmare had started and, indirectly, led to the slaughter of her family. Although, ever since her Testing, she couldn't condemn someone out of hand.

'Quite true. We have had to adopt brutal measures to continue our survival. It's not the first time and I'm sure it won't be the last. Just think, how many babies, deformed or sick, have parents discarded as nothing more than a burden to their lives? In that sense it isn't very different. But that is a discussion for another time. What concerns us now is that for whatever reason, the Possessed that *my kind* have become, are displaying behaviour none have heard of before. Of immediate concern to my friend Donald is whether or not we can expect the same sort of event to happen here. And finally, of personal concern to me,' Tenn pointed a crooked finger at Enna 'is why you are not telling the whole truth?'

Enna knew this had been coming. It had been in way he had looked at her whilst she told the tale. But if she didn't admit to anything, how would they know? They only had her word for it.

'I've told you everything!' She said in a voice that was rather huffier than she had planned. It made her sound like a petulant child.

Tenn scowled and rocked on his haunches.

'Very well, Enna. I really don't have the time or patience for theatrics or temper tantrums. So, I'm going to be completely honest with you. That way you might understand that we are not so different as you would believe.' He stopped himself for a moment and grunted, 'I am more than just a magician. I was once the Archmage to the Dukes of Albair. In fact I am the uncle to the current Duke. And I was probably the most powerful sorcerer on this island. But I'm willing to argue the point. That's if there was anyone left to argue it with.

The thing is, young Enna, by all the laws of this land, I shouldn't exist anymore. I, more than anyone, should have willingly surrendered myself to the very laws I advocated. But I didn't, because being the most powerful sorcerer in the land does give one a different perspective. But,' he placed his hands palms down on his thighs, 'I am here only because of the trust of the Laird. If he wished to he could cast me out or report me. Troops would come and it would make no difference to them who I might be related to. They'd make sure of me, make sure I wouldn't be a danger to anyone anymore, and they'd have every right to. But instead, I'm alive because of trust. And now I have trusted you with this knowledge. And I hope that you will not go running from this place and bring a Hunter Band upon my head. So, Enna, I say again. Tell me the whole truth. It will go no further.'

She sighed and dropped her head. It was true. This old man had placed himself in a difficult position. His life truly was in her hands now. She had to take a chance. Maybe it would be alright and if not, she would tell everyone what Tenn had just said to her.

'I'm sorry. I didn't want the same thing to happen to me again. I don't want to have to run again. But I think I know the reason this is happening.'

'Which is?'

'I think they're after me.'

'And why?'

'I think, somehow, I draw them to me.'

'Hardly seems likely. What makes you special?'

'At my Testing. I did lie. It was less than two months ago. The Testing, I...it...failed.'

'Ah, so you are a potential then? Well, I can understand you running. And makes your earlier comment rather hypocritical don't you think? '

'I didn't fail it exactly,' Enna clenched her fists in frustration. Why does this have to be so difficult to explain? 'I was there in the inn, and the Magistrate was there, and he touched me with the Stone, and it just blew apart!'

'It did what?'

'It shattered all over us. And then everyone started shouting and some wanted to kill me there and then. But others said that they should wait and get help. And that night the creatures attacked.'

Tenn had shown surprise in his face but had now replaced it with a calculating look.

'Well, that shouldn't have happened. I was responsible for the creation of some of those things myself. They were virtually inert in magical terms. Nothing more than a lodestone.' He tapped his finger against his lips, turned and walked over to a small chest resting against a pile of blankets. He opened it up, rummaged inside and withdrew a cloth-wrapped object. Leaving the chest open he returned to stand before Enna.

He unwrapped the cloth to reveal a small black stone the size of a pebble.

'And here is the mystery revealed. A Testing Stone and the reason why the good folk of these parts are so accommodating to me. Well, one of the reasons anyway. So, let us conduct an experiment. I presume, Enna, that you do not object?'

'I guess I don't have much choice. You are going to try and Test me again.'

'Quite so. It'll help to determine just what level of involvement you truly have in these disturbing events. Ready? Hold out your left hand, palm up.'

Enna nodded.

Tenn leaned forward and placed the Stone against her hand. It instantly blew apart, sending shards flying out in all directions away from her palm. Tenn reeled back, trying to ward his face with his other arm. He was too slow and a piece struck him in the forehead. He fell back, his legs buckling underneath him and he collapsed to the floor. Enna got on all fours and crawled towards him.

'Are you alright?'

Tenn propped himself up on his elbows and Enna reached forward to help him.

'Well, some hurt pride,' he reached up and his fingers came away with blood on them. 'And some potential scarring. At my age that doesn't matter that much. Don't worry, I'm still alive.' His voice dwindled off and his face assumed a puzzled expression. 'Wait, I…I feel something. Enna, let go of me.'

Enna complied with the gentle command. Immediately Tenn's face changed again. This time she could see relief. He gently touched his forehead again, patting the edges with his fingers. 'I don't think I have concussion. But I could be wrong. Enna, touch me again.'

Enna started to worry for the old man. Perhaps the shock had been too much for him but she did as he asked. She placed her hand on his shoulder. In response, Tenn sat very still and closed his eyes. His breathing became regular and calm. 'Now, remove your hand.'

She pulled back and sat on her haunches. Tenn opened his eyes and exhaled, ending with a long drawn out sigh. He looked at her and smiled oddly.

'Do you believe in fate, Enna?'

Enna shrugged. 'Never thought about it really.'

'Neither have I. Of course, in my profession, I know well enough that there are powers at work in the heavens beyond our control. But the gods have seldom played a part in the affairs of men or magic. Any fate stems from the decisions that lords, mages and priests have taken. It is all cause and effect. And yet here you sit.' Tenn sat up straighter. 'What is the likelihood of you turning up at my door? Of all the places you could have run to?' He shook his head and laughed with genuine warmth. 'Well, let's say you've certainly given an old man something new to think about.'

Enna threw her hand up. 'I really don't know what you are talking about but I think you have gone mad!'

'That's as may be. But I'll explain a little more. After some tea, I think. Be a good girl and go fetch us both a fresh mug.'

'Okay.'

Enna stood and walked back to the exit. Things were

taking a really odd turn. After the stone had exploded, she had expected him to call Merrett back. His reaction was the last thing she had in her mind. Outside she found the other man sat before the fire. Jagger was laid beside him and looked up at her, his tail wagging. She explained her presence and while she held the mugs, he poured out two more teas. As she entered the cave, she found Tenn, his forehead cleaned up, sat cross-legged on the rug.

'Ah, good. Here,' he reached out and took the two mugs. She sat before him and her passed here one of the mugs back. They sat there sipping in companionable silence. Enna didn't feel the need to restart the conversation. Tenn took one final sip and placed his mug down. 'Well, I don't know about you but I feel a bit calmer now. So, I think we should start with all the bits you left out in your tale and take it from there, shall we?'

Enna launched into her tale again and this time she left nothing out. She included as best she could every moment from the testing going wrong to their escape and the help they had from Mistress Tabawic; the loss of her father, her discovery by Merrett. During her telling, Tenn would interrupt with questions. He seemed especially keen to hear about her apparent sensing of the Possessed during the attack on the caravan. Once she had finished, Tenn sat back, pressed his finger to his lip, and rocked back

'Enna. Firstly I wish to sympathise with your loss. It has been many years since such devastation has been wrought on a community. Sadly many families still do suffer the way yours has. But it does not detract from what you have experienced. I would that I could say something that would ease your pain. Sadly, what I believe I must tell you will not do that. Trust me when I say your arrival at Cormant and then on to me may well have been fate. Because I am perhaps the last person left alive on these shores that can give you an explanation as to why these things have befallen you. But before that, finish your tea. I would like to tell you a little more about what brought me here and the effect your coming has had on me.' He picked up Enna's mug and handed it to her. It had become quite cool but she drank it anyway. She was becoming used to the sweet taste.

'As I have already told you, I am a mage, a magic user. A potential monster. So why am I still alive? Why haven't I turned? Someone of my power would make quite a beast, don't you think? The simple answer, and what I wish a few more of my colleagues had done, was that I stopped using it. After thirty years residing within the Ducal Palace, I left. I left and travelled as far as I could go on this island. I shed my old rank and position 'til at last I fetched up here. It was quite a journey in those days. You have to remember that the land was not as… adjusted, as it is now. There were refugees, running fights, law and order were collapsing as state and local troops tried and failed to contain the plague. The only safe place was to be as far away from humanity as possible. There were occasions when I was tempted to use my powers but I knew the risks, I couldn't help no matter how much I wished to. Bah! The others tried so hard to find a way to use their magic to turn things around. To bend events to their will. You see it was my world that was falling apart. A different world to now.' Tenn paused. 'Perhaps not so different. In the old days countries warred against each other. Now we just have a new enemy. One we have spent a long time losing against. From what I hear, which isn't much, many things on the mainland have begun to revert to how it used to be. I digress. The world was in chaos. I fetched up here, at Cormant. I knew the old laird, Donald's father, and came to an arrangement. We came up with a cock and bull story about me being a physician having come from Albair city with a testing stone I had acquired. My living in a cave was put down to me having witnessed my own family's destruction and being no longer entirely of sound mind. In return for letting me live nearby I would Test for potentials. The old laird knew the truth, as does Donald. The truth being that magic is about control. About tapping into a source of energy and molding it to your will. I was one of the strongest mages in Albair *because I had the will*, the mental control to command powerful energies.

'A student in magic spends their life trying to develop this. It is that same will that allowed the strongest of us to resist the plague and its desire to take us and turn us. The power of this force is persistent, strong and all darkness. When you open yourself up to the energy, you open yourself up to the evil. It pushes at you, probes your defences, looks for a way in and takes hold. What you are is consumed, your body taken over, changed. It is possession, but a kind there is no coming back from. No one can release you from it. So we resisted. It gave us time to fashion things like the Testing Stones. Our last legacy, an attempt to do some good and help the people we had inadvertently cursed with our ability. A bloody legacy nonetheless, where we condemn our own kind to an early death.' Tenn spread his hands and looked about him. 'My last great work of magic was this very chamber. I imbued it with energy, created a barrier, a bulwark between myself and the energy stream.

'You perhaps know about the Testing Stones? That those who use these things are themselves safe from possession? I took this principal and created my own item – with me inside it. While I am in here I am afforded some protection from the plague, power, whatever it is. I can, in small measures, employ my skills. In so doing I have been able to perform small services to local people, healing and the like. The barrier is not total. I can still feel that darkness on the outside, so I must be subtle and careful with what I do. When not in service, my time is spent using small amounts of my power to explore the darkness outside the barrier. To learn more about its purpose, its origins and what intelligence guides it. So I am a willing exile. As long as I am within these rock walls I can still wield a modicum of magic. That is until you, my dear, came along. You did something that I gave never seen or heard of before. When you touched me I felt a sensation I have never felt before. My link, that ever present sense, my ability to engage with magic, was gone. It disappeared. Having had that ever present relationship all my years, I suddenly felt that I was missing a limb!'

Enna couldn't understand what he was saying. Tenn was more animated than she had thus far seen of him. He leaned forward.

'You blocked me or...' he waved a hand in the air, 'severed my ties. You are a void, a null force. You reject magic, you repel it. No wonder the stones reacted in your presence! You are a force of nature unlike anything that has gone before! Do you know what this means?'

'To be honest, sir, I not even sure I understand anything of what you are saying.'

'It means that potentially you have the ability to block all uses of magic. The question is can you control it? How far can your influence spread?' Hah!' he smiled. 'The truth is, I have no idea of what this might mean. But it does present us with a reason for why the Possessed may be attracted to you.'

'If I touch them, do you think they might explode too?'

Tenn laughed. 'Now that would be a fine thing. But to be honest, I doubt we would be so fortunate to have such a power. I do not believe that to be the case. It is my belief that whatever the force is that corrupts the streams of magic, the Possessed use it as bridge to possess us. Their power is different from ours. I used a Testing Stone on one before it succumbed to its wounds. There was no effect. But then the stones were designed to detect our magic. But the issue still remains; why the Possessed would wish to attack you. We will need to think on this and its significance. If any.'

'We?'

'Why yes.' He looked down and clasped his hands. Enna thought he looked like someone at prayer. 'Now that you are here it is important we take this opportunity to discover as much as we can about you. You are as safe here as anywhere. I suggest you return with Merrett to the island. I would like to spend some time thinking about what must happen next.'

Enna grew angry and frustrated, events were spiralling out of her control and now Tenn was behaving like she was something to be examined. 'Am I a prisoner now?'

Tenn looked up at her, with surprise on his face. 'Why no, Enna, of course not. And now that we have a better idea of what you are about, I will personally vouch for you to Donald. No one needs to know that you failed your testing. However, I would suggest to you that it is in your best interest to allow us to work together.'

'Do you think that we could find a way to stop the Possessed coming after me?'

'I can't promise that. But hopefully we might find a way. Not just for you but anyone near you. If the Possessed are drawn to you then no one will be safe around you. Here though, you have the benefit of being off the beaten track, with a defensible position on the island and the benefit of my knowledge and sadly much reduced powers. These things should give us some time to play with at least. Besides, I'm not as young as I was, so there really is no time like the present.' Tenn clapped his hands together. 'So, shall we give it a try?'

Enna, thought hard about this new turn of events. On one point she was happy to know that she wasn't likely to be turning into a Possessed now. But whatever this thing was that she had inside her, it meant that it was probably the reason her parents had died. It was her fault. She felt tears welling up inside if her. She couldn't stop them. Wiping her eyes she looked up at Tenn. 'Do you think, maybe because of my thing, that the Possessed are hunting me because there are scared of me?'

Tenn nodded solemnly. 'It is quite possible.'

'So maybe there's a way I can hurt them back?'

'That's something that you and I can explore together.'

That night, as she lay in bed, she considered the implications. On leaving the cave, Tenn had informed Merrett that she would need some time to get over her ordeal and that she would be coming to visit him every day. He also added it would be good to have someone to train up in the healing arts and general chores. Merrett had said that she was welcome to stay as long as she wanted but she would have to earn her keep around the home. And that no, Jagger couldn't sleep with her because he'd get the sheets dirty and Mary would go mad. She had agreed to the conditions and had also established a reason for spending time with Tenn. The old mage had said he would speak to Donald and ensure her secret was kept. So she was, according to Tenn, a null void, almost the reverse of the wizard himself. In which case it seemed to her that anything that opposed to what possession and Possessed were all about, it had to be a good thing. And that meant she had a reason to keep going. She could find a way to get vengeance for her mother and father. She fell asleep with a fresh resolve burning inside her. She would make them pay, one way or another. And if she could, she'd kill them all.

CHAPTER NINE

Over the course of the following month, Enna found she had little time to be bored. Her day would begin early, getting up and helping with breakfast. She'd then help out with general housekeeping chores all morning. Sometimes she'd be working on her knees weeding in the small garden by the house where various vegetables were in constant cultivation. In the evenings she would help prepare dinner. This was much like a return to her old life, helping her own mother. But back in North Downs she did seem to have more free time. Here there was always something needing doing. This included taking her turn working within the castle. While in olden times there would have been a larger staff serving the laird, in recent years a more collective approach was taken. There was a small family who acted as cooks and retainers, and people who lived within the walls of the island lent a hand.

She learned that the Laird had two daughters, their

mother having died in childbirth. Both were able-bodied and not afraid to muck in. There certainly weren't any airs and graces. There was always plenty to do and the laird definitely liked the place to be well kept. This included the well-stocked armoury. One day she was sent to assist Raff, the retainer, to check the state of the weapons. She was impressed by just how many they had. There were swords, axes, halberds, bows and crossbows, suits of armour, helmets and jerkins. Raff had told her that many of these weapons were hundreds of years old and that most had seen conflict at one point or another. The lairds had always been sticklers for ensuring that they were all cared for. So now, the island had amassed quite an arsenal. But it meant that blades must be kept well oiled, scabbards and binding repaired, bow strings kept dry and fletching replaced.

Every week Raff would do a complete inventory whether work was needed or not. Whilst many of the folk kept their own weapons like the droving spears kept by Merrett and his companions, they would also be expected to arm themselves from the keep in times of strife. That included the youngsters and the womenfolk. One day a month, everyone was expected to down tools and engage in weapon practice, each choosing the implement best suited to their strength and skills. Enna had already spotted a large broadsword with a two handed grip. Raff had allowed her to wield it and had burst out laughing when the blade had clanged to the ground.

'I like the way you think, lassie. It's a fine weapon. But

I'm thinking you might need to build up those dainty wee arms of yours first. Maybe in a couple of years,' he had advised in his booming, broadly accented voice. 'But, no one leaves the walls of Cormant without some means of protection. So here, this will get you started.' Raff walked over to a rack and retrieved a leather belt with a sheath attached to it. 'Wear this when you're out and about. Get used to having a blade in your hands. Better you arm yourself with this,' he pulled a knife out of the sheath. It was a simple blade, eight inches in length and double-edged. Enna held out her hand and he placed the handle into her palm.

Raff nodded. 'We call these things dirks. They are a bit of a cross between a dagger and a sword. See how the hilt is more like that sword you held? They can get pretty long. Better for the rough and tumble. See the lines running down the middle of the blade? That's for helping the blood to flow. Means your weapon doesn't get stuck in the fella you stabbed! Stick it in hard then twist and pull.'

Enna ran her hand over the blade and gingerly felt the sharp edge. She looked up at Raff. 'You get used to that blade first and see how you do.'

She nodded. She strapped on the belt and let the dirk hang from her left side. It felt good hanging there.

One of the other interesting things about living on the island was that every seventh day the entire population would come and have supper within the hall. Apparently the old laird had started this in response to the horrors of the Possessed plague. A chance for people to come together in companionship and forget what was happening in the world. These evenings were raucous affairs. All the families - bar a solitary lookout - would gather together. The hall itself was tightly packed. Whilst the adults would sit at the tables, the children were given free rein to run wild or set up secret hideaways in the corners of the room. They were even allowed to charge about the keep itself, the only places being off limits were the quarters of the laird and his family on the top floor and the armoury, which Enna had been surprised to learn from Raff was never locked. 'No bloody good having a room full of weapons you can't get to when you are attacked, and the one and only key holder has just fallen off of the roof with an arrow in the back.' It was a testament to the community that the children respected those rules. Enna suspected that she probably would've broken them once or twice, just to see what would happen.

The kitchens within the keep would have been preparing for the occasion for the previous two days and during the meal, the resident family and the daughters of Donald would bring out trays laden with steaming vegetables, joints of meat and fish from the lake. The table would already be laden with bread, cheese and jugs of water. On one side of the room a table carried three tapped barrels of ale, brought up from the lower level. Everyone was free to help themselves and Enna found the brew cold and refreshing, the taste malty and sweet.

The laird himself was sat at the head of the long table and appeared relaxed, comfortable and clearly enjoying the affair. He never once spoke to Enna about the secret that Tenn had confirmed he had shared. Instead, he only ever enquired about Enna's health and happiness.

All in all Enna found herself settling into the routine of Cormant Castle quite nicely. Merrett and Mary were kind and accommodating but strict enough with her when the commitment to her chores started to wane. She felt that in any other circumstance she could have called this place home. As it was, she always made sure to remember, last thing at night, to play through the events that led her to Cormant. That way she kept the fire of hatred burning.

Her daily visits to Tenn were the one part of the day that would jar her from the peaceful domestic existence she was living. She would walk around the lake following a well-defined track; the walk did her good and was the only time she felt she had some privacy and space to think. At first, Tenn had done nothing other than simply ask questions of her. He had asked her to think back to the days of the attack on North Downs and her pursuit. He wanted to know more about what happened, how she felt, what she had seen of the Possessed. Once they had done that to death, he wanted her to think back to earlier years of her childhood. Had she ever had nightmares? Had she thought of things before they had happened? Had she been able to influence the behaviour of animals? This questioning was tiring and caused her head to ache.

Each time she had answered in the negative and each time he came back with further questions. After hours of these questions, and on her fourth visit, he had declared himself satisfied.

'I am sorry for the incessant demands, Enna. And unfortunately they are but the start.'

Enna flung her hands up in the air. 'What more can you want? I have nothing left to tell you!'

Tenn nodded solemnly. 'That is true. What I have attempted to do is probe you for evidence of any magical ability your might have had or displayed in the past. I wanted to know if your nullifying force was brought about through an incident involving magic. If so, there may be a way of replicating the effect. Because of your gift, I cannot learn the things through my own arts. So I have had to do it the hard way. And, sadly, from my point of view, I feel that what you have has not come about from any method that I can define.'

'What happens now? Is that it?' asked Enna. She felt almost disappointed that her power could not be used like magic.

'Hardly. We have but eliminated one avenue. What we have to do now is discover just what your potential is. So. Let us see what happens when I do this.'

Tenn stood up slowly, the grimace ever present, and took a couple of paces back. He held out his left palm and gazed at it. A spark of light jumped into existence, hovering an inch above his hand. The spark grew brighter until it appeared to Enna more like an orb of light, akin to the size of a small pebble. Tenn looked up at her. 'And now, let's see what happens.'

The orb lifted higher and then slowly moved towards Enna. It travelled the distance between them keeping at an even height. It stopped six inches from her and rose to eye level. It then fell a little to the level of her nose. Enna felt herself going cross-eyed and she glanced at Tenn who smiled wryly.

'Now, Enna, I want you to concentrate. I want you to concentrate on two things actually. I want you to reach out with your senses. You know how you had a feeling about the attack on the caravan? See if you can get that sensation again.'

Enna did as she was asked. She tried to concentrate on the light. She shut her eyes and attempted to reach out with her mind. She wasn't actually sure what that meant. She already knew the ball of light was there.

'Don't try too hard! Your face looks like you've eaten a whole lemon. Relax.'

Now that he had mentioned it, Enna could feel how her face had tightened. She forced herself to be calm; she let the tension from her face drop and allowed herself to breath evenly. Again, she began to feel for the ball of light before her. It helped that it made no noise. She still couldn't sense anything. She slumped her shoulders and scratched idly at the end of her nose.

'Nothing.'

'No matter. The second thing I'm going to do is send this light towards you and it'll touch your skin. Don't worry, it won't be too hot. Let me know when you feel it.'

Enna gathered herself again and sat upright. She readied herself, even though he had assured her it wouldn't hurt. She waited. Nothing happened.

'I'm waiting,' she announced .

'Open your eyes,' ordered Tenn.

She did and found the ball of light had disappeared.

'You did it already?'

Tenn nodded, a smile playing on his lips.

'Well I don't see what's so funny. I was worried about it hurting. As it was, I didn't feel a thing.'

'I wouldn't say that exactly. I played with you a little just then. You see, when I told you I was going to touch you with the light, in fact I already had.'

'When?'

'Recall back to when you told me you couldn't sense anything? That was the moment I did it and if I'm not mistaken you did react.

'No, I didn't!'

'Really? Well, when I sent it crashing into your nose, didn't you give it a scratch?'

Enna's eyebrows arched. 'Yes! But that was just a little itch.'

'And that little itch was your body telling you that you had just cancelled out my magic.'

'Next time I'd like to watch, please,' said Enna. 'I'd rather see what's coming.'

'As you wish. But this is positive news. It means that your body does have a physical reaction. So we now have a way of measuring your power.' Tenn lowered himself back down onto the rug and took up his cross-legged position. 'Can you guess what we are going to do next?'

Enna shrugged, although she figured she already knew.

'We are going to do the same exercise over and over again. We have two pieces of evidence that your power isn't completely passive. First, your ability to sense the Possessed. I class that as a reaction and secondly your little itch. What we have to do now is see if we can repeat these reactions.'

'And what will this prove?'

'Firstly, that they are not just random chance. Secondly, it means we might be able to train you to control it, to strengthen it.

'Why?'

That stopped Tenn. He looked at her with a confused expression.

'You know, I really couldn't say. A lifetime ago, your ability would have had useful applications. Just think you would have been the ultimate protection against any magical interference. Powerful folk could have used you to block any magical intrusion or threat, thieves to unlock the most warded door, mages could practice the most dangerous of experiments with the knowledge it could be contained. Sadly, Enna, you do seem a little out of Time. As do I.'

'So again. Why are we bothering?'

Tenn sighed. 'Because if nothing else, Enna, perhaps

we can find a way to hide or cut off the lines of power. Perhaps that will no longer draw the Possessed to you.'

'I'd rather they come. That way I could kill them.'

'Yes, well. I really don't think that is something you wish to pursue just yet. Maybe in a few years when you have grown. Until then I would recommend you stay well hidden. Let's limit our ambitions for the time being. We shall begin by seeing if we can create any expansion of your null field.'

She would visit Tenn and conduct the same tasks over and over again. He also taught her techniques for focusing her concentration that she had to practice each night before sleeping. It was tiring, frustrating and often very boring. Sometimes they would have to stop to allow the old man to rest. He explained to her that there was a price to pay for using magic; it took its toll on the body. Use too much and the body would break down. Combining his age with his need to maintain strict controls on the use of his power meant that the former arch-mage could not keep up with the constant demands of even the simplest forms of magic for too long. Finally, it was the physical strain that marked a change in proceedings.

Enna was often bored and felt tired because of it. However, one day she arrived at the cave feeling completely exhausted. She had done her normal day's chores and had not put in any physical effort, but for some reason her whole body ached. She had thought perhaps she was coming down with a sickness and had hoped Tenn might be able to help. Instead he got excited and asked her to describe how she felt. As best as she could discern, it wasn't just the physical exhaustion, she felt just like she had during the last days of flight with her mother. Tenn had immediately sent her back to the island with orders to get a good long rest and he'd see her the next day.

That next day followed and Enna, feeling more refreshed and less achy, had begun with the same old sequence of calming her mind and trying to focus on the ball of light before her. It rose from Tenn's hand and moved slowly towards her. She stared at it and thought hard about creating a wall about her like she had been shown to do. The light winked out of existence. Enna sat back in surprise. It had happened so quickly. She looked at Tenn who was smiling triumphantly.

'Now we're getting somewhere.'

Woodhall and Miller dismounted, the latter turning and spitting out a stream of chewing tobacco, narrowly missing Woodhall's boot. He gave his leader a sour look but said nothing of it. Miller was just jerking his chain.

Before them was the wreckage of a trader caravan that had been attacked by a band of Possessed sometime in the recent past. The state of the bodies suggested at least of couple of weeks. What hadn't been scavenged by local wildlife was well on its stinking way and had turned black from putrefaction. Most of the dozen or so wagons had been left intact although one had been pushed over, its contents spilling out onto the ground. Some of the wagons had been canvas covered. Woodhall figured that the excessive shredding of these coverings meant the drivers had been sleeping inside them. Dumb really. You wouldn't catch him napping with his arse hanging out to the wilds like that. 'You got to wonder at these folks, Avery. They had guards who were all stood by campfires. Haven't they heard of night vision? They should have had their backs to the flames and their eyes to the front.'

'Guess they never figured on the bastards operating in packs,' replied Miller.

'Sure, but come on, everyone knows; it only takes one.'

Miller didn't reply but instead hefted his crossbow.

'Let's take a look.'

Woodhall signalled to the men gathered behind. He detailed five to stay with the horses whilst the rest dismounted, armed up and followed them into the camp. Miller led them through the opening created by the upturned wagon and once through the group fanned out, picking through the remains. In the rough centre of the encampment was a crude and blackened fire pit. Around it were bundles of sleeping rolls, blankets and personal effects. Many of these stained with blood.

Miller walked over to inspect the cargo and Woodhall joined him. A smashed up crate lay on its side, a collection of brass pots and pans lying scattered on the floor.

'Just like the survivor said,' Woodhall said as he

squatted to inspect a bloodstained pan.

The Hunters had been overnighting in the Port of Longhaven to the south-east. The day before, they had been summoned by the local baron to hear the statement of a caravan guard. The man had come into the settlement two weeks before riding hell for leather on an unsaddled horse and terrified out of his wits. The story, now well known from the retelling by a hundred gossips amongst the townsfolk, was that the caravan he had been part of had been attacked by an unknown number of Possessed their second night out from Longhaven.

It had been so quick that everyone had been overwhelmed before they could react. The guard had been on the far side of the wagon circle, near the horses, and had time to mount the nearest and make his escape, riding through the night and following day. A relief column had been sent out to find other survivors. None had been found. The guard was a regular visitor to Longhaven and known by many as an honest man, so there was no reason to doubt his claim. Woodhall acknowledged the fact that one beast could easily wreak the havoc required to take out an unprepared encampment. It wasn't usual for this to happen these days but it was always possible. So the baron had wanted them to go hunting.

That was all well and good, but what had caught both Miller and Woodhall's attention was the part about it being a group of beasts. Woodhall's first guess was that the guard was trying to justify his decision to run. Part of him couldn't blame the man for that. But then you shouldn't be a damn guard if you didn't have the balls for it. Jess knew that any man in the group would rather go toe to toe with a Possessed than turn their backs. They all had scores to settle.

They had gone to question the man to get directions, description of the trail and any more details about the attack. Miller pressed him on the numbers involved. It turned out that he was likely telling the truth. The guards had been awake but had all been clustered round the fire. The survivor had been taking a leak by the horses. When the Possessed came he had seen at least four coming over and across the wagon barriers. Two had gone straight for the guards. At that point he was already untying a horse. Miller asked if he had seen any others escaping. The guard had nodded. That was the thing; he'd seen two people running past him just before the attack and he'd called after them. But they hadn't stopped. They were a couple of women who they'd picked up earlier the day before. A mother and daughter, survivors of a Possessed attack. No one in the caravan was unduly worried. No one had expected a repeat of that on them. At that Miller had looked at Woodhall with a raised eyebrow. Two incidences of assaults by large bands of Possessed; it was unprecedented. Miller had asked the guard if he had gotten a name. The guard thought for a moment then replied. 'Enna'.

Now, standing amidst the ruined camp, it seemed to Woodhall that history had repeated itself.

'Jess, I doubt we'll get any sign left but take some of the men with you. Head north east then swing round to the west and come back.'

'We still looking for the girl?'

'That or the pack of hounds after her.'

'Okay, I'll get on it.' Woodhall stopped. 'So two attacks, both involving a girl called Enna. What do you reckon?'

'Trouble follows her whether she invites it or not. Time was I might've stopped to ask why. But we don't have that. Fact is she's already responsible for the deaths of at least two hundred people. That makes her dangerous. If these things gather around her, wherever she goes, people will die.'

'So we've got to catch her,' said Woodhall.

Miller shook his head and spat. 'We've got to kill her.'

CHAPTER TEN

As the weeks passed, Enna continued to make slow progress. At first it took a number of tries to maintain the null wall just a few inches from her, but it began to come to her more easily and the mental concentration she needed became simpler to attain. Tenn had then encouraged her to try and push this barrier further out. And so, inch by inch, she had been able to extend her influence out by some two feet. Physically, it was still draining, and she would go to bed with her joints aching. Fortunately, each morning these aches would fade away and by the time she arrived for her next lesson they would be virtually gone. Of course, two hours later, they'd be back again. The mage pushed her hard but always took care never to over-tax her, for which she was grateful.

Keen to see more of the land around Cormant, one morning she been allowed to go out to collect firewood, accompanying a large cart drawn by oxen and several men carrying long woodcutting axes. They headed out to woodlands an hour or so away. On arrival, Enna wandered amongst the fringes of the wood - with warnings not to go too far in - and collected smaller branches that could be used for kindling. Nearby the men worked quickly to fell certain trees and haul them onto the cart.

She had been told by Merrett the night before that it would take most of the day, and her trip to see Tenn would mean having dinner with him. No one ever travelled across open ground at night, so instead she was allowed to take one of the rowing boats with her, and Jagger was allowed to tag along as company and protection.

Dusk was already well begun when she rowed the pair of them across the lake and trooped up to the cave to find a pot of stew already simmering gently. Tenn still required her to train before they ate, but afterwards they relaxed by the cooking fire. While Jagger stretched out by Enna, Tenn told her stories about the old world and his life as an arch-mage. It all sounded terribly exciting and there were a number of tales to do with wars, court intrigues and the mage's own adventures. What she loved the most was hearing about his apprenticeship. It felt good and reassuring to know that he had gone through his own trials and frustrations when he was learning his craft. She found it funny when he talked about how youngsters today, including herself, wouldn't know how good they have it now. It reminded her just how old

Tenn was. After eating, he bade her goodnight, and she walked back down to the lake edge.

Enna gently rowed across the lake in no hurry to return to the other side. Reaching the middle, she pulled up her oars and lay back, absently stroking Jagger's head. She would dearly love to see the stars but there was too much cloud cover. So instead, she contented herself with enjoying the moment but her thoughts quickly drifted came back to her present situation.

She knew she was getting better at using her power. She hadn't mentioned it to Tenn yet, but she believed she was starting to understand how to sense magic around her. It wasn't easy to put words to it, rather it felt like an instinct thing. She just knew. It was the same feeling she had after the caravan attack, not as strong or alarming but a lot more persistent. She felt it when she passed through the entrance to the cave, an ever present sensation, not unpleasant, just different. And when Tenn used his magic, it would increase a notch. She could definitely see the value in this aspect of her power – the more warning she could get of Possessed approaching the better. It would give her more time to be ready for them. As she drifted in the silence of the lake, her thoughts drifted to an image of her, armed with the longsword from the armoury, slaying Possessed with nothing more than a swipe of her blade.

Two days later, Enna was returning from the cave. She had been ambling along the high path running parallel to the lake enjoying the early evening breeze. She was starting to get used to the bracing conditions and didn't even mind the inevitable wet weather. In fact, she found herself starting to think of the landscape as having its own special kind of beauty as well. She reached the last bend before the shoreline cut back paralleling the western side. One of the fishing boats was tying up. As one man was making good the knots, another was already unloading the catch. Ahead, she saw three figures running quickly from the western path, others were gathering by the bridge to meet them. The two groups met by the bridge and Enna watched as the larger group huddled together with much finger pointing and hand waving. Yet more people were joining them from the settlement, streaming out from the gateway. Enna entered earshot and a babble of voices hit her. Then, almost as one, the group fractured and made their way purposefully towards the gate. There was a knot gathered round the three who Enna suspected were the recent arrivals. She was finally able to recognise the men as her rescuers, Conor, Adrian and Merrett. Enna called after him. He turned, a frown on his face. Then, seeing her, he quickly turned to Adrian, spoke into his ear and then strode over to her as the group continued onward. Although she hadn't noticed him before, Jagger padded along excitedly next to his master.

'You alright, lass? Have you seen anything?' he said, placing a hand on her shoulder.

Enna shrugged. 'No, nothing. What do you mean? Has something happened?'

She felt his hand tighten on her shoulder.

'You haven't felt anything?'

A dread feeling awoke inside of her. Surely not again. Not already.

'No. Nothing. What is it?'

Merrett's face looked grim.

'We found some of our cattle. They were butchered. If it had been one, we would've put it down to wolves. But the dogs, they got wind of 'em. Then we found the tracks, at least three different sets. We followed one for a wee while, got to a stand of rocks. A large outcropping, plenty of cover. Jagger here was going crazy. Conor swore he saw something in there. I was tempted to try something but then thought better of it. Now listen. We are gathering in the Keep to speak to Donald. Come along in now. We are closing the gates.'

Merrett gently propelled her forward and together with Jagger they ran to the gate. As they passed through the doors were shut behind them by another man. He placed a wooden bar in the holding slots and as Enna hurried on, she looked back as the man climbed up into the watchtower. It reminder her far too much of North Downs.

The dining hall was in uproar. The place was pretty much as full as it ever was with all the families gathered together. At the head of the table stood Donald, listening to three conversations at once. He looked up and caught sight of Enna and Merrett as they entered. He raised his hands in the air and commanded silence. He beckoned Merrett forward.

'Merrett, let's hear the story from you and then we'll

decide what must be done.'

Merrett left Enna by the door and bid Jagger stay with her. As he passed through the crowd he whispered to Mary who looked round, saw Enna and moved back to stand by her, a protective arm round her shoulder.

Merrett stood before them all and related the story he had told in a briefer form to Enna. It was punctuated with much murmuring from the crowd as he spoke. Once he finished the murmuring broke out into fully fledged conversation.

Once again Donald quieted the crowd.

'Alright, friends. It's been a while since we've had to deal with this problem. But this shouldn't come as a shock. We can never afford to become complacent.'

'Aye, Laird, we know how to deal with these things. So why don't we get out there now and finish 'em?' asked Padraig, a burly long-haired man who Enna had helped to cut trees with.

'One, aye, I'd agree,' said Donald. 'But this is new. I've no reason to doubt Merrett when he says they found three sets of tracks. That is a number we've never had to deal with before. We don't have the men to fight them all.'

'We can hunt them individually, then,' said Merrett. 'We know where one is now – we arm ourselves and flush the thing out. After that we follow the tracks and kill them one by one.'

This bought a chorus of approvals.

Enna could tell by Donald's face that he was troubled by this. He knew well enough why they were banding together. It was because of her. Even though she was at the back of the hall, his eyes met hers and held them for a moment before moving on. Merrett was also looking at her, his face unreadable.

'That is a question we can debate another time,' said Donald. 'For now we deal with the immediate problem. It's too late to go hunting now. It'll be dark soon and those creatures will have the advantage. Let's make sure we get everyone back in from their work and then we look to our walls. Raff will go down to the armoury and begin issuing weapons. Tonight we'll put four men on watch. If any of you wish, you can sleep the night in the keep. Tomorrow morning we will put together a hunting party and track these things down, one at a time. It seems they are not hiding together which is to our advantage. I know that we have not had to live through this for some time now and it is easy to forget that the world is still as dangerous as ever and that evil is abroad. Now, I suggest you continue about your business as best you can. I will decide who will go on the party tomorrow and who will stay. Until such time as I am confident, no one must travel beyond the immediate vicinity of the lake and island.'

'I'll go and put these monsters down!' shouted Padraig. Further voices joined his.

'As will I!'

'And me!'

'I'll smack the bastards down!'

It seemed to Enna that every man and young boy was volunteering to go out; she noted that a number of the women and girls were also shouting out their desire as well. She was tempted to volunteer as well but then wondered if she might well be more of a hindrance than a help. Her presence might just bring more of these things into one place. It would be a death sentence for everyone.

'Thank you, everyone, for your enthusiasm! I'll make my plans and inform you of them presently. Now please, let's prepare accordingly,' said Donald. He then turned to speak to Raff and Merrett. Everyone else began to filter out of the hall, talking loudly amongst themselves.

'Come on then, Enna,' said Mary.

'What is everyone going to do?' asked Enna

'Well, the same thing we always have. Look after each other. Keep a watch out and weather the storm. We have done this before, Enna. I think we've gotten used to things being quieter of late.'

Emma nodded. 'Aren't you worried about the Possessed?'

'I've always been worried about them,' said Mary. 'Trust me, Enna, we're safe here. Not one of them has ever gotten into the keep. And we're bred tough up here. None of us will turn our backs from a fight.'

CHAPTER ELEVEN

There was a palpable sense of anticipation amongst the folk of Cormant. Enna could clearly feel it. The last few workers had returned from the hills without incident. As was expected, no Possessed walked in the daylight. Now torches burned along the island wall and upon the keep. At the far end of the bridge two braziers burnt brightly, casting wide circles of light. She had been upset to see that one of the cattle dogs was settled by one of the braziers. Merrett had said that it was a necessary evil; they needed the dog to act as an early warning if it caught the scent on the wind. At night-time folk needed every advantage they could get. Besides, the dog had been left untethered and was more than able to take care of itself. The watchtower was manned whilst three other men stood before the gate. A further brazier was lit, not just to provide warmth to the night but also to light the pile of torches clustered next to it. Enna watched this scene from her window, with the shutters thrown back, a light breeze carrying the smell of the lake blew into her room. Although she couldn't see it from her side of the cottage, she knew that the roof of the keep was also manned with lookouts. Their vantage gave them excellent fields of vision across the tops of the surrounding hills. Within the keep itself, a number of the families with much younger children had taken up residence. Mary was still over there, helping out in the kitchen. They were laying in supplies for the possibility that entire population had to shelter within the keep. Those already present were in the minority, however, as most preferred to stay in their own homes. Everyone was confident that they would have ample warning to get to the keep. Enna was certainly comforted by the preparedness of the community. It didn't look like they would be caught unawares as North Downs was. But then, her village had had lookouts and a much higher wall and it still hadn't done any good.

A knock on the door distracted her. Merrett walked in and smiled at her.

'Come now, lass. Time to sleep, we have plenty of watchers already this night.'

She noted that as well as the dirk he always wore, a hand axe was looped into his belt on his left hip. She had also seen him taking a whetstone to his spear earlier in the evening.

'Are you going out tomorrow morning?' she asked.

Merrett folded his arms and leaned against the doorframe.

'Certainly. We found the beastie's lair. We'll be the ones to lead the hunt. Well, no doubt Jagger'll be leading us.'

Enna smiled. Thinking of Jagger jolted her memory. 'Oh. I forgot. What about Tenn? We should go and get him?'

Merrett shook his head.

'No one has had the time to do so. Knowing him as I do, he may well already have gotten wind of them. And to be honest, I really don't think we need worry. He wouldn't come even if we insisted. He likes it in his cave. And whilst I've never pried and have no desire to, I suspect that old man can look after himself.' He gave Enna a knowing look. She realised that perhaps Tenn's secret was not as closely guarded as he might have thought. But it also reassured her to know that Merrett and the others thought well enough of him to allow his privacy and past life to be kept that way. 'Do you think I can go see him tomorrow?'

He chewed his lip then shook his head.

'Sorry, lass. I can understand why, but the laird has already ordered that we keep to the walls. I know you could row across and walk the short distance from there. Now, if Jagger was with you... no' he shook his head again. 'I'll need him tomorrow. Just wait a day, let us go deal with those things, and then you and I can go together.'

Enna wasn't happy with that answer. She needed to speak to Tenn desperately. She needed to know if the arrival of the Possessed was, as she suspected, because of her. But she also knew that she wouldn't get any change in Merrett's view. The time she had spent in his home had taught her he was fair but firm in his decisions.

Merrett pushed himself upright again. 'Anyway, to bed, young lady.'

'Good night.'

'And goodnight to you.'

Enna turned, closed the shutters of the window and climbed into bed. She would have to see about things in the morning. She felt she would be able to find a way to see the old man. A few white lies here and there would do the trick.

She awoke early the next morning to watch the hunting party leave. It would have been hard not to as it seemed everyone was gathered to see them go. She stood at the front door next to Mary. Both of them had wrapped shawls around themselves to ward against the chill. As was usual, dawn had only just started to break, but already the place was a hive of activity. The party numbered a dozen men. All of them carried spears or pole arms as their main weapon. Added to that was an array of different items. Some carried bows, others axes and a few large swords. Many of the men had shields strapped to their backs. Accompanying them, Enna counted at least four cattle dogs. She spotted Jagger, sat at Merrett's side. His master was in conversation with Donald. The Laird would not be going with them. He and the rest of the able-bodied men were needed to guard the island and keep the community safe in case of an attack. She watched as the laird leaned in, whispered something in Merrett's ear, then leaned back, clapped him on the shoulder and stepped away. The gates were opened up and the group filed out, Donald speaking to each man as they passed. There were shouts of encouragement and the occasional whistle from the watching crowd. As the last man passed under the portal, the gate was shut.

Enna looked over at Mary. The older woman's face was set, her mouth tight. She glanced down at Enna and forced a smile.

'They'll open the gate up later today.'

'I thought the laird had said people weren't allowed out?'

Mary waved a dismissive hand. 'People still have business to go about and it's safe in the day. He was just being cautious. But life has to go on and those lads will need their supper ready when they return.'

The two of them watched Donald walking back towards the keep in conversation with one of the others. He nodded to them both before proceeding on. Enna felt pleased. Mary's comment suggested that she may well be able to get away to see Tennebran.

'Now, shall we have some breakfast?' asked Mary.

The two of them returned inside the house.

Enna's moment came a few hours later. She was walking back to the house with Mary from the keep having joined most of the others left on the island. True to Mary's promise, the gates were open, albeit with three men on guard, and people had being going about their business.

'Well, I think I'm going to go and visit Tenn now,' Enna declared brightly.

'Oh, I'm not sure that's a good idea,' responded Mary. 'I don't think Merrett would want you going off by yourself to the other side of the lake.'

Enna feigned a puzzled look. 'But I thought you said it'd be fine. It is daylight. Besides I'm not going far. And Merrett and others all headed the other way so it must be safe in the direction I'm going.'

Mary's face showed her indecision so Enna pressed her attack.

'It's okay, Mary. How about if I row over? That way I haven't got far to walk. Back at home I used to be out all the time and back well before dark.'

Mary relented. 'Alright, go see if one of the boats is free and whether you can take it out. You might as well take some provisions over to Tenn, just to be sure. But I want you back soon after, at least an hour before dusk.'

'Thank you, Mary,' Enna beamed.

'And,' Mary continued with an upraised finger, 'I'll be stood by the dock waiting for you. So, I mean it – an hour before dusk.'

'Yes, Mary,' nodded Enna, solemnly.

Returning to the house, Enna helped Mary pack a basket with some meat, cheese and bread. She also took a flagon of ale with a reminder to bring back any empties.

Then she was off. She passed under the arch of the gateway and smiled to the men on watch. On the other side of the bridge some cattle were being driven down the hill into a holding pen by the graveyard. She was tempted to go and visit her mother but continued on. She then followed the path round to the pier. Two boats were tied up. Walking to the nearest, she put her cargo on the pier and lowered herself in. Reaching up, she grabbed the basket and flagon and tucked them underneath the seat before releasing the mooring. Gently pushing herself away from the side, she busied herself with the oars. Once ready she was off, pulling with gentle but steady strokes. As she swept across the water, she waved at the third boat that was off to the north side. The figure in the boat waved back. Enna once again marvelled at how, being on this lake, everything felt natural and normal. You wouldn't ever know that right now there are Possessed prowling nearby, she thought. I wonder why people don't live out in the sea?

She was soon tramping up towards the boulder field, still musing about the possibilities of having an entire village of boats all tied up together. Maybe in the channel between Albair and the mainland? It would be perfectly safe, and Possessed that popped up could just be thrown into the water and drown. She was pretty sure they couldn't swim. At least, she'd never heard of it. It wasn't until she reached the passage to the cave entrance that she remembered where she was. She stopped herself and felt the shock of what she had almost done. What if a

Possessed was already in there, had found Tenn, killed him, and was now waiting for her? She was now at a loss for what to do. Perhaps she shouldn't have come alone.

'So are you going to stand out there till nightfall? Wait for a Possessed to come along and finish the job you've worked so hard to avoid?' Tenn's voice came from the passage. 'Sound does carry very well into here in case you're wondering.'

Enna smiled with relief. She hurried through the rock passage and emerged at the cave entrance proper. Tenn was leaning against the wall, his arms folded in front of him and an eyebrow cocked.

'You alright, young lady? You seem positively flustered.'

Enna nodded her head vigorously and stepped up to him.

'They're here, Tenn.'

The old man's face turned hard.

'Inside. Tell me everything.' He stepped back from the wall and ushered her in.

Settling down into their usual positions, Enna explained to him the events of the last day. She knew how inquisitive he would be, so took care to relate as much as she could remember as clearly as she could. In response, Tenn sat impassively, watching her intently.

'I thought Duncan would have sent word to you. But I guess he was too busy,' she added when she had finished her news.

Tenn nodded. 'No doubt. It's been a while since he

has had to think about such issues.'

'Well, him and Merrett do think that you can take care of yourself.'

Tenn's frame shifted as he grunted in humour.

'Well, not as much as I would like!'

'So what do we do now?'

'We? I'm not sure it's we, it's more about what can you do.'

'What do you mean?'

'Are you ready to run again?'

Enna reeled back in shock and she felt her head swim. She didn't want to even entertain the possibility. But now that he had raised it, suddenly she felt a familiar, cold sensation in her stomach.

She shook her head.

'I don't want to.'

Tenn smiled sadly. 'Believe me, I don't want you to either. But we must all do what we can to survive. Look at me, twenty years in a cave!'

'But, Merrett and the others, they've gone off to kill them!'

'That's true. And I wish them all the luck of the gods. But will it be enough? Think about the Possessed and how they have banded together. Perhaps Duncan's people will take one, maybe two, today. But then what? How many of them are there? How many will come? The walls of the Cormant are strong but it has never had to deal with a siege the likes of which may transpire. Possessed, attacking, night after night. How long before there is not enough to hold them off?'

Tears began to fall from Enna's eyes. He leaned forward and wiped them away from her cheeks.

'I'm sorry, Enna. I did not wish to upset you. But you must understand, I try to paint the worst possible picture of what may come to pass. I do not truly know. Perhaps you are right, perhaps our friends will hunt down all the Possessed that come this way. Maybe we will just end up returning to the vigilance of the first days.' He leaned back from her and sighed. 'Then life can continue here, very much like it does in the lands further south.'

'I hope so. I don't want to see more people die because of me. Not again.'

Tenn grasped her shoulders firmly. 'That may be out of your control, Enna. Your power is a threat to the Possessed. How, I still do not understand fully. But, if you are willing, I want to try something with you.'

'What?'

Tenn folded his arms. He smiled and there was an eager glint in his eyes.

'Up 'til now, all we have done is to try and exercise your powers in a limited way. Working your "non-magic" muscles in a way. It is something that we all had to learn as magic users,' he held a stern finger up. 'Control is everything. Without it we are just as likely to burn ourselves up or turn into something unpleasant.' He then threw his hands in the air to punctuate the point. Enna smiled in spite of herself.

'Now, tell me. You feel stronger, yes? More aware of

your ability?' he asked.

She nodded. 'Yes, I've started to feel I can use it now. Not like before when it just happened...'

'And?'

'I think that I'm getting better at sensing when the Possessed are about. It's a bit like you. I know when you are working magic, I can sense when you use it, and it's a bit tickly on my skin, especially on the back of my neck.'

'Ah yes, the nape is truly our sixth sense!'

'And I can feel this cave. There is a slight pressure when I come in here. Not painful, just I know that it's there.'

'Very good, Enna. It's what I was expecting.' Tenn rubbed his hands together. 'Let's try something different. I want you to start focusing your power. Don't just think of it as a wall about you. Use it.'

'I understand.'

'Of course you do – you're a bright girl!'

He raised his hands and four pebbles rose from the floor behind him. They began to spin slowly around a central axis.

'Concentrate. I want you to pick one and cancel my influence on it. Just one, mind.'

Enna nodded. She wasn't at all surprised at this new task. She reached into herself and sought out her power. She felt the warm sensation of it pulsing out from her body and then checked it. Normally she would let it extend as far she could, this time she held it close and sought to shape it. She wasn't exactly sure has this was supposed to work so she just tried to think hard about what she wanted it to do. She imagined it forming a straight line out from her forehead, like a spear or an arrow. She was encouraged by the sensation around her head; it seemed to be warmer, like heat gathering. She threw it out from her with an exaggerated thrust of her head. The four pebbles were thrown out of their circle and smashed against the wall.

Tenn raised an eyebrow and glanced behind him.

'Sorry,' said Enna smiling. As a first time it had been pretty impressive.

'Don't be, my girl. You might have over-egged it a bit but I think the principle has been proven. And did you notice?'

She shrugged. 'What?'

'You have just beaten your own distance record by about three feet, I'd say!'

'Really?' She hadn't even thought about that. Now she thought about how far away those pebbles had been, her barrier had never gone that far out from her.

'Absolutely. But I think we may need to work a bit on your accuracy. Next test. You've only ever worked on stones. But what about other things? Can you, for instance, cancel out the shield of magic around my home? No, no,' he said responding to the look of panic on her face. 'I've no intention of putting that to the test – not after all the bloody effort it took putting it in place to start with.' He walked to the far wall. 'I wonder whether your power has a finite range, whether it losses efficacy at a certain limit. I doubt we'll ever know for certain here. But it'll be something for you to think about in times to come.'

That got her attention. Enna fixed Tenn with a stare.

'What do you mean, times to come? You're sounding very gloomy all of a sudden.'

Tenn shook his head.

'I'm sorry, Enna. That is not my intention. But you have to understand something very important. Something you don't want to hear. You won't be able to stay here forever.'

It was Enna's turn to shake her head in denial.

'But why? I'm as safe here as anywhere. Where can I go? Back out into the wild again. I'll get torn to pieces!'

'Nonsense! I want to you to travel to Albair city. Present yourself to the Duke. I'll be sending a letter of introduction,' Tenn paused, looked wistful and forced out a throaty cackle. 'Now won't that be a surprise? He's my nephew you know. I had better make it a good letter, full of family secrets. It'll be the only way, else he'll think you are some charlatan.'

Enna's mind was spinning; it was one revelation after another. Albair city!

'Perhaps, if we chase off the Possessed, we could go together? Sometime soon?'

'Oh no, young lady. I'm far too old. I'd die of exposure out there! And you won't be talking anyone into going with you all that way south.'

Enna felt her excitement fade as quickly as it had

come.

'No, you can stay here for a while yet, said Tenn. 'Grow up a bit and then you can join up with a caravan. Besides, until that time we have much more work to do!'

CHAPTER TWELVE

Enna rowed back to the keep. She felt odd about how things were turning out. On one hand she was acutely aware of the danger that she was in, that she had brought upon the settlement. But by the same token, her mind was filled with possibilities, that her ability may well lead her to a new life in a city she had only dreamed of. So busy was she imagining her future that the trip across the water was swiftly over. She hopped out and tied off. As she did so she noted that dusk was soon approaching. The sun was beginning to drop behind the high ground to the west. It brought her thoughts into more immediate focus. Were Merrett and the others alright? She finished off and hurried round the walls. Her fears were quickly scorched when she saw the crowd of people gathered at the bridge. There was much chatter and cheering. She ran to join them and watched as coming down along the track were the hunters. The men were waving and shouting and lifting their spears in salutes. Cattle dogs were bounding around, tails up and barking excitedly. It's like a party, thought Enna. She did a headcount. An even dozen, they had all come back.

'How many you get?' shouted a boy next to her.

'Two!' came the return cry from the fast approaching group.

Two! Enna was really impressed. She'd heard it said you needed an entire Hunter Band to take on a Possessed and yet these Highlanders were so tough they could do it with half that number. And some brave dogs of course.

At the head of the welcome party was Donald, he strode forward to meet them at the far side of the bridge. He clasped hands with Merrett and leaned in close as the other man whispered to him. Donald nodded his head and turned to lead the group in. He raised a hand to the gathered throng. 'Everyone, these lads are tired and hungry. Let's all go to the hall and listen to what they have to say.'

The crowd parted to let the band through. Enna could see now that not all of the men seemed in as high spirits as she had thought. The young ones were flushed with the excitement of the moment well enough but some of the older men bore grim faces, Merrett included. She also spotted a white-faced Conor, his right arm, encased by a thick woollen sling, was held tight against his chest. He carried his spear in his left hand, using it to support himself. He continued to walk gamely forward, not wanting to show any weakness in front of his friends and family. He even shooed away his mother who came running up to him, tears in her eyes. Brave, thought Enna. She gave a small start as something wet touched her hand. Looking down she found Jagger gazing back at her, tongue lolling and tail wagging. She laughed and leaned down to hug him.

'I knew you'd make it back okay. You're far too smart for that,' she said as the dog started to lick her face.

'Stop being so bloody soft, Jagger,' Merrett said to the dog as he walked past. 'Bring him along, Enna.'

She nodded, though he had already walked past, his back to her. She had heard the strain in his voice. Continuing to rest her hand on Jagger's head, she waited until the crowd had moved on and tagged along behind. She waved at a concerned looking Mary, who had turned to look at her and then beckoned for Enna to hurry. She took her time and deliberately loitered at the back. She found herself falling back into her old habit of checking the defences and looked around to see if the gate was secured. There were two men on guard. Together they closed and barred the stout doorway. One of them then climbed the lookout tower whilst the other went to work stoking up the fire pit. Satisfied, Enna made her way to the keep entrance. On reaching the main hall, she noted that she really hadn't missed much, there was a fair hubbub going on. Most of the hunting party were scattered about, talking to friends and helping themselves to ale that was pressed eagerly into their hands.

Enna worked her way down one side of the hall,

grabbing a chunk of bread as she did. She got to within a few feet of where Donald and Merrett stood together.

Merrett sighed and leaned wearily on his spear. 'We didn't have too much trouble finding the bastards. The dogs picked up the scents easily enough. Found the first one holed up nearby to where we found young Enna. Smoked it out and skewered it. The animals took care of it when it hit the ground. The second one we found not half a mile away. That one took some digging. That's where Conor got smacked; the Possessed gave him a backhand swipe, near breaking his arm, the daft bugger.' Conor looked suitably abashed and shrugged.

'Then all in all, a successful day,' announced Donald looking about him.

'No, Laird. You don't get me, it was a lucky day. I said that the dogs had no trouble finding the scents. It was because they were *everywhere*. We spent the last few hours scouting out other caves, holes and hideouts. Donald, there is a gang of them out there.'

'We reckon we found one cave where there are at least three of 'em skulking inside!' added Adrian.

'Aye, and that's two more than we would want to handle. We shouldn't risk going in there and there'd be no guaranteeing that we'd not lose some of us in the way of doing it.'

There was a visible slump in Donald's shoulders. Enna felt her own mood start to grow darker. She had hoped that perhaps they could have been able to deal with the Possessed; that these men would be able to hunt them down one by one and they'd never be able to get her.

'Listen to me everyone,' announced Donald raising his hands. 'Let's put this in perspective. We killed two of them today. That is a feat few outside of these lands could attest to in recent times.' He looked around as if waiting for agreement, there were a few nods and muted 'ayes' from the crowd.

He nodded. 'This means that we have done everything right. We know how to handle ourselves and our dogs know their business. But most importantly, we have Cormant itself. There'll be the hells to pay if any beast tries to get in here. We killed two today. We'll kill more tomorrow.' He turned to look Merrett and clapped a hand on his shoulder. 'Tell you what, old man, how about if I come with you?'

Grim-faced Merrett locked eyes with Donald for a moment, then smiled. 'Watch who you're calling old, you pampered lordling. No, you stay here, someone needs to make sure that the bread is made and the meat is cooked for our victory supper!' This caused a roar of laughter from the crowd and much catcalling. Enna was pretty sure that she had just seen a very difficult situation be averted. Merrett was really worried, but Donald had successfully calmed things down. As far as she was concerned, Merrett's fears were well founded.

'But,' Donald continued, 'the night is almost upon us and we know that they will be on the prowl. We must be vigilant. But after today's success, I hardly think we need worry. As fearsome as they may be, they'll know not to try their luck with us!'

The gathering filed out of the hall. In contrast to the animated discussions of before, these were gentle, lower-key conversations. Family groups huddled together as they passed Enna. She hung back from the throng to wait for Merrett. Once he was done speaking to Donald, Mary walked over to join him. Together they moved towards her and Jagger.

'Come on then, lass. I'm about done for the evening and I'm hoping that there is some steam on a plate waiting for me at home.'

'A dinner fit for a hero,' announced Mary. Enna could see that the smile she wore was strained. It was the same kind of look her mother had had when they were waiting for the Hunter Band to arrive. Enna wasn't sure who the show was actually for. Merrett didn't need it, he knew well enough what the situation was, it was probably for her, and she appreciated the effort but it wasn't particularly effective. She felt bad enough about things as it was.

'Will you be taking a turn on the walls tonight, love?' continued the older woman.

'Bah, not likely. The lads will have the night off. We're back out tomorrow.'

'What?' cried Mary, stopping in her tracks. 'But you've done your bit, let someone else do it.'

'Come on, now. You know it doesn't work like that. We all take our share of the risk. One way or another. It's always been that way.'

'I know, that but it's not as if you are a young man anymore.'

Merrett grunted. 'Well thank you for your vote of confidence, my love.'

'You know what I mean!'

'I do, but I can heft a spear as good as the next man. And more importantly,' he tapped his head, 'I've got more sense than most of the younger ones put together.'

'Then you should have more sense than to be putting yourself in harm's way.'

'Ah, of course I do, I always put the younger ones at the front.'

Enna enjoyed listening to them bicker as they made their way home, Jagger sticking closely by her side. There were more torches lit now. There was even a look out posted on the top of the keep. Donald wasn't taking any chances.

Shortly after the meal, Enna excused herself and went to bed early. She could hear the two of them talking quietly next door. She lay on her bed, closed her eyes and concentrated on her power. Without the presence of Tenn's magic, she found it a lot harder to actually shape it in the way she had done in the cave. She had no real point to refer to and think about. Instead she focussed on the sensation of warmth that told her the power was within her and tried forcing it into the spear shape she had used earlier. She sent it out at imaginary targets.

After a short while she started to feel a wavering in the intensity of the heat within her body. She guessed that that might mean it was working. She continued practicing until at some point she drifted off to sleep.

Feeling disoriented and confused she was awakened by the shouting that seemed to be coming from directly outside her window. She looked about her in the darkness, there was no light coming from the room next door and, as she climbed out of bed and threw open the wooden shutters, she saw no predawn light in the sky. Instead, people were rushing to the gateway carrying torches, weapons and a fair few domestic implements like shovels and pick axes.

The door to her room opened and Merrett peered in, he was struggling to throw on a shirt and do his belt up at the same time.

'You okay?' he asked.

'Uh huh.'

'This hasn't happened for a while. They've no doubt spotted something.'

'I want to see,' said Enna.

'I'm sure you do. Go to the keep, climb up to the roof. Probably best place for you.' He turned and ran out the door, his footsteps pounding on the wood. Though she lost sight of him, she could feel the vibrations under her feet. There was a pause, no doubt he was collecting his weapons from where they rested against the wall and then she heard the door open and slam back into place. She jumped out of bed, grabbed her cloak, threw it about her and then placed her bare feet into her boots that rested under the bed. She passed through the main room, rushing past Mary who was peering out of a window, a shawl wrapped about her.

'I'm off to the keep. It's okay, Merrett said I could!'

'Enna...'

Enna opened the door and bounded down the steps, she didn't want to give Mary the chance to stop her. More people ran past her as she made for the keep. She kept moving as glancing back she saw how a crowd formed at the wall. She reached the keep entrance, passed through it and onto the stairway. She heard voices but saw no one. She passed the top floor and arrived at the staircase leading to the roof of the keep. The stairs spiralled up and lead to an open doorway. She could feel the chill breeze against her face and saw stars shining above her. She stopped when she found a figure already looking out over the island towards the mainland. She couldn't quite make out who it was, the figure wore a cloak. She could just back up...

'You might as well come on out and join me, Enna.' It was Donald.

Enna stepped out onto the roof and pulled her shawl tightly about her. She hurried over.

'You made all sorts of racket coming up those stairs. And I know none of my folk charge around at that sort of pace – they're far too old and far too sensible. And none of the children would ever think to come up here. So that leaves you.'

'Sorry,' she mumbled. Not that she was really.

Donald smiled down at her.

'Not to worry. Look.' He pointed to the notch in the hill line where the trail leading to the keep began.

Enna strained to see anything but it all seemed like a dark stain to her.

'Let your eyes adjust. Move them left and right.'

She did so and after a few moments, was able to discern more of the landscape about her. The notch seemed more defined now; she could tell where the trail met the slopes to either side. Movement! A black shape detached itself from the shadows, then another! They moved down the slope aways and then pulled back. There on the hilltop to the left, another one, no two. She gasped. She could hear a dog barking. Looking towards the bridge, the cattle dog was crouched low.

'You've seen this before, haven't you?'

Enna, her throat tight nodded. 'Yes.'

'Did you have warning of the attack?'

'Not really, just what happened with the Magistrate.' Damn. She realised her mistake straight away.

'What do you mean? What happened?' asked Donald, looking at her.

'Oh well, it was the Testing. They came the night after. I guess that's what I meant. It was odd that it happened then.'

'Indeed.' Donald was quiet but continued to study her. He gazed back to the hills. 'They'll be more wary of us. We are prepared. It seems they do have a sense of self preservation. None of them appear to be of the truly large kind. I only saw one of them once – when I was young. It took out half the men of a clan before they brought it down.' He went quiet again. Enna was starting to feel a bit awkward. Nothing much else seemed to be happening. Even some of the crowd were drifting off back to their homes. 'Enna, do you know why this is happening. Truly?'

The tone of his voice caused her to pause before she answered. There was sadness and she was pretty sure there was some desperation in his voice. It was like he wanted to find an explanation, no matter how terrible. It seemed out of place to hear it from him, he seemed so assured usually.

'I'm sorry, Laird. I don't know why they come,' she felt terrible. She knew that had been a half truth. She knew she was the reason. But in all honesty she still didn't *really* know why they were doing what they did.'

Donald sighed; he placed his hands on the parapet and leaned forward.

'It's not easy you know, Enna. Being in charge. Being responsible. I've led my folk for a long time. And we've always prevailed. This time, well, this is new. Ah! Listen to myself. I'm getting too old and wistful.' He placed a hand on her shoulder. 'Don't listen to me, lass, I've been around Tenn far too long, he used to lecture me all the time when I was younger. Now I suggest you head off back to bed. Mary is no doubt prowling the streets looking for you now. There'll be no beasties getting in here tonight. Mark my words.'

Enna nodded, then leaned forward and, getting onto tiptoes, kissed him on the cheek. He backed up with a look of surprise then chuckled warmly. It seemed to her that he needed pepping up a bit. She was glad to see that it had worked. She hurried back down the stairs of the keep. He was probably right, she thought. I'm going to get an earful from of Mary. Maybe Merrett will be back in, he'll take the edge off, big hearted softy.

Enna slept in that morning. She woke with a start. Hang on. This isn't right, she thought. Why wasn't Mary ploughing through the door to get her up? She rolled out of bed and threw open her window. The sun was up and high in the sky. Pausing for a moment she listened for anything unusual. At first it all seemed far too quiet. Where was everyone? Then the normal sounds of everyday life on Cormant filtered through. She heard a child giggling off to her right. Somewhere cattle were braying. Someone was hammering, a dull thud against wood. A gentle breeze blew against her face. Closing her eyes she breathed deeply. The world hadn't ended last night. No one had died. And life went on. She opened her eyes again and saw Mary gazing sternly up at her.

'Oh, so you decided to get up have you?'

'Sorry Mary, I didn't realise. I'll do my chores now.'

'Oh d,on't bother. I've done most of them.'

'Thank you.'

'Thank Merrett. He's the one who said you should

have a lay in after last night's excitement. Now get dressed. You can at least help me with preparing tonight's stew. At least that way you can tell him that your day wasn't completely wasted.'

Enna grinned at her and went to get dressed.

CHAPTER THIRTEEN

She was peeling her first potato when a shout came from near the gate. Enna and Mary shared a look and stood up from the table.

'That sounded like the hunting party was on its way back,' said Mary, thoughtfully.

'Isn't it a bit early?'

'Maybe they've gone and killed them all. Yes, there'd be no other reason.'

Enna detected the doubt in her voice.

'Come on, lass, let's go welcome them in.'

Enna put down the semi-skinned vegetable and knife and they swiftly made their way to the gate. There was a buzz of excitement amongst the rest of the crowd. As they filed through to the bridge, that excitement was replaced by silence.

'Oh Gods, no,' whispered a woman next to her.

'What's happened?' asked Mary, pushing forward and

squinting at the line of men moving slowly down the trail. They appeared to carrying something bulky – a Possessed corpse, perhaps?

'Look at what they're carrying,' said Conor, pointing with his good arm.

As the hunting party got closer, Enna could make out that the men weren't carrying a Possessed corpse, they were pulling a stretcher. Not just one. She could see three. And a quick count of the men still walking came up with only seven. Nobody moved until the men had reached the bridge. At that point, everyone on the island had gathered. Donald, a sword strapped to his side, stepped forward to meet them. Someone screamed. Enna didn't register who it was at first. The howl had been guttural; it reminded her of how a wounded animal sounded. Someone pushed past her. It had been Mary. The woman rushed to the first stretcher. Oh gods, was that Jagger? It was. The dog walked, tail hanging low, next to the second stretcher. A crudely made affair of two spears and a blanket. A man to each spear pulling the passenger at a low angle across the ground.

'It's Merrett,' whispered Conor.

The crowd surged forward leaving Enna in its wake. More cries and shouts of anger erupted as the group was surrounded.

'Give them some room, dammit!' roared Donald. 'Get them inside.' The crowd parted somewhat and the entourage continued to where Enna stood. As the second stretcher moved past she looked down on

Merrett. He looked calm and serene. A large strip of bandage had been wrapped around his stomach. It was sodden red. Mary walked alongside, her face white. Enna was at a loss what to say. Perhaps he'd be okay? What had happened? Had it been a Possessed? A loud voice dominated the babble. 'The bastards ambushed us. Suckered us in and jumped us,' shouted Padraig.

'Impossible! They aren't that smart!' argued another.

'You weren't there,' growled Padraig. 'We saw one. It was in a small wood, one of the ones by Grey's Cairn, moving within the trees. We sent the dogs in to drive it out. That they did. We had it surrounded. Then two more dropped out from the bloody trees. They grabbed Willy and Declan and pulled them back into the trees. Then the thing we had trapped went berserk. Took Merrett in the guts, Thomas had his arm ripped clean off and Liam his throat torn out.'

'Alright, Padraig, I think we should talk about this inside,' said Donald, trying to push the man forward.

It was clear that the big man was in no mood to quieten down.

'I tell you, I've never seen these things come out in the open like that before. If it hadn't been for them turning up right then we'd have lost more of us. Hells we were this close to turning tail. They went and charged straight at the beast, drove it away. '

'Stop. Who turned up?' asked Donald.

Padraig pointed. 'Them.'

A band of horsemen appeared at the top of the hill

line. They proceeded down the track at a canter. Enna studied them closely. By the gods, but these men were armed to the teeth! They weren't soldiers. There were no uniforms, unless you could call black a uniform; no crests, flags or emblazoned shields. They seemed more like the caravan guards she and her mother had joined up with. She watched as Donald moved ahead to wait for them at the landward end of the bridge. The horsemen, she counted at least twenty, slowed to a gentle trot. One rider pulled forward and went to meet the Laird.

The crowd had quieted except for the choked sobs of Mary and the other wives. Enna moved away from the grieving women and pushed her way through the gathering so she could get a better look at the new arrivals. The man speaking to Donald had yet to dismount but he looked a rough sort. They all did. She spotted the crossbow that was hung off his saddle, it looked a monster. The other riders had an odd array of weapons. What caught her eye were the nets that some carried. It seemed an odd choice to fight with. Then it hit her. It wasn't an odd choice at all if you wanted to trap something. *Gods, they were a Hunter Band!* A chill swept through her. Perhaps they were the ones sent to find her. Maybe they had tracked her here. She fought the rising panic. Now hang on, what could they know? They'd never seen her. No, they probably had a lot more than that; they might have a name and a description. She just couldn't be sure, the magistrate had sent word but she had no idea what that meant.

Donald finished his discussions and stepped forward. 'Everyone. Please listen. These men are a Hunter Band. They have been tracking these beasts for some time, and if it wasn't for them we may well have lost more of our friends and family. They are welcome to the protection and comforts that our home offers. And bearing in mind what we face right now, we could not have asked for better assistance. Let us all go back inside. There is much to do for our fallen kin and to prepare for their burial tomorrow. These men will stay in the keep. I would ask that if you can, spare us some of your time and your cooking skills. We have many mouths to feed.' He turned to look at the larger man behind him. 'Bring your men inside, friend, I'll show you where to stable your horses.'

The man nodded.

'You got any spare timber?'

'Yes, we have some stored.'

'Good. Show me where. And we'll need woodworking tools; axes, hammers, nails and the like.'

'Can I ask why?'

'This place isn't ready for what's coming.'

Donald's face paled but he said no more.

The crowd parted as the riders dismounted and led their horses across the bridge. They waited as the bodies were carried through the gateway and then continued inside. Those that remained by the bridge watched them quietly. They were hard looking men alright. Most were unshaven and looked like they never washed themselves. Their weapons on the other hand: clean, bright and sharp.

I could leave now, Enna thought; go grab my cloak and a sack full of food. Yes, I could go out and hide in Tennebran's cave. But she'd have to do it without anyone asking questions or raising the alarm. She'd need to speak to the Laird, let him know she was going. Think of some excuse or story that she could tell which would stop him being suspicious. Yes, she'd do that.

Donald's man, Raff, took over the settling of Miller's men within the island keep known as Cormant. They were being placed throughout the keep, at least a dozen were put in the Hall with others scattered wherever there was space. Miller and Woodhall followed the Laird into his private chambers.

Miller glanced about him appreciatively. 'Got yourselves a good, strong position here, Laird.'

'It has served us well for generations. This latest foe has not been the first to test us.'

'I don't doubt it, but I reckon you haven't suffered so many losses for a while.'

Donald walked around his table and slumped into a cushioned, high backed chair and run a hand through his greying hair. 'It's true. We have never been complacent, but perhaps we believed we were safer, more able to deal with these beasts than we truly were.'

'Heard your men took out two of them yesterday. I reckon you can handle yourselves if you could do that,' said Woodhall as he eased himself back against the door, arms folded.

'But what they did today. It's unheard of.'

Miller took the chair opposite the table. He released his sword strap, swung it over his shoulder, sat down and cradled the scabbard between his legs. Gripping the hilt with both hands he leaned forward and rested his chin on the pommel.

'We've seen it before. They're getting smarter. You can't treat 'em like beasts any more. They're working things out. They learn.'

'But you stopped them, yes? Your arrival turned the tables.'

Miller huffed.

'We startled 'em some. Though we only caught one. The rest scuttled back into the woods,' said Woodhall, adding rather more meat to the comment.

'So that is four we've killed. There cannot be many more. In living memory, we have never heard or seen more than three run together.'

'That's because you live in the middle of nowhere. But you're right. Time was they never used to pack together. Time was, it would only take one or two of them to rip through a place like this. Back in the first days people weren't ready, weren't organized. But we learned to defend ourselves.'

'So you think they've just adapted to that?' asked Woodhall.

Miller shook his head.

'You know better than that, Jess. You've seen 'em. What they're doing now, it isn't animal cunning. They're working together, they are planning.'

'Gentlemen. You must forgive me. I don't understand what you are saying,' said Donald.

Miller fixed him with a hard stare.

'We've followed a trail of destruction and death. We saw an entire settlement taken apart, as well as a trader caravan. But what we did not see, until now, are the beasts that have been doing it. This is the thing. The kind of trail we've been blazing along, we would know where the fuckers usually hide. But here's the stinker. They weren't there.'

Donald leaned forward clasping his hands tightly.

'They're here, aren't they? All of them.'

'That's what we figure,' said Woodhall.

'They've been moving this way, gaining strength. All of them that are along the path have been joining the pack. I can't tell you how many. But it's a shit load more than the few you've put paid to and the others in that wood.'

'Merrett said as much' said Donald, his voice shaky. 'Will they attack here?'

'How long they been around?'

'Three or four days. At least that's when we started to see signs.'

'Then my guess is they'll be coming tonight.'

'My gods.'

'Like I said. You got those wood working tools?'

'Yes, Raff can show you where. Most families have more.'

'Okay. Jess, go to it.'

'Done.' Woodhall pushed himself upright and returned to the Hall, shouting as he went. 'Alright. Dump your stuff and stop loafin'. We got about three hours to sort this place out.'

'This place is a good defensive position. It can also be a deathtrap though. We need to hold 'em off for as long as we can before they get to the keep. That bridge of yours will help. But your wall is a pile of crap. It's useless. They'll be over it in a second.'

'So what do you want to do?'

'We're gonna beef your defences up a bit. Start by barricading the bridge. My men will do that. Your folk will need to work on the walls. You got to find a way of raising 'em higher otherwise you'll get Possessed swarming from all over. If that happens, then the keep is your only refuge. Likely you'll have to burn your homes.'

'What?' cried Donald rising from his chair.

Miller shrugged.

'You can do it now or when the bastards get over your wall. They hole up anywhere they can during the daylight. We'll be in the keep, they'll be in the outbuildings. Gonna make it tricky going about your daily business.'

'Then why don't we just root them out during the day? If we must lose the houses, at least do it for a good reason,' pleaded Donald.

'If you'd asked me that a few months ago I would have agreed. But not after today. Think about that ambush,' said Miller. 'They came *out* of the trees. First time they've done that too. Looks like they aren't as afraid of the daylight as we thought. What's to stop 'em doing it again?'

Donald's shoulder's slumped. 'Seems to be that a lot of things are changing.'

'It does. So I leave it you. What would you rather do?'.

'You're staying to help us?' asked Donald.

'It's our work. The Possessed are here, so this is where we kill them. I should point out we got a lot of horses that we'd rather not lose.'

Donald rubbed his chin. 'The stables are large enough and an annex of the keep. I daresay that we can fortify it, even seal it off. There is a doorway leading into it from here. We can block off the outer doors from within.'

'Good.' Miller stood and walked over to the window overlooking the lake. 'The Possessed will be more interested in getting to us anyway. This keep is a good place to defend. But I've seen some of these things climb near sheer walls. The outer works are just there to give us some time. Maybe we can kill some of them there. We hold until the morning and then me and my men will go out and hunt them down. Defence is not what we're best at. Be prepared. The night will be hard.'

Donald moved to the window and looked at Miller.

'Why?'

'Hmm?'

'Why here. Why would they travel this way and single us out?'

'Now, that is the question. Here's what I know. We were summoned by a local magistrate to investigate a Testing gone wrong. When we arrived we found a village of corpses and changelings. We followed the trail and found a caravan, protected by many guards torn to shreds. And now we find the Possessed gathering in numbers around this place.' Avery joined Donald by the window. 'There is only one link. The Testing involved a girl. We got it figured that for some reason she attracts them. She was from the village, we thought her dead, and then a survivor from the caravan says they picked up a girl of the same description with her mother, just before they were attacked. So I got a question for you. Seen anyone like that around here?'

Donald stiffened. He glanced at Avery but the man had noticed.

'No. What does this girl look like?

'Never seen her. Redhead apparently, according to a survivor of the caravan attack. Enna.'

'Sorry?'

'Her name is Enna.'

'We have had no one come this way for some time prior to your arrival. We are off the beaten track.'

Miller grunted.

'That explains why you've had a quieter time of it. But the attack on you follows the pattern. I think we'll be basing ourselves here for a while. I want to see if there are any signs of this girl passing through.'

'I think our chances are better with you and your men.

And you are welcome to stay as long as you please. Who's to say that more of these creatures won't come here?'

'If we find this girl, I will. She is drawing them along in her wake.'

Donald had had enough; this man was far too intense for his liking. He had to get away and think. He had lied to this man. Not only was he leading a force of men that could overwhelm his people within moments, Miller was an agent of the Duke. He would no doubt consider Donald a criminal. If he had not given his word to Tennebran, he would have told the Hunter about Enna immediately, but he owed Tenn and trusted his judgement. The old man had said this girl was special.

'If you'll excuse me, Master Miller. I'll go check on how your men are settling in. Oh by the way – you might like to have a look at our armoury. Another reason we have been seldom troubled.'

'Thank you, I will.'

Donald nodded briskly and left.

Miller watched him go, then settled himself in the Laird's chair. The man was lying. The laird had fidgeted like a child with fleas, probably thought he was doing a good job of hiding it. So, perhaps the girl had passed this way. But there seemed no useful reason to lie to him. Well, whatever, there was no point in dealing with it now. They had a fight coming. Despite what the Laird might think, his men weren't used to this kind of scrape. Hells, they'd go toe to toe with a Possessed wherever they found it. But defence wasn't their business. Be that as it may, these people looked tough and their backs were against the wall. They looked like they'd hold the line. He had no doubt at all about his own men. Might as well go and look at this armoury, see if they have anything big or interesting. He stood up, stretched, buckled his sword against his back and left the room.

CHAPTER FOURTEEN

Woodhall tested the point of the wooden stake, the fourth he'd shaped. He nodded; pretty sharp. He looked along the line. 'That's us. Pull back to the gate,' he ordered.

Around him the other half dozen of the Band gathered their weapons and moved back from the bridge. They left a crude barricade that ran the width of the bridge, about midway along its span. The barricade itself was a wall about six feet in height, made from planks, half-formed logs and crates. It was easily scalable. Its purpose was simply to slow anything crossing the bridge down. The spikes they had set up were a few feet beyond the wall, nailed into a log that ran widthways. The second part of the plan would be to keep the things busy as they climbed over. Knock a few of 'em off balance with some well-placed shots, give them a nasty scratch on the way down.

He stopped at the gateway and turned right. He followed the line of the wall along the path leading to the jetty. This part of the defences was a problem. The Possessed could try and get up the wall anywhere along here. There would be no point in trying to defend the settlement itself. To try would be a bloody slaughter now that these things could coordinate. He found Hall and the other heavies finishing off a crude extension to the wall, coming out at right angles from the stone and running six foot into the sea. Several of the locals, stripped down to britches, were forcing long wooden spikes into the lake bed near and around the end of the wall. Damn but that water must be cold! Jess didn't like cold water, something that Avery loved to take the piss out of him for. Whatever, these lads didn't seem to mind. Well done. Good for them.

He joined the others at the wall. It was made up of various pieces of planking but looked sturdy enough. Hall wiped his hands and nodded towards the wall.

'What d'ya think? Propped up from behind with bracing and spikes littering the place.'

He left forward and knocked the wood. 'Nice and sturdy too.'

Jess nodded appreciatively.

'Nice work. Probably won't stand up to a charge though.'

Hall gaped at him.

'It bloody would.'

Hall shook his head and looked at the others.

'What do you think?'

They responded with a barrage of thoughtful 'ooh's and 'ah's. Dougie, a shaggy, brown-haired Hunter rested his mallet across his back. The man had been a carpenter back in the day. He sucked air through his teeth. 'Well, now you mention it, Jess, we did kind of rush it.'

Hall looked fit to explode in indignation.

'What d'ya mean? That's bullshit. This thing is bloody tight.'

'Says you.'

'That's right says me. Want me to prove it?'

'Reckon I do.'

'Right. Back up lads. Watch the sledgehammer!'. Hall turned round and strode purposely away.

Jess winked at the others. 'Better back up lads.'

He and the others moved back to the corner of the wall where the side trail began and fanned out away from the track. The locals in the water stopped to watch.

Hall turned, stared hard at the wall, cricked his neck and rounded his shoulders. Bellowing madly, he launched into a charge speeding towards the structure. Heads turned to follow him as he passed by at speed.

Leaping into the air, he smashed left shoulder first into the wall. And bounced off. He crumpled onto the ground and half rolled into the water.

The crowd burst into laughter. Jess looked about him. Dougie was actually weeping. The folk in the water were joining in too.

'Ah, that sight warms the cockles!' cried one.

'Hall, you are the brawn of the brawns of the outfit. Just don't ever get confused with the brains!' laughed one of the heavies.

Ah, good, thought Jess. Needed something to lighten the tone. And it brings us a bit closer to these folks. We'll need that tonight. We'll no doubt be shedding some blood with them.

'Come on,' he said. 'Let's pick him up.'

Miller stood next to Donald supervising the finish of a small fighting platform that stretched roughly half the length of the front wall. Wherever it met one of the abutting buildings, their roofs would be used instead. Behind them, many of the highland folk were piling up kindling and brush against their homes. At the sound of the laughter Miller leaned over and spat.

'Sounds like Hall's been set up again. Bloody idiot. Never learns.'

Donald sighed.

'When must we burn our homes?'

'When we see them at the top of the rise. That'll give us time to fire off some salvos then retreat back into the keep. When they get over the walls the fires will have taken. Once in, their movement will be restricted, they'll be penned and we'll be able to spot them easier. They won't like the fire.'

'I suppose it will work.'

'It will, but only the once.'

Miller looked up at the sky. 'Almost time. You got

that pitch coming along?'

'Yes, it should be. I'll go and check.'

Donald turned and walked to the keep.

Miller walked out through the gate. 'Hey, Jess! If you boys have stopped pissing about, you just got time to get supper.'

Enna held tight to Mary. The woman was completely grief stricken. Enna had had to pull her out of their bedroom where Merrett now lay. She had had to help some of the others prepare the building for burning. She had stacked bundles of pitch-soaked branches around the house but had deliberately kept to the rear; there had been less chance of being spotted by any of the Hunters. As it was they had pretty much gone into the keep and quickly set about working out the front of the island. She had used Mary's refusal to leave the body as a chance to gather some belongings and pack. She positioned herself to look out the doorway and saw her chance when Donald passed. She kissed Mary and hurried out to catch him. The man was deep in thought.

'Donald?'

'Mmmm. Ah.' His face was pinched, pained. It was clear he was wrestling with something.

'Are you alright?'

'That remains to be seen.' He placed an around her shoulder, guiding her, with an urgent pressure towards the keep. He remained silent and Enna thought it best not to push the issue. They entered the keep and headed to the rear of the structure. Passing through the empty kitchen into one of the storerooms, Donald gently pushed her through the doorway and then shut it behind him.

'Enna. I want you to be honest with me. It doesn't matter what you may have said in the past. Do you know those men out there?'

Enna knew that she should stick to her story, that Tenn would most likely be angry with her if she told. But there was something in Donald's tone of voice. Something that told her he wasn't going to cause her harm.

She nodded.

'They're looking for you.' It wasn't a question.

'I don't know why this is happening, Donald.'

'Hah, well, that makes all of us, doesn't it?'

'I want to leave, Donald. I don't want this to happen.'

'So you are the cause?'

'I am but I'm not like them. I haven't turned. I won't.'

Donald turned his back to her. She tensed when she saw his right hand drift to his sword.

'I have seen two children die because of the testing. From what I understand from Tenn, it is more often the case than not that those children who fail the Testing, those who are susceptible to the change, still won't turn. That they never develop their powers. Apparently, the bloodlines of magic run wide but often shallow.' He turned back towards, his face intent upon hers. 'How many do you think we have sacrificed over the years? All those ones that would never have used their power, those that would have lived long lives. Those that would never have turned. Those that are innocent. Are you innocent, Enna? Are you another one we should sacrifice so the rest of us survive?'

'I'm not innocent. I know that I have a power. But that power doesn't work the way you think.'

'It's true that if you have been using this power, you should have turned by now,' he acknowledged.

'I've used it lots. I've gotten better at it. I think that is why they are after me. I didn't want to accept that at first.' Enna said.

Donald folded his arms. 'So what should we do, Enna? Shall we give you to them? Do you think that would work?'

'I don't want to die, Donald. But I don't think it'll stop them anyhow. They aren't the same anymore, they are organised. I think that they have gotten cleverer somehow. I think that even if I were to die, they would still come. I don't think they'll ever go back to how they used to be.'

'I agree. If I didn't, then we may not have had this conversation. I respect Tenn and his opinion, but if I thought there was a way to save Cormant, then I would take it. As it is, there seems little point. They are coming whatever we do. So the question remains, what do we do with you?'

He walked to the back of the storeroom to where a number of crates were stacked. To one side was a barrel, it was one of the ones that was brought out for the community gatherings. He beckoned to her with both hands.

'Come on.'

Gingerly she stepped forward until she stood directly before him. What was he going to do? Put her in a barrel and throw her off the roof of the keep? Donald placed his hands on her hips, bent his legs then boosted her up onto the barrel.

'Reach up and grab that top crate.'

She reached across and finding the crate was empty, lifted it of the rest and handed it down to Donald. By moving it she revealed a small set of shutters.

'Open it up,' he commanded.

She leaned against the remaining crates, twisting her torso slightly and flipped the retaining bar and tried to force them open. The hinges, either rusted or just long unused, protested with a grinding noise but yielded after she applied more pressure.

The shutters opened to a gentle wind and light flooded into the room. She looked out and saw the waters of the lake. They must be at the back of the Keep!

'Most don't ever think about this small window when they row about the lake. They look at it as just one of many overlooking the water.' Donald said behind her. It was true; Enna only vaguely paid attention to the keep walls backing onto the lake. Her attention had always been fixed on the jetty, the boat always angling to that side of the island. He tilted his head up.

'Climb through and lower yourself down. Don't worry, you won't sink. There is solid ground, a ledge, just a few inches below the water line; it'll lead you round to the far side of the jetty. Jump in a boat. Head out across the water. I'm sorry, there isn't anything I can give you here. There isn't time. It's going to be dark soon. I'd say the best place to hide would be in the middle of that lake. I imagine the Possessed will be too busy with us to notice you. Wait there 'til morning, then head over to see Tenn. He can help you from there.'

There were tears in her eyes as Enna leaned forward and hugged him. The irony wasn't lost on Enna. This was the second time that she was being spirited away through the walls of a settlement. Now she was truly fearful that the same fate would befall this place.

'I'm so sorry. I didn't mean for this to happen. I really didn't.'

Donald smiled and patted her back before pushing her back.

'There was a time when magic was part of life. Before it became a curse, I used to marvel at what could be done. To command such power. Now I would pity such souls. Maybe, in years to come, that sense of wonder will return. Perhaps you are part of that?'

Again, another hint. A suggestion that what she could do might actually have some use. Some reason to exist. She was at a loss and far too terrified to think much on it.

'Now go on, lass. I haven't mentioned you or that we even found a girl. But I can't keep the Hunters from finding out about you. Someone will talk. Then they'll want to talk to me. They'll be after you again. That is if any of us survive the night. Go, go.'

Enna wiped the tears from her face and clambered onto the crate, twisting around so that she went feet first. Wriggling out of the window, she braced against the window edge and looked down. She guessed she was only a foot or so from waterline. *Time to get wet.* She let go and dropped with a splash into the lake. She was standing on firm ground, the water not even close to coming over the tops of the leather boots she wore. Ahead of her the lake was growing dark as the sun started to dip below the hills to the west. The keep cast a long black shadow upon the water.

Enna splashed her way around the edge of the walls. The jetty was just ahead of her, and as she had expected, boats were tied up to it. She could see no one about. They had all withdrawn inside the keep. She felt terribly exposed out here, in the deepening gloom. The Possessed were probably already on the prowl. Reaching the jetty she ran to the end boat, untied the mooring rope and climbed in. She shipped the oars and headed out. As the light faded she thought she could see movement on the roof of the keep, but no one was looking her way.

Streaks of red and orange spread across the sky as the sun made its final retreat. About her the lake and hills were dark, becoming formless and immense. Her sense of scale was diminished, even though she knew what surrounded her well enough. There were torches glowing on the walls of the island and on the keep itself. They seemed to Enna weak, insubstantial things that could never hope to hold back the dark. But then light bloomed: a flickering, moving mass of yellow and ember. It came from behind the walls, first at one spot, and then another as individual sources came together, each one adding to the strength of the whole. In what seemed like a minute or so, the keep had become a pulsing beacon. They had set light to the houses.

Miller stood with his back to the settlement. He kept a steadying hand on his crossbow where it rested on the top of the gate. He felt the heat of the flames against his back. The nights were chilly up here and the warmth was welcome. None of his men wore cloaks, they needed their mobility. All of the Hunter Band was upon the wall. His men and most of the local lads were mixed in together. Every man carried either a bow or crossbow. The armoury had indeed proven to be well stocked. His heavies and spearmen were given the crossbows although they weren't that hot at marksmanship. They and the highlanders kept their personal weapons close to hand. If anything got to the walls too quickly then they would have to keep them off. He heard someone climbing the ladder up to the crude firing platform he was standing on.

'That's the lot, Chief.' Woodhall blew into his hands and rubbed them together.

'What good is that doing? You've got gloves on.'

Woodhall shrugged. 'Makes me feel better.'

Miller spat over the wall.

'Reckon this should get their attention.'

'See anything.'

'Nah. They're biding their time.'

On the far side of the bridge torches burned on either side. These marked the start of a procession of lights, tied to poles and driven into the ground.

The lights ended where the trail met the top of the hill line. Flanking them on the hill tops nearest the trail, bonfires had been built, and they too were now blazing merrily away.

'Maybe they won't come.'

Miller looked to his left. The Laird had followed Woodhall up the ladder.

'If so, it would've made our slash and burn policy a bit pre-emptive,' said Woodhall.

'You been reading books on military strategy again? That stuff will rot your brain.'

'But if they don't come tonight, perhaps they won't at all. We could combine and go after them tomorrow.' Donald was persistent. Foolish hope, thought Miller. If what I'm thinking is going on here, every night they don't come means we're just storing up more trouble. No point in worrying the man, though.

'Possibly. There is a part of me would rather they come to us. Saves all the effort. Besides, we should be safe enough in that fortress of yours. Long as no one panics.'

'My people know what's at stake,' said Donald. The

defensiveness in his tone was clear. Miller conceded that. They were brave enough to go take on Possessed on their own turf.

'Well, if it's effort you want to save, this should be easy,' murmured Woodhall.

'Why?' asked Donald.

Woodhall pointed as the lookout in the tower to their left cried out.

Miller squinted and scanned the hills. At first nothing was obvious, then he saw the light from the left beacons blur. Black shapes flitted past at speed. At first this movement was intermittent, suggesting that there was only one Possessed moving about up there.

'Another. On the right side this time!' cried the lookout.

The men on the walls strained forward, some talked quietly to each other, most remained silent. As the moments passed, more forms appeared, they were still too far to discern properly but Miller spotted a couple of big ones, looming over the others, standing farther back in the light. Some were moving onto the trail itself then up the bank to the other side.

'They're gathering. Don't seem too interested in coming down yet,' said Woodhall.

'Uh huh. Making a nice show of things. How many you count?'

'Ten, a dozen or so?' replied Woodhall

'Have you ever seen that many in one place?' whispered Donald. He sounded awed by the prospect.

Miller was pleased to detect no fear there. He shook his head.

'Nope. Never have, seen maybe half a dozen once. Most we ever encountered in one place was three. That was back at that village and again at the woods.'

'We do this for a living but even our guys don't want to tangle with more than one critter at a time. Three's the most we could manage I reckon,' surmised Woodhall.

'We'll be challenging that notion tonight,' said Miller. 'And I'll be happy to oblige 'em.'

A dog starting barking behind them. Many of the cattle dogs stayed with their masters, waiting patiently below them. More joined in, teeth bared and hackles raised.

'I think we get it!' shouted Hall from further down the line. 'We know where they are!'

'The dogs are trained to alert us if one gets near,' said Donald. 'We had one posted at the end of the bridge the night before.'

'Seen 'em in action this morning.'

'Pretty good sense of smell, them beasts,' said Woodhall. 'I'm surprised they can get a whiff of the things all the way up there. What with the fires burning behind us.'

The men watched the Possessed in the distance for a few moments longer. The dogs continued to bark, the noise increasing as more of them joined in. Their respective owners were now actively trying to quiet them.

'I'm sure they are just agitated by the fire and

excitement,' said Donald. He stopped for a moment. 'But you know, the distance, the fires. They shouldn't be able to sense those things at such a great distance.'

Miller shot Woodhall a warning look.

'And, what?' Gods, here it comes, he thought.

Donald shrugged. 'It's just odd that's all.'

Miller couldn't risk it.

'Stand to. They're already here!' he bellowed.

'There on the on the shore line!' cried a man further to the right.

'And on the left!' replied another.

'Oh shit.' said Woodhall.

'You got that right,' said Miller.

Coming from both sides, at speed, were a bunch of Possessed. They were racing across the shingle and would swiftly converge at the bridge head. As he watched, Miller saw yet more shapes bound through the graveyard. The bastards had caught them by surprise.

'Listen up! No bastard runs till I say so. When they reach the barricade, wait for my order then you let loose with what you got. Then you run. Don't stop 'til you get inside.'

He knew that his men would hold. The others, well, he wouldn't waste the shot. He'd kick their arses later.

The dogs, now forgotten by all, continued to bark; their owners were focussed on what was coming. Men lifted their weapons and drew beads at the leading Possessed. Behind them the conflagration was complete. Only the central path through the island was clear. Try to take any other course and the heat and flame would quickly drive you back.

At the far end of the bridge, the first of the creatures bounded onto the structure. There were four of them in the pack; three were like wolves, a kind the Hunters had encountered many times before. A fourth, hairless and bald, seemed to be a tangle of human limbs but leapt with inhuman strength. Within a few steps, they were at the barricade. They launched themselves at it, quickly finding purchase and momentum.

Miller already had one of the wolf-like Possessed in his sights. He breathed deeply, making sure of the shot. He let loose. As he did so, those nearest him followed suit and a ragged ripple of shafts and bolts followed his. With more than thirty projectiles in the air, many found their mark. He saw his own stagger back, its body a pin cushion. A second lost its footing and fell into the waiting ground spikes, impaling its body in several places.

'Fall back! Fall Back!' he shouted. As his order was taken up with cries along the line, he stole one more look at the bridge. Two down. A decent tally on any other day. Already the beasts were moving forward again, and behind them more followed. Many more. He didn't have to check to know that they would soon be joined by the others on the trail. They could never hope to hold off as many as this. It would only take one of them to get up, create a gap in the defence and they were all dead. They'd break and run, and half would never make it to the keep.

He turned, crouched down. Holding the side of the

platform with his right hand, he grabbed his crossbow tight in his left, and leapt to the ground with a grunt. He bent his knees into the landing but it still knocked his breath out. He heard the thuds of others dropping down, but he was already up and running for the keep. Behind he could hear the snarls and screams of the Possessed hitting the wall. The gate itself shuddered as something heavy smashed into it. As he sprinted hard along the cleared passage, the heat of the flames was almost unbearable. At the midpoint he forced himself to stop and turn round. Coming right at him was a mad mass of men and barking dogs. Damn, can't tell friend from foe in this heat. It was so hot he had to squint to see. 'Come on, come on, move your bloody arses!' He pushed stumbling figures past him. Then he saw them. Forms climbing over the wall and jumping to the ground.

He'd seen enough and recommenced his dash to the keep. Ahead of him the men were streaming through the gate. Woodhall was stood by the portcullis waving them on. As the sound of pursuit grew nearer, Miller felt an old fear crawling up his spine. The heat and the flames reminded him of some kind of childhood nightmare. He passed by Woodhall and through the small gatehouse. He moved into the room holding the portcullis wheel. It was already manned by a Highlander. A few more figures ran by him and he turned to look out into the hamlet.

'Come on! Fucking move!' Woodhall was screaming at a pair of men still a few metres away from the keep. One man was supporting the other who half ran, half hobbled.

Must have twisted something getting down.

'Woodhall, get in here, now' he ordered.

Woodhall turned gazed back at him, his face flushed. He then took another look at the two men who were but a few feet away. A large black blur appeared in the air above them. It smashed into the injured man, driving him onto the floor. It leant forward and bit into his neck, ripping out a hunk of flesh with a savage jerk. His helper was thrown to one side. Another larger Possessed quickly appeared and swept a taloned hand across his face. The man screamed as his face whipped round in a spray of blood.

'Drop it!' ordered Miller and the highlander unhooked the quick release mechanism of the portcullis.

Woodhall turned and threw himself head first towards Miller. Behind him another Possessed was closing the gap fast. Woodhall rolled into a ball and smacked into Miller as the portcullis fell at speed. The creature slammed into the metalwork. The metal barely reacted to the impact. Miller hauled Woodhall up. The thing was only feet away from them and it clutched at the metal bands with all too human hands. It slavered and screamed, its deep red eyes blazing with hatred. It reached an arm through, straining to get at them, blood dripping from its fingers. Dougie ran past them brandishing a spear, two more men followed behind.

'Give it a taste!' he shouted. He skewered the creature through the grate, the others crowded round him jamming their own spears past him, trying to get a decent jab into the thing. It roared at them, withdrew its hands, grabbed the spear where it was embedded in its stomach and stepped back, yanking the spear out of Dougie's hands.

'Woah, someone get me another sticker!' he announced. Miller reached forward and pulled him back as three more Possessed crowed outside the portcullis.

'Leave it, let's pull back and get this door shut. Woodhall, get upstairs and start laying down fire.'

'On it. Come on you lot!' As the defenders raced down the corridor, Miller turned back to the gatehouse room.

'Alright, let's get this door shut.'

The occupant nodded and come out. His left arm was in a sling.

'You alright?'

'Aye, sir, just a wee scratch from yesterday. One of them backhanded me.'

'Uh huh. Scratch you?'

The younger man shook his head,

'Name?'

'Conor.'

'Ok. Well, watch you don't get smacked again.'

Conor grimaced. 'Once is enough, it's stinging like hell.'

Together they moved to either side of the passage and took hold of the thick wooden doors that rested against the walls. Miller had to put some effort into getting the thing moving. He moved it forward a few inches and then braced himself against the door and pushed it forwards and outwards. Opposite him, Conor had to perform the same actions but with one hand. The lad's face was straining with the effort. Working with the momentum, his half of the door slammed firmly into place. Conor had pushed his door forward a little way and Miller reached across to assist him. Together they closed the gap.

'Where's the cross-brace?'

'Back through here.' Conor indicated the gate room.

Miller noted that the lad was breathing heavily.

'I'll get it. Just put your weight on the door.'

Conor nodded and settled his back against the gap.

He went inside, grabbed the beam where it rested against the wall and returned to the door. Conor stepped forward and helped him to drop it into place.

Miller patted the door.

'That'll keep 'em busy for a time.'

He studied the younger man; he looked exhausted.

'Come on, get yourself with the others in the hall. Rest up a bit, then make yourself useful.'

Conor could only nod. Miller led the way. They passed three of his men who were already setting up a barricade along the corridor. He turned to speak to them.

'If you hear anything like grinding metal you holler and get yourselves back up the stairs.' The men nodded.

He quickly outpaced Conor as he ascended the stairs. He looked into the Hall on the next level. Most of the women and children were gathered together in there. Conor caught up with him.

'In you go, lad.'

He continued up the stairs and onto the spiral stairs leading onto the roof. As he emerged, he was assaulted by the voices of a score of men. Woodhall and Donald were directing operations. Most were at the sides facing onto the hamlet below. Many were firing bows whilst others were hauling and dropping large rocks over the side. In the centre of the roof a cauldron was suspended over a large fire.

'How we doing, Jess?'

Woodhall ran over to him. The bastards are crawling all over the place down there!'.

'How's the gateway holding up?' He found himself having to shout over the noise around of the men, the Possessed and the fire below.

'So far so good, they've left it alone for the time being, trying to find another way in. I'm worried about those stables. They aren't getting access through the doorway, it's sealed shut. But if they figure out they can get through the roof we could lose the horses.'

'Not much we can do about that now. But you've got to figure they'll work it out. Those bastards caught us out, Jess, they played us.'

'Damnedest thing. Never seen it before.'

'They truly are cunning,' said Donald joining them.

'They sure aren't stupid anymore. Jess, better take someone and double check we got the stable entrance locked up good and tight. Might be a weaker spot than we thought.'

Woodhall looked about him. 'Hall, you're up.'

Miller looked towards the cauldron.

'Donald, that pitch ready?'

'It's boiling a treat now' said Donald.

Hall stopped as he walked by. 'Ah shit, Avery, I'm gonna miss the fun?'

'Fuck off.'

'Now you've just gone and pissed me off, boss!' said Hall with a smile. He ran to the tower exit where Woodhall waited.

'Good.'

He walked over to the front of the roof. As he looked over he was greeted by a wave of heat. He raised his arm in a warding gesture. Completely bloody useless, he chided. Forcing himself forward, he scanned the base of the keep. The men were keeping up the pressure on the Possessed. He had thought of putting shooters at the windows but thought better of it. These things had been known to scale walls; there was no point in making it easier for them to get in. He had sealed the windows with stone and wood.

They prowled around below, flitting amongst the flames.

'After that initial try at the gate, they haven't done much more than dance around to avoid our missiles,' commented Donald.

Miller stared down thoughtfully for a moment.

'I think they were waiting for him.'

Donald raised an eyebrow and looked down. Striding

through the flames was a huge Possessed. It was at least twice the height of a man, horned, muscled and cloven hoofed.

'I've only ever heard of these things.'

'It's a night for surprises. Best get the pitch ready.'

'Yes.' Donald turned and shouted orders to his men.

Miller watched as the Possessed reached the gatehouse.

'Target that one!' he ordered to the defenders. A rain of missiles was launched at the thing. It roared its defiance and shrugged off the impact of the hits. The rocks bounced off without leaving a mark and arrows failed to penetrate its hide. It took hold of the portcullis. It began to rise slowly off the ground. Once it had gained a few inches it began to rock backwards and forwards.

'The bastard's trying to rip it out the wall,' observed a local next to him, Miller vaguely recalled hearing him called Padraig.

'It will if we don't kill it.' Miller set his crossbow on the ground and pulled the string back. He pulled a heavy bolt from his pouch and placed it in the groove. Hefting his weapon, he took aim and let fly. His bolt struck the thing in the left shoulder and held. It let go of the portcullis and it dropped to the floor with a clang.

'Nice shot.'

'Yeah.'

The thing reached over with its right hand and yanked the bolt free. It then bent down to continue its work.

'Ah,' observed Padraig

'Yeah.'

'Coming through!' shouted Donald's man Raff, leading the way for two men bearing the pitch between long poles fed through twin loops on either side of the cauldron. They manoeuvred it onto the ledge directly above the gate house and the creature.

Raff looked toward Miller, an excited look on his face. 'Ready,' he said.

'Pour it on,' ordered Miller.

The outside pole was pulled out of its loops and men grabbed either side of the remaining pole. Maintaining their control, they tilted the cauldron forward and a gentle stream of pitch began to pour out. Gaining confidence the men tilted the cauldron forward and the intensity of the flow increased. Miller and the others leaned over to watch the hot pitch splash over the Possessed. This time its reaction was more acute. It screamed in pain as the pitch burned and bonded with its skin.

'Torches!' ordered Miller. He held out his hand and was passed a burning torch. A few others were passed out along the line. 'Make 'em count!'

He and the others sighted and dropped their brands towards the Possessed. Some failed to find their mark but fell amongst the pool of pitch at the gate. Three more struck the beast itself. It flailed about as the fire took hold both on its body and upon the ground around it. The way the thing was crashing about, it looked to Miller like they had blinded it, as it piled into one of the buildings. The gathered men cheered as it continued to thrash about the place for several minutes, its size and strength making it easy to follow, before it finally collapsed.

'Gods, that took a while to die,' said Raff.

'They never die easy,' said Miller.

'There's more coming,' observed Woodhall. Down below other Possessed had worked their way around the smouldering body. Another large one was moving towards the entrance whilst two more were probing their way up the first few feet of keep stonework.

'But we don't have any more pitch ready!' said Donald, an edge of panic to his voice.

'Then we break out the good stuff,' replied Miller. 'Jess?'

Woodhall nodded. 'Yep,' He turned around. 'Bring 'em out.'

Donald gave Miller a questioning look.

'We carry supplies of special, burning mixture. Very volatile. Doesn't like to be banged about. We call them stinkers. The stuff smells like the worst kind of shit, but it puts your pitch to shame. It sticks and it literally burns through Possessed flesh.'

'I've heard of it,' said Donald. 'Why didn't you use it before?'

'I said its special stuff. By that I mean it's damn rare, damn expensive and damned hard to get hold of. We only use it as a last resort, when we know it's going to work. I think we've reached that moment.'

Beside him, eight Hunters gathered. Each carried a small round clay container, the top tapered to an opening, about two inches in width, with a wooden stopper in place.

'Open up,' ordered Miller. Then men wrestled and twisted the stoppers off as gingerly as they could. Then, to a man, they held the pots out at arms length.

'Stuff ain't as bad if it's not burning, you can get it off, but it still stings like a bastard,' commented Miller.

Dougie moved along the line with another torch. He placed the flame against the stopper, after a short moment, sparks and blue flame erupted from the top. The bald-headed Hunter strained to hold the pot further away from him.

'Don't be a girl, Derris', remarked Dougie.

'Piss off, Dougie,' said Derris. 'You never bloody carry this stuff.'

'Not that stupid,' said Dougie, with a wicked grin, as he continued down the line.

Once each man's pot was lit, Dougie nodded to Woodhall and stepped back.

Woodhall leaned over the wall. The two climbers were halfway up and the larger Possessed had started on the gatehouse.

'Right, you two and you two,' he detailed Hunters, 'aim for the climbers. If you miss, we can still probably handle them. You four go for the big one.'

The Hunters moved forward and lined themselves up.

'Stinkers away!' cried Woodhall.

The eight pots were released and men gathered to watch their fall. One pot hit each of the climbers, the impact causing the pots to crack and spill their contents out over the Possessed. The shrieks as the substance coated and stuck to their flesh was blood curdling. As the things reached to brush it off, the substance spread to their limbs. Both quickly lost their holds and fell back to the earth in a writhing, tumbling mess. The pots that missed and those that aimed at the larger Possessed had a far more impressive result. Two pots struck the Possessed and the four impacted into the ground around the base of the walls in a loud, blue-flamed explosion. The creature roared as the stinkers hit home and a large part of its body was encased in the blue fire. The thing charged off into the night. The watchers charted its progress as it passed through the burning buildings only to stall in its attempt to climb over the wall. It fell back to the floor and after a few more half hearted attempts to brush the substance off it finally ceased to move.

'Eat that,' muttered Miller.

'And that's our big surprise all used up,' said Woodhall.

'They're pulling back,' said Donald.

'I guess they're still trying to figure out what to do,' said Woodhall.

'Gods forbid.'

'Yeah' Miller spat over the edge. 'You ever seen any of them swim?'

'No, can't say that I have.'

'Me neither, let's hope they never figure out how to do it. In fact,' he paused and looked behind him. 'Hey,

Reed?'

A tall redhead with a long, tasseled beard looked over from the south side.

'Yes, Boss?'

'I want you to stand look out on the lake side.'

'They won't come from that way, will they? They'd have to swim it.'

'Yeah I know, just do it, last thing I want is to get blindsided again.'

'Yes, sir.'

The fires below had eventually burned out and the mood on the roof had quieted. The Possessed had gone to ground and withdrawn from the walls. Donald's men placed the cauldron back over the fire and had refilled it with pitch.

The Hunters stood at ease, watching the local men at work.

'Good fun that was,' observed Hall.

'See that bastard go up? I hear tell they got rows of those things on the walls of Albair City' said one of the others. 'Hey, Derris, you're from there.'

'I seen 'em, they got these huge cauldrons and runnels that feed the stuff off to a dozen different spouts,' said Derris.

'Pity we only got a few portable ones,' remarked Woodhall.

'Makes life easier in room clearance. Just hose the bastards down,' said Miller. He looked behind to the lake.

'Reed. Anything?'

'Nothing. Caught sight of a boat. It's floating there in the middle of the lake.'

Miller walked over to join him and leaned forward to get a look. Damn, his eyes were failing.

'I can't see shit. Oh, hang on. Yeah, got it.' He could make out a dark shape on the water.

'Not doing much you say.'

'Nope. Just bin sat there.'

Miller turned his head slightly and spoke over his shoulder.

'Hey, Donald, one of your boats is out on the lake. You got anyone doing some late night fishing?'

Donald, stood by the cauldron, turned toward Miller.

'I shouldn't think so. Someone must have been careless in tying it up.'

'Guess so.'

CHAPTER FIFTEEN

It was... unearthly? It was a word that Mistress Tabawick had used a few times. Enna felt like she was cocooned. That she was watching events she wasn't part of. That were happening in some place that had no effect on her. That she was safe here. *Hah! I know that's not true!* The boat bobbed gently upon the black water of the lake. It made a lapping noise against the side of the boat, which answered with its own occasional creak. That was her world. She shivered a little and wrapped her arms close around her body. She'd gone right out to the middle of the lake like Donald had asked and now sat watching the Keep. There was so much light coming from the island, it reached across the lake, like the moon did on cloudless nights. Sounds drifted across to her – shouts, screams, howling. She could feel the Possessed; the prickling sensation was clear, strong and insistent. If she had been unsure about this before, it was no longer the case. She *could* sense them. Just like they could her. That at least gives me a chance, she thought. I'll know if they are coming.

She couldn't see what was going on but she could spot the occasional black shape flit across the roof. The shouting was coming from there. It meant someone was still alive. That they hadn't gotten inside. She knew that there was no going back for her. But she wished the people of Cormant well; they had taken care of her. And had lost too much in the process. A breeze blew across her face and she felt streaks of cold against her skin. Reaching up to her face, her fingers came away wet. She'd been crying and she hadn't even noticed.

Donald leaned over Conor and touched his brow. His skin was cold and clammy to the touch. The younger man had rapidly deteriorated in the last few hours.

'Hang in there, lad.'

Conor was drifting in and out of consciousness but he raised a smile.

Donald stood and gently took the arm of the woman who was caring for him.

'There is little we can do for him, but I've got Raff sorting out some of our herbs from the stores.'

'Thank you, Laird. What do you think he has?' asked Jenny. She was Conor's childhood sweetheart. A good-natured girl but with only a modicum more sense in her head than Conor had.

'Ah, could be anything, lass. Those creatures have all sorts of corruption in them. But with the fever he's got running, I'd say his body is fighting this thing at its peak. I daresay if he makes it through the night, he should pull through.' Not that I know anything of the sort, he thought. This lad could die in the next five minutes. But this night of all nights, they needed some hope.

'Laird?'

He looked around. 'Ah, here is Raff now.' Donald's retainer had arrived bearing a steaming mug. A bitter smell emanated from it. Donald took it off his hands, inside a number of leaves and roots could be seen floating around the top.

He laughed and passed the mug on to Jenny.

'Sometimes the cure seems just as bad as the disease.' He smiled at the both of them and moved away. Conor did not look good, but they'd have to address that later. They still had to survive the night.

Jenny gently cupped Conor's head and tilted the mug to his lips.

Conor looked up at her.

'I'm sorry, Jenny.'

She shook her head.

'Not your fault, you lummox.'

'No, I didn't tell anyone. But the beastie caught me better – scratched me it did. But I hid it, didn't want to scare anyone.'

'Oh, Conor. You know these things carry illness and

worse. You should have said.'

'I know. But I felt fine.' He gasped and closed his eyes.

Jenny looked around. She knew she should tell someone but they might react badly. She'd just have to hope for the best. Conor was still with her. He'd pull through.

On leaving the hall Donald ran into Woodhall.

'Everything alright?' asked the Hunter.

Donald nodded and ran a hand over his head.

'Got a sick man back there. I don't think he'll last for much longer.'

'Oh?' Woodhall's hand drifted to his sword. 'Something we should worry about?'

Donald shook his head. 'No, he's got a fever but I don't think it is infectious.'

'Even so, you might want to think about moving him.'

Donald nodded. 'I will.'

Woodhall jerked his head back, 'Least those things are holding off. The fires are starting to die down out there now; they're keeping themselves tight against the outer walls. We can't hit them but they can stay there all night for I care.'

'Then that is a mercy. Perhaps we should talk about what is to be done tomorrow?'

Woodhall shrugged. 'That's for Miller to decide. Problem is there is a lot more of them than we have ever had to deal with. It's going to take a long time to hunt 'em all.'

Donald was surprised but impressed. There was no hint of cutting and running from these men. They'd stay for as long as it took. Even though it was obvious to all that there were far too many Possessed to ever hope to clear from these lands. The Hunters would take casualties. It was inevitable; their numbers would dwindle over time until they would no longer be effective. But no doubt they'd keep trying anyway.

He felt a light touch on his arm.

'Donald?'

Mary's face was a picture of anguish: her eyes were red-rimmed, her hair ragged.

Donald placed an arm on her shoulder.

'What is it, Mary?'

'It's Enna, Donald. I can't find her.'

He felt a cold sensation in his stomach. Damn, this Hunter had to be here. He'd have to brazen it out.

'Now, you've been mourning your loss. I'm sure she is in here somewhere.'

'Gods help me, Donald, I was so distraught, I've no idea where she's got to. I've looked and asked and no one has seen her.'

Mary held out her hands in supplication and he reached out and took them firmly into his own.

'You and I both know what a wilful spirit she is. No doubt she is stood on the battlements or guarding one of the doorways downstairs. I'll go look for her myself.'

'Thank you Donald. I've lost my husband. I couldn't

bear it if we lost the wee girl as well.'

He patted her hand and gently pushed her away.

'Go on now Mary, I'll take care of it.'

'Thank you, Donald. Here, you best take this one with you. He knows her scent.' She leant down and ruffled Jagger's head. Donald hadn't even noticed the dog.

'He's been by my side all day. I've never seen him so low.'

'Of course I will. Thank you. Come on, Jagger.'

The dog lifted its head, sniffed his hand and moved to his side.

Donald led the way out of the door and headed for the stairs with Jagger and Raff in tow.

'Where you headed?' asked Woodhall. He had followed them out.

'I think we'll start downstairs. Apart from your men, it's empty, no sign of life.'

'Uh huh. Fine. I'll take a wander upstairs and look for, what was her name again?'

'Enna.'

'Right. I'll come find you.'

Duncan watched him go. The man had not appeared to pick up on the mention of the girl's name. Hopefully they could brazen this out for a while longer yet.

'So where shall we start, Laird?' asked Raff.

Donald, sighed heavily, blowing out a large gust of air. He felt some of the pressure ease off.

'We'll start downstairs, work up. Don't be surprised if we can't find her, she is crafty that one.' Together the two men and one dog filed down the stairs to the ground floor.

'She was here.'

Miller looked round at Woodhall. 'What?'

'The girl. The Laird ain't good at lying. One of the older women came up to him worried about a girl called Enna who had gone missing. Donald tried to hide it but I could tell he was rattled. Made pretence of going to search for her round the keep.'

Miller heaved his crossbow and walked to the rear of the keep where Reed kept watch.

'We won't find her inside.'

He gazed out across the lake to where the small boat sat.

'But I'd wager she isn't far away.'

'He got her out?'

'Looks like it.'

'Why'd he do that? It makes no sense.'

Miller shrugged. 'Nuthin' much about any of this is making sense lately. All I know is, we're close to our prey. Something tells me, we get that boat we might just stop this happening again.

'Want you want to do?' asked Woodhall. 'I could get some guys out the back, and into the water. We should be able to work our way round, get a boat whilst none of them are looking.'

'Worth thinking about,' agreed Miller. 'Problem is, she sees us coming, she'll run. Might make it to the other side.

If we get into a chase on the ground, there wouldn't be enough of us to deal with any Possessed turning up.'

'So we wait until the morning, huh?'

'Seems the safer option. We'll take the horses; it'll be easier to track her.'

' And Donald?'

'Yeah, go find him. We need to have a talk,' replied Miller. He hated being lied to.

Conor's breath was ragged and laboured. His eyes were shut tight but she could see rapid movements behind the lids. His skin had drained of colour and was almost translucent. Veins and arteries showed clearly through the bloodless layer. Jenny dabbed his forehead with a wet cloth. The herbal brew had seemed to do no good at all. Turning around she looked to try and catch someone's eye, anyone's. She really didn't know what to do. As she tried to stand, she felt a sharp, ripping pain in her stomach. She gasped and looked down. An arm was embedded in her belly, blood seeping out of the edge. It withdrew, it's hand clutching a string of guts. She raised her head and looked into black, soulless eyes. Conor's mouth was now a mass of jagged teeth. A triumphant hiss escaped from his lips and a forked tongue emerged. The thing that had been Conor proceeded to run his tongue over the intestines clutched in his hand. Jenny felt her head tilt back and her body start to fall to one side. As her world started to go black she heard another woman scream.

Donald jerked his head back in the direction of the stairs. He was in the kitchens with Jagger. The dog had gotten agitated and started barking a few moments before he had heard the screams. He ran back out into the main corridor and looked at Raff who was in conversation with the three Hunters by the barricade.

'Laird?'

'Quickly, Raff.'

'I know that sound,' said one of the Hunters. All three of them started to move.

'No,' countered Donald. 'Stay at your post.'

He ran up the stairs, turned the corner onto the landing and met several figures stumbling towards him. Women and children escaping from the hall. He shouted at them to make way whilst trying to draw his sword. As he neared the door a woman, it looked like Paidraig's wife, Lilly, ran out in front of him. A long, white arm, snaked round her neck and yanked her back inside. Donald drew up at the entrance and peered inside. It looked like a charnel house. Blood sprayed the walls in a dozen places; bodies lay limp upon the floor.

Donald could not believe his eyes. My gods, children too! The Possessed, rangy and white skinned, bearing misshapen humps upon its back, was bent over Lilly, eviscerating her. She was already dead. How many others? He couldn't count. It had to be stopped. It couldn't be allowed to get into the rest of the Keep.

'Raff, get Miller,' he said firmly.

He stepped across the threshold yelling a challenge to the creature. It turned and stood to meet him.

Several terrified women emerged from the stairs and onto the roof of the keep. Miller and Woodhall took but moments to realise what was happening.

'Heavies and spears to me now!' ordered Miller.

His men reacted quickly, swiftly followed by the locals as they interrogated the women.

'Woodhall, keep everyone else here. The sneaky bastards will take advantage,' said Miller.

Raff collided with him halfway down the spiral staircase leading to the third floor. 'Inside,' he said, breathing hard. 'There's one inside.'

Miller, pushed him away, 'Come on!'

He led the charge down the steps followed by Dougie, Hall and several others. They passed no one else on the stairs leading down to the first floor. The screams had died down. Either everyone was dead or had found hiding places. They emerged onto the first floor landing and he drew up his party to a stop. Charging around blindly down here would do them no good. The entrance to the hall was directly ahead. The row of torches along the corridor showed several glistening droplets of blood on the floor. Two more of Miller's men emerged from the ground floor stairs.

'The Laird said to hold our position and we figured we'd wait for reinforcements before coming up,' said the lead Hunter.

'Oldfrey, keep position here,' Miller ordered. 'If things get out of hand, don't weigh in, you head for the roof. Tell Woodhall to stay up there and hold the steps 'til morning. Then make a crack for the stables.' He looked to the men gathered behind him. 'We go in. Usual game.'

Taking up position in the front, Miller lowered his crossbow and edged slowly along the corridor. Behind him his men formed up, spears extended and heavy weapons readied. He stepped up and peered inside. It was a slaughterhouse. Bodies lay scattered, they were torn and sundered. The door at the far end, which led into Donald's private offices, was ajar. The man himself was lying face down in pool of guts and viscera, his sword lay a few feet away. They'd never know what he was up to now, thought Miller. Another scream emanated from the offices. Miller and his men moved quickly into the hall.

'We got it cornered. Get that door shut,' he said.

One of his men closed the door and pulled across the restraining bar, a new addition put in earlier that day. It was supposed to have kept the Possessed out if they had gained access to the keep. Something of a failure on that front.

His men fanned out.

'This table is going to mess up our defence,' whispered Dougie.

'I know,' Miller whispered back. They needed to present a united front otherwise the line would be too thin and the beast would get amongst them. They'd have to fight with their backs to the entrance wall. He took stock of his Hunters. He hadn't taken much notice of how many had come with him. A quick count showed he had three heavies, three spears, two of the local lads and Raff. The man must have tagged on the end. He looked white as a sheet, his colleagues didn't look much better. Guess seeing the Laird would have that effect. Okay, ten, a good number. He silently pointed out his dispositions. He stood in the centre flanked by the spears. The heavies took one flank, the locals the other.

He lifted his bow up to eyeline. 'Hey, shitface! Over here!'

A half growl, half whimper came from the far room. The door swung back and the Possessed emerged. A tattered, bloody woollen shirt covered its upper half whilst the trousers finished two thirds down the legs where they had stretched and thinned out way beyond their previous size. The legs looked stick like, like an insect. It stood there regarding them with black eyes and a mouth that was split open in a rictus grin. Bloody bits of flesh fell from the maw.

'I... I think that's Conor,' said Raff quietly.

The Possessed stepped forward and in one bound, leapt onto the table. It loped towards them impossibly fast. Miller fired just as the thing launched off the table and smashed into them.

CHAPTER SIXTEEN

Enna awoke and rubbed her eyes. She looked up into the sky and watched as it gently rocked backwards and forwards with the motion of the boat. She couldn't remember falling asleep. She must have just lain down in the bottom of the boat and drifted off. Her head hurt a little. She sat herself back up onto the duckboard and looked about. It was still night but she could see the tell-tale signs of approaching morning. The air smelled different. There was a sense of expectation. She looked towards the island. There was a still a glow coming from the roof and the remains of the houses, probably nothing more than piles of burning embers. She couldn't tell if there was any life left over there though, it all seemed dreadfully quiet. She didn't want to think about what might have happened just yet. She didn't have the strength. But morning was coming. That was good enough for her. She didn't want to stay out here any longer. She shipped the oars and started for the far side of the lake. She wanted to see Tenn, she needed to know she wasn't alone out here.

She pulled hard and quickly, intent on her task and she reached the far side in short order. She climbed out of the front end of the boat but didn't pull it further out of the water like she normally would have done. There didn't seem much point. As she strode towards the rock plateau, she gazed again at the sky. Red streaks from the east were plainly visible. Yes, she was safe enough.

Enna arrived at the rocky outcropping that marked the start of Tenn's domain. There was no way of telling if he was still alive or if a Possessed was now lying in wait for her. She followed the route through and entered the small cleared area before the cave. A warm glow emerged from the entrance.

'Tenn,' she called quietly. Surprised how timid her voice sounded, she thought she was braver than that, after all she'd been through.

'Come in, child.'

Relief flooded her as she scrambled up to and through the entrance. Tenn was sitting in his usual spot, cross-legged and still. His arms folded and his hands hidden within the sleeves of his robe. His face radiated concern and fatigue in equal measure. The cave was brightly lit but there were no torches or flames within. Instead, the glow came from the very walls themselves.

She looked at the mage, her mouth open.

'I've never seen this before.'

'No indeed, I thought that I'd stretch my muscles a bit, as it were.' He indicated for her to come and sit before him. 'Besides, I've been waiting for you.'

'Really?'

He nodded. 'Things have been happening haven't they?'

'Yes. Terrible things.'

'Tell me.'

As tears ran freely down her face, she recounted the death of Merrett and the others, arrival of the Hunter Band, the fortifying of the island and Donald's hand in her escape.

Tenn looked grave and had a sad, faraway look in his eyes. 'Donald was always a good man, but even I did not reckon on him staking so much on your safety,' he stood stiffly and began to pace. 'Enna, we've run out of time. The Possessed have gathered in numbers that have never been witnessed before. The Hunters have come to bring judgement to you. And now we must flee.'

Enna, her head spinning, stood as well.

'Really? We are going?'

'Yes, come along. We must gather some supplies,' he stopped and scratched his ear. 'Well, I packed already, actually.'

'We're going to Albair City?'

'We are indeed.' Tenn walked to the far side of the cave and retrieved two small knapsacks. 'Here we are. Yes, Albair City. It's time for my nephew, the Duke, to take charge of you.'

'But what about everyone here?' Enna asked.

'They will have survived the night. That keep has weathered the storms before,' he threw his knapsack over his shoulder. Enna thought it quite out of place. Tenn looked positively sprightly. 'We've got a fully days travelling ahead of us. The first stop is Longhaven. Get ourselves passage down the coast. Did you know, a lot of communities started living in floating enclaves... wait.'

Concern clouded his face.

'What is it? Tenn?' asked Enna. He didn't answer, the knapsack slipped back down his arm and crumpled in a heap. 'Tenn, what is it?'

'Get behind me,' he said, keeping his eyes trained on the entrance to the cave.

'Tenn, please,' Enna felt hopelessness building. Her senses finally telling her what had halted Tenn. No more, she couldn't face anymore, not today.

He turned and looked at her with sad, sympathetic eyes.

'I'm sorry, Enna, it looks like I won't be coming with you.'

'I don't understand.'

'They've found us. The Possessed. They're outside, a few of them. They're being cautious, they don't know what is in this cave, but they sense power. They're right.'

'What can we do, Tenn?'

'The glow from this cave wasn't just a friendly light to welcome you in. I was charging the barrier between me and the outside world.'

'Why?'

'So that I can teach these bastards *a lesson.*'

Enna had never heard such force in his voice before.

'Now stand well back,' he ordered.

She wasn't about to argue. Instead, she drew her dagger and stood against the wall.

'Oh, and Enna? For this to even remotely have a chance of working, I need you to take command of your power utterly. I need you to rein it in and keep it locked inside of you. I know you are afraid, but can you do that?'

'Yes, Tenn, I can.' She was frightened but she didn't want to die. She had a good idea what Tenn was going to try and do. And, trapped as they were, she knew that he had no choice.

'Then do so now.'

She closed her eyes, took a deep breath and reached into herself to find the power. She felt the familiar tingling sensation and concentrated on forming a hard shell about it. All the practice she had done over the past few weeks made this a relatively simple process. She was surprised how far she had come.

In front of her, Tenn raised his hands above his head. Enna felt a pressure build around them. It was like the very air itself had grown heavier.

Thin strands of amber lights formed in the gap between Tenn's hands, they twisted, curled, spread and joined to his fingers. It looked more like a web now, and in its centre, a glowing red ball of fire.

Enna gasped. She couldn't help it. This was real magic! Not the stuff they had been playing with. This was the Gods' honest magic. The smiting kind that her father would tell her stories about. Oh, how he would have loved to see this.

'Come on then,' growled Tenn. 'I haven't got all day.'

Outside the cave a chorus of howls and shrieks erupted. Suddenly a huge shape blocked the entrance, all muscle and horny growths. The thing growled at Tenn and stepped forward into the cave. Crowding behind it were many more shapes; claws and arms sought out purchase on the side of the cave entrance as too many Possessed tried to gain entry at once. They were literally blocking the hole.

'Ah, this will do nicely,' grunted Tenn with obvious effort. He flung his arms forward and the ball of flame shot from his arms in a tight line straight into the lead Possessed. It threw him back into the others and they in turn were thrown back. The fire engulfed them and pressed on, Tenn continuing to control its passage out of the cave and into the area beyond. It seemed nothing so much like a stream of water, the like of which she would see coming from a pump, yet this was running horizontally. Tenn kept this blaze going for some moments. The force of the flames was incredible; it must have completely engulfed the clearing outside the cave and would have continued through the passage back to the rock field beyond. And all the while she listened to the scream of hideous things dying and of an old man howling against an unseen force that was trying to take possession of him. Then, with barely a sound, the flames disappeared and the web of ember strands faded away. Tenn collapsed to the floor.

Enna scrambled over to him and cradled his head on her arms.

His breathing was laboured and his face was bathed in sweat. His eyes fluttered open.

'That's it. The best I could do.'

'You killed them all, Tenn. That was amazing.'

He smiled weakly. 'Yes, it was rather. It felt good to do that. You know, in all my years I have never had the chance to face one of these creatures down? I'm glad that I gave them a taste of their own medicine. Showed them that magic is not their sole domain. Not yet.'

'So what do we do now?' Enna asked.

'Do? We wait. I doubt I have killed them all but perhaps those nearest to us. Perhaps you'll gain some time.'

'Well, we shouldn't be waiting. We should get started!' Enna said loudly.

'No, Enna. I told you. I can't come with you. I've used myself up. All I can feel is that relentless pounding of the Possession trying to enter me, trying to take me. But I've used all of my life force to do what I did. Not that I had much left anyway! I went and made myself an empty vessel, useless to the power trying to possess me. I'm useless to you as well.'

'No! I can't do this alone, Tenn. I've lost everyone.'

Tears, again, flowed down her cheeks and splashed onto the old mage's robe.

'Now, now, enough of that.' With effort, he raised his hand and brushed her cheek. 'You are stronger than you look. Besides, you won't be alone. Although it won't be the friendliest company you could keep.'

'What do you mean?'

'You'll see. Now listen closely. There are a few things I need to say before I say goodbye.'

Miller dismounted carefully and brought his crossbow to his hip. Behind him, a half dozen of his men followed suit. Miller pointed to one of them and then the horses. The man nodded and took hold of the reins of each mount. Walking steadily forward, he stopped at the smoking form that lay just in front of a narrow passage through an outcropping of rock and boulders. The body was still smoking, thoroughly blackened and crisp, sections of bone showed through where flesh had been sloughed clean away. An exposed jaw revealed two lines of serrated teeth. He kicked at the thing and small clouds of ash rose into the air.

He cocked an eyebrow at his men and turned to walk the passage. Inside he found three more bodies, just like the first. After a few more yards he found a cleared area before the entrance to a cave mouth.

He turned to look at the man behind.

'This the place?'

Raff nodded. A bandage covered his head. A dark

stain showed on the material above his right eye.

Miller tried to count how many Possessed had been in this area. He gave up after six. They were way more of a mess than the ones outside. These things had caught the blast point blank. It looked like parts of different Possessed had actually ended up fusing with each other. Gods, it must have been hot.

He looked upwards; dawn was with them. The sun was just beyond the hills to the east. He squinted his eyes a touch, then stepped up to the threshold. Walking, heel to toe; he kept silent as his entered the cave. The place was gloomy. No lights burned inside. He waited for his vision to improve and centred his gaze on the middle of the cave floor, where a young woman, or girl, cradled an old man in her lap. He swiftly raised his crossbow and stepped through. His men quickly entered behind him, the two armed with bows taking up firing positions. Another held his spear tight against his side. Raff held his sword in both hands. He was shaking so much the blade waved in the air before him.

The girl turned her head sharply and gasped when she saw them enter.

'It's alright, Enna, it's alright. Our guests have arrived,' said the old man, his voice quavering.

Miller took a few moments to see if anything nasty was going to happen. Nothing did.

'There is one reason that the pair of you aren't dead yet. And that is because something just took out a dozen or so Possessed. We saw it go off on the other side of the lake,' he lowered his bow slightly. 'So what I want to know is which of you just used magic and why the hells haven't you turned?'

'Enna, help me up.'

She got an arm around under his shoulder and pulled him upright.

He groaned and squeezed his eyes shut with pain.

'My name is Tenn. Have you heard of me?'

Miller shook his head. 'Should I have?'

'Well, perhaps not. You are the Captain of the Hunter Band, yes?'

'I am.'

'Charged with hunting and destroying the Possessed wherever you find it. To protect human kind against the Possessed and the curse of magic that flows through the veins of those unlucky few. To do so with your very lives if necessary.'

'Verbose son of a bitch, aren't ya?'

'Something you clearly do not suffer from. My name, sir, is Tennebran, Archmage to the court of the Dukes of Albair and uncle to Lord Henry. Who, I believe, still holds the throne?'

'Bullshit,' replied Miller. 'What you are is a fugitive from justice. Someone who we should have caught a long time ago. Someone who has been working with this girl to bring death on innocents.'

'Miller, I must protest. I've known this man for years!' cried Raff.

'And this man just got your Laird killed.'

'Oh nonsense man, use your eyes!' The man claiming to be Tennebran admonished. 'There happens to be a number of dead Possessed out there, who did that do you think? A freak accident? A bolt of lightning? The girl? What power is there in the world that could achieve such a thing? Magic is what, and look, I haven't changed.'

'You're not looking so good to me.' Miller was taken aback. It had a while since anyone had actually gone and laid into him. His job and the authority it carried usually engendered the kind of respect that didn't provide much argument. He actually felt himself getting defensive.

The old man chuckled. 'That's true enough. And you don't need to be waving that thing in my direction.'

Like hell I bloody won't, thought Miller.

'My name *is* Archmage Tennebran, relation to the Duke. Your lord and master.'

'We're a long way from Albair City.'

'What is your name?'

'Miller.'

'Then come here, Miller, and I'll show you evidence that I am who I say I am.'

Miller hefted his crossbow and regarded the old man and girl. They looked harmless enough. If you ignored the charred corpses outside. Tennebran raised his right arm; he appeared so weak, he could barely lift it more than six inches off the ground. Miller noticed Tennebran wore a large signet ring.

'If they do make any kind of move, I want them impaled and beheaded before I spit.'

Derris, carrying a barbed spear, moved closer. 'You got it'.

He stepped forward and hunkered down. He studied the ring. It bore the Ducal seal. The same seal that was upon the Band's letter of commission. He had seen the Duke once, years ago when he had first joined this Band. The man had insisted on going through this ceremony way back when the Hunters were first formed. Miller hadn't been in charge then. He was just one of the many men, driven by rage and grief to sign up. The old leader, Captain Smats, had told him that the reason for this was to give the Band legitimacy. Smats was a regular soldier, just doing his duty. He had explained to Miller that the work the Band was commissioned to do was unpleasant and went against many codes of decency. People needed to know that they pursued their hunts with the full support of the Duke, that any actions they undertook were fully sanctioned. People needed to know that they weren't just a bunch of lawless vigilantes.

When the Captain died a few weeks later, Miller had taken command of the Band in the field by election. He carried the letter now, but had seldom thought of it and what it meant. The Bands had fallen into their own routines. No one had ever thought to question them and no word had ever come from Albair City regarding his assuming command.

'So you have the same seal as the Duke.'

He stood and shrugged. 'Don't mean nothing. Our mandate covers everyone, the Duke down. You've just admitted what you are. My job is to stop you from changing.'

'And that you shall. But before you do that, hear me out. What harm can it do? After all I appear to have done your job for you tonight. A word, just between you and me. But first, will you take this lady outside?' Tennebran coughed weakly.

'I was planning on doing that anyway,' replied Miller. 'Raff. Take, her.'

Raff stepped forward and placed his hands on the girl's shoulders.

'No wait!' she shrugged them off and lent down to the old man.

'Tenn, what's going on? I don't understand! We can't trust these men.'

Tenn patted her hand. 'Enna. There is nowhere safer than with these men now. I can't protect you. They can. Now remember what I've told you and what you learned. Carry on with your exercises.'

'I don't want to go.'

'I know you don't. But it really is no good you staying here. Now listen. Make our time together worthwhile. You have a gift. Let's not waste it, hmm?'

Miller had had enough, he wasn't sure what was going on and he didn't like not knowing.

'That's your goodbyes. Raff, get her out of here. And don't let her go. In fact, all of you get out.'

'That wise?' asked Derris.

'I got a bolt aimed point blank at his eyes. He turns,

he's not gonna have a chance.'

The Highlander grasped her shoulders gain and pulled the girl off Tenn. Miller stood back and waited until they were bundled outside. Cradling his crossbow he picked up a stool that was pushed up against a wall and set it a couple of feet from Tennebran. He lowered himself onto it, the bow resting lightly against his lap.

'One move, wizard. Give me the excuse.'

The old man coughed again; there was blood on his lips.

'Oh, I think you already have that. Tell me, Miller, who did you lose?'

'None of your damn business.' This old man was greatly testing the limited patience Miller had to offer.

'Please?'

He stared hard at Tennebran. Fine, and damn him for making me remember. 'My family. Got ripped apart by a neighbour, funnily enough. A witch practising some healing arts. Thought it wouldn't affect her. Seems like you all thought that way before it went and happened to you too.'

'I'm sorry.'

'I don't care.'

'Perhaps you don't. But what would you do to see this ended? What would you give?'

'The same thing every member of my band would give. What many have already done tonight.'

'Then listen to me,' Tennebran's breaths were becoming ragged, his voice a whisper. 'This girl is the cause of all that has happened. But the question is why. And the answer to that is intriguing. They are *hunting* her. They have intelligence, they have understanding. And I believe they have fear.'

Miller leaned forward, intrigued. What was the old man up to?

'This girl, she has a gift. Ask her. She is the antithesis, the negative of what I represent. I believe she represents a great threat to the creatures that possess my kind. And I believe that the answer lies far to the south of here.'

'The answer?'

'My nephew, the Duke. He is the only man who can help, his palace, the only place where we can learn more about what the gift means.'

'Her gift is a curse!' spat Miller angrily.

'Yes, it is, for her, for us. Because we have to live with it. But what if we can end this nightmare. What if we can use her? And her powers?'

'Why not kill her and let those things scatter? We can hunt them down, like we always have.'

'No. Don't you understand? Things have changed. Again. Perhaps it is Enna that caused this, perhaps it is pure chance that she appeared when she did. It doesn't matter. Those creatures are our future. They are too strong, too fast and they comprehend. They understand and they learn. Our very existence is more at risk now than ever before. They may well remake the world in their image. Perhaps that was always their intention.'

'You talk a lot for a dying man.'

'You don't give me much choice. Miller, you have Enna now. You can kill her whenever you wish. If that is what you choose. But take this chance. Go to Albair, let the Duke decide.'

'And what makes you think he'll listen?'

'Ah, because of me!'

He lifted his hand again.

'Take my ring. He'll know what it means and he'll listen to what I have said. Trust me on this.'

Miller regarded the old man. All his senses screamed at him to end this. To do his job and finish them both off for all the death they had caused. But Miller was no fool. His rage he kept for the Possessed.

'If we take her, they'll be after us.'

'Yes.'

'There'll be too many of them for us to handle.'

'Probably.'

'You're a bastard.'

'Yes.'

Miller snorted. What about you?'

'Ah well, this you'll have no issues with. You have to finish me off. Don't take the risk that I'll turn. I'm dying. I don't feel them trying to get in. Perhaps I am too useless as a vessel. But do it.'

Miller leaned forward, and fired his crossbow into Tennebran. It punched straight through into the brain. It would have been too quick to feel pain. It was perhaps a mercy the man didn't deserve. I guess I'll find out soon enough, thought Miller. What a bloody fool. Did he really think that I'd listen to the ravings of a wizard who had hidden from his fate for all these years? He placed the crossbow down, picked up the man's right hand and worked the ring loose. He reached down, collected his weapon and stood. He regarded the ring. It was a damned good copy if it wasn't the real thing. Should be worth something at the very least. He placed it into his pocket and walked out of the cave.

Outside his men waited.

'Everything okay?' asked Derris.

He stopped and studied Enna. Raff held her close as she gazed up at him with a pleading look. Her face tearful, her eyes red rimmed, black circles prominent underneath. How many times had he seen a face just like that? He sighed. *Am I getting tired of this?* Not yet. He looked up. 'Raff, hold her still.'

Enna gasped as he drew his dagger from its sheath. Raff's arms drew tight around her.

'I'm sorry, lass,' whispered Raff.

A man's scream rent the air.

'That was Walker,' said one of the men.

'Hold fast,' ordered Miller.

The group drew weapons, the archers held there bows ready, scanning the path and the rocks to either side.

Enna could hear the rapid breathing of Raff to her left. The Hunters seemed steady and calm. Miller stood to her right, his crossbow raised high.

For a few moments, nobody moved, nobody spoke.

To Enna, the expectation was palpable. There was a Possessed out there. And it was coming for her. She felt a rage build up inside of her. She just felt so tired, so angry. After all this. After all the bloody effort! Her parents died for this, Merrett and many others died for this. Tenn had died for this. She hated the Possessed, but not like before. Back home they had been the stuff of nightmares. Monsters who came at night, never seen, never heard. Safe in her bed within the walls, it had almost been a game. Not anymore. She had seen these things up close. And now she truly hated them, wanted to hurt them. She had felt such glee when Tenn had unleashed his power on them. Miller pushed his weight into her side.

'Right. Everyone back up into-'

A Possessed, in a blur of fur and talons, careened into the groups from the left. Men were pushed aside in a chorus of shouts and curses. Someone let out a scream. In the chaos Enna felt herself pushed backwards and she stumbled and fell onto her behind. And then it was in front of her. A slavering creature with blood dripping from its claws. It leapt towards her. Enna flung her hands out, not in a warding gesture; she held her dagger in front of her. She wanted to hurt this thing, she didn't care about herself, she just wanted to hurt it. Kill it. Enna felt the thing crash onto her, felt the foetid breath issuing from its mouth. She cried her defiance. And in that moment she felt her power rise, felt it roar in her ears, felt it escape from her. And then the beast's weight was upon her, pinning Enna to the ground. She lay there; her eyes shut, body tense, holding her breath. Waiting for the inevitable. Which did not arrive. Instead she heard a grunt and the weight was lifted off of her. Light played on her eyelids and she opened them to the dawn sky.

Miller loomed over her, regarding her. Then he leant down, grabbed her wrist, and hauled her up. Around Enna, men were picking themselves up. To her left, Raff stared up into nothingness, his skull smashed. On her right lay the Possessed. It was dead. Not a mark on it that she could see. No blood, no damage. No spear thrusts, no arrows. But it was dead. There was no way her dagger could have done that! She looked back at Miller.

'How?' he whispered.

'I don't know,' she replied. 'I'm not sure. I just got angry and I think I just pushed it into the creature.'

'Remind me not to piss you off,' muttered Derris.

'Is this what the old man was talking about? Your gift?' Miller asked.

Enna shrugged. 'I suppose so. But I've never done that. Never thought I could.'

Miller reached into a pouch and pulled out some tobacco. He took a bite, replaced the rest and chewed for a few moments. 'You earned yourself a wee bit of credit, lass. You were a lodestone. Now you've turned yourself into a weapon.'

CHAPTER SEVENTEEN

Enna had never ridden a horse before. Sure, she had sat on a few and walked a short distance on the old plough horses back at home. But not these horses, not proper riding mounts. She wasn't entirely convinced. The saddle seemed really big and she was pretty sure that she was going to get a bruised behind. There was cushioning but the up and down motion made it quite painful. Added to that her legs were stretched far too wide.

They had found Walker, torn to pieces, but the horses had been spared. They were well trained and didn't stray too far. Miller had made a remark about how they should have kicked the Possessed to death if they had had any balls. She had been given Walker's old mount and had cantered back all the way. One of the riders had hold of her reins and led her horse. She was pleased about that, she was pretty sure it wasn't happy to be carrying her. No one had said much more to her on the way back. They just eyed her warily. She had two riders behind her and she knew they had bows readied just in case. Miller had called her a weapon. That somehow she had killed the Possessed. Well, I suppose I must have done. So why are they treating me like a bloody prisoner? What do they expect me to do? Start creating balls of flame like Tenn? Oh. She felt a pain in her chest. The same pain she had felt at losing her mother and father. Had Miller done it? Probably.

But she was looking forward to seeing everyone at Cormant. There was a kind of relief coming back to something familiar. As they rounded the shoreline and the front of the island came into view, her mood swiftly darkened. The horses had stopped by the bridge. A portion of the barricade had been removed. Horses were being led out by grim-faced Hunters. She strained to see through the gate.

She had seen the smoke coming from in front of the keep but had not expected the vision in front of her. Whereas Cormant had always seemed full of life, now it was dead. An empty shell. From what see could see, nothing was left standing, even the stones of the castle looked stained and cold. Figures moved through the smoking piles of their homes. But there seemed so few of them. She turned to one of the riders. 'What happened? They didn't get in did they?'

The man looked at her then dismounted.

'No, they didn't get in. They were already there.'

Enna chewed her lip. Already there. What did he mean? Was there a secret entrance?

'He means that one of the locals turned,' said Miller, as he drew his horse next to her.

She couldn't believe it. Turned? But everyone was supposed to be Tested and clean. Tenn himself would have known it.

'Woodhall,' said Miller to the man she knew to be Miller's second. 'We ready to ride?'

Woodhall approached them from the gate. 'Almost, got the last few coming out now. Lucky those things pulled back when they did. Found a bloody great hole torn through the roof of the stables. They would have made a mess of the nags.' Woodhall stopped and inspected Enna. 'Got her then.'

'Yeah, hiding out with the old man,' replied Miller.

Woodhall did a quick inspection of the gathered Hunters behind Miller. 'Two men short.'

'Those things pulled back because they got a scent of her,' said Miller. 'They tracked her to the cave Raff told us about.'

'Then you ought to be dead,' observed Woodhall.

'Almost was, 'cept her and the old man did for all the Possessed. Those nearby at any rate.'

Woodhall raised an eyebrow.

Miller raised a hand in response. 'I'll tell you when we're away.' He leaned forward and looked into Cormant.

'Got any new recruits?'

Woodhall shook his head. 'None that are ready.

They're still in shock. I'd say they've lost half the population, all down to that one Possessed. Damn near could have been the rest if you hadn't stopped it.'

'Lost three doing that.'

'Yeah, it's thinned our numbers a fair bit.'

'So what are they gonna do, now they've lost Donald?' asked Miller.

'No!' Enna cried out as if stung. That was it then; she had no friends left in the world. She tried to compose herself as she received stares from both the men.

'Reckon they'll sort themselves out,' shrugged Woodhall.

Miller leaned back in the saddle.

'Well, they'll not get any more trouble, I'd wager.'

'How so?' asked Woodhall.

Miller scratched at his head. 'I'd say that anything left alive out there will be after us pretty soon.'

'Best we get going, then.' Woodhall turned and shouted at the last couple of Hunters stood at the far side of the bridge. 'Come on, lads. We're done here.'

'Let's go,' Miller ordered. He turned his horse and urged it forward onto the path leading back into the hills. Enna's own mount was led into line with the rest of the Band. As they walked up the hill, Enna turned in her saddle to look back at the island. A number of the survivors had gathered to watch them go. After all that had happened, this Band was just up and leaving them to their fates. Although Miller was probably right in what he said. The Possessed would be after her, she would draw them away from Cormant. It was all she could do to help. But it was not enough. After what she had bought down on them, she could never make right. As her horse crested the hill she said a silent goodbye and sat back into her saddle.

As the Hunters disappeared from view, a small shape ran out of the gate and trotted after them.

Miller estimated it had been dark for around four hours, which meant that midnight was still some way off. The winter nights were always hardest, the sun always longer to rise into the sky. The danger increased the longer they were out in the dark. But there was nowhere safe for them to hole up. Nowhere defensible. So instead, Miller kept his men on the move. Each one of the group led their horse in a slow walk. He was satisfied that they'd shaken any pursuit from the rear. For now. The concern was dealing with the things in front and to the sides of them.

He slowed down to allow his mount to draw level. He ran a hand down its nose and whispered a few words. 'Good lad, Bane. Now be ready to run like the hells if needs be.' A good animal. Almost as mean as him. He looked behind him to where the group walked in a tight circle. It was no good having them strung out if they got attacked. Numbers were the only defence. In deference to early warning, he had men ranged a short distance on all sides. Depending on the terrain they would pull closer in to the relative safety of the group or further out if visibility permitted. Woodhall walked up to him, mount in tow.

'How we doing, Jess?' asked Miller.

Woodhall rubbed his eyes. 'Alright, so far. Just done the rounds with the lookouts. We got Reed in the rear. He hasn't seen anything, but he's pulled in a mite closer. The others all report the same. John's in front, says that we're starting to head downhill. Be coming out of the Highlands soon.'

'Good. We'll turn east, head for the coast.'

'You haven't asked about who we lost yet, Avery.'

'We've lost five. I know my own men,' he replied, his voice brusque.

'Sorry, just you've been a bit distant since we left. But you're right, by my reckoning you've been there when every one of ours has died. You got lucky with that thing in the keep.'

'Could've been worse.'

'So we haven't spoken yet.'

Miller walked on silently. Woodhall waited before pushing on. Timing was everything with Avery; you didn't push him.

'The old man was a wizard alright. Claimed kinship with the Duke.'

'Desperation will make you say anything.'

'This guy burned a bunch of Possessed to a crisp. It backed up his claim a bit. But as far as I cared, that girl was responsible for the deaths of our men. I was all set to kill her. Then the Possessed attacked, never seen anything

276

like it before.'

'What she do?'

'She killed it.'

'What with? Her bare hands?' asked Woodhall.

'The old man reckoned it was something else. I didn't believe his bullshit. But then she did this thing,' he rubbed his head. 'Killed it with nothing more than a dagger. That kind of move makes you stand up and take notice. He said she's got a gift.'

'The type of gift that gets everyone around her killed?' asked Woodhall, doubtfully.

'Jess, sometimes I'm a little slow on the uptake. But when it smacks me in the face, I gotta take notice. Too much is happening. You can see it yourself.'

Woodhall shrugged. 'Something's changed.'

'We can't do things like we used to. These things are intelligent now. If they kept to themselves we could still hunt them. But they pack together. We can't handle that.'

Woodhall reached into a saddlebag and took out an apple. He took a mouthful then fed the rest to his horse. 'So what do we do? Get larger bands, join up with the others?'

Miller shook his hand.

'We haven't got the time. If what the wizard said and everything we've seen is true, then this is new. And we've got the one thing that they want. A girl who can kill them. And what's bad for them is good for us. He said the Duke could figure out what's going on. So we get her there.'

'Is she worth dying for?'

'There's only one thing worth dying for, Jess. The only thing. And that's the chance to take at least one of those evil fuckers with us.'

'Then she'd better do a lot of killing. By my count we're about even so far.'

Woodhall stopped and turned. It was the sound of a horse being ridden hard. A Hunter pulled up before them.

'Reed?'

'Spotted one, not far back.'

'Just one?'

'That's all I could see, boss.'

Woodhall and Miller shared a look.

'Do you think they are playing us again?'

Miller spat. 'Not gonna take the chance. Pass the word, everyone mounts up.'

Woodhall nodded, climbed quickly onto his horse and walked it back down the line, speaking to each of the men in turn. Miller mounted Bane and then looked on as Enna's watcher helped her onto her horse.

'Reed. Take up position at the rear. But stay close. I just want you to make sure we don't get any stragglers.'

Reed turned to follow Miller's eyeline and nodded.

'Got it.'

Miller figured the girl was probably getting one hell of a sore arse. Couldn't be helped. As long as she hung on. He debated putting her behind one of his men. They might be in for a wild ride.

He turned his horse around and urged it forward to the head of the line. Perhaps it was because they had a sighting now, or maybe it was just the years under his belt, but he could sense that the night air had changed. It had become still, quiet, anticipating. He raised his hand up to signal a canter.

There came a shout from his left.

'Two coming in!'

'Ride!' Miller shouted. He kicked his heels into his Bane. 'Yeeaah!'

Other shouts echoed behind him as the Band followed his lead. The horse bolted forward. He lowered his body and lay close to Bane's neck. He looked behind him to see the rest of the Band close behind him.

They were thundering towards a notch between two hills, the land closing in to either side. He couldn't see the end, couldn't see if it opened up or constricted them even further. Damn, these things were funneling them in there. His mind raced. Do they risk it? Had they sprung the trap too early?

'Fuck!' He pulled the reins hard and angled Bane to the left. They had to do something that the Possessed wouldn't expect. He led them up left hand slope, towards the east. He knew that two of those things were coming from that direction, but there was a good chance they could out manoeuvre any waiting within the gap and get past them. They just had to outpace them. Bane reached the slope and noticeably slowed as his momentum was stalled.

'Ride, you bastards. Ride!' Millar kicked hard at Bane's flanks once more.

Enna wiped the hair from her face. With her other hand she held onto the pommel for grim death. In front and to either side she was surrounded by men shouting and swearing, horses snorting with effort, hooves pounding onto the earth. And beyond that, the howls and shrieks of the things in pursuit. She didn't know whether to feel terrified or elated. The wind whistled into her face and beneath her she could feel the power of the animal, the sheer strength of the thing, and it just didn't seem to tire. She almost felt safe, that nothing could catch her. This must be how a cavalry charge felt. Then the horses hit the slope and she felt herself fall backwards as the angle increased. She leaned forward, wrapping her arms around the horse's neck. The man holding her reins tuned backwards to look at her. 'You al-'

A blur smashed into him from the left, the momentum carrying him off his saddle and he disappeared into the night, as both horses continued their forward charge, the reins of both now dangling free. Enna didn't know what to do. All she could do was hang on, but she saw her own mount was angling away to the left, away from the main group. She knew the reins were trailing free on the right side and she let go with that arm, trying to locate them. But she didn't feel steady enough and she couldn't help herself but whip her arm back whenever her body began to wobble. She turned her head at the sound of something coming up behind her. Another rider! The man leant down and gathered her reins up.

'Good work. Reed, get her back in the centre.' The man, Woodhall, was riding along her left flank. Between the two of them, they guided her horse to the main group, cresting the rise as they did so. Before them the hill began a steep descent, way into the distance, Enna couldn't see any more high ground.

'Come on, boys, let 'em run!' shouted Miller.

Yet again the riders urged the horses onwards.

'Hold on tight, lass, we're going hell for leather!' warned Woodhall, slapping the rump of her mount.

She leaned in tight again and felt the animal pick up speed. She turned her head to look back up at the crest, now drawing further away. Three dark shapes drew themselves up against the skyline. They paused for a moment and then continued in their pursuit. Enna closed her eyes and concentrated on willing the horse on, as fast as it could go.

Miller stretched out. He threw his arms wide and pointed his toes. He opened his eyes and glared up at the noonday sun. Lifting his head from where it rested on his saddle, he leaned himself forward into an upright position and yawned. Scratching absent-mindedly on his beard, he reached for his tobacco pouch. He fished around and pulled out a small plug. He cursed under his breath, he was almost out. With his free hand he stuck his forefinger into his mouth and rubbed viciously at his teeth and gums for a few moments. He then withdrew the finger, inspected it closely, then reached across for his water bottle, pulled the stopper out with his teeth and took a swig. Sloshing it around in his mouth, he tilted his head to the sky and gargled before spitting it all out onto the ground. Satisfied that his morning routine was complete, he stuffed the plug into his mouth.

'Not sure that's the right order it's supposed to be done,' remarked Woodhall wandering over from a nearby cook fire. He handed over a mug of steaming tea. Miller looked at it sourly and then took a swig.

'And don't go leaving any of your foul weed in the mug like you usually do,' advised Woodhall.

Miller eyed him and then looked around. They were camped on the side of the road leading east towards the port of Longhaven, not far from the site of the caravan massacre. They were on open ground, the sky was bright and there was no cover for a hundred yards, the forest way over on the other side. If they pushed hard today, they'd reach the port tomorrow morning. Just one night to survive.

'Another man down,' said Woodhall.

'We got lucky last night,' responded Miller.

'Yeah. Damn me, but I wouldn't have believed it if I hadn't seen it. They almost trapped us. Driving us into that narrow gap like that. Shit, that's our tactic,' said Woodhall with a shake of his head.

'And they'll try again if they get the chance.' Miller

looked over at Enna. The girl was asleep by one of the other fires, she was wrapped up in a blanket and her mouth lay open. These things really wanted her bad.

'She okay?'

'Uh huh.'

Miller pushed himself up and turned round. They'd need to start moving again, there was no telling what these things would try next.

'Looks like we have a visitor,' remarked Woodhall.

Miller looked back into the camp. Walking carefully into the camp from the north was a dog. It looked pretty miserable, it was wet and its tongue lolled.

'He's been traipsing behind me since we left. One of the cattle dogs,' said Reed, as he walked by.

The men watched as the dog picked its way through the camp, others joined in to watch its passage, and none tried to get in its way. Head low, it sniffed the ground and walked towards Enna's bedroll. It spent a few moments running its snout around her body before giving a quick wag of its tail and settling down closely next to her.

Miller grunted.

'Those dogs don't abide the smell of a Possessed,' said Woodhall. 'Guess it's more proof that she ain't what we thought her to be.'

'I'd still like to know what she is,' he replied, chewing thoughtfully. 'We can think about it more when we're safely rid of her in Albair City.' He scratched his crotch and sniffed hard. 'Best get everyone up. We're leaving as soon as I get on my horse.'

Enna found herself in that warm half dream before waking. She had been completely exhausted after the wild ride the night before. They had galloped harder and faster than she had thought a horse possible of doing. After leaving the crest, they had started on a downhill run that never seemed to end. And behind them the sounds of pursuit continued. She wasn't sure at what point those sounds had left them but after a while she had registered the fact that the only noise was the horses. Even then they had carried on. The land had eventually levelled out but instead of stopping, the group had simply slowed their horses to a walking speed. Her horse had been breathing heavily; she saw foam around its mouth. She was very concerned that the poor beast would collapse on her. She looked about and saw that most of the others seemed in a worse a state than hers. She figured this was due to her slighter frame. Eventually Miller had called a halt, they had stopped next to a stream and for a short while, they dismounted and allowed the beasts to drink deep and feed from supplies of oats that the men took from their saddlebags. Anxious to help her own horse, she'd located the feed and had cupped a pile into her hand. She had stood in front of the animal and held the food out in front of her.

'There, thank you for carrying me,' she said quietly. The horse eyed her momentarily before dipping its head into her hands. Once it was done, she led it to the water where it drank noisily. She was aware of being watched and looking around she could see a number of the men eyed her warily. Her checks has flushed with colour, she was embarrassed by the attention and ashamed by the reasons for it. She dropped her gaze and stroked the neck of her horse. At least it had accepted her. Miller had pushed them hard until dawn. She had collapsed into her bedroll then, sleep taking her swiftly.

Now, with the sound of the camp waking up around her she stretched out and felt a warm weight pressed against her side. At first she thought it was one of those "sleep ghosts", her mother had called them; the sensation of weight that she sometimes had felt when waking up at home. She would thrash and struggle to wake up only to find the terrors always turned out to be just her sheets, tucked far too tightly about her.

Enna swung her arm round to banish the ghost and instead connected with warm, wet fur.

She opened her eyes in surprise and sat up quickly. He ghost followed likewise and proceeded to lick her face.

'Jagger!' she cried. He must have followed her all the way from Cormant. She threw her arms around him, face nuzzling into his flank, getting a big whiff of musty dog. She drew back and ruffled his ears, he responding with enthusiastic panting and a furiously wagging tail. She felt a genuine surge of joy such as she hadn't felt since before the attack on North Downs.

Miller appeared in front of them, his arms folded, regarding them both. 'Seems you got a friend.'

Enna felt a wave of bitterness. 'Seems like my only

one.'

Miller shrugged.

'You're probably right about that.'

'Nobody trusts me around here, do they?'

'Nothing personal. People just seem to end up dead around you.'

Enna glared at Miller. 'It's not my fault, you know.'

'Maybe not. It's the fault of people like your old man. And if it wasn't them, it would be those who would have turned into them in the future.'

'So people who haven't done anything have to die for something they *might* do?'

'You've seen what happens. If you could stop it happening. If it meant protecting the lives of your family. If it meant that you could save them from the terror and the agony of being torn limb from limb, to stand there and watch their own children be ripped apart. Tell me, lass, what would you be willing to do?'

Enna stood a little straighter. 'I'd be willing to die for it.'

He smiled coldly. 'That part's easy. Would you be willing to kill a child? Could you wield the blade even as innocent eyes look upon you with fear and pleading.' He shook his head and grunted. 'We are willing to do whatever is necessary to protect this land and its people. Because every single one of us failed to protect the ones we love. So now we do what others cannot.'

'How can you live like that?' Enna asked wonderingly.

Miller chewed and spat.

'We don't ask for thanks or forgiveness. We're damned souls. But we do it because we know it's the right thing to do. The only thing to do. And we'd gladly die to see just one of those things bleed out in front of us. It means we're still human.'

'So what about me? Am I human enough for you yet?' Enna asked.

Miller didn't answer. He looked around the bustling camp, all the time chewing thoughtfully. 'I've lost good men because of you. And you're still here. Get up. We're leaving.'

He turned and stalked off. Enna thought about what he had said. She was still here. That was his answer, he hadn't killed her. That meant he didn't think of her as a potential Possessed. Which was a good thing at least. But she severely doubted that he'd ever get much friendlier with her than that.

'Well, Jagger, I guess we'd better get going.' She gathered up her blanket and took it over to her horse. 'Oh,' she realised she had left the saddle back where she had slept. Walking back, she bent over and got two hands round it. She leaned back and pulled the thing up. It was so heavy! She had to crab walk it over to the horse. She stumbled over and dumped it back onto the floor.

A shadow fell across the saddle. 'Need a hand with that, lass?'

She looked up at a large, well-muscled man, with long hair and a thick bushy beard. She nodded her head.

He smiled leaned down and lifted the saddle

effortlessly. He threw it over the horse and started to buckle it up. 'You're gonna have to learn to do this if you want to ride with us.'

Enna brushed back a lock of hair. 'But I can't lift it over him. I'm not tall enough.'

Dougie stood and folded his arms.

'Good point. If I ever get the chance, I'll make you a stool. Until then, what with John taking a fall last night, I'm in charge of leading you today. `I'm Dougie, by the way.'

'Was that the man that got killed?'

'Yup. Silly bugger. Should have ducked.'

A horse drew up, Miller astride it. 'Get her on it, Dougie. We're leaving now.'

'You got it, Miller.'

Miller urged his horse forward with a click of his tongue.

Dougie knelt and cupped his hands.

'Put your foot in here.'

Enna did so and in one swift motion he stood up and propelled her into the saddle. She swung her leg round and into the stirrups.

She watched Dougie take her reins and place them into her hands.

'Hold onto these a mo whilst I get my nag.' Enna watched him walk away. That was the nicest anyone had been to her. She wiggled in her saddle and the soreness in her behind and in her thighs reminded her how uncomfortable the thing was.

'That dog with you now?' asked Woodhall, riding up to her.

'His name's Jagger. I guess I'm the family he's got left.' She shook her head sadly. When would it end?

'Well, being that he's not gonna jump on the saddle with you…' he twisted around and leaned into a saddlebag, 'can't imagine he's eaten much – reckon he's been on the move since we left.' He withdrew a fistful of something. 'Here.' He threw it on the ground, a number of strips of dried meat. Jagger jumped on it immediately and it disappeared within seconds.

'Heh,' smiled Woodhall as he watched the dog eat, then he turned his horse around and cantered off.

'Right you are,' said Dougie, now mounted. 'Let's have 'em.'

Enna handed over the reins.

'Now, I'll lead you for a while but after that, you'll be riding him on your own.'

'What's his name?'

Dougie made a face. 'Blowed if I know. Walker never said. "Boy" tends to work.'

Another man, bigger than the others she'd seen, drew up.

'Or "bastard" if you're Bane,' he said.

Dougie laughed. 'Right enough, Hall.'

'Bane?' Enna asked.

Dougie nodded.

'You know. Miller's horse.'

'Good name, isn't it?' said Hall. He leaned forward.

'It's named so because it's the bane of the Possessed,' he said conspiratorially. He then rode forward, trying to carry an air of mystery. Enna felt he didn't quite carry it off. Dougie tapped her on the shoulder. 'Horsepiss. Miller calls the horse Bane because it's a surly bloody creature that tries to take a chunk outta him every time he puts his ass on its back.'

Enna smiled and Dougie winked. At that he gently slapped his heels into the flanks of his horse and made a clicking sound. It moved off and the pair of them worked their way forward into the line of Hunters.

Miller sat quietly on the road. He looked up into the sky and gauged they had about two hours of daylight left. He leaned back and acted casual. But he wanted to get moving again as quickly as possible. Ahead of them the road was flanked by trees, which extended far back left and right. This was the choke point, the one place on the road to Longhaven that you really didn't want to be after dark. Too much cover, too many hiding places. And they were too late in arriving. Now he was waiting for Woodhall, Reed and two others to return from their scout. If there was anything waiting for them, they needed to be through and out the other side fast. If these things were braving short periods out in the sun to get their prey, then they'd love the shadows cast by the damn woods.

Behind him, the Band rested their mounts. They all knew the score; this would be the last chance to do it before they had to make the run.

Miller inwardly relaxed when the scouting party, all four of them, rounded a corner in the bend, moving at a steady trot.

They pulled up in front of Miller and dismounted. Woodhall walked up and placed a hand on Bane's neck.

'How we doing?' asked Miller.

'Went about a half mile in, just before it gets really close and scary. Didn't spot anything. But that doesn't mean much.'

'No signs.'

Woodhall shook his head.

'Alright, we go in. If we don't stop for a piss, we can be out of the thick of it in an hour. You guys make up the rearguard.'

'Right you are, Avery.'

Miller turned round.

'Mount up!'

The Band quickly reorganised and was off within a minute. Miller took the lead and held his crossbow ready. He urged Bane into a trot, and watched the woods closely as they followed the road. As the woods closed in around them he considered why someone hadn't just come in here and cut these things back from the road? Or better still, just set fire to the whole damn thing. Well, he did know why. No one would have the balls. Why risk your neck? Besides, right up until recently the risk hadn't been that great during the day.

'Miller?'

He looked to his left as Dougie drew up next to him.

'You'd better listen to this.'

Miller raised an eyebrow then looked at Enna, who had followed up behind Dougie. He noted that she was using the reins herself. He thought of saying something but then, it was easier that way. It meant they didn't have to babysit her so much.

'Listen to what?'

Dougie threw a thumb back towards Enna.

'She says she's got the spooks. Says these trees ain't right.'

'Whoa there, Bane,' he said, gently pulling back on the reins until the horse slowed and the stopped. He turned his gaze to Enna. He had to admit, the girl looked frightened.

'Go on then,' he ordered.

Enna opened her mouth, trying to form the words.

'It's a feeling huh. Something that I've been getting better at. There's Possessed out there, pretty nearby too.'

'A feeling, huh?' Miller replied skeptically.

Enna nodded.

'One of your gifts?'

'I've felt them before. When they came at the caravan. Then even stronger at the castle. I can sense them. It's like…like my skin goes cold and prickly.'

'I call that fear.'

'Not when you don't think there's anything out there to be afraid of,' she countered. 'I don't have to see them. And just knowing that they exist doesn't make me afraid.'

Miller sighed. Here he was; having to make another judgement call again. But unlike what she did back at the cave, he had no proof.

'Listen, we've got a way to go and we've still the time to cover it. It's still daylight. We'll keep going.'

Enna tried to respond but he shot her one of his best glares. That seemed to shut her up.

'Okay, Dougie, get her back in the middle. Everyone else, look sharp,' Miller ordered. 'C'mon,' he said to Bane. They moved forward, Miller increasing the speed slightly. He didn't want to tire the horses too much. They were pretty near exhaustion as it was.

'Miller!'

What now? He turned and this time saw Reed cantering up to him. 'Yeah?'

'Woodhall sent me forward. Saw something back in the trees. Missed it the first time, only saw it as we moved off. So I took a look.'

'And?'

'It's a body. Local militia by the look of it.'

That figured, thought Miller, the authorities at Longhaven said they'd be sending some patrols out after the attack.

'Just one?'

'Yeah, fresh kill too.'

'How fresh?'

'Today.'

'Shit.' He sat back in his saddle and scanned the woods around him. He hadn't noticed it before. The place was quiet. 'Shit.' He looked back at Enna, her face was as white as a sheet. The dog crouched low on the ground and started to growl, it ears lay back against it's head, hackles were raised and it let loose a short bark.

'Turn around. Everyone turn back. Reed, lead us out. Quick as you can.' Reed swiftly turned his horse and took off at a run. The others began the same manoeuvre. Damn but they were making a bloody racket. 'Come on, move!'

Howls erupted from the wood to either side. Miller looked into the trees. He couldn't see anything but they were close.

'Come on!'

Spurring his mount onwards into a run, the mass of horses galloped back they way they had come. Miller didn't even bother looking back. If they were coming, there wasn't a damn thing he could do about it.

The gallop ceased only when they had returned to the point they had started from. Smoke rose from the recently doused campfires. The group reined in, horses whinnied and stamped hard as riders tried to soothe them. Miller pulled Bane around and watched the road intently. Woodhall and some of the others joined him.

'No pursuit,' stated Woodhall.

'No, not yet,' replied Miller. 'But they'll come. Once it's a little darker.' He turned Bane around and walked him over to where Enna waited, Dougie close by her side. He saw the dog had wandered over to the stream and was lapping at the water with gusto.

'Seems you got yourself another useful skill. How reliable is it?' he asked her.

'I don't know, it hasn't failed yet and it seems to be getting stronger,' she replied.

'Keep it up and let me know the minute you sense something.'

'They're out there now. Just a little deeper into the woods,' she said.

'You know how many?'

'Nope, just a lot.'

'Great. They're trying to block us again. This time, they've gone and worked out that if we can get to the port then we'll be out of their reach.'

'Sneaky bastards,' observed Dougie.

'So we got two choices. Go through 'em or round 'em,' said Miller.

'The first doesn't sound like a good option,' suggested Woodhall, joining the group.

'Not now,' agreed Miller. 'They'd jump us and have the girl.' He leaned forward, 'So we go round 'em.'

'Question is can we get to the port?' asked Woodhall.

Miller looked at Enna again.

'No,' he shook his head. 'I don't reckon we can. So we head south. Straight for Albair City.'

Dougie whistled. Someone muttered 'Shit' behind them.

'Bloody long way, boss,' said Woodhall.

'The horses will keel over before we get there,' added Hall, in a rare flash of common sense.

Miller spat. 'Any other suggestions? I'll hear 'em because right now we got a bunch of shit eating Possessed sat waiting for suppertime to start.'

'The Ebb,' said Woodhall

'Huh?'

'The Ebb River ain't far from here,' mused Woodhall. 'We get ourselves on that and it'll take us within a day's ride of Albair. Get some boats and we can keep on the move for a couple of days.'

'Where we gonna get the boats from?' asked Hall.

'Oh, there's a few settlements on the way. Nearest is going to be Hove. Could be there the early hours of tomorrow morning.'

'Oh pissing bloody great. Another night ride!' said another of the Hunters.

'Quit it,' ordered Miller. He looked back towards the road, then around at his men. This was all new to him. Before life had been simple; hunt Possessed, die if necessary. Now they had to survive. At least until they could get this girl to the Duke. They had to run when he'd rather fight. His men were sacrificing themselves for her now. And there was no promise of killing any Possessed that was hunting them. It grated like a bastard. He turned his gaze to Enna. She locked eyes with him. She's getting more balls, he thought.

'Whatever we do we're going to have to cut through the forests. I know your dog can smell 'em if the wind's right. How much of a warning can you give us?'

'I'm not sure, but I think that I've got a couple of

hundred yards on them.'

Miller nodded his head in approval. 'Not bad.' They had no option but to move on. He wasn't happy and he was damn sure that he'd lose a few more men and horses, through sheer exhaustion if nothing else. 'Alright we head for the Ebb. Woodhall, lead on.'

The Band turned westward and trotted along the road for a mile or so. Miller joined Woodhall at the head of the column.

'What you thinking?' he asked.

'We got maybe an hour of daylight left. We won't clear the forest before that. Clear country south is still a way yonder.'

'So?'

'So it's your call, Avery. We cut through the woods and we could slice off a chunk of time and hoof miles.'

'Nice description.'

'Just thinking about Bane there – he's the one that has to carry your heavy arse.'

'Fair point. You know if we go in there, they'll be all over us.'

'I know, Miller, but it seems to me that right now, we need to get ahead of them, not just keep dodging them. Whatever way we take now it'll go hard for us. At least this was, it's the faster road.'

'I know. I just don't like this running.'

'It's like you said, maybe this girl is worth it. Maybe we get to make a real difference, really end it.'

Miller sighed.

'Everyone, listen up. We're gonna turn into the woods. We move as quickly as we can. Light torches, there won't be any point in trying to hide. If it turns to shit, protect the girl, if you can. If you can't, ride like hell and I'll see you on the other side.'

Around him the men talked quietly as they dismounted to secure kit and prepare for close-quarter fighting. In the trees many of their weapons would prove to be unwieldy. Bows were limited, nets useless. Swords, daggers and spears would be the best defence. But even then, it was more about maintaining their spirits, making them feel they had the means to deal with what was waiting for them. Miller knew that if they got drawn into a fight, they would be lost. This was the enemy's ground. Some of the men took out prepared brands which they doused with oil, using flints to spark them into life, before they passed them up to comrades.

'This is going to be the most fun yet,' remarked Dougie as he adjusted Enna's, saddle.

'How far do we have to go through there?' she asked.

Dougie pulled down hard on a strap and shrugged.

'Woodhall reckons the thick goes on for a mile or so. Then it starts to broaden out a bit, then we've got meadows, brooks and woods the rest of the way. Very pretty.'

'Pretty? You're strange, Dougie. It's just land,' remarked Hall, wandering over to them. He carried two torches, one he handed over to Dougie.

'Hall here has never stopped to appreciate the beauties of life,' Dougie said winking at Enna.

'Ah, now if you're talking about pretty ladies. Then I get your drift!' announced Hall, chest visibly swelling. 'I can appreciate them all day long.'

'Well lookin's all you'll ever do. You're far too ugly to get your hands on one,' observed Dougie.

Hall looked indignant.

'Huh, look who's talking. A woman wouldn't know where to find your face, it's all just a mess of hair.'

'It's true. Although some may say that not being able to see me too well is a blessing.'

Enna laughed at that.

'Besides we shouldn't be talking about such things in front of the young lady. What will she think of us?' observed Dougie.

Hall sniffed. 'Well, I'm getting on my horse. And woe betide anything tries to grab me.'

Hall wandered off, muttering to himself. Dougie laughed.

'He's not that bright, is our Hall. But he's handy with an axe. There, you're good to go.' He handed her up a torch. 'You hold onto this with one hand and tight to the saddle with the other. Things are going to get pretty messy in there if we get jumped. So I'll take the reins off you.'

'Why don't you hold the torch, I can ride him fine now.'

Dougie shook his head. 'The horses are brave and

used to dealing with Possessed, but they'll get skittish in the woods, in the dark. I'll be needing one hand on my own horse. If things get bad I'll try and lead you on.' He held his hand out. 'Come on, give.' Enna smiled and handed them over.

Woodhall, carrying his own torch, joined Miller at the edge of the treeline

'This is going to get messy, Jess,' said Miller.

'I know it. But I don't see a way round.'

Miller sighed, handed his torch over and climbed onto Bane's saddle. 'So, you know the way?' he asked, reaching down to take the brand.

'Pretty much,' said Woodhall, handing it over.

'Then you lead. I'll take the rear.'

Woodhall laughed.

'I don't know which one is worse.'

'What would you rather have me or a Possessed chasing your sorry arse?'

'That's easy, I'd rather get torn to shreds than have to deal with you in a foul mood.

The riders entered the treeline at a brisk pace. The forest itself was thickest at the edge and once through, it opened up enough for horses to navigate without hindrance. The woods itself were dark and shadowed, even though there was still daylight, it was giving up its battle to penetrate and only in the high branches could the glow of fading rays be seen.

The torchlight marked the passage of the riders. From his station at the back, Miller could discern his men only by the trail of flames, bobbing along in the darkness. The group was trying to maintain close contact with each other but was inevitably becoming splintered due to the terrain. He was rapidly losing faith in this whole enterprise. He felt very exposed at the back and his imagination was playing tricks on him. He knew damn well that anything coming up behind him wouldn't piss about; they'd be on him in a heartbeat. There, he chided himself, nothing to worry about, see? The sun was down, he knew that they were necessary but he hated the fact that those torches give away their position. Again, a stupid fear. The Possessed didn't need the torches to find their way. He spurred Bane forward, drawing level with Reed. 'You got the rear.'

'Great,' muttered Reed, pulling on his reins to slow his horse.

Moving on, he passed his men, acknowledging each with a nod. In the flames their faces were stern and taut. Everyone was on edge. He found the girl. She gazed over at him, eyes wide, and the fear palpable. He leaned in close.

'You did good on the road. But it ain't over by a long shot. We're dead men in these woods. You know that?'

Enna nodded.

'Then what I need from you is to concentrate really hard. The more warning you have the better.'

'I'll try.'

Miller looked behind him at her dog, it was keeping close to the horse.

'I doubt he'll be able to pick up much of a scent in here. Probably a fair few old trails.'

He looked back at her.

'Give it a try now.'

In the flickering night he watched her eyes close and her face screw up in concentration.

He glanced at Dougie who had slowed his horse down to ride on the other side of her.

Enna bit her lip and shook her head.

'I can't. I think it's clear,' she said slowly.

Miller didn't feel reassured.

'Wait. Something,' she said sharply.

Dougie flashed Miller a concerned look.

'Something, I'm not sure. Like it's right on the edge. Not really strong,' Enna continued.

'Like they're hanging back? How far?' asked Miller.

'I know that when I've felt them before they were quite far away, maybe two hundred yards? I think I'm stronger now though, so maybe further than that?'

'Possessed can cover that distance in a minute no problem,' said Dougie.

'And normally they don't bother to wait before attacking,' added Miller.

'They've changed their tactics. Maybe there's only couple of them. They're afraid to attack?' asked Dougie.

'Doesn't sound right,' said Miller.

The rider ahead twisted in his saddle. It was Hall.

'Maybe they're scared of us? We've killed enough of them, maybe words gotten around?'

Dougie snorted. 'Yeah, now we're the bogeymen. And the young lass here, well, she only has to look at them and they crap themselves.'

Hall gave him a sour look and turned back round.

Miller found himself giving Hall's words some credence. These things were hanging back. Maybe it was because they lacked numbers. Maybe they were starting to worry about their own survival; another, very human, trait. But they sure wouldn't be afraid of his Hunter Band, even though the lads were all vicious bastards when they wanted to be. No, it was just the girl.

Another rider from the head of the group waited for them as they drew near.

'Miller? That you?'

'Here.'

'Woodhall says he can see a break in the treeline ahead.'

'We're out?'

'He doesn't think so, probably just a clearing. Might be a good place to take a head count.'

'Fair enough. Enna, you let me know if they start getting closer.'

He spurred his horse onwards and got to the head of the group. Woodhall had already passed into the open area. He waited, torch raised high; Miller knew the man was deliberately trying to draw attention to himself. To see what kind of moth would be drawn in. Usually, they would be waiting to close the net about it. Miller paused a few moments, giving Woodhall time. Finally he lowered his torch and. Miller moved out to meet him.

'Looks like am not tasty enough,' Woodhall said.

'I could've told you that.'

Woodhall shook his head. 'You're a wonderful human being. I'll bring 'em in.'

Miller walked Bane forward and looked about. Like Woodhall, he raised his torch and tried to gauge the land. This was nothing more than a small clearing with some smaller bushes and low lying trees. No, a glade. On the northern edge his flames reflected off a small stream which wound its way from somewhere back in the woods across the clearing and continued to the west. Good, that was probably on its way to the Ebb. They were on the right track.

The rest of the Band entered the glade. There was so much torchlight now that he could see everyone clearly. It also meant his night vision was buggered again. He counted the men in and waited for Reed, the last man to arrive. Miller nodded, satisfied.

'Jess, see the stream?' he asked.

'Yup, not far off now.'

'Let's get on then.'

Enna stretched out in her saddle and relaxed. They were all here and not far to go. She looked down at Jagger and made an affectionate clicking sound. He gazed up at here with a lopsided, quizzical expression.

'Don't think he gets it,' observed Dougie.

Enna sniffed. 'Of course he does, he is a very clever boy.'

'He's a good Possessed hunting dog, and that counts for a lot with this crew,' admitted Dougie. He gazed at her intently. 'Speaking of which. How we doing?'

'Oh, sorry.' Enna had completely forgotten to keep her senses up. They couldn't be close, it would've just happened. She closed her eyes again and pushed her focus outwards. Suddenly she touched them, two at least, but these weren't on the edge of her range. She could feel they were moving and not far away, they were coming right at them and the cold feeling started to well up. They weren't alone! She felt many more presences hurrying up behind them. She snapped her eyes open.

'They're coming!' she whispered.

Dougie's eye grew wide, he turned and shouted. 'Boss. Possessed!'

Miller snapped his head round. Riders turned to scan the tree, weapons raised.

'Everyone, get moving, we aren't far.'

The next moment the sound of crashing foliage heralded the arrival of the lead Possessed. It ploughed into the riders causing chaos. Horses reared, one screaming as its belly was raked open. A second Possessed appeared swiftly after the first, latching onto the rider of the fallen mount.

Enna felt the reins grow tight as Dougie pulled her horse close.

'Right, we're off. Oh, shi- '

A Possessed clawed at his mounts' flank and Dougie was thrown clear as it reared up in pain. Another Hunter charged the beast with his spear and thrust it into his side; it whipped round and broke the weapon in two. Howling in fury it barreled into the man, teeth snapping at his throat.

Enna looked about her as men and horses tried to deal with the Possessed in their midst. She had counted at least two of the beasts wreaking havoc, and she knew the rest would be here in moments. They were too exposed here.

As the Possessed slaughtered the Hunter, Dougie appeared, yelling incoherently, slamming his hammer into its back. It reared upwards and another Hunter, the one called Hall, ran in from the side and swung his axe from waist height in a wide circle, burying it deep into its stomach. Dougie raised his hammer high above his head. He turned and looked at her. 'Go!' he shouted.

Enna pulled at the reins, trying to turn it about. A hand reached out from the darkness and snatched them from her. Her horse gave a jolt and she was thrown back in the saddle, the torch flying from her hand. Looking behind her, the fallen brand fought with the shadows. She saw Hall and Dougie, the weapons raising and falling. About them, other indistinct figures writhed and struggled. Trees closed in about her vision; the scene receding into the darkness.

Once again Enna's world was filled with the sound of

snapping branches and the whistle of the wind. She couldn't tell if the noise of laboured breathing was her own or someone else's. In the midst of it all her horse continued to drive onwards, the reins taut then growing slack as her guide had to negotiate an obstacle. And then they were off again. As she rode, she glimpsed other riders before they were swallowed up back into the night. She couldn't hear any pursuit, but she knew it was there all the same. And what about Jagger? The thought struck her suddenly. She'd completely forgotten about him. She felt ashamed of herself. She looked about, desperately trying to catch a glimpse of the dog. Perhaps he was right next to her. Ducking low, eyes straining, she couldn't spot him. Perhaps he'd stayed with the others? She'd just have to trust in that nose of his.

Up ahead, there appeared another clearing, the trees thinning out before a stretch of empty ground. Beyond that, another line of trees, a darker smear against the night, ranged left and right.

'Whoa!' cried the rider in front of her. Her horse continued on but as it broke the tree line, it rapidly halted, this time Enna having to throw her hands onto the horse's neck to stop her forward motion. Other voices were raised in warning as more Hunters emerged. The gap, as she now saw, was not open land, but a wide, gently flowing river. The water appeared calm and serene, glints of light sparkled upon the surface from the few starts visible in the light sky.

'Which way?' shouted someone.

'Left!' cried her leader. In the open air she finally recognised Woodhall as her rescuer. 'Come on, heeyaa!'

The group, she couldn't tell how many, turned and ran down along the river back, heading what must be south. The tree line was uneven, sometimes standing well back from the water's edge, sometimes encroaching upon it. Horses weaved their way around them, having to enter the water, submerging almost to their bellies. Enna was getting splashed and sprayed by Woodhall's horse. She ducked her head and held on tight. They were making quite a racket and Enna expected a Possessed to come flying out of the forest and smashing into her side, carrying her right into the water. She could think of nothing worse, being torn apart *and* drowning.

Then they were through. The treeline veered sharply to the left whilst a bend in the river moved it off to the right. They were back in open territory. The horse picked up speed and turned to follow the line of the river.

'It's there!' cried Woodhall. He spurred his horse forward and Enna's followed suit. Silhouetted against the sky was a familiar looking shape – a stockade. This must be the fishing village. As they drew near, Enna expected to hear challenges or questions form sentries, none came. And there were no lights either. No beacons, or torches. No warm glow from the homes within. They were almost at the entrance before anyone noticed that it was wide open.

'Hold up!' ordered Miller from somewhere behind her.

Riders gathered around them and Enna tried to count how many were with them, it was but a handful. She could not see Dougie or Hall. Another horse cantered in, a small black shape following close by. *Oh thank the Gods, Jagger.*

'Reed, we got followers?' asked Miller.

'None past the trees yet but I can hear 'em coming.'

'This place looks dead,' said Miller

'Could be the same thing happened here,' said Woodhall breathlessly.

'If so it might be a trap,' warned Miller.

'But that's where the boats will be,' replied Woodhall.

'They're out of the trees!' shouted Reed,

'Fuck it. Ride for the boats!' growled Miller.

The Band entered the village and followed the main path through the settlement. To either side empty houses stood bereft of any sign of habitation. Enna noted that many doors had been forced or smashed open. That answered the question. The Possessed had attacked here as well. The dock quickly came into view. It was a slightly raised platform running along the bank with a parallel platform built further out into the river, connected by a central walkway. There were a number of vessels tied up. These included a number of the rowing boats, resting on the bankside walkway, with larger boats on the outside one where the water was deeper. Some even had their own masts. Enna had never seen any so big and certainly didn't expect to see them on a river.

'Grab weapons and food, leave everything else,' said

Miller as he dismounted.

'What one we going for?' asked one of the men.

'I can't sail,' responded one of the others.

'That one,' pointed Woodhall. The boat he indicated was about twice the size of the rowing boat, she was used to. Even so, they'd be pretty tight in that one.

Around Enna, Hunters began dismounting and grabbing items.

Woodhall took Enna's hand.

'Come along, lass.' As they ran towards the boat which lay on the outer dock, Enna turned and called for Jagger. She saw she hadn't needed to; the dog was already following them.

'In you go. Get up front. Take the mutt with you.'

Enna climbed onboard, holding onto Miller's arm. She steadied herself and clambered up front.

'Come on, Jagger,' she said. The dog bounded in and hurried across to her. The rest of the group were piling in unceremoniously.

'Get those oars out and be ready to row for your lives!' directed Woodhall. He was already untying the mooring ropes.

Enna counted six others in the boat with her and it was already full.

'Miller, we got a full ship,' shouted Woodhall.

Miller stood where the horses were gathered. She saw him lean in and whisper something to Bane and then pat his back. He waved at their boat. 'Get going!'

'You heard the man, we're off,' said Woodhall. He

leaned down and pushed the boat away from the side and stepped smartly in to the back where he took hold of the tiller. The oars were lowered and in a ragged uncoordinated fashion, the two sets of oars located on the boat guided them into the middle of the water. The current took hold of it and the boat began to pick up speed.

'Alright, keep rowing and try and stay in time,' said Woodhall from the back of the boat.

'Listen to the bloody skipper,' mumbled one of the rowers.

At the front, Enna kept her arm wrapped around Jagger. She kept her gaze locked on the dock. Miller and it looked like Reed ran over to one of the rowing boats, released the moorings and climbed onboard. Reed took control of the oars and guided them out, sat in the back, his crossbow at the ready. Their boat was only a few out when the first of the Possessed appeared, running four-legged; it was quickly closing the gap. Miller raised his weapon and fired a bolt at the creature. Enna didn't see it hit but the thing was knocked back. and it allowed their boat time to gain a safer distance. Reed rowed furiously as Miller quickly reloaded. The Possessed paralleled them along the dock until it hit the village wall. It was not alone. More Possessed arrived and gathered to watch the two craft as they drifted away. The thought struck Enna that in the dark, as their shapes become indistinct, the gathered Possessed looked almost human.

The two boats glided down the river. No one said

much. For the first time in many hours there was no howling, no shouting, no panicked crashing of horses careering through forests. Each man seemed lost in their own thoughts. Enna stroked Jagger's head as he sat next to her, his ears pricked up but his body was at rest. She thought back to Miller and his horse. He must have been saying goodbye. There was a softer side to him after all.

'That bloody horse cost me a bloody fortune.'

Woodhall laughed. Miller glared back at him.

'Saw you spending some quality time with it before you left,' said Jess biting into an apple.

'I told Bane that if he got out alive, he'd better find his way to Albair city. If not, I'd hunt him down and use him for glue and bowstrings.'

'Ever the sentimental one you.'

'Not in this job.' Miller leaned back against the side of a tree and closed his eyes briefly. They had continued down the river all night and late into the day. The two boats were drawn up on the river bank where the landscape had changed to wide open spaces and fields. They wouldn't stay long but he'd been getting cramps in that boat. 'We got decimated back there, didn't we? '

Woodhall threw the core into the river.

'Yeah. Lost a lot of the old hands. You know, the girl asked me this morning if there was any hope for the ones we left behind. I don't think she really got it till then. That they got themselves tore up to get her away.'

Woodhall paused, waiting for reply. None came. That

was Miller.

'What do you make of that?' he continued, pointing to the settlement on the far bank, a half mile downstream.

Miller opened his eyes again and pushed himself forward.

'No sign of life,' he said, squinting.

'That's the second we've passed since we've been on the river. Think we should take a look?' asked Woodhall.

Miller shook his head. 'No. We don't have the time or the manpower to deal with anything we might find. We're all far too strung out to fight properly.' He looked over at what remained of his Band. The rest of them and the girl were all sleeping. Only nine of them left. The rest lost in little more than three days. Those men had been experienced Hunters and it still didn't make any difference. Except the fact that they'd got their licks in before they went down. He hadn't seen or heard of human life lost on this scale since the start of the nightmare.

Woodhall shrugged. 'Makes sense. But I'd still like to know what's happened. Why did the Possessed attack here? If they were all heading our way, why waste their time?'

Miller conceded that it made no sense. Perhaps things were worse than they had imagined. Perhaps this wasn't just about the girl. Maybe things were worse than they thought.

'Doesn't matter.' Miller looked up into the sky. They'd been lucky with the weather, but it wouldn't last, it would get colder and wetter. 'I'm going for a nap. Let the man taking over from you know that I want him to wake me up. We need to be back on the river by midday. If we're lucky we can hit the jump off point early tomorrow morning.'

'And then we need to find ourselves a means of transport,' said Woodhall.

'If that horse of mine has got any bloody sense, he'll be waiting for us. Miller settled back down against the tree and closed his eyes. He slowed his breathing and listed to the sound of birdsong and the gentle run of the river.

CHAPTER EIGHTEEN

'Miller?'

'What?'

'Company,' said Reed. He was manning the oars, rowing at gentle pace. Miller pushed himself up with a wince, from where he had been curled up in the back of the rowboat, his limbs stiff and protesting. It was daylight again. The night on the river had been a bloody nightmare. Everyone was bone tired and struggling to keep up the pace. Both boats had turned to shifts, two men on the larger boat, and him and Reed taking turns on theirs. They all slept fitfully. They had passed another village on the way. This one as empty as those before it.

Miller watched an otter, disturbed by their passing, slide into the water by the river's edge. The few, gentle ripples spread out sedately and merged with the more vigorous one generated by the sweep of the oars. A river bird, Miller didn't know which species, leapt from the high branches of an over-hanging tree and flew across to the other side. The snorting of a horse drew his attention back to the eastern bank of the river. A number of horsemen waited, fully armoured, visors down, pennants attached to spears fluttering in the breeze. Those carried the symbol of the hawk, which was also emblazoned on their shields. One of the riders stepped forward from the group and raised his gauntleted hand in greeting. He had full armour: helm, breastplate, chain, leggings, identical to the other riders around him. What stood him out was the long sword strapped to his right side and a black cloak made out of fine velvet. Clearly the boss.

'Good morning,' he called. The voice was slightly muffled by his helm but it sounded friendly.

Miller raised his hand in return. 'It's looking better now.'

'Where are you headed?'

'Albair City. Going to jump off the river when it bends west and head inland from there.'

'You've reached your destination, then. The river bends just beyond this village. There,' the rider raised his hand and indicated further downstream, just beyond the walls to where the river did indeed bend.

'Yeah, this looks like the place, Avery,' said Woodhall from the other boat.

'Then I guess, you don't mind if we jump off here, then?'

The rider raised his hands, took hold of his helm and

removed it.

'Not at all.' The rider turned. 'Sergeant, give these gentlemen a hand with mooring up, will you?'

Another rider, with a white edging running around his black tabard nodded. 'Yes, Sir. You two, get over there.'

A couple of the horsemen dismounted and walked to the edge.

'By the looks of you I'd say you men have seen some excitement,' said the now bare-headed rider.

'You might say that,' said Miller as he climbed onto the shore, helped up by one of the soldiers.

'Hunter Band?'

'Yes. That's us – what's left of one.' He held up a hand. 'Avery Miller.'

The rider reached down and took it. 'Ah yes, you lead the northern Band. You and your men have been quite efficient during the last few years.'

That was interesting, thought Miller; usually people didn't refer to his Band's reputation in quite that way. The rider dismounted and Miller studied his face. Brown eyes, intelligent, focused and friendly. Big, straight nose. A forked goatee style beard well speckled with grey. Well into his middle years, Miller reckoned, though he still looked healthy enough.

The rider released his grip. 'Duke Henry. I believe you work for me.'

Hah! He knew it. 'M'lord. Our wages are late.'

That brought a smile.

'And you were coming to collect them?' asked the

Duke.

'Thought we'd sweeten the deal.'

The Duke raised an eyebrow.

Miller hiked a thumb back towards where the larger boat was drawing up.

The Duke looked around. His eyes rested on Enna briefly and he turned back to Miller.

'I'm not immediately sure what you mean by that. But I recommend we talk on the road. He looked around him and gestured at the village.

'We've been evacuating all the local settlements. This is as far as we can safely reach. You're lucky to have caught us when you did.'

Miller, taking his crossbow from Reed, squinted at the Duke.

'So it ain't just happening behind, us then?'

'If you mean the Possessed attacks? No.'

'We had to leave the horses, back up north, if you can give the girl a lift, I'd appreciate it.'

Again, another raised eyebrow and a confused look from the Duke.

'I can do better than that. We have a couple of spare wagons. You and your men jump on. We'll talk on the road,' he responded.

Miller bowed his head as the Duke turned and walked away to talk to his sergeant.

Woodhall, now disembarked from his vessel, joined Miller to watch the conversation.

'Well, this is a turn up.'

Miller reached into his tobacco pouch, rummaged around and pulled out a small limp of the weed. 'Just in time.'

'Yeah, looks like they were just about to pull out.'

Miller looked up. 'What? Oh…no, this is my last plug.'

Woodhall shook his head.

'Right. Of course. Stupid of me really.'

The sergeant nodded his head and turned.

'Bring up those last two wagons!' he shouted to an as yet unseen listener.

The Duke turned. 'Gentlemen, your transportation is coming, I suggest you move along to meet them. Time is of the essence.' He moved over to his own horse and mounted up. 'Oh and my apologies, we have gathered together some remaining foodstuffs from the village. It might be a tad, ah, odorous.'

Miller and Woodhall looked at each other and then at Jagger who came jogging past.

'Do you think the Duke has noticed how bad we smell yet?' as Woodhall.

Miller just shrugged.

'C'mon boys, we got ourselves a royal escort.'

There was some ragged cheering and the odd sarcastic comment as the group trudged their weary way towards a pair of small wagons, each pulled by a pair of draft horses, that had appeared from behind a small copse. The group split into two and climbed aboard. They made themselves at home amid baskets of bread, fruit, dried meat and relatively fresh fish. Miller elected to ride up front with the driver. Woodhall, he noticed, did the same. Knew there was a reason he was second in command, he thought wryly. With everyone on board, and Enna deliberately on the second wagon, they rejoined the main party. As the wagons rounded the copse, the main party was in fact much larger than they had first thought. There were at least a hundred cavalry as well as another half dozen wagons of varying sizes.

Without further delay the convoy moved off eastwards along a well-worn trail. The other wagons carried not only supplies but a number of people, looking disconsolate and in some cases ragged and wounded.

Miller turned and looked at their driver. An older man, in his fifties, stubbled and pockmarked, had probably been doing this all his life.

'Got quite a party here, what's been going on?'

'Everyone left alive out here is on these wagons. If they ain't then they're dead anyway,' said the driver, not for a moment taking his eyes off the road.

'Possessed attacks?'

The driver snorted. 'You could say that. Ain't seen nothing like it before. Whole towns been overrun, hardly any survivors. Possessed in numbers you ain't never seen. At least that's what I hear. The city's safe enough. So the Duke ordered everyone who could to get behind its walls. Nothing's ever getting over them.'

'Surprised to see him out here.'

'He wanted to see for himself. He's got balls, I'll give

him that.'

Miller had yet to make his mind up on that front.

'So how far we got to go?'

'Well, if we don't keep stopping every five minutes, we might just make it in before nightfall.'

Fair enough, thought Miller. He settled back and allowed himself to relax some. A hand tapped him on the shoulder and a chunk of bread was handed over. He took it with a nod and took a bite. The driver gave him a sour glance but kept silent.

True to the driver's word, the wagon train continued for a couple of hours without stopping and Miller judged they'd covered a fair distance. Though he was guessing at that, having snoozed a couple of times. Later that day one of the Duke's men rode down the line and fell in step with the wagon. He had another horse in tow.

'Duke wants you,' said the soldier curtly.

Miller gave him a blank nod and passed his crossbow over to one of his men. 'Cook, keep hold of this and don't go shootin' yerself with it.'

'Yes, Boss.'

He jumped off the wagon and climbed aboard the horse. It was saddled and equipped like a cavalry mount.

'What happened to its owner?'

'Killed. Was part of a guard detachment for a village back yonder. It was the only thing we found left of them that weren't dead already. Come on.'

The two cantered forward. As they passed the other wagons, Miller took a closer look at the refugees aboard.

Some were soldiers, many of them bearing wounds. As they reached the head of the column, he saw the Duke. He was flanked by two men on either side and up ahead rode a flag bearer and two more men. He already noticed a half dozen riders ranged out to either side of the column and had seen a half dozen more ride ahead by perhaps a half mile. They weren't taking any chances. He and his escort drew up next to the Duke's group. He looked over and waved Miller forward.

'I want to speak to this man in private.' This statement was clearly taken as an order and his protective shield of riders spread themselves out so than there was a clear space between them and the Duke.

Miller brought his horse nose to nose with the Duke's.

'Had some rest?' asked the Duke, looking over at Miller with a smile.

'Some, M'lord.'

'Good. So let's cut to the chase shall we? Things must be as bad up north as they are here? Otherwise why would I find the remnants of one of my Hunter Bands skulking along the river, miles away from their usual patch?'

'I don't know what's been going on here. But I've seen two well-defended settlements torn apart and I've seen Possessed working together in a way I've never seen before.'

The Duke nodded. 'Then it's the same.'

They rode in silence for a few moments.

'It was the local Band that spotted it first,' said the Duke. 'They sent reports back that the Possessed were getting cleverer. Setting up traps and ambushes. I wanted regular updates. They stopped over two weeks ago and then things got worse. Coordinated attacks on villages, Possessed in unprecedented numbers, not seen since the start.'

'It's what we've faced too,' said Miller.

'I've been piecing it together. Trying to make sense of it. It seems this began a few months ago. It started small, just isolated incidents, then bigger,' the Duke leaned back and sighed. 'So tell me. Is the north overrun? I have had reports from the largest settlements but the situation has been confusing of late.'

'I don't reckon so, M'lord. Don't think they're so interested about that.'

'Oh really?' asked the Duke, his eyes, sharp as a knife, boring into Miller's. 'I imagine this has something to do with your rather cryptic greeting earlier this morning.'

Miller reached into his pocket and withdrew Tennebran's ring. He had forgotten about it over the last few days.

'I think you might want this.' He said, handing it over to the Duke.

The older man took the ring and studied it for a moment. When he looked up again, Miller wasn't sure how to read the look in Duke Henry's eyes.

'I suggest you tell me everything.'

The rocking of the wagon reminded Enna a little of her time on the boat. But somehow the boat had always seemed a lot more comfortable than what she was experiencing right now. Enna was nestled in between two baskets of apples on the wagon floor. Jagger sprawled across her legs, completely conked out by the look of him. She was feeling slightly sick, not from the rocking she suspected it was probably from the half dozen apples she had wolfed down earlier. The rest of the passengers were sprawled over the cart, all in a similar state to Jagger, although the snoring was worse. Even Jess up front appeared asleep. His head lolled from side to side as the wagon swayed. She couldn't blame them for that. They were all exhausted. She would have liked to have slept herself, it weren't for her tummy. She was also worried. They were soon to arrive at Albair City. The place Tennebran said she should go to, the place where she might be safe. Where she might get answers. But the thing was she wasn't sure if she really wanted to know what those answers might be. Earlier a man had ridden up behind the wagon. She recognized him as the one who had spoken to Miller. Apparently he was the Duke.

He had looked at her for some time, regarding her with an intent, thoughtful expression.

'So you knew my uncle?'

She had nodded in reply.

'What was he like?'

Enna had thought for a few moments.

'Sometimes he was serious, sometimes he was sad.

Often he was grumpy.'

The Duke smiled thinly. He had turned his horse away and disappeared. Miller must have told him everything. So I bet the Duke is really mad at me now, Enna thought. I bet he blames me. Enna closed her eyes. Why does everyone blame me?

'Wake up, lass.'

A rough hand gently shook her.

She opened her eyes and blinked. The hand belonged to one of the Hunters.

'You'll not be wanting to miss this,' he said.

Blinking sleepily she struggled to get herself up of the floor. Jagger was rolled off her feet unceremoniously and looked at her with an accusing expression.

'Sorry,' she mumbled.

Looking out the back of the cart, the sky was darkening, shadows were forming. She felt some tension begin to build inside her. Were they there yet? Would they make it in time? She focused, trying to get her bearings. They were on a well worn road, built on a bank higher than the land surrounding it. The land itself was a patchwork of fields and farm buildings as far as she could see. There were buildings on the side of the road with signs denoting inns and blacksmiths. She had never seen order on such a scale before.

'You're looking the wrong way, lass,' said the Hunter, an amused edge to his voice.

She turned and, open mouthed, took in the sight

before her.

Albair City rose up from the earth. It literally sparkled as the sun, going down in the west, sent it rays horizontally into the city. She could make out little detail but could see high spires and towers framed in the gloomy sky. It took them another ten minutes to reach it, and as they drew near she could make out the city walls themselves. They were famous. Her father had said they were so tall and smooth that no army, let alone a Possessed, could ever breach them. They were so high! They were at least four times the height of the old stockade walls around North Downs and made of stronger stone than Cormant. Lights and watch fires blazed all along the battlements. She made out a variety of constructions ranged along its length. Things that looked like larger versions of Miller's crossbow, with large wicked looking points poking out, catapults, and other things she had no idea of.

As the convoy reached the main gate, the wall cast a deep shadow over them. The gate itself was an incredibly complicated affair, spouts and trap doors were arranged over the ceiling. She guessed this was to drop things on would-be attackers. As the gates themselves were pulled back they entered what seemed to be a passageway before arriving at another set of doors. Passing under the first portal she looked up to check. Yes, there was a portcullis. Arranged along either side of the passage were arrow slits and above them, more chutes and wooden doors. She nodded approvingly. Anyone getting in here would be trapped, shot at, have rocks dropped on them and be covered in boiling pitch. It was only once the wagon had passed through the second set of doors did she finally get to see the city itself. Her companions all seemed to be similarly impressed. Woodhall whistled.

'Finally, some civilization,' he announced.

The city itself crowded almost right up to the walls themselves. Everywhere Enna looked there were houses, shops and big official looking buildings. Lights blazed in windows and all about her people milled about. It was the sheer scale of the place - there were no single storey buildings, there were a few two storey ones, but they were mostly three of four storeys, big towering things that seemed to lean against each other for support. And the noise! There was a constant sort of roaring sound; she had never heard the like before. It wasn't unpleasant, just unusual. Such was the racket she could only ever make out the conversations near to her. Someone, she couldn't remember who, had said that you could get lost within moments in a city. No one need know your business. She could well understand it now. They proceeded down a wide avenue where traffic flowed both ways. She noted that most of the traffic going the other way consisted of men on foot, heading towards the walls. She didn't need to ask why. She noticed that some of the wagons were peeling off down side streets, she guessed to drop off supplies and the like. The main party continued on. The nature of the buildings changed. The residential houses and shops were replaced with grand buildings made of stone and marble. She passed one where steps led up from the road to a wide veranda where a triangular roof was supported by stone columns. The place looked old and unused.

'That's the Temple of Dawn,' said Woodhall. 'Lot of folk died in there at the start.'

'How so?'

Woodhall scratched behind his ear. 'Ah, magic and the priesthood have often gone together. It's hard to spot the difference between priests and wizards. A lot of them thought they were immune. That the gods would protect 'em.'

'It didn't work.'

'Bloody right it didn't!' said Reed from where he sat on top of a pile of boxes, his legs dangling over the side of the wagon. 'My old mum got killed that way. Her priest tore her apart when the change came on him.'

'So people still worship?'

Woodhall shrugged.

'Some do, it depends on which god they pray to. A couple of gods died out – mainly because they killed all their parishioners.'

That drew a laugh from the rest of the men.

'The smarter religions have had a bit of change to how they ran their priesthoods. They tend to avoid anything too mystical and go light on the prayers.'

Enna watched the temple as it fell back; then watched the next one come into view. This had braziers burning brightly and people were gathered around the entrance talking quietly.

'Ah, now this one we like,' said Woodhall. 'Temple of Mistra – goddess of war and peace.'

'War and Peace?' asked Enna.

'Sure. You have a war then you have peace, makes perfect sense to me,' replied Woodhall.

'I suppose,' said Enna.

'We're still waiting on the peace bit to happen,' chipped in Reed.

'Yes, the way things are shaping up we might get a resolution on that,' said Woodhall.

The wagons left the temple buildings behind them as the road reached a crossroads. Directly ahead was a short but very ornate looking, very steep, humpbacked bridge. And beyond that an incredible sight – the Ducal Palace; grand and imposing. The road running parallel went north and south along a river bank. There were a number of barges and small craft moored to either side.

They continued over the bridge, past two armed guards and a burning brazier. As they reached the highest point Enna leaned over to study the river. It was about forty yards wide and looked quite lazy. A few boats were still afloat, lights bobbing at their prows. They were pretty high up, watching one craft passing underneath; she guessed that the construction was entirely deliberate to allow the flow of traffic. She could just make out further bridges and judging by the lights, they lead to more parts of the city on the far bank. It was even bigger than she had first thought. It was odd but she drew little comfort from the press of people around her. She had seen how quickly it could fall apart and how lucky they had all been to have survived the arrival of the Possessed.

On reaching the apex the tilt of the wagon shifted as they proceeded along the downward slope. Before her the castle loomed – she was impressed. She'd really only had Cormant to compare it to and that hadn't been a real castle. Its walls were built right up to the river itself and unlike Cormant, they appeared to go into the water. She wondered why it didn't flood and fall down inside. Coming off the bridge, it was only a few more yards and they were entering the gate house - or the barbican – she remembered that's what it was called. It was smaller than the one by the city walls but looked just as solid. It was just wide enough for the wagon to pass through. On the far side they entered a wide open area. There were various buildings built into the walls on three sides of the square courtyard but on the eastern side was the most impressive structure she had ever seen – it wasn't a keep. It was like a…well she'd just have to say it was a palace. She didn't have much to compare it to. A series of wide steps lead to an impressive looking entrance, large torches sat in stanchions to either side and she could see beasts and monsters carved into the walls surrounding them. From the entrance, the main structure spread out to incorporate a series of towers and behind them she could see a series of rooftops and spires silhouetted against the darkening sky.

'Impressive, isn't it?' a voice asked.

Enna turned to face the Duke. He had dismounted and stood waiting by the wagon tailgate.

'It is, um, M'lord,' said Enna, remembering the honorific.

He smiled. 'It used to be just a single keep, just a few levels, a long way back in the past. A bit like the ones you might find in the outlying territories. But time and prosperity saw the addition of extra halls, bed chambers, barracks and kitchens. And of course, a few artistic embellishments. So eventually it turned into a palace. I think the builders got envious of our cultured neighbours across the sea and felt us in need of some whimsical decorations.'

'How many people live here?' she asked.

The man shrugged. 'You know, that is a very good question! Sometimes I do wonder. But I am assured that there are some three hundred souls employed in one capacity or another. It takes a lot of people to run the affairs of a state.' He held out his hand to her. She took it and she clambered off the back of the wagon. 'Even one as ravaged as Albair. Come.'

He walked across to the steps. Miller and his men were gathering at their foot.

'Hunter Band,' The Duke addressed the group. 'I daresay the lot of you could do with food, ale and no doubt a wash?'

'We'll take the ale,' muttered someone from the back.

The Duke gave Miller a stern look and then shook his head.

'If I wanted manners from my Hunters, I would imagine you wouldn't be half as effective as I needed you to be.'

Miller tilted his head in agreement.

'Very well – ale first. My sergeant will see to your quartering. Rest up tonight. The city is safe. But your fighting skills will be needed soon enough. I do not intend to stay hiding behind the walls forever.'

Enna saw Miller and Woodhall exchange looks.

The Duke placed a hand on Enna's shoulder and steered her towards the steps.

'You, on the other hand, are going to avoid watching this lot lose what dignity they have. I'll have quarters for you inside. You'll like it, it's in a tower.'

'Can Jagger come?'

The Duke didn't miss a beat.

'He can. I doubt the two of you can be parted. Just make sure he doesn't terrorise the castle dogs too much.'

The Possessed came three bells into the night watch. Previously they had hung back from the wall, preferring to stalk the fields and hamlets that supplied the city. It was no accident that the cleared area extended many miles beyond the city walls. There was nowhere to hole up during daylight hours. The city itself was well protected; there was no way those things could get in without being seen and targeted. Sentries watched intently all along its length. In addition, both the river gates lowered a portcullis below the waterline.

At first those sentries on the battlements sent back a few reports of sporadic sightings, Possessed seen skulking just a few hundred yards away, nothing more than what had been witnessed over the last couple of nights. Then the reports started to tell of Possessed coming together, in pairs and small groups, gathering together in packs. At first the commander of the watch didn't accept this and demanded clarification. There had never been such sightings before, but then his aides reminded him of the reports given by the evacuees, that the same behaviour had been witnessed by them. The survivors too, not many of them to be sure, had also told of devastating attacks on settlements that were overwhelmed within minutes. The commander ordered a general stand to, moments before a group of Possessed made a move towards the western gate. The guards there let loose a volley of arrows and spears as the things drew close. Ballista fire from the towers flanking the gate scored a direct hit on one of the beasts, the long wooden shaft driving straight through its chest, pinning it to the ground.

This group withdrew, only for reports of further approaches at several other points of the city wall to come in. Alarm bells sounded across the city, and squads of troops could be seen scurrying to reinforce those already on the walls. The city garrison had diverted all its resources to defending the city during the night hours. They had been augmented by local militia and spare Ducal troops from other settlements. It was these troops who maintained order and calm during the days. It became apparent to all, that these attacks were coordinated, and designed to test the defences and reaction times of those manning the walls.

The probes continued throughout the night. Each time the Possessed moved forward, they were repulsed by the defensive positions, many that had been put in place years ago to counter human foes. Murder holes poured hot oil, overhanging hoardings built at intervals along the walls gave men access to shoot at lateral angles or drop stones. The Possessed quickly learned to avoid these places. Bales of flaming hay were thrown over the side to add illumination, while catapults launched pots that burst into flame, the substance sticking to anything it made contact with. Most of this was for show; noise and lights to scare and intimidate. Sometimes it worked. Sometimes it didn't.

Woodhall rocked back on the chair he had acquired and rested against the wall of one of the castle towers. It was set into the rear of the old keep where the distance between the castle wall and the city wall was nothing more than about fifty yards. There was a missing chunk of masonry directly in front of him that allowed a clear view of the action. He took a slurp from the cup of tepid mulled wine he had been nursing.

'I could smell that shit from the bottom of the stairs,' announced Miller emerging from the doorway.

'Well, there had to be some reason you found me.'

'This place is a bloody maze,' said Miller hunkering

down next to him.

Woodhall had rather liked wandering around the place – it was steeped in history and had lots of nooks and crannies.

'How are the lads?' he asked.

'Most of them have sparked out. They'll claim it was doctored in some way tomorrow morning.'

Woodhall laughed. 'Surprised you're still up.'

'Same reason you are. Wanted to see for myself how things are.'

'I think this is the first night they've had like this,' said Woodhall.

'Won't be the last.'

'They're testing out the walls, looking for a weak spot. I get the feeling that they know our little package is in here.'

'Did you see where they took her?' asked Miller.

'Yeah, I found it. Private quarters, one of the towers at the front.' Miller had asked him to make sure he knew where Enna had been taken. That had surprised him a bit. He'd have thought Miller would have been happy to hand over the burden and be done with it. 'Why so keen on keeping tabs?' he asked.

Miller reached over and took the wine from Woodhall's hand and took a sip. He made a disgusted face and handed it back over. 'If it wasn't for the alcohol I would've spat that out.' He paused for a moment. 'We got a lot invested in that girl, Jess. We lost good men getting her here. But it ain't just that. There's something bigger at stake. When I spoke to the Duke, I could see the wheels turning. He's got a notion.'

'Did he share it?'

Miller shook his head. 'I imagine he is still fairly annoyed with me for killing his uncle.'

'He can't blame you for doing your job.'

'It would be a bit hypocritical. But then nobles and men of power often are,' replied Miller.

'What about the girl. What do you think?' asked Woodhall.

'The girl is valuable, that much is clear. And I almost killed her up north. If it wasn't for what she did.'

'She kills Possessed with her thoughts. I like that in a woman,' said Woodhall, with a grin.

'And attracts them like moths to a flame. I tell you, Jess, they'll be making another play for her. We got to be ready when they do.'

Woodhall sighed. 'A Hunter's work is never done.'

'Til we drop dead.'

'Aye, until then we kill as many of the bastards as we find.' Woodhall waved his cup towards the far wall. 'Nice of them to come to us, then.'

Miller looked over at his friend. 'I could swear you are enjoying this, Jess.'

Woodhall grunted. 'It's nice to be back in civilisation, Avery. You have to remember, I'm a city lad by heart. I grew up amongst people, amongst commerce and industry. Believe it or not I actually had an education.'

Miller snorted. 'Don't you dare get civilised on me,

Woodhall.'

Woodhall smiled. He had been the son of a merchant and had something of a more rounded experience of the world. Miller, on the other hand, had never felt comfortable in the larger towns they had visited. Woodhall could imagine he must be feeling downright antsy being in the biggest city in Albair. 'Ah, Avery. We are getting old, slowing down and mellowing out. You can't stay angry forever,' he said.

Miller didn't respond. Woodhall figured he might be right.

CHAPTER NINETEEN

A muted bang roused Enna from a deep sleep. She rolled over in the bed, pushed her head to the side of the pillow and allowed her arm to fall out the side. A wet nose was immediately pushing insistently into her palm. It withdrew and moments later it was inserting into her left ear, accompanied by a loud sniffing.

She moaned and eyes squeezed shut, flailed her arms out in the nose's general direction.

'Jagger!' she moaned.

This only encouraged the dog more and he leapt onto her bed.

'Alright, alright,' she pushed herself up and made a fuss of the excited cattle dog. Jagger rolled over onto his side, allowing access to his stomach which she duly ruffled.

'You know, I'm pretty sure you were a lot better

behaved back with your mum and dad. When did you get so soppy?'

Jagger looked back at her with wide black eyes and a toothy grin.

After a few more moments she stopped fussing over him and in a rapid movement, Jagger flipped himself over onto his stomach and jumped off the bed. Emma sat back to look around the room.

'So, this is how the high and mighty live.'

Enna lay in a plush four poster bed, draped with purple overhangs and a semi-transparent muslin curtain which was tied back against the poles. The room was furnished with an ornate wardrobe on the left side of the bed whilst on the other side a glass window allowed light to stream in. In one corner by the door was a red cushioned chair, with carved arms ending with what looked like dragons. Upon the chair was a pile of material she suspected of being garments, the presence of freshly polished boots placed by the chair reinforcing that belief. She threw the sheets back and walked over to the wardrobe. There was a small key in the lock. She turned it and opened the two doors together. Inside she found a collection of robes and undergarments, clearly for a man.

The wardrobe smelt musty, the clothes had a layer of dust upon them. Wrinkling her nose, she shut the doors and wondered over to the chair. Yes, they were clothes. A plain white tunic and trousers. Oh, that made a change – she had gotten tired of wearing her old shabby dress which had been falling to pieces. She quickly pulled the clothes on and opened the door. She had remembered that her accommodation had been described as 'rooms'.

She entered what could best be described as a study. There was a table covered in all sorts of papers, objects and vessels and behind it sat a very grand, high-backed chair. Along the wall behind it was row upon row of books, tomes and scrolls. Beneath a window to her left was a smaller high legged table that held an empty decanter and two finely cut glass goblets. A fireplace fronted by two more chairs – rather more comfortable looking than the one behind the table – was just to her right. A man was on his knees, and was energetically prodding the remains of last night's fire with a poker. After a few more stabs and some vigorous blowing he sat back on his haunches with a satisfied look.

'There, that's got it,' he announced.

The man looked over and smiled. It was the Duke.

'One of life's important skills,' he said, 'always know how to start a fire and keep it going.' He reached into a basket and withdrew some small, wooden blocks that he tossed into the grate. Standing, he brushed his hands and turned to regard her. Though unarmored, he wore sturdy-looking garments: a dark brown shirt, black trousers and a long leather coat that reached to his knees. Her first thought was that he didn't really look much like a Duke.

'There's usually a fire on in here – I tend to use this place as my hideaway and if I want to get some research done.'

'This used to be Tennebran's, didn't it?' she asked.

The Duke nodded.

'Well guessed. Yes, this is my uncle's room. No one's used that bed until you. It seems fitting that as his pupil you should have it.'

Enna was taken back, she'd never thought of herself as his pupil but she guessed it did make a kind of sense now that she thought about it.

The Duke sat down in one of the chairs and indicated that Enna should take the other.

'There'll be some food up soon – you've missed breakfast so it'll be lunch.'

'What time is it?' asked Enna. She thought it was still early in the morning.

'Oh, I believe it is around ten o'clock or so.'

'I didn't think I'd slept so much.'

'I shouldn't worry,' said the Duke waving a hand. 'You've been through a fair bit.'

He sat back and steepled his hands, bringing the tips of his index fingers to his lips.

'You are very lucky to have gotten here you know. If we hadn't found you, I doubt you would have made it to the city before dark.'

Enna sat back in her chair, absently reaching over to Jagger, who had quietly taken up a position beside her, and stroked his head.

'I've been riding my luck quite a bit,' she said.

'Indeed you have, but from what I've gathered, you had the best kind of help getting here. Not least the intercession of my uncle and the Hunter Band.'

Enna nodded.

'They gave everything. Just like the people of Cormant and,' she felt her throat constrict, 'my parents.'

The Duke nodded gravely. 'I'm sorry for your loss, Enna. Sorry for all of them.' He paused, looking thoughtful. 'However, things have changed. We are entering a new time. I can feel it.' Another pause. 'Tell me, is it true Tennebran let loose and burned a bunch of those things to a crisp?' he asked with sudden intensity.

'Oh yes,' said Enna, enthusiastically. 'You should have seen it. It was incredible. A huge jet of flame shot right out from his fingers. They never stood a chance.'

The Duke beamed and slapped his thigh, 'Hah, good for him. I knew that wily old bugger wouldn't go down without a fight. If only we still had that kind of power. Sadly, Albair has been bereft of such things for so long.' He leaned forward, eyes gleaming. 'Do you know that on the mainland they still have magic?'

'Really?'

'Indeed. Not wizards, but they have people, just normal people, who have been gifted with weapons. Infused with magic, much like our testing stones, but much more powerful. They are mighty warriors whose sole purpose is to seek out and destroy the Possessed. One on one. Can you imagine that? I've never seen them but they must be a sight to behold,' The Duke shook his head in wonderment then pointed at her. 'Still, now we have you.'

Enna was waiting for this. She knew that the Duke

342

was taking a very special interest.

'I'm not sure what I can do. I'm just a kid.'

'A kid with a very special gift. Avery Miller tells me you killed a Possessed yourself.'

Enna shifted uncomfortably. 'It wasn't much of a fight.'

The Duke shrugged and raised his hands. 'It doesn't have to be. But what you did. What you can do. Well, you have much potential.'

'To do what?'

The Duke smiled ruefully. 'To turn the tide perhaps?'

Enna couldn't hide her feelings. This was too much. What did he expect from her? She couldn't fire a bolt of lightning from her finger tips or conjure magical shields.

The Duke seemed to pick up her thoughts. 'I'm sorry, that does sound rather dramatic doesn't it? I'm just excited even in the midst of all that is going on.' He leaned forward. 'The Possessed want you. They have gathered here in great numbers. And that is their mistake. You saw how the land lies outside the city?'

Enna nodded.

'The Possessed still mostly fear the daylight, thank the gods, yet they stayed at the walls 'til near dawn. Where do you think they would have retreated to?'

Enna thought quickly. 'The houses on the roads leading in.'

'Exactly! I've been out this morning with the troops. We've been burning them out. Every tavern, outhouse. Every smithy and stable. We piled the wood high, doused them in oil and let them burn. And stood by ready to deal with anything that came out. My men continue the task as we speak. We've only found a few but there will be more no doubt. That'll thin their numbers down a bit.' He stood and knelt down to the fireplace, picking up the poker and prodding at the small pile of wood that had caught alight and was burning steadily. Reaching into the wood basket again, he pulled out larger logs, and placed them against the smaller blocks.

'They'll no doubt come again tonight and once again we'll play their game. But when they try to withdraw we won't make it so easy for them. For too long we've danced around, my Hunter Bands doing what they can in the daylight hours. But we have never been strong enough to handle a major confrontation, to think about a time when we are free of them. But now they come to us on ground of our choosing. I intend to ride out and hunt them down.' He spoke the last few words slowly emphasizing the importance of the fact.

Enna was impressed and excited. She had never heard such an aggressive speech against the Possessed. All her life people had sheltered and survived. But here was the Duke talking about actively wiping the Possessed out. At least those that had turned. There would still have to be Testings. A thought struck her.

'How come there are so many of them? I mean, they come in packs now, but how come. I was always told they dwelt in small numbers.'

The Duke looked at her gravely then smiled with a

look of almost fatherly pride.

'Yes, you are right. How is it that in the past thirty years we haven't been able to extinguish them? That their numbers have increased? The answer is simple but one that many have not really had much opportunity or perspective to think on. For many years the Possessed have been wild creatures. Solitary even. The ones the Hunter Bands have caught and killed were the smaller of their kind, usually the weaker ones. Even without their new found intelligence, they were always cunning.' He shifted in his seat, tugging at his long coat. 'Miller also told me of how Cormant almost fell. Apparently one of the young men from there turned after being wounded. One fact that many communities have yet to learn is just how virulent the Possessed plague has become. It is something that we have become aware of only recently. I blame myself that this knowledge has yet to reach everyone.

'At first, when the magic users of the past changed, their rage left all it encountered dead. Then something new and very troubling started to happen. We noticed it first in survivors, and then it started to occur in our wounded soldiers. At the start, it didn't affect everyone but we had some turners. We put that down to the untapped magic in their veins. Tennebran once told me that the bloodlines are long but faint. But, recently, anyone coming into contact we these things gets the infection in their blood. They change, not straight away, some can stay human for a while, but eventually it takes them.'

'So they're going and spreading it now?' Enna asked. The Duke nodded. 'Yes, they are actively doing this, going into settlements, wreaking havoc but deliberately leaving wounded. That's another reason why I've evacuated as many people as I can. There is no reason to give them more troops.'

'So what about the wounded?' Enna was afraid she already knew the answer.

The Duke looked away into the fire.

'We do what we've always had to do.' His face was hard, unreadable when he turned back to her. 'Those that bear the marks of claws or teeth must be quarantined, if they do not show the symptoms after two days, then they can go free. Otherwise they are put out of their misery. I've sent word out to the other cities of Albair. And to the Hunter Bands, although I fear that there are none left.'

'They're pretty tough and smart,' Enna countered, surprising herself by the pride in her voice. She hadn't realised how much she'd grown to depend on them.

'That they are,' acknowledged the Duke. 'It is a wonder what desperate and angry men can do when faced with such terror.'

Enna bit her lip.

'Lord Duke.'

'Yes, Enna?'

'Are we truly safe here? I mean, can we stop them?'

The Duke thought about it for a moment. 'Yes, I

346

believe we can. These things are focused on getting to you. We know their intent and that gives us an advantage. I suspect all the remaining Possessed will be flocking here. I hazard that our outlying lands have never been safer.' He pointed a finger at her. 'But, this goes much further than just Albair. Come over here.'

He stood up and walked over to the desk and sat himself behind it. Enna rose and stood quietly in front of him. He opened a drawer and pulled out a large leather bound book. 'Now, let's see.' He fussed about trying to locate pages within it. Enna stood on tiptoe trying to examine the leaves as they flicked over. The Duke looked up.

'Oh, don't stand there, come round here.' He beckoned her to join him. She took up a position on his right side and peered over the book. It appeared to be full of writing, with the occasional sketch. 'Believe it or not, I have become a man of action through necessity rather than desire. It has never been my first love; I'm rather more the studious sort. Now that I'm getting older, people don't expect me to be leading the charge so much. This is my journal. I said to you that the mainland have their own methods of dealing with Possessed? Like us, societies have had to baton down the hatches and hide behind their walls. It was incredible to imagine but entire cities fell to the creatures. Provinces lost their administrations and settlements became islands, no longer linked to the idea of a nation. Mounting a defence against such things was not easy. We would have almost lost

Albair city – if it hadn't been for Tennebran. He was powerful, but more importantly he was wise. Tennebran himself counselled that we had to cut the problem off at its source. Hence the Testing Stones. It cost us dear, but we maintained control. Hard decisions had to be made. Many were lost. Many had to be sacrificed so that we as a nation might survive. This country almost fell apart, governance was all built impossible. The plague and starvation took us almost to the brink. For many years contact between our major cities, those that did not fall, was scant. It took time but our society has been rebuilt.' He sighed then smiled at her. 'We have even re-established links across the sea. Things have become fragmented, new orders have sprung up. But, more importantly, the light of learning hasn't gone out. Go and pour me some wine, would you?

Enna walked across to the small table, unstopped the wine and poured the wine almost to the top of the glass. She placed the vessel in front of the Duke. He glanced up and grunted. 'I know it's the middle of the day but are you trying to get me drunk?'

Enna felt her face flush.

'I'm sorry M'lord I...well, we never had wine at my house. Only ale and my dad always used to have his mug full to the brim.'

'Wine is a little more potent, Enna,' the Duke said with a laugh. 'Many folk in the cities drink the stuff. I'm sure you've had mead before?'

'Oh, yes. I love honey. We get it sometimes. It's

brought in from an island to the East apparently.'

'That's right. The drink was made by some religious orders and the tradition has continued in their absence. Wine is a lot like that. Do you drink a lot of ale?'

Enna nodded. 'And tea.'

'Well, the substance in ale, wine and mead, which causes people to get drunk, also has another useful property – it is excellent at preventing bugs and sickness within the liquid. An irony, don't you think? That the stuff which causes men to lose their minds is in fact important to staying healthy?'

'Yes, Lord.'

'You'll find, Enna, that there are many ironies in life and nothing is ever as simple as it seems. There are links, causes and chains all around us. We just never notice them.'

The Duke gave Enna an odd look. She didn't quite know how to describe it. Like he was weighing her up.

'You not having some?' he said, resuming his light hearted tone. 'Go on.'

Enna went back to fill the second glass as the Duke continued talking.

'Many people water down the wine. That way it becomes their staple drink. Personally I don't like what it does to the taste – I prefer it the way vintners intended. At least the Possessed plague hasn't wiped out that noble art.'

Enna took a sip – the taste was strong, the liquid itself quite thick. It warmed the back of her throat as she swallowed it. She thought it quite sour but then another, sweeter taste hit her, like blackberries.

'Now, back to the book. As I said, contact with the mainland has been re-established, has been for a number of years in fact. We have trade and ships sailing across the sea just as before. It is, after all, the safest place to be against Possessed. The gypsies have prospered by retreating to floating settlements and in so doing, have helped to keep communications going. I have devoted much of my time to discovering the cause of the plague – it was clear that this was no naturally occurring affliction. Just think, it only affected the wielders of magic. There had to be a link, an event that sparked this. I have made contact with a number of likeminded individuals; together we have pieced together our knowledge. I have sent agents to research and gather scraps of information, small clues. And, I think we have had some success.'

Enna found herself being caught up in the passion and enthusiasm of the moment. The Duke had a light shining in his eyes, an intent expression on his face.

'You found an answer?' she asked hopefully.

He nodded and then shrugged.

'Not so much an answer but perhaps a location. Here.' He turned to another page and pulled out a folded folio, twice the size of the book itself. On it was sketched a map. She had only seen a few maps and those had been little more than sketches. This was much more detailed but also unfamiliar. She recognised none of the features, none of the settlements or place names indicated. Dotted liberally around the map were small circles and writing. 'Where is this?' she asked.

'This is the mainland. Look,' he pointed to the top left corner of the map. 'Here's Albair, the coast of it anyway.'

Now that he'd indicated it she could see Albair City, marked almost on the edge.

'How long does it take to cross the sea?' she asked.

'Oh, about a day if the wind is right.'

She compared the relative size of the portion of Albair to the rest of the drawn map; there was a stark difference!

'This is all one country?' she could not believe the size of it.

'What?' The Duke said, surprise in his voice. 'No, no. In times past this used to be several countries. Yorven, Olifers, Imray, and down there, the start of Gower.' His finger traced around the map indicating the rough boundaries. 'Each one had its own state, ruler, bureaucracy and army. The plague changed all that. Gower had it bad by all accounts. It had a long tradition of mage craft, had its own college. Can you imagine the havoc that was wreaked? This map is of the new world. It doesn't have the old borders. I have indicted the locations of the new city states that have grown up from the wreckage. They are many and no can contest or hold the land that they aspire to claim. See here? And here?' He pointed to the circles and dates. 'Can you read them?'

Enna leaned forward and squinted. 'Yes, I can understand the writing.'

'So, can you spot the pattern?'

Enna, looked around the map, her eyes flitting between the circles.

'Take your time,' said the Duke, no hint of agitation in his voice.

She quickly worked out that the dates were all very similar to each other, within a month or two, thirty years or so ago. A thought struck her. She checked the dates near Albair, and then swung her gaze across to the far side, yes! They were roughly the same. She then worked her way inwards. The dates reflecting earlier days.

'This is a chart! It shows when the Possessed appeared,' she said proudly.

The Duke nodded and smiled indulgently.

'Yes indeed. Clever girl. This is a chart. One that I have painstakingly put together over the years. It is not entirely accurate, but the pattern is clear. So what is that pattern do you think?'

Enna resumed her study. It did occur to her that the Duke was always asking questions. She supposed that was a good thing but it did remind her of Mistress Tabawick on a bad day. She concentrated on trying to find the earliest dates. After a few seconds, she placed her finger on a circle slightly to the right of the map's centre.

'This is the earliest spot. So, this is the first place that they appeared?'

'Right again. And so the pattern is obvious. The plague *spread* Enna. It started at one point and radiated outwards. The question is why? Why there? What might have caused this point to be originator?'

Enna made to answer but the Duke clearly wasn't waiting for her answer.

'It is my belief, that perhaps this curse has as its precursor a very specific event. Something happened, something was done to spark it. And if this something was done by a human action, then perhaps it can be undone!'

'You think someone made this happen?'

The Duke shrugged. 'That I cannot say. I cannot think that anyone would intentionally wish this upon us. What would they have to gain? No, I would imagine that it was a mistake. Perhaps a wizard delved into places he should not have done? Perhaps he did something that created...a portal? A way into our world completely unintentionally. Tennebran once explained to me that magic is not gifted to humans in the same way that intelligence or great strength is gifted to some. Magic is a thing, an element that exists beyond us. In a place that perhaps the gods inhabit or maybe somewhere else. What humans are gifted with is the ability to access that place that... realm. So then perhaps other things can as well? That is their bridge to us.'

'And we can knock it down?'

'Yes, in a manner of speaking. Or at least we can seal it off. Now believe me, I am no wizard, I am no great thinker, and much of what I saw may well just be my own mistaken conjecture. But I'm sure you have thought this yourself. At the same time that your abilities started manifesting themselves, the Possessed began to develop a level of self-awareness. And then they come after you. None of this can be coincidence. They are now far more dangerous. They have an agenda. They may no longer be content with hiding in the shadows. It may be that you hold the key to this.'

The Duke stood, took his glass and sipped from it. 'I fear that these Possessed wish to claim the world for themselves. They are not the same things of mindless rage that they began as. But I believe we do have the means to step them. The Captain of the Hunters described to me how you were able to kill the Possessed. This combined with the means to cancel out magic and its effects lead me to the conclusion that at the very heart of these things, the Possessed need the link, need magic, to exist in our world. You cut off that link and they cannot stay.'

Enna found it hard to keep up with the Duke. The man seemed to have something figured out but she didn't like the implications.

'So you want me to go and kill all the Possessed myself?'

'Hardly. That would take an age to do. And I don't think we have that much time. But what if you could stop it at its source? That, I am beginning to believe, may be the answer. Your power could do that.'

'So you think that this place on the map. Where the date is written, this is where it comes from?' Enna asked.

The Duke shrugged.

'It's unlikely that we would be that lucky. But maybe

somewhere nearby.'

The Duke put down his glass and placed a hand on Enna's shoulder.

'This is all to be considered another time. More thought and research before we can decide what to do next. And we have the rather pressing matter of our nightly sieges. Rest up. You have the freedom of the palace. Though I would ask you not to go beyond the bridge. The city is safe but people do not change, there will be those who would take advantage of someone who isn't streetwise.'

'I will, M'lord.'

'Good. We will speak again.'

The Duke gave her a slight bow and exited the room. She watched him go then, blowing a guest of air out of her mouth, gazed around the room. She took another sip of the wine, made another sour face and put her glass down on the table. She sat on the chair and flicked through the journal. And quickly got bored. It was all very well the Duke talking about stopping the plague and finding secret bridges and her single handed ending of the Possessed menace. But it didn't actually give her much reassurance. It didn't sound like she would be particularly safe in all of this. In fact, it sounded very much to her that she would be thrust into even more danger.

A short while later a servant arrived bearing a tray full of bread, cheeses and meats. A pitcher of milk was also provided. This was more like it. She felt her stomach rumble and realised she hadn't eaten anything substantial in days. Tucking into the food with gusto she watched another servant arrived with a bowl full of scraps for Jagger. He left his very attentive station next to Enna and buried his head in the pile.

After a very pleasurable meal, she finally pushed the tray away from her, rubbed her now stuffed stomach and sat back and looked at Jagger. The dog, his bowl emptied within two minutes, was laid out on the floor, head resting on his paws, watching Enna intently. He had a hopeful look in his eye, the tail dragging back and forth on the floor.

'Come on. Let's go for a wander. I need to walk some of this off now.' Enna stood and together the pair exited the study.

Woodhall found Miller, Reed and the rest having taken over a corner of a tavern in the poor quarter. It wasn't that they were short of coin; the Duke had been very quick to cover their back pay. Rather, most of them had humble origins and felt comfortable in these earthier environs. They also felt it their duty to spread the wealth with those that needed it most. That and the fact that the ale was always cheaper.

He nodded to the barkeep and swirled his hand in the direction of his group's table, indicating another round was in order, though judging by the state of some of them, not necessarily needed.

He joined them at the table, taking a chair by Miller. Avery gave him a lopsided stare. Woodhall stared right back and relaxed into his seat. There were a few chunks of bread on a platter in the middle of the table. He reached over, grabbed the largest piece and began to tear bits off; popping them into his mouth one after another. He chewed away with what he hoped was a thoughtful, distant, expression. Miller glared at him and looked away. Woodhall felt smug, he knew how much that would wind up his friend.

Three pitchers of ale arrived along with another mug for him. He was quietly pleased with that, showed the innkeeper was switched on enough to notice, Woodhall appreciated that level of service. He took one pitcher and filled his mug and then leaned over and filled Avery's. He replaced the pitcher, took his mug and swallowed it down. He put his mug down and reached for the pitcher again. He noted the others had already shared out and emptied the second one. He wasn't surprised. With what they'd been through, even the toughest nerves were frayed and needed some release. Poised to refill his mug, a second one was pushed in front of it. He sighed and poured the ale into Miller's before his own. 'I had a chat to the gate commander. He's been talking to the hunting parties going in and out all day. They've burnt down almost every structure for three miles around. There's some pretty pissed off people out there.'

'They'll live with it,' said Miller in best surly mode.

'Well, they'll be more pissed when they hear that the big swathe of Possessed exterminations they were expecting hasn't happened.' That got everyone's attention. 'From what they've been saying, they haven't been going in at all, they just set the buildings alight, surround them and wait for whatever comes out.'

'Nothing?' asked Derris.

Woodhall nodded. 'Most of the places were empty. Either that or the Possessed would rather burn to death than face a bunch of ducal guard quietly wetting themselves.'

'Tough choice,' chuckled Reed.

Woodhall threw back another chug of ale. 'As it turns out they only had a half dozen times when a Possessed did appear.'

'Casualties?' asked Miller.

'One group got chewed up. Lost eight men. Possessed headed off to the north when reinforcements showed up. Other parties lost a few here or there, bunch of injuries.'

'They keeping them quarantined?'

'Nope. Put them out of their misery. Got told that the Possession can affect anyone these days.'

'Best way. We've seen what happens one someone gets cut.' Miller drained his mug and taps his fingers in the table. 'Doesn't sound right, those Possessed getting caught like that. Seems to me most of them were smart enough not to hang around.'

'No, sounds like the Possessed pulled back farther than the Duke thought,' agreed Woodhall.

'Looks like a stalemate. They hold the ground at night and then we take it back in the morning. Eventually one side is going to have to push matters.'

'Go after them in the woods? It'll be a bloodbath,' said Reed.

'Or maybe they won't wait. Do you think they'll try and get over the walls again tonight?' asked Woodhall.

'They might try. They got the climbers to do it. But they'd need to take a gate. Without it the Duke's men should be able to deal with the wall-huggers. Eventually.'

'The Duke's guys already figured that one out. You should have seen the place. Damn near impregnable. Reinforced the doors, extra manpower,' said Woodhall.

'What are we going to be doing?' asked Reed.

'Now, there's a thing,' said Miller. 'I kind of expected us to be manning the walls tonight. They'll be stretched thin. But the Duke has asked me to pass on a request.' He leaned forward and refilled his mug again. 'Seems like our wee girlie was quite the prize. He believes that keeping her alive is of the utmost importance. More than that, he told me that she might possess the means to end it all.'

'After what we've seen it does make a kind of sense,' said Woodhall.

'Perhaps. We are the last surviving Hunters, according to His Highness. There's the Band they lost contact with and the other got chewed up somewhere to the south. The Duke has requested that as the Hunter Bands have ceased to exist, we become the girl's personal bodyguard instead.'

Woodhall sat back and scratched his chin. Reed whistled.

'Do we get a pay rise?' chipped in Derris.

'This isn't what we signed up for. We all became Hunters to kill Possessed. That's it. Nothing else mattered. We throw our lives in the way of harm just so we can see one of those bastards die. And now, we're being asked to babysit.'

Everyone was silent for a moment. Woodhall looked about him and noted that everyone gathered were calculating the implications. The others who weren't here would no doubt feel the same. 'We stay with the girl, I'd say we'd be in exactly the right place to kill Possessed. They'll be coming right to us.'

'It ain't the same as hunting,' said Reed. 'Out there we had numbers on our side and we had a method. We had it down pat. Now we got less than half of us left and we have to fight 'em on their own terms.'

'In a close quarters fight we could take on one. Maybe get away with a few scratches if we were real lucky and had a bit of distance between them and us,' said Cook. 'Why don't we just wait this out and recruit some more guys, start up the Band again?'

'Surely the Duke's men are better at the close quarter stuff?' asked Derris.

'Fine when they got a shield wall going – crumble to shit when it breaks,' replied Reed.

'We're brawlers. We fight dirty and we got nothing to lose. That's what makes us different. If one of those things starts feasting on me, I'd still be biting its fucking ears off,' said Miller.

'And spitting your tobacco in its eyes,' smiled

Woodhall.

'I swear the stink of that stuff is what keeps 'em off of you, Avery,' said Reed laughing.

Miller grinned evilly.

'So boss, what are we going to do?' asked Derris.

Miller shrugged and looked at each man in turn.

'I guess you're leaving the decision up to me? I don't know. This is a call I didn't think I'd have to make.'

'We'll follow your lead, Avery,' said Woodhall.

The others nodded.

Woodhall studied his friend – there was doubt in the man's face. That didn't surprise him. Avery's world had become a lot more complicated than he had wanted it. For his part, Woodhall had grown tired of the hunt. The rage that had burned in his soul for so long had dimmed. He'd continued with the Band more out of a sense of duty. It had become his job. He no longer wanted to throw his life away as recklessly as he had in the past. Maybe some of the others felt that way too. Though he doubted Miller was one of them. They hadn't had much opportunity to talk about it of late. But if he had a chance to really make a difference? Well, that was something worth dying for.

CHAPTER TWENTY

Enna stood on the battlements overlooking the bridge to the city. She had been there for some time watching the world go by. Life had seemed quite normal, the comings and goings from the castle as servants, functionaries and visitors went about their business. On the other side she watched boats offloading their goods – fishermen with the daily hauls, merchants transferring boxes, crates and large bails of wool and other textiles. She sighed. All her life she had wanted to come here. Had dreamed about what it would be like, the wonders and excitement she would experience. And now she was here, she felt almost disappointed. Yes, the place was huge and impressive. But actually, it was just people. Just doing the same things they would do back at home.

Somehow she had expected something more. She laughed at herself then. What, like fighting magical monsters for a living? That particular fantasy had quickly vanished when faced with the reality of it.

Earlier she'd gone for a wander around the palace. Although, with all the defensive works built into it, it seemed more like a castle. Word had clearly gotten around about her and wherever she'd gone, people had been polite but cautious. True to his word though, the Duke had clearly made it plain to his people that nowhere, except his private apartments, were off limits. She'd been able to look in storerooms, grand looking reception rooms and the busy kitchens.

The armoury was particularly impressive, putting Cormant to shame. They had blacksmiths working in an adjoining chamber, soldiers were stood around waiting for armour to be fixed or a weapon sharpened, while grubby looking apprentices scurried about fetching fuel for the fires or working the bellows. It was hot and sweaty and smelt of charcoal and iron, reminding her of her father. She had gone and found a corner to cry in for a bit, hugging an acquiescent Jagger. The dog did his seemingly favourite thing of sticking his nose in her ear. It had the immediate effect of bringing Enna out of her mood. She still carried her knife, but when no one was looking had helped herself to a shortsword. She could just about hold it without becoming too tired too quickly. It came with a sheath, belt and buckle. She wore it now on her side. She liked the weight, it reassured her somehow. It felt like she was dangerous. She gotten a funny look from one of the soldiers as she had walked out but another had laughed and sent her on her way.

She'd also discovered the main hall that the Duke used for public audiences. She couldn't remember if it should be a throne room but decided only kings got them. She had come across the place when it was in use and had listened to the Duke dealing with rather mundane issues. Having gotten bored she wandered off to discover other nooks and crannies including a small but lovely chapel, dedicated to some deity she had never heard of. Returning later, the hall was empty and having the place to herself she took the liberty of inspecting it. There was a very impressive chair at the far end although, on seating herself, Enna decided it was not a particularly comfortable one. Perhaps the Duke had a pillow bearer or something?

'There you are,' said the Duke breaking her out of her reverie. As he approached he raised an eyebrow at her weapon. 'Nice sword.'

'M'lord. I didn't think you'd mind,' her face flushing.

He joined her at the wall and leaned against the parapet. He was wearing the same set of armour he had on yesterday, ready for the night ahead. He clasped his hands; they made a slight rasping noise as the gauntlets he wore rubbed against each other.

'Oh I don't mind at all. I'd prefer it if you didn't sit on the chair though, people might get the wrong idea.'

'Ah, um, sorry,' said Enna. How did he know? She thought she'd been alone.

The Duke took a moment to breathe in the air and

gaze across the city. 'It's getting dark. Best you get to your room. No doubt there's a fire lit and some hot food waiting for you.'

Enna didn't respond. She wasn't ready to go yet.

The Duke coughed. 'I usually expect a more vocal response from my subjects.'

'Sorry, M'lord. I'll be along soon.'

'Yes…well. I'm going to walls. We can expect a major assault.' The Duke pushed himself away from the wall and adjusted his sword belt. 'Please don't go running off, we can't afford to lose you.'

As he turned, Enna reached out and touched his arm. 'My lord?'

'Yes?'

'What's going to happen to me? I know you have a notion.'

The Duke sighed and folded his arms. 'I have already sent word to my contacts across the sea. They are going to start preparing the way.'

'The way?'

'We have to investigate the source. If it indeed exists. And that means sending you.'

Enna stepped back. It was what she had feared.

'You want me to go halfway across the world?' How on earth did he expect her to survive a journey like that?

'I never said it be easy, Enna. But that is our only option. We might only get one chance at this. Rest assured I will do everything I can do prepare you and to provide the right protection for your journey.'

'What if I don't want to go?'

The Duke shook his head sadly. 'It is not a question of wanting, Enna. Choice is a luxury we lost a long time ago. We do this out of necessity. I do this because it is my responsibility to do all I can to protect my people. That requires sacrifice.'

'And I am the sacrifice?'

'You are what you are, Enna. Whether you do this willingly or not. Is the sacrifice being asked of you any less than that of your parents? Of the people of Cormant? Or the Hunter Band? They chose to sacrifice themselves so that you might live. Will you now turn your back on them?'

'Not much of a choice then,' she muttered.

'No. But be thankful you have a chance to do some good,' said the Duke sternly. 'Now, go get some rest.' His whole demeanour changed, he stood straighter face was calm and cold, eyes flashing. This was new. It reminded Enna who she was dealing with. She dipped her head.

'I am sorry, M'lord. I keep saying that a lot don't I?'

'You do. Now run along.'

'Yes, M'lord.'

Enna turned and hurried off, Jagger at her heels. She felt angry, ashamed and frustrated all at the same time. Angry, because it was unfair of the Duke to put this on her; none of it was her fault. Ashamed because the last thing she wanted to do was let the Duke down. And frustrated because no matter what she did, it would seem that she couldn't win. She walked back through the castle in a funk. There were only a few souls about. She climbed the several flights of stairs that led to Tennebran's rooms. Inside she did indeed find a tray of hot stew, half of loaf of bread, some fruit and a jug of cool water. She grabbed the platter and lowered herself into one of the chairs by the fire. It was well ablaze and the heat washed over her. She grabbed a piece of bread, dunked it in the stew and took a bite. She chewed thoughtfully and swallowed. It occurred to her then that she wasn't hungry. She picked up the bowl, leaned forward and placed it on the floor. Jagger appeared in front of her. He sat on his haunches, looked at the food and then cocked his head at her.

'Go on,' Enna ordered. She had never seen anything, including a Possessed, move so fast.

She sat back and watched the flames.

The attack came on the southern wall only an hour after nightfall. There was little finesse about it. They came in a howling pack, at least twenty of them. Those watching on the walls raised the alarm, as the artillery pieces and shooters opened up. Bales of flaming hay and incendiary pots were flung high, blazing in the night sky before smashing to the ground, lighting up the darkness.

The Possessed didn't retreat as they had done before. Instead they came on, to the very walls themselves, and started to climb. The lithe ones used their sharp claws and feet to find little cracks and gaps between the blocks. They scrambled up quickly. Other, less agile Possessed used their immense strength to smash chunks out of the wall and fashion their own handholds. Now rendered ineffective, the crews switched to the secondary weapons, hefting rocks and boulders over the side. Others operated the cauldrons of hot oil, ranged at intervals along the wall, tipping them over the side, coating the stone blocks in the slick, viscous liquid. Crossbows fired straight down, whilst ballista on the supporting towers turned their fire, the large spears smashing and splintering into the stone as they missed their targets. Many weapons did strike home. Oil splashed onto exposed skin and fur, bolts embedded into shoulders and heads. Many of the creatures lost their purchase and fell to the ground.

Many others did make it and were soon at the top. They were met by a wall of spears as defenders banded to drive them away from the parapet. In this way two Possessed were forcibly pushed away to fall and smash against the ground below. A third slashed at the hedge of sharp points, breaking many and driving their wielders back. It leapt onto the battlements and fell up on the defenders to its left. Some fell over the side as it ripped into them, another dropped to the ground clutching his throat. And then its path was clear. It raced along the walkway, opening up the belly of another defender. As it stood, it heard a series of loud thrums, before it was hit several times by heavy bolts. A roar went up as a half dozen men closed on the beast. Reinforcements had arrived; one of the Duke's flying companies. As they engaged the wounded Possessed, more soldiers poured onto the wall. A second Possessed had followed into the undefended gap and was now wreaking havoc along the line. The soldiers and crews struggled to seal that gap. On the ground below, those Possessed that had been unable to climb or driven off the wall, quickly took advantage of the chaos and began the ascent once more.

On the eastern wall, a short way from the gatehouse, another pack appeared. The Duke himself led a flying company to reinforce the defenders. They arrived before the Possessed were able to get too far up the walls. The greater numbers of men were able to keep them from gaining the battlements. Word reached him that a third group was attacking the western gate. That was a mistake. The gatehouses were the most heavily defended. Then another messenger arrived. The north wall, on the western end, was now under assault. He had precious few reserves left. He ordered a squad of his company to head straight for the north wall and sent the messenger to summon a further squad of troops from the castle garrison.

The barbican sergeant stood on the short, central battlement that overlooked the gate and bridge. Below, the clink of chain and the thud of boots announced the departure of a bunch of the castle guards. A dozen of them, hotfooting it to the north. They passed over the bridge and the two guards stationed at the far end and heading along the river road to the right. That thinned the numbers a bit. He looked down to where another guard rested against his spear.

'Hey, Conrad.'

The man looked up at him. 'What?'

'Getting a bit chilly. Want some tea?'

'You're life saver.'

The sergeant nodded and walked back into the main structure, down a flight of steps into the main chamber. Beneath it was the passage leading into the courtyard. The floor of the chamber had a number of murder holes and stairs on either side leading down to the lower passages built into the barbican walls where men had access to firing ports. The chamber also controlled the two portcullises and served as the guardroom for the barbican troops. A younger man, barely old enough to be a serving soldier sat on a bench oiling his sword with a dirty-looking rag. A stove was continually on the go. He retrieved the kettle resting on top of it and poured out a mug of steaming tea.

'Barney. Stop that for a minute, the thing is so bloody slick it'll probably slide out yer hands soon as you try to pull it out.'

The younger man jerked up. 'Sorry, Sarge.'

'Make yourself useful and find some more clean mugs, let's keep the boys outside happy.'

He continued out the doorway and down a set of stairs which in turn led to a stout doorway opening onto the courtyard. It was the only entrance to the Barbican and was heavily reinforced with steel bars. He walked round into and through the passage.

'Here you go.'

Conrad rested his spear against the outer wall and accepted the tea with a nod.

The sergeant looked about him and listened to the sounds of fighting drifting through the night air. 'Sounds desperate.'

'Aye. Don't see why we all haven't been called up to fight. Not that I'm complaining,' replied Conrad.

The sergeant shrugged. 'Someone's got to look after the place. If it goes badly, everyone will come running straight back here to hole up 'til daybreak.'

'With that squad gone, there can't be more than a dozen of us left in here,' said Conrad.

'I'd reckon so.' The sergeant clapped the man on the back. 'So don't expect to be relieved anytime soon. Don't worry though. I'll keep you supplied with tea and good conversation. Now, go and give the boys over the bridge a shout that I'll be bringing them a brew in a minute.'

'Sure.'

The sergeant turned and walked back to the barbican.

Conrad took another sip of his tea, gathered up his spear and walked up to the bridge.

'Hey!'

He waited for a response. None came. Sometimes the sound didn't carry too well.

So he walked onto the bridge and up to its apex. He looked down onto the far side. The two guards were nowhere to be seen.

'What?' He looked up and down along the bank. There was no sign. No one was about. They must have got dragged along with the rest of the squad. 'Nice of them to tell us,' he muttered. He turned and walked back down the bridge towards the castle. He stopped at the end and saw the dark figure of the sergeant coming through the passageway.

'Hey, Sergeant. Nobody mentioned they were taking the guys on the far side.'

'They didn't. I saw 'em just-' something made the sergeant stop in his tracks. Conrad saw him spill the mugs of tea he held in his hand and heard the spatter of water on the cobbles. But that wasn't right. He heard dripping water to his rear as well 'What?' he turned.

Rising out of the water, a huge black-skinned Possessed pulled itself onto the bank. It stood and towered over the guard who stared back open mouthed. It reached forward and gripped his throat, raising him into the air and crushing his windpipe. It then threw his body into the water like it made of nothing more than straw.

The sergeant watched it all, terror rooting him to the spot.

Coming over the bridge another one: smaller, lithe and red-coloured.

'Oh...shit,' the sergeant whispered as the first creature turned its eyes on him. The soldier threw the mugs down and raced back to the barbican door. Behind him he ·

heard the pursuit, cloven hooves smacking against stone. He turned left and a further two paces saw him into the doorway and slamming the door shut. He thanked the stars the thing was so well oiled. The thing had a simple looking mechanism, a single key, which he turned just as his hands were thrown back with the powerful vibration of something large smashing into the door from the outside. The lock had engaged three iron bolts into the wall. The door held.

'Sergeant? What?' said Barney.

'They're fuckin' inside! Help me!' The sergeant was bracing himself against the door as another powerful blow caused the door to shudder. Barney charged down the stairs.

'Get the bar,' ordered the sergeant. The young soldier reached down and grabbed a timber cross brace. He raised it and slotted into the top brackets. Again the door shuddered.

'Hurry!'

He picked up another and the sergeant moved away from the door so Barney could slot it into a second set of brackets in the middle. The sergeant repeating this with a third brace into the bottom section. Again another loud smack and the door shuddered but with less force. The extra reinforcement seemed to do have done the trick.

The sergeant, breathing heavily looked at the wide eyed soldier.

'Come on.' He led the way at speed up the stairs. He closed the door behind them locked it. He opened the slot which doubled as a firing hole and squinted down the stairs – the door still held. 'Get your weapon.' Barney hurried to the bench and started to belt up his sword.

'How'd they get in? Have the walls fallen?'

'The water. It was the bloody water.'

'But that's blocked too,' said Barney.

The sergeant shook his head. 'The portcullis only blocks entrance by boats. It barely goes into the water.'

'But Possessed don't swim!'

'They've bloody learned to.' The sergeant ran over to the portcullis winch. Should he release it? No. It was too late, they were inside. Oh gods. He could seal them in but then no one could escape. It'll be a slaughter. Shit, it would be anyway. Those two could wipe out everyone in the castle.

'What should we do?' asked Barney, panic clear in the pitch of his voice.

'We got to get help.'

'How?'

'Come on.'

He led the way upstairs to the battlements. He looked over the side, waiting to hear the creature beating on the door. Nothing. Then a scream. Muffled, coming from the palace.

'Alright.' He looked at the young man, the lad's pupils were expanded to almost total black. 'I'm lowering you over the side.

'But what if they're more of them?'

'They've gotten inside already. I'm going to ring the

bell. You head north, try and find help. Understand?'

The soldier nodded quickly.

'Over you go.'

Barney climbed onto the battlement, sat down and pushed himself forward, he then turned and clasped the proffered hands. The sergeant took the weight, feeling his face flush with the effort as he bent over and lowered Barney as far as he could.

'Dropping you now,' he whispered.

He released his grip and watched the lad fall the ten feet or so onto the ground with a muted thump. He scrambled up into a crouch looked towards the passageway and then signalled a thumbs up to the sergeant.

'Okay, lad. Run!'

The soldier was up and sprinting across the bridge. Once he made the far side without incident, the sergeant turned away and ran to the stairway leading to the top of the southern tower. Up a short flight was a bell tower. Used in older times to signal the approach of visitors or enemy soldiers, it was seldom used now.

Behind him he heard an almighty crack. *Oh Gods.* The creature was still there. And now it was inside. He had no time. He took the stairs swiftly and reached for the rope that hung down from where the bell hung, just above his head. He started to pull it back and forward. The peal was at first lacklustre as the weight inside struck the metal with little force, but swiftly momentum was built and a decent, clear sound echoed forth. He counted the seconds. Each one a small victory, adding to the chance that someone would hear and send help. He closed his eyes.

'Come on, just a few more seconds.'

He felt a crushing pressure on his ankle, he screamed. He was yanked backwards down the stairs, his hands torn free from the rope. The bell struck once more before its force was spent and its peals faded away.

Enna woke up from a dark dream. She couldn't recall much about it. She was being chased. The feeling they were close tingled away, that didn't surprise her, who knew how many were outside the walls. She could remember there was a bell. It was odd though. As she struggled awake and rubbed her eyes, she could have sworn she heard it toll. Not in her dream but for real. She sat up and looked about. There was no light in the room except that coming from an open window but her night vision was easily able to pick out where everything was. She got up and headed through to the study. A warm glow emanated from that room, where the fire still burned. She yawned and looked for Jagger. She saw him and started to worry. The dog was stood facing the door leading into the landing. His hackles were raised.

'Jagger.'

The dog turned and looked at her briefly, his eyes reflecting the fire.

She didn't need any more warning. Something had happened. The Possessed were here. She stilled her mind.

Yes, now she could feel them. Nearby. In the palace. The bell hadn't been a dream. It was just like before, that night back at home, it was happening again. She quickly dressed, buckled her sword and returned to the landing door. Jagger was literally shaking with tension, his tail high. She listened at the door, straining to hear any tell tale heavy breathing. She shook her head. Like a Possessed would spend the time to be waiting patiently behind the door, ready to pounce when she obligingly came out. It really wasn't how they did things. She grasped the handle and firmly pulled it forward. A slight gust of colder air swept into the room.

'Come on, boy,' she said to Jagger.

She stepped onto the landing and started down the stairs. The tower was not particularly high and she passed onto one more landing before they took her down to the main passageways and corridors of the keep itself. Halfway across that second level she heard a scream. Long and bloodcurdling. She'd heard that scream before. This was swiftly followed by shouting and a high, shrill-sounding squeal. She couldn't be sure where it was coming from. The sound carried in odd ways around here.

She drew her weapon. If they were hunting her, then she and Jagger could turn that against them. She pushed out with her senses and sought them out. No, they weren't as close as she had thought. Motioning to Jagger, the pair hurried down the stairs and into the main passage. Looking left and right, the corridor was lit intermittently with torches, no one was in sight and there was no evidence of any Possessed passing. Now which way? Right led towards the palace's main entrance. And she felt two Possessed prowling around in that direction. Left it was.

She jogged along the passageway, down another set of stairs and emerged onto a large hall with doorways and two more passages leading off of it. A bloody body lay in the middle of the halfway, one of the castle servants. Sightless female eyes stared back at her. Another howl, drifting down the stairs behind her. It was on her trail. She turned for the right hand passage. Ahead would have been quickest, but her senses told her it wouldn't be a good idea. Her route took her through the kitchens. From there she could get to one of the flanking buildings that abutted the main keep. She passed through a T-junction. Another body. This time, wearing the armour of the Ducal guard.

The passage she was in continued for another few yards before ending at an open door. The smells that greeted her confirmed she was in the right place. She hurried on into the large kitchen chambers. Earlier in the day this place had been a hive of activity. The room was long and wide, incorporating baking ovens, open fires and preparation benches. Big enough to feed a small army. The kitchens were still well lit, the ovens warm, but it was deathly quiet. On the far side, the wall was smeared in blood. To the left of her, an arm lay amongst plates. She moved to the door leading to the barracks blocks. She spotted a body near the ovens. Then another, just off the right of the door. The owner of the missing arm.

She wrinkled her nose. She had become used to the sight and smell of blood, but this one had let loose their bowels too. As she reached for the handle, Jagger barked. She pulled her hand away. But it was odd; she couldn't sense anything behind the door. She grabbed the handle once more and tentatively pulled it toward her.

'Oh!' she jumped back, as at least two crossbows and various sharp implements were pointed in her direction.

'Bloody hell, girl!' announced a voice.

'When that dog barked, I almost wee'd myself,' said another. She knew that voice; it was Derris.

'Let's get in there,' said Miller, raising his weapon as he stepped inside.

She felt such a wave of relief as the Band crowded past her, the last man shutting the door as he came through.

Woodhall placed a hand on her shoulder. 'Well done, lass. Made our job easier.'

'What, were you coming to find me?' she asked.

Woodhall nodded.

'Reed, check that door.' Miller ordered.

Reed ran to the door Enna had come through and looked out.

'All clear'.

'Okay, close it up.' Miller moved to stand before her. 'The Duke asked us to protect you. I thought it would get us out of manning the walls for a while. Didn't think we'd have to start work straight away.'

'There's a Possessed back that way,' she pointed towards the keep exit. 'I was going to get out through the barracks.'

Woodhall shook his head. 'One back that way too.'

'Came in and started tearing into some of the Duke's men. We hightailed it out of there,' said Miller. 'Not a good place to get into a fight.'

'How do we get out?' she asked.

Miller thought for a moment. 'That bell means someone saw these things come in. So there's a good chance we might get help. Maybe we should try and hole up, find somewhere secure.'

'Or we make a break for the bridge,' said Woodhall. 'Easier to held them off and nearer help.'

'Means we have to go through the palace to get there. Lass, you know this place better than the rest of us. Seen any good spots?' asked Miller.

Enna thought about it then looked up. 'There's the hall. I think there's a route up. Its doors looked pretty strong.'

'Hmm,' Miller looked at Woodhall. 'Had too many bad experiences fighting in buildings recently.'

'We could always just lock ourselves in the dungeons?' suggested Woodhall.

Miller returned him a withering look.

'We make for the bridge. Enna and the dog can check the route. You can do that?'

Enna nodded.

'Good. Let's go. I'll take the lead, Woodhall, the rear. Everyone else, I want sharp things facing out in all directions. If something jumps us, run like hell for the bridge and we'll hold them there.'

Woodhall moved to the door and placed a head against it. He looked towards Enna. She shook her head. Miller looked towards his men then opened the door wide; he stepped through and brought his crossbow to bear. The group filed out of the kitchens and back the way Enna had come. Past the first T-junction and then on into the hall.

'That's the way to the entrance,' pointed Enna.

'Clear?'

'I don't know. They're so close, I can't really tell.'

Miller blew his cheeks out. 'Come on, we move fast.' He stepped over the body and set out down the passage at a brisk pace. Jagger bounded forward at his heels. The passage was wide and well lit.

Up ahead he spotted another cross passage and beyond that the entrance hall. He stepped onto the threshold looking left and right. Nothing. Almost there. He sped up, now running into the entrance hall. Three more dead, but no Possessed. He leapt over one and reached the main doors, ahead of him he could see the courtyard. He stopped at the door to count his men through.

'We got one, it's coming!' shouted Woodhall from within the hallway.

'Move! Move! Make for the bridge,' shouted Miller.

Enna and the others charged through. She looked back. A red-skinned Possessed was advancing towards them.

She ran into the back of a Hunter. They had all stopped and were looking up. A large black mass stood atop the barbican roof. They could never get past.

'Miller!'

He looked behind as the Possessed emerged from the keep.

The group drew themselves into a circle, Enna being gently forced into the centre. Jagger, crouched low, teeth bared, eyed the black Possessed. It leapt from the roof and landed onto the courtyard with a thud.

'Big bastards, aren't they?' whispered Reed.

The one behind them made their way slowly down the steps. Claws extended, teeth bared.

'Bigger means badder,' said Woodhall.

'Really wish we'd kept some of those stinkers handy,' said Derris.

Miller looked around. 'Move to the wall. There. They come at us like this we got no chance. Get something solid at our backs.' The group edged towards the wall of a stable building. The Possessed slunk towards them but made no move to attack. The Hunters reached the stable and spread out in a line. Enna was pushed up against the wall. Miller took position in the centre. She watched him as he transferred his crossbow into his left hand and pulled his sword from its sheath. Enna marvelled at the strength it took to carry both weapons at once. The nine hunters, a girl and her dog faced off against two

Possessed. She knew how this would end. It would be no contest. Woodhall gently touched her shoulder, she hadn't realised she'd been shaking so much until she felt the pressure of his hand. He smiled at her. 'Get that sword ready, lass.'

Miller glared at the beasts stood before them. 'They don't get through,' he said, his eyes never leaving the Possessed. 'They don't take this girl. They don't get to win. Not tonight. Not ever. Show them they picked the wrong men to fuck with.' Tilting his head to one side, he spat out a stream of tobacco juice onto the ground. 'Take them down.'

He gave a guttural roar and charged towards the middle Possessed, the other Hunters crying out in unison and following their Captain. The Possessed howled at the challenge and went to meet them. Enna stood there and watched the men storm to their doom. She had never seen anything as brave. They didn't care about defending themselves, they just through their bodies at the creatures. Jagger went too, she tried to call him back but he was already away. Time slowed down, she could see it all clearly.

A Hunter was swept from his feet caught in the face be a backhand swipe of the black Possessed. Another was smashed to the ground and leapt on by the red Possessed, its face burying into his neck, claws raking his side. The Hunter howled and stabbed at the thing even as he died. There was Derris rolling on the floor screaming as his guts spilled out of a ragged wound. Reed and another man grappled the beast to the ground. Miller, his foot on its chest, shot his crossbow point blank into its face, the bolt punching clean through and out the back of its throat.

To the other side, the black Possessed faced off against Woodhall, who thrust a spear at it. The Possessed batted it away and thrust its clawed hand into his chest and lifting the body high into the sky. Woodhall was thrown back against the wall smashing hard into it and landing before Enna, his neck twisted at a horrible angle. She looked back. The red one was down. There were five Hunters left.

Miller, using his sword two handed, charged at the black Possessed, swinging his weapon into its chest. Another Hunter buried his axe into its back. It swung round and gored the man. She watched Reed, locking into an embrace with the Possessed, jamming his dagger into its neck whilst it bit into his shoulder. She saw his mouth open, teeth in a bloody rictus grin as he thrust again and again. His legs were locked round the creature, not allowing it to break free. Jagger slammed into the side of it, biting into its calf. She could see the dog's flank was torn and bloodied, she cried out in dismay as he was swatted away to land in a crumpled heap. Miller, weapon held high stabbed into the Possessed. It punched his face, she heard a crack and then Miller was down. And then there was no one left.

At some point Reed had let go. He too was lying in a broken heap on the ground. The black Possessed stepped slowly towards her. It was covered in blood, red merging with black as it leaked from at least a dozen vicious-looking wounds. It limped slightly, favouring its right side. But it came on; its bright red eyes glowing in the night. Enna gripped her sword tightly. She knew what she could do, she just had to summon up her power and drive the blade into the creature. It sounded simple, but it had been so fast the last time, she hadn't had time to think. But as the Possessed advanced, the terror gripped her so hard, she couldn't think. It loomed before her, its arms reached out. It was over. She couldn't fight this thing.

A shape appeared behind it, wrapping a bloody arm around its neck. A hand fell across its eyes, fingers digging into the eyes. The Possessed reared up and screamed. It threw its arms over it shoulders trying to grab its assailant. 'Do it!' cried Miller.

Enna knew she had one chance. She aimed at the Possessed's exposed stomach. Summoning her power, she screamed her rage at the beast and plunged the blade in. The skin was hard and the muscled tightly packed, she had to lean in to penetrate it. She pushed her null magic along the sword, directing the tingling energy straight into the heart of the beast. It howled in range and collapsed.

Enna released the sword as the creature fell backwards.

Breathing hard she looked about her. Nothing moved. There was no sound. The entire castle was dead. She heard a groan. Miller lay face down next to the Possessed. His left hand flexing as if reaching for something.

Scrambling over she placed her hands against his side and tried to roll him over.

'Steady, lass,' he whispered. He pressed down and pushed as she pulled. After a few moments his shoulders flipped over and his head moved round. She cradled it between her legs. His body looked wrecked, his nose was smeared over his face, his breathing hard and ragged. 'Aw this hurts.' He tried to lift his head but gave up. 'Anyone else make it?'

'I don't know. I don't think so.'

'Probably best. You're clear. Don't hang around. Finish me off and get out of here.'

'What?'

He reached up and grabbed her arm.

'I've been cut in a dozen places, I'm going to turn.'

'You don't know that!'

'Yes, I do. Come on. Get it done. Otherwise it's all been for nothing. You want that on your conscience?'

Tears stung Enna's eyes. Now she was being asked to kill another human being. Possessed she didn't care about but this was different. She thought frantically.

'Maybe they can quarantine you. I heard they're doing that. We can wait...'

'There isn't time!' he shouted gruffly. 'Take a bloody knife and slit my throat. So help I'll do it myself, probably fuck it up and die in agony.' Coughing racked his body.

Enna wiped the tears away and nodded.

'Okay, I'll do it.'

She raised his head, pulled away her legs and lowered

him down. Looking around she found a bloody dagger. She rubbed the blade against her trouser leg. It seemed a silly thing but she felt it important that the metal be clean. She knelt back down. And studied the weapon then looked at Miller. His eyes were closed, his chest rising and falling unsteadily.

'Come on. I'm still here,' he said.

'I'm sorry.' She raised the blade, and then stopped herself. She found a tear in his side, a ragged flap of skin covering an exposed rib. She drew the dagger over her finger tip, creating a small cut. Blood welled up. She threw the dagger away and placed the finger into the wound.

Miller opened his eyes and hissed. 'What are you...?' He tried to get up.

'Stop. Hold on,' said Enna quietly. She placed her other hand down onto his chest and pushed him back gently.

A thought had struck her. If she could sever the link with Possessed and make them vulnerable, then she could stop the possession taking hold in the first place. But would it work forever? She didn't think so. She could only hold it a bay by being present. So she would just have to be with Miller all the time. Or at least part of her. She felt that Tenn would be pleased with her thinking. Now her blood would mingle with his. An ever present means of nullifying the Possessed's bridge to the world. She smiled at Miller.

'There, I don't think you are going to turn anytime

soon. As least for as long as I need you.'

Miller stared at her with a look of bewilderment and pain. His eyes rolled up in their sockets and his head fell to one side.

CHAPTER TWENTY-ONE

Miller awoke to find he was resting upon something soft and comfortable. He opened his eyes a fraction and tried to focus. He felt disoriented and unsure as to where he actually was. As his vision cleared he could make out he was in shadowy room. A window allowed in a subtle stream of light, not daylight, but rather the light that comes before the dawn. He was conscious of his body being tightly constrained and under covers. He wriggled his toes and experienced a sensation of stiffness. He rolled his ankles and the subsequent movement initiated a wave of pain and nausea.

'Shit,' he muttered. Now he remembered. For a moment he had thought perhaps he had passed on. As afterlives went, it hadn't seemed too bad. So he hadn't died. Instead he had been picked up and patched up. Bearing in mind the beating he had taken last night, he wasn't surprised by how uncooperative his body was being. He conducted a slow and deliberate check; his head carried a bandage, one arm had been splinted and from the way he felt a stabbing sensation in his chest, it suggested a broken rib. That was the serious stuff; the rest of him was just one big bruise. He couldn't be sure how long he had been out for. The state of his injuries meant it couldn't have been too long. But what about the others? It sounded like he might be the only one left. Did Enna make it? Damn but what did that girl do to him? Went and mixed her blood with his. He didn't know whether to be angry or grateful. There was a time when he would have felt he had been tainted, infected. Things had changed. By rights he should have already turned, he had taken enough of a beating from that Possessed to have made possession pretty much guaranteed. But now, the blood of the girl he had once planned to kill because of what she was, the danger she represented, was in his veins. And by the looks of it, her blood had stopped him from turning. At least for now.

He wasn't given to spending much time mulling over things; that was Woodhall's job. But it looked like he'd be having plenty of time to think about Enna and what she might mean for the future. He had chosen not to take her life and in turn she had saved his. As for the Duke's charge for the Band to become her protectors; they had done their duty. It hadn't been as long as he had expected. It would be up to someone else to take on that responsibility. Good luck to them. He turned his head towards the window and closed his eyes.

A voice intruded on her peaceful slumber. 'Enna?'

'Hmm?'

'I'm sorry Enna. It's time to wake up.'

'Uh.' She struggled to get up fighting a wave of exhaustion she hadn't felt since, well she couldn't remember. Even when she had been found by Merrett, she had been worn out, but not like this. Her head felt empty. Like it had been drained of all emotion. She opened her eyes and blinked in the gloom. She felt disoriented at first and her vision was blurred, a gentle light flickered in one corner, shadows played against the walls behind it. A dark figure was sat on the edge of the bead. She could feel its weight and her body wanting to fall towards it due to the slant in the mattress. She rubbed her eyes and blinked a few more times. The image took a firmer, recognisable shape.

'My Lord?'

'Yes, it's me.' The figure shifted and pushed itself off of the bed. 'It's almost dawn.'

'Oh.'

'You'll find a fresh set of clothing. Good hardy travelling gear, on the table. I've got some hot water being brought up for you. Everything else you'll need is already being put onto your horse.'

Enna nodded. She still felt groggy but her memory had returned. But she still didn't really have a clue what the Duke was talking about.

'What?'

'Ah, yes, of course. We didn't get a chance to discuss earlier did we?'

Realisation started to come to Enna.

'I'm leaving?'

'Yes. It is far too dangerous for you to stay here. The events of earlier has made it obvious that we cannot protect you. We lost many lives and I fear that a second attempt on your life would be successful.'

'Where am I going?'

The Duke smiled.

'We start your quest! I'm sending you to search for where this nightmare began. All the research I showed you must mean something. With luck and your ability, there is a chance we can turn events. We might just be able to end the nightmare.'

'But, Miller. Is he okay? I don't think he would be ready?' she asked.

The Duke put his hands up. 'Miller is a stubborn brute and is more than likely to recover from his injuries. But that won't be for some time yet. I have arranged for a new guardian for you. If things go according to plan, you'll pick up more help along the way. Right now, speed and the daylight are your best protection.'

'So, where am I going?'

The Duke moved to the door.

'To the coast. A hard day's riding will get you there. Then, a swift boat to the gypsy colony of Shanty. You'll be safe there whilst you wait for transport to the mainland. Now, up you get. The guard outside will accompany you when you are ready.' He opened the door and stepped through. He stopped and looked back at her. His face was obscured by shadow. 'You've got a very long road ahead of you. I do not know what the outcome may be. But I place my trust in you to do the right thing. For everyone we have lost. It is possible may never see each other again, so I wish you good fortune, Enna.' He turned and shut the door behind him.

Enna stayed where she was. She didn't want to get out of bed. To do so would mean taking her first step into the unknown. She wasn't sure she was ready. But what choice did she have? The Duke was right. She would go. For everyone that had lost. She felt tears form in her eyes. No. No more. She had to stop that now. She had to grow up. She had to keep her emotions tightly locked, deep inside. She had to be strong. Enna climbed out of bed and began to dress.

Duke Henry returned to his private rooms. A fresh goblet of mulled wine had been placed on a table, steam rose from its surface and he breathed in deeply of the spicy, warming aroma. Looking out towards the eastern side of the city, most of the fires from that evening's fighting had dies out, a few smoke trails persisted, black and dirty, rising lazily up from ground beyond the walls. Smaller wisps of smoke were appearing from a number of chimney stacks scattered amongst the tightly packed dwellings. The city was waking up. He could hear the shouts of carters and merchants as they commenced their working day. Crews of men were already moving along the ramparts, replenishing stocks of stone, pitch and missiles. The horizon was coloured a rich red, and hues of orange and yellow spread upwards and outwards. The sun was lingering just behind the edge of the world.

There was a knock on the door.

'Come in.'

He listened to the latch lift, the gentle creak of wood, followed by a firm thud as the door was shut and the soft footfalls of his visitor. Then silence once more.

He took a sip from his mulled wine and turned to look at the man stood before him. Tall and rangy, the man had mid length brown hair, and plain, unremarkable features. The kind of face you would quickly forget in a crowd. At parade rest, the man wore functional, travelling garb, a mix of tans and dark green. A black cloak was worn over one shoulder, the neck clasp resting upon the opposite side. Dulled chainmail was visible under the hems of his jerkin's sleeves. A shortsword rested against each leg, the pommels were black and the grips covered in dark brown leather. The scabbards themselves were similarly black. No bare metal was visible, nothing to reflect the light of a torch or gleam in the darkness. The Duke knew that secreted about the man was at least one throwing dagger in a boot and a selection of smaller blades resting against his torso, hidden by the folds of the cloak. He did not doubt that there were many others he was not aware of.

The man inclined his head.

'My Lord.'

'Are you ready?'

'Yes, Lord. The horses are ready up and I have already sent a rider to ensure preparations are underway for our arrival.'

'Good.' The Duke rolled the wine between his hands, feeling the warmth spread between his palms. 'Leyburn, I haven't had a chance to fully explain your task.'

The man did not respond, his face impassive. The Duke expected nothing less. It was always difficult to read him, anyway. An inevitable requirement of the work Leyburn was often asked to undertake.

'I want her out of this city. Now. She brings death with her wherever she goes. Another night will see us overrun. My first concern is the survival of our people.'

'My Lord, it would seem to me that there is a quicker way to this.'

The Duke nodded. 'I know. It would seem the quickest and simplest solution. But it may not be enough to stop the attacks. The Possessed are gathered here and are likely to remain until they break through. No. We use her like a huntsman uses a lure. I believe they will follow you to get to her. It will draw them away from us.'

The man raised an eyebrow but nodded his assent. The Duke continued.

'This girl must reach the coast and then on to the mainland. Once there, you will need to meet with our agents and accompany her on the journey. Here,' the

Duke indicated a leather pouch resting on his desk. Leyburn leaned forward and took it.

'You'll find more extensive notes and details in there. I've given you as much as much as I know. But you will have to use your own judgement and initiative. The location I have marked is sketchy at best and may be nothing more than a goose chase.'

'And what if it is?' asked Leyburn.

'Then, if there are no more leads, do what you feel is necessary. I do not know how bad things will be over there. If it gets difficult I suggest you cut your losses and run.'

'And do what with her?'

'At that point she becomes a liability and a danger to any with her. It would be best for all concerned that her curse is ended permanently. In truth it will be a kindness.'

Leyburn bowed and turned to leave.

'Leyburn?' asked the Duke.

The man stopped.

'I suggest you ride hard, Leyburn.'

He nodded and walked out.

The Duke turned looked out the window once more. He had had to make hard choices in the last thirty years. Tennebran had taught him that. Before he had departed, Tennebran had provided him with the lists and locations of as many magic users as he could recall. His uncle was never one to shirk from responsibility. Neither was he. It meant doing things that he took no pleasure from. Leyburn was a necessary evil. He needed men like that to help maintain order and ensure there was no dissent. If he had not, then it was likely the city and Albair itself would have fallen. He would not let that happen now, all because of a girl and the faint promise she brought. His first duty was to the people and their protection. So he must be rid of her. The world was changing again. That much was obvious. Perhaps the expedition he was initiating would prove to be successful. If not, well, better the mainland bore the brunt of the Possessed's attentions. He would have time to build new Hunter Bands and counter the creatures. Albair could weather the storm. As for Enna, he wished her luck. And if he was wrong, then he knew that Leyburn would give her a quick death. He sighed and took a swallow of the wine. It had grown tepid and cloying.

'Well, Uncle. Let's see if you were right to trust in this girl.'

Dawn broke and the sun appeared on the horizon. Beams of bright autumn sunlight speared into the room, banishing shadows and lighting up dark corners. Dust motes sparkled and danced within the rays. The night was ended. But outside, hidden and patient, creatures with evil intent waited. Their time would come again.

THE STORY CONTINUES IN:

A CRIMSON DAWN

COMING SPRING 2015

www.ingramcontent.com/pod-product-compliance
Lightning Source LLC
Chambersburg PA
CBHW051313250626
47155CB00007B/2309